HAND-FASTING
and
OTHER HAZARDS

L.L.
CAMPBELL

I0635745

Copyright © 2025 by L.L. Campbell

Cover design by Charlotte @charlotteslegers
Map and shop art by Mel @melissa.martin_art
Chapter and page design by L.L. Campbell
Art of Lochlan and Nia by Bia @amimbia

All rights reserved. No part of this publication may be reproduced
or transmitted in any form or by any means, electronic or mechanical,
including but not limited to, photocopying, recording, and/or any
information storage or retrieval systems—except in the case of brief
quotations embodied in critical articles or reviews—without written
permission from its publisher.
The characters and events portrayed in this book are fictitious and/or
used fictitiously. Any similarity to real people, living or dead, is purely
coincidental and not intended by the author.
All brand names and product names used in this book are
trademarks, registered trademarks, or trade names of their respective
holders. L.L. Campbell is not associated with any product or vendor in
this publication.

Cataloging-in-Publication data is on file with
The Library of Congress

ISBN (Paperback): 979-8-9997081-4-4
ISBN (eBook): 979-8-9997081-6-8

Content Warning

This story includes explicit sex scenes (all open door), past parental loss, and kidnapping.

But mostly, it's meant to be cozy, spicy, and a little bit fun.

Welcome home, Smutlings.

xx L

Scan for playlists
chapter breakdowns, and more.

VIDET ARCHIVES
Department of Literary Development
Magical Research & Library Division
Stella Rune | ST-444 | Confidential

CLASSIFIED

TRANSFER RECORD
FILED BY HEAD ARCHIVIST

Inventory: Hand-Fasting and Other Hazards
Condition: Pages and binding sound.
               The story itself, however, is left to be determined.
Status: Important — requires secondary inspection.

Note: *I cannot account for this record, as it is apparently about me. I pass it on to you for your own interpretation.*

Signed by: Head Archivist
Lochlan

RECORD OF RETRIEVAL:

This book is now the property of:

Immediate Thoughts:

Notes:

Story Evaluation:

	POOR	FAIR	FINE	GOOD	EXCELLENT
Magic	☐	☐	☐	☐	☐
Setting	☐	☐	☐	☐	☐
Vibe	☐	☐	☐	☐	☐
Spice	☐	☐	☐	☐	☐
Overal	☐	☐	☐	☐	☐

Playlist

Chasing Shadows – Alex Warren
Close To You – Gracie Abrams
The Archer – Taylor Swift
Rhiannon – Fleetwood Mac
Hunger – Florence + The Machine
All I Wanted – Paramore
Ribs – Lorde
willow – Taylor Swift
Feels Like – Gracie Abrams
Dandelions – Ruth B.
Guilty as Sin? – Taylor Swift
Crystal – Stevie Nicks
Slow Burn – Kacey Musgraves
Honeysuckle – Addison Grace
Gold Dust Woman – Fleetwood Mac
we fell in love in october – girl in red
I know it won't work – Gracie Abrams
Call It Love – Picture This
This Love (Taylor's Version) – Taylor Swift
Think I'm In Love With You – Chris Stapleton
Butterflies – Kacey Musgraves
If You Ever Did Believe – Stevie Nicks

Words & Runes

Nia — knee-uh
Videt — VEE-det
Charis — starts like Charity: CHA-riss
Pyronia — pie-ROH-nee-uh
Lunaflor — LOO-nuh-floor

Promises   Sex   Love

Hex   Bind   Goddess

Veil   Protect   Ward

I hope you like thicc plant daddies who want you well-fed, and hot shadow mommies who would stab someone with a fork for you without hesitation.

WELCOME TO
Stella Rune

Lochlan

"Is It Now Taboo to Wear Clothing to Equinox Events?"—THE WEEKLY HEX

"The witches are already naked," Lochlan groaned into his phone.

On the other end, Becket crashed to the floor with a grunt, probably tripping over his own feet in excitement. Naked anything tended to short-circuit his friend's brain. Lochlan rolled his eyes and stepped behind a bush of honeysuckle to hide from the jiggling boobs and flopping dicks. The late-blooming flowers and their vivid orange colors did nothing to lessen his annoyance at having to attend a Mabon celebration alone.

"You're shitting me. Isn't the sun still out over there?" Becket asked. "Who's naked?"

"Maybe if you didn't miss your train you'd know."

"How many witches are we talking about?"

"Beck," Lochlan grumbled. A few of the blooms wilted with his mood.

He took a breath and stroked the petals back to life. "I wouldn't have come if I knew you weren't going to be here."

"Go home then," Becket said over the sound of a suitcase zipping. "I'll be there in five hours—we can have a nightcap."

Lochlan should have known better than to trust his friend to catch his train back to Stella Rune, let alone make it to the celebration on time.

"I was going home, but Nancy from Magical Resources spotted me in the parking lot and she's a gossip." He glanced over his shoulder toward a middle-aged woman who was talking animatedly to Ben from accounting—who, like many of the witches, was already naked.

Lochlan tugged at his collar, feeling the gentle warmth of heating spells and the weight of glamours thick in the air. Most attendees had arrived preheated by liberal amounts of spiced mead consumed during private celebrations at home. Being naked wasn't a strict requirement, but when you combined alcohol, tradition, and supernaturals' love for anything fun and primal, clothes simply became optional.

Which was exactly why they gathered in a specific section of Stella Rune's park. Regulars—non-magical humans—weren't supposed to see magic, much less naked nymphs dancing. Most regs lived in blissful ignorance, and those in charge wanted to keep it that way for their safety. Allegedly. Only regs who married into a supernatural family were allowed to know the truth. It was a rule, and though Lochlan wasn't sure he always agreed with it, he could see how it might keep everyone safer.

He turned his attention back to the honeysuckle, bringing a few more buds back to life while healing others caterpillars had chewed on.

"I hate coming to these parties." He usually worked from home, but his boss had forced him to attend to network. He was the lone archivist of the Videt; there was no need to make connections over drinks and nudity. And if he did, no one would remember a thing by morning anyway.

"I know, I'll make it up to you," Becket said, breaking him from his thoughts.

"If you don't, I'll hide leadwort in your bed and underwear drawer."

Becket's deep laugh brought him a little comfort. "I'm guessing that's some kind of plant that makes you itchy?"

"It's a Plumbaginaceae."

"I deal with stars Lochlan, I have no idea what a plumbie-whatever is."

"We've been friends for almost eight years." Lochlan sighed, realizing how often he'd listened patiently while Becket talked endlessly about stars, planets, and constellations. Clearly, plants hadn't quite made the same impression in return. "It's a blueish-purple flower. The oil from it can cause blisters. Or vomiting, if ingested."

"Lovely. So much for being friends for *almost* eight years then."

"Yeah, yeah. How's your mom doing?" He had wanted to go with Becket, to sit with her, cook, fold laundry, do anything at all. Just like she'd done for him since his freshman year of college. But work had gotten in the way.

"She tripped my stepfather with her crutches this morning. I'm still not sure if it was an accident or not. Probably not, considering he said he was thinking about trading her in for a model that *ran better*."

"That's not very funny."

"Mom didn't think so either. But she's good other than that." Doors slammed in the background. "Listen, I'm sorry I didn't make my train. I'm leaving for the station now and I don't have any clients in the morning, so you have me all to yourself. Go make some rounds for the lords in power and head home. I'll call you when I get in. We can go from there."

"I'm expecting top shelf bourbon."

"Only the best for you."

They said their goodbyes and hung up.

Lochlan peered around the honeysuckle bush, taking in the scene before him. The equinox celebration was in full swing—joyful music swelled through the crisp evening air, lively banter carried from clusters of supernaturals, some clothed, some decidedly not, and the bonfire roared, painting the sky in hues of orange and violet. Tables sat a safe distance from the flames, crowded with dishes and half-finished drinks, giving people a place to eat and rest between dances. Despite the revelry surrounding him, Lochlan would rather have been home with his dog, Jade, tackling the set of old diaries he was restoring. Though, if he was being honest, that felt lonely. No offense to Jade.

Historically, Mabon was a time for gratitude: a celebration of the harvest and preparation for the coming winter. Witches had come a long way from thatched roofs and no plumbing, but the spirit of the season remained unchanged. So, he'd celebrate, make his rounds and head home.

Lochlan scanned the crowd, searching for anyone he could tolerate small talk with, when the flicker of deep red hair caught his eye. A sudden, senseless ache filled his chest as he recognized the woman it belonged to.

Nia, the Duchess of Charity, stood in the shadows on the far side of the bonfire.

Lochlan had never officially met Nia, though he'd seen her often. As the only archivist in the area with a knack for repairing books, he frequently helped the Stella Rune bookshop restore old volumes, and the shop was located in the same building as her offices.

Nia was stunning, driven, and always in motion. What Lochlan—and everyone else—admired most was the way she inspired people to care. To donate when they could. To show up. She fought for housing access, food equity, and the kind of rights most people didn't even know were being stripped away. Nia stood for everything he struggled to believe in: hope, connection, belonging.

Maybe that was why he couldn't bring himself to walk past her office without stopping.

Now, in the fading light, her hair caught the fire's glow, and her presence pulled at something in him he couldn't name.

Nia turned.

As their eyes met, Lochlan felt an inexplicable familiarity, as if some thread of connection had existed between them long before this moment. He didn't know if it was fate, magic, or his imagination. He only knew he wanted more than this quiet glance. It was a need that unsettled him more than the thought of approaching a stranger.

He stepped out from behind the honeysuckle, his focus entirely on Nia, and walked straight into naked Nancy.

"Lochlan!" Nancy looked delighted as she grabbed his arms to steady herself. "I thought that was you in the parking lot. I haven't seen you since that cauldron explosion in the staff bathroom. How have you been?"

He kept his gaze above her chin but the blur of so much skin haunted his periphery.

"Erm," he choked on his words before he could form a greeting.

"My, I cannot believe you are here. Listen, I have this nephew, and I know you haven't seen anyone in a while, right? I could set up a coffee date. Just casual."

"Well..."

"Janet!" Nancy waved at someone and Lochlan looked for his escape as three naked women surrounded him. "Look who's here. Our prince!"

"Lochlan, I can't remember the last time I saw you," said Janet, who also worked in Magical Resources. Unlike Nancy, who handled community outreach, Janet was in charge of keeping the town's long-term glamours stable. "Susan, didn't you say your granddaughter just graduated summa cum luna or whatever it was. She's single."

Since Lochlan was looking anywhere but at the woman who'd just joined them, he didn't know if it was Susan from accounting, or Susan from the tourism department.

He prayed to the goddess for mercy and a way out of this conversation before it turned into a matchmaking catastrophe.

Just then, a tray of spiced mead passed by, heading away from him and the cluster of unclothed women.

"It was good to see you," he said, seizing the opportunity to escape, "please excuse me while I grab a drink before the dancing starts."

"The dancing has already started!" they complained in unison, but Lochlan was already slipping through the crowd, focused on the man bringing drinks to another group. After he placed his order, he found a table with mostly clothed supernaturals.

Lochlan had nothing against nakedness at celebrations—or in general. It was more that he didn't know where to look, how to react, or how to avoid making a misstep. When he'd left home at eighteen and traveled to Stella Rune from Dover, he had been thrust into witch life and hadn't found steady ground in the eight years since.

Nia crept into his thoughts, slipping past the guard of his better judgment.

She made it look easy, as if she'd always known who she was. Like she didn't have to try. He scanned the gathering, but she was nowhere to be seen. The ache that had spread through him, the glint of something new—something he hadn't felt before—faded to a dull longing.

His drink arrived, a welcome distraction. He'd let himself finish it and then he could leave the chaotic field and put the night behind him. Or at least pretend to. He doubted anything would make him forget Nia.

The way she made something in him stir.

The way she made him *want*.

At least his boss would be satisfied; tomorrow, he'd scribble a brief note, seal it, and send it off with the next available messenger cat to confirm he'd attended, had his drink, and fulfilled expectations.

Nothing more, nothing less.

He downed the chilled liquor and a distinctive fizz tickled his throat. It tasted like bourbon, but bourbon didn't make the world feel more colorful or hazy at the edges. The warmth spread fast, loosening the quiet caution within him. Strange. He didn't hate it. In fact, he liked the way it softened the world.

Suddenly, he wanted to stay a little longer.

2

Nia

"How to Detect Fairy Wine at Your Next Celebration." —*A PAGANS BLOG*

Nia stood far from the bonfire, where darkness welcomed her and her shadows prowled.

"How much are you willing to pay for your transgressions?" she asked, her voice calm, almost bored. "What are you willing to do?"

Jackson, her latest mark, swallowed hard. "T-transgressions?" he echoed.

Nia rolled her eyes. Shadows coiled around him, slithering up from the ground, winding like smoke around his throat. They whispered to her, revealing what he tried to hide—his fears, his secrets, the things he thought no one else could see.

Movement in the distance caught her eye.

A man, tall, broad-shouldered, and entirely out of place lingered at the edge of the gathering, half-hidden behind a bush. *Was he... talking to it? Petting it?*

Curiosity flickered over Nia, sharp and unexpected. Without thinking, she let her magic tighten around Jackson's throat, silencing his blubbering as she turned to study the stranger.

Who was he here with? Why wasn't he joining in like everyone else? And why was he so fascinated with that bush?

His gaze lifted and locked onto hers across the bonfire.

The noise around her dimmed. Her pulse skipped. An odd feeling stirred beneath her skin, slow and certain: like she'd found something hidden, something meant only for her. It settled deep in her chest, a familiarity she couldn't place and didn't trust.

Jackson's choking shattered the moment.

The spell was broken, leaving her with a flicker of irritation. Nia's gaze snapped back to her mark, her magic coiling tighter around his throat, punishing him for daring to break her focus. His face turned a lovely shade of blue before she pulled her shadows loose.

"I—I can't believe they call you Saint Nia, Duchess of Charity," he wheezed, glaring with watery eyes. "What would people say if they found out you threatened and terrorized for your donations?"

Nia's lips curved into a cold smile. "And what will they say when they learn that the so-called king of happy and healthy chickens is a fraud? That his birds are living in squalor and fighting off rats? That those organic chicken breasts they're feeding their children come from animals covered in lesions and riddled with disease?"

His eyes went wide. Nia gave him a wicked grin.

"Ten thousand dollars," he said, his voice barely a whisper.

"Oh, Jackson," she said, shaking her head. "No."

"F-fifty thousand."

"You think fifty will absolve you of your cruelty?" she asked, her tone cool and unyielding. "That amount is a drop in the ocean for someone like you." She paused, watching horror dawn on his face. "I know about your illegal gambling. And the money laundering."

"You're a monster."

"No, I just grew up with one," she backed him farther away from the party and tightened her powers once again. He was right where she wanted him. "Here's the deal, Jack. You're going to clean up your farm, get proper veterinarian care for those poor chickens. Then you're going to donate fifty thousand to Feeding Children, twenty-five thousand to the Stella Rune Pantry for the Unsheltered, and then, for pissing me off, ten thousand to the Stella Rune Animal Shelter."

His mouth opened and closed, but no words came out.

Nia leaned in. "What? Cat got your tongue? Spit it out."

"Eighty-five thousand?" He shook his head, incredulous. "That's insane."

She pulled her phone from her dress pocket and pressed play on a video of one of his farms. The sound came first: the restless clucking of chickens and the creak of old wood. The footage showed overcrowded enclosures, the birds packed too tightly, their feathers ruffled and dull. Some perched uneasily, shifting as they tried to find space, while others remained still, their heads tucked down.

Nia watched his face pale. "How much would you lose in sales if I posted this? If, say, the media got their hands on it?"

His jaw clenched. "Fine. Fine."

"Niiaahh," a singsong voice called from the distance.

"I expect the funds in five days. Now tell my business partner how pretty she looks tonight."

Nia linked her arm through Jackson's and smoothed the creases from his shirt. She turned to Ivy, who was skipping toward them in a shear opal dress. Her white-blonde hair gleamed orange in the firelight and her eyes sparkled with delight.

"Nia," Ivy said with a breathy sigh. "I've been looking for you."

"I'm right here." She pinched Jackson's rib.

"You look lovely tonight, Ivy."

She pinched harder.

"Absolutely stunning, if I wasn't already mar—"

"Thank you so much, Jackson," Nia cut in. "I look forward to working with you."

She released him and he stumbled away as Ivy waved an uneasy goodbye.

"What were you doing with the CEO of the largest poultry distribution company this side of the continent?" Her delicate hand continued to wave.

"Talking to him about the best places to donate his money." Nia glanced at her nails, her tone casual.

She and Ivy had founded The Charis Foundation six years ago, back when they'd shared a tiny apartment on the verge of foreclosure. The building's owner, an elderly woman, had fallen behind on her payments. A large corporation was circling, eager to buy the property and turn it into a parking garage. A parking garage in Stella Rune—how obscene.

Determined to help, Ivy and Nia had worked tirelessly to raise the money needed to save the property, eventually returning ownership to the older woman. That victory had sparked the creation of Charis, an organization dedicated to supporting causes close to Stella Rune and in the surrounding area. Years later, when the woman had passed away, she left the building to Ivy and Nia.

On the surface, Charis matched small charities with donors and helped them find creative ways to raise funds. They worked with wealthy individuals who had a genuine heart for giving—but that was only half the story. Off the books, Nia targeted corrupt individuals and forced them to pay for their sins.

It was the only way she knew to atone for the damage caused by people like her father. She'd never let Ivy in on what she really did, or the kinds of people she convinced to donate.

"Nia," Ivy scolded, spinning to face her. "You were roughing him up, weren't you?"

"Me? Never."

"If people want to donate, let them do it out of the goodness of their hearts."

Nia arched a brow. She never judged Ivy for how she got her donations. Her best friend had once bought them groceries—and quietly funded three food drives—by sending a few spicy videos to some exceptionally generous individuals. Not one of them knew their money ended up feeding the hungry.

Ivy had no idea how far Nia went to secure donations, and it was better that way. Safer.

Nia smiled, deflecting. "Oh, go dye your eyebrows."

"How dare you!" Ivy gasped, her hands flying to cover her brows. "You know how much it bothers me. You can't even see them unless I color them every other week." She stomped her foot for emphasis. "That's it."

"What are you going to do?"

Ivy's lips curved into a mischievous smile. "I'll order you decaf for a month!"

"You wouldn't do that to me."

Satisfied, Ivy turned her nose up and strutted off toward the growing crowd, where people had begun to dance beneath the now-dark sky. On her way, she passed one of Stella Rune's few remaining elders: a wiry old witch with shoulders curved from years of hunching over spellbooks and mediating petty squabbles.

The elders carried weight in town, not just in the supernatural community, but even in the Videt's decision-making. They weren't lawmakers, exactly—that was the Videt's domain—but their words held enough sway that few dared to ignore them. They had a way of charming humans, too, securing goodwill, influence, and occasionally funding for magical initiatives.

They also officiated hand-fasting ceremonies and other romantic rites, which made them particularly popular during celebrations like Mabon. Something about the air—whether it was magic, moonlight, or just an excess of wine—had a way of stirring up romance. Someone always ended up married before the night was through. Because nothing said *true love* like exchanging vows while your drunk uncle accidentally turned himself into a toad in the background.

Nia cupped her hands around her mouth and yelled after Ivy's retreating figure, "Make good decisions!"

Ivy was the only reason Nia bothered coming to these celebrations. Left to her own devices, her could-not-be-single best friend would end up married off to an ancient oak, a fairy, or—like last time—a wood devil.

Nia shivered and was thankful when a man approached with mulled wine. She grabbed a glass and made her way toward a shadowed tree. Settling onto the ground, she adjusted her skirt so it pooled around her and turned her attention to the dancing. Ivy swayed to the music, her movements fluid and carefree as she and others circled the fire, their laughter rising into the night air.

Nia always came to these gatherings as an observer; she never got naked, never let herself indulge, dancing and reveling, the way others did. Everything was business to her. But she still enjoyed watching the supernaturals cut loose, chasing things she told herself she didn't need. Love. Connection. The luxury of being fully known.

She had spent the first eighteen years of her life hidden, a secret kept for her own safety. And though she had built a new life in Stella Rune, she was still keeping that secret. Just like her father had.

Nia lifted the glass to her lips, but before the wine reached her tongue, a halting movement, out of place in the easy flow of revelers, snagged her attention. A tall, awkward man hesitated at the edge of the crowd before reluctantly stepping in. His brow furrowed as he tried to find the rhythm, his movements stiff and uncertain.

Nia recognized him immediately: the man who talked to bushes.

Now that she had a proper view, he wasn't terrible to look at. Actually, as his face relaxed and a small smile curved his lips, he became devastatingly handsome. Not that Nia was interested. She had a duty to help as many people as possible, and she wasn't about to get tied down. Not after what happened to her mother, and not for some tall—

He turned and her brain short-circuited.

Thighs. Thick, strong, and unfairly distracting under tailored pants. Her gaze trailed up and down, her breath catching as she took in the rest of him: broad shoulders, a solid, grabbable waist, and an ass that could only be described as perfect.

She could almost feel the rough press of his thighs under her palms, her hands gliding upward to dig her fingers into that infuriatingly faultless curve. The thought burned through her, sudden and unwelcome, leaving her stomach tight and her heart racing.

No. She would not be tempted. Dancing led to flirting, flirting led to dating, and then bang! You were married against your will.

Nia downed half her drink, though the burn and fizz almost made her spit it back up. She looked to the sky as her eyes watered, but—instantly and irrationally—she missed the sight of him. When she looked back toward the supernaturals, he was staring at her.

Her breath hitched as she swallowed a hiccup.

He was so handsome with stars dancing around his head. When he gave her a welcoming smile that felt comfortable and familiar, she was suddenly on her feet. Which was a horrible idea, because as she stood, her vision blurred. It felt like her feet left the ground as colors swirled around her in a vibrant tornado, and all she could hold on to was her absurdly desperate need to get to him.

That wasn't normal. It was rom-com-level nonsense. A part of Nia knew this was how people got cursed, or worse—married. She'd need to see the eraser witch first thing in the morning to sort out whatever this was.

But first, she'd dance.

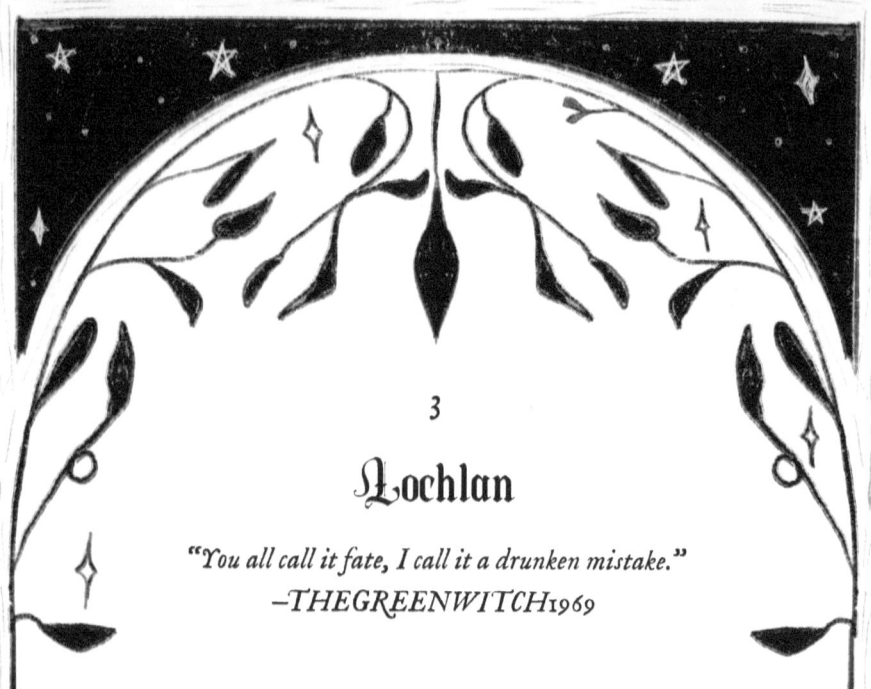

3

Lochlan

"You all call it fate, I call it a drunken mistake."
—THE GREEN WITCH 1969

L ochlan groaned. His bed was wet and itchy, and a blinding light assaulted his eyelids. He remembered dancing, a blazing fire, and—

"Click-click-kra!" a crow screeched, scrambling his thoughts.

"I will use you in a damn potion if you don't cease your jeering," Lochlan snapped, his words slurred with sleepy irritation.

"Kra-kra!"

He opened his eyes to glare at the dark bird.

The sun hung low in the sky behind the creature and gray smoke rose in the distance. He could hear the sounds of birds and insects waking, which meant he'd never made it home last night, and this was not his bed.

"Shit, Jade." He ran a hand across his face and discovered a braided rope wrapped around his palm. "What the—?"

"Jade?" a woman's voice interrupted, husky with sleep. The sound brought Lochlan an unexpected sense of relief. He reached down, fingers brushing through her silky hair, and felt a sudden, fierce longing to stay like this forever. Not that he could move, even if he'd wanted to. Her warm body was draped over him, legs tangled with his, her bare stomach pressed against his side.

Bare.

Naked.

They were both naked.

Everything stilled around him; he didn't even breathe as he realized his situation. Their situation.

Moaning rang in his memory, along with grinding bodies, and a desperate need for release. He put his weight on his elbows and looked down to find deep red hair. Tired green eyes blinked up at him.

It was Nia.

She had been using him as a pillow.

Her eyes widened and she scrambled back with a yelp, but didn't get far. The rope still tied around their wrists snapped tight, yanking him forward. He hit the grass with a grunt, then pushed up onto his hands, dragging her part of the way back with him.

She landed face-first in his bare lap.

Lochlan went very still as his brain went blank and blood rushed south. Ache bloomed, harsh and sudden—a reminder that he'd never found relief. He hadn't let himself. But now he hardened instantly, involuntarily, and completely inappropriately. His body didn't care. It knew exactly what it wanted, even as his mind scrambled to slam on the breaks.

"I'm sorry," he blurted.

She jerked back. Darkness gathered around her and hid her naked body from him. He blinked rapidly, desire battling with awe as he watched her magic come to life. The dark shadows moved like smoke.

It was mesmerizing. Trailing petunia suddenly appeared alongside her shadows, the dark velvet petals and vibrant green leaves cocooning her chest and thighs.

"Stop it!" she snapped, attempting to shuffle farther away. Her power sliced through the rope, then the flowers, giving him one more accidental view of her body before it vanished again in blossoms and darkness. He caught a glimpse of faint fingermarks—almost certainly his fingermarks, he realized with a pang—bruising her hips. Her voice echoed in his memory, low and breathless, begging him for more. But he hadn't let them go that far. They were too drunk. He'd stopped, even when it nearly broke him. Still... the way she'd wrapped her legs around him. He hadn't meant to leave marks. But seeing the evidence of their night while she looked so wounded filled him with uneasy doubt. "Leave me alone!"

"I'm not—" Lochlan stopped and couldn't breathe past the pounding in his chest. He brought his right hand up: a thin wisp of darkness danced across his knuckles, twirled around his fingers, and twined with the rope still wrapped around his wrist.

It was a hand-fasting rope.

There were rumors of hasty marriages during supernatural events, but it was laughable to think that could happen to him.

"What the goddess is this?" Nia's voice was edged with panic as she looked between him and the hand-fasting rope. She had stopped struggling—whether from exhaustion or the weight of their intertwined magic, he wasn't sure. Her gaze burned into him, demanding answers he didn't have. "Tell me we didn't actually do this."

"What's mine is yours." A memory flashed, filled with the sound of husky laughter and the taste of a sweet drink.

Oh fuck, he was married to Nia—practically a stranger. He pushed himself to his feet, swaying slightly as his head throbbed. Hastily, he covered his front with his hands and turned his back to her, scanning the grass for his clothes.

She gasped and his skin prickled with heat. His hand shot to cover his ass, but it was a futile effort; his palm barely concealed one cheek. He could only imagine what she was seeing—and thinking. Unease flared in his chest, leaving him feeling more exposed than ever.

Did she notice the scars winding up from his ankles, fading as they reached his knees? Would she ask? Would she care?

The thought made his steps falter, and he nearly missed the scattered remains of a piece of clothing: his underwear. A spot of denim caught his eye a few feet away, and he walked toward it, gathering his scattered belongings. When he picked up a silky purple dress, he hesitated, then brought it to Nia with his eyes firmly shut.

"This can't be happening," she muttered, snatching the dress from his outstretched hand. He turned away to give her privacy, pulling his shirt on—inside out, of course.

"Wait," she said, a note of accusation in her voice. "Are you a wood devil?"

Lochlan froze. He turned back to her, his shirt halfway over his face. "Wood devils don't exist."

"A wood devil would say that." She rubbed her bare arms, shivering.

Without thinking, he gave her his jacket. "I'm a witch," he said, his tone flat. "If you didn't notice, my magic has mixed with yours. Which means—"

"Don't say it." She covered her face with both hands, stepping back. "If you say it, it's real."

Lochlan flinched. Would he ever get used to the sting of being unwanted?

"I'll fix this," he offered quietly.

"No, I will," she snapped, then added under her breath, "I fix everything."

She stormed off in the wrong direction, muttering curses to herself.

"The parking lot is this way," he called, gesturing over his shoulder.

She grumbled something unintelligible but adjusted her path, trudging ahead without looking back.

They walked in silence. Now and then her eyes slid to his, lingering before looking away. Was she piecing together moments from last night, like he was?

It was blurred images, slurred conversations, and heated touches.

How did this happen?

"I'm Nia," she blurted, stumbling. He reached for her instinctively, but she raised a hand to stop him.

"I'm Lochlan," he offered.

"The Unwanted Heir?" she asked, her brows scrunching as if she'd expected someone different.

A flush climbed his neck, and he looked away, focusing on the path ahead.

The title would never leave him. Even after all these years carefully fading into the background, it still found him: a reminder of a past he had no control over and a kingdom that had begun to fall the moment the world learned he existed.

His mother had kept her pregnancy a secret. After his birth, he'd been quietly placed in his father's care, raised unseen among the castle's staff. He grew up never knowing he had a half-sister and brother—two children the queen had claimed and presented to the world while he remained hidden in the shadows. Lochlan had been thirteen when his father died, leaving him alone with servants who had no idea what to do with a boy who was never meant to exist. Then one of them had talked.

One whisper turned into many, until the truth spread beyond the castle walls.

The scandal had been immediate, a wildfire that tore through the monarchy. The queen's affair with a castle gardener, they'd called it. But his father had been far more than that. He was a powerful herb witch— his magic hidden, just like the child they had conceived.

Lochlan's thoughts swirled through the dark memories until Nia broke the silence.

"I actually have experience with this kind of mess," she said.

Lochlan grimaced. *A mess.* That's what his mother had called him—a problem she'd tried to hide.

"Not for me," Nia added quickly. "I would never get caught married."

He raised an eyebrow.

"Well… never again," she muttered, waving a hand in the air. "Ugh, I need coffee and a lawyer."

The mention of a lawyer made him think of Becket. Had he made it home safely? Lochlan would call him as soon as he found a charger and this was all sorted out. At least he would get a good laugh out of the situation.

Lochlan held a low branch up so Nia could duck under it safely. She blinked up at him, her expression briefly thankful before shifting into frustration. It was oddly endearing. The darkness that had clung to him moments ago loosened its grip, even as she grumbled about the mess they were in. *A mess.* That's what she'd called their predicament. Not him.

"Anyway," she said, "someone I know got into a similar situation, and I was able to get her out of it easily. Half an hour of paperwork, and this whole thing will be annulled. Then we can just forget it ever happened."

Forget it ever happened. He could never forget Nia, or the way it had felt to hold her in his arms, or the shape of her body beneath the stars. She was seared into his memory.

"Shit," she said. They arrived at the parking lot and all that waited for them was his ancient truck. "I came with my partner."

"Partner?" he asked, startled.

"My business partner," she clarified. "And best friend."

He nodded in understanding, breathing a little easier.

"I can drive us." He gestured to the truck.

A question flashed in her eyes and he wished he had the courage to ask her what it was, what she felt, besides regret.

They got in, buckled their seatbelts, and when he turned the key, the engine roared to life.

Lochlan hesitated.

Though they'd just met, he already knew the ache of losing Nia to an annulment would haunt him forever. He had finally mustered the courage to approach her before the liquor took over. What if he hadn't been derailed by Nancy? Would he have woken up with a number in his phone and the possibility of getting to know Nia instead?

She turned to him with an awkward smile. He was taking too long to leave, but putting the truck in drive would begin the process of saying goodbye. What reason would she have to talk to him or seek him out when this was taken care of? It felt like so many experiences he'd had before, and he wanted something different. Something new.

But that was impossible. Unless...

"Lochlan," she said, quiet and pleading.

He wouldn't get what he wanted today.

But at least she would.

4

Nia

"The Duchess of Charity Marries The Unwanted Heir." –THE STELLA RUNE GAZETTE

"You won't be the only ones coming in today," Vinny said. He was a local Stella Rune lawyer who'd handled Ivy's hasty annulment. An energy witch, Vinny could sense emotions in a way humans might call empathic. It probably made him an excellent lawyer, able to read people in ways they couldn't even read themselves.

He sat behind a large mahogany desk, sorting through the paperwork to finalize the annulment.

"They should pass a bill pausing all marriages during equinox gatherings," he muttered.

Nia flinched at the word *marriage.* She couldn't believe she was sitting here. This wasn't her.

It could be worse. As far as husbands went, Lochlan was hot—no denying that. He was the classic tall, dark, and handsome cliché, all sharp cheekbones, broad shoulders, and just the right amount of scruffy stubble. And, well… that ass.

She swallowed a groan.

He also seemed sweet, in a quiet, barely talking kind of way. But she had vowed to never be in this position, no matter what. Now she had to vow that it would never happen again. Maybe she should do a spell, or find a potion to help make it stick.

"How is your friend Ivy doing?" Vinny asked.

"She's amazing, and happily *unmarried*," Nia gave him a pointed look and then dropped her gaze to the papers in his hands.

"Right, right. I'll just take these to the back, confirm the information, and get you out of here in time for brunch."

Vinny walked away and when the door closed behind him, Nia bent over and rubbed her eyes. Once this was taken care of, she would have to make sure nothing leaked to the media. They loved following anything she did, for some absurd reason.

"Are you okay?" Lochlan asked.

She waved the question away. She wasn't okay, but she would be, and either way it wasn't any of his concern.

"You'll be rid of me soon."

Memories of the night before flickered through her mind like elusive flames, impossible to hold on to, yet they left her burning all the same. She had never enjoyed an equinox celebration so much, never danced so freely, never been so… carnal.

They hadn't had sex. He wouldn't let them. But they had been naked, tangled together, her legs spread over his thighs as she chased relief with desperate, breathless urgency. He'd held her through it but refused to take that final step, no matter how many times she'd begged. Her moans had pressed against his throat, her teeth had sunk into his skin. The marks she'd left were red and angry, and yet, she couldn't bring herself to feel ashamed.

What would it feel like to have all of him? To feel him inside her, with nothing between them but heat and want? When they woke up, he'd been sweet and attentive, but he'd marked her as roughly as she'd marked him, and she wanted that side. That darker, hungrier part of him. The one that would leave her sore and aching in all the ways she craved.

She blew out a shaky breath, her cheeks flushing as the images swirled too vividly in her mind. *Stop it.* There was no good in dwelling on what couldn't—wouldn't—happen.

She forced herself to look anywhere but at him.

On the lawyer's desk sat a plant, its leaves drooping and dull. Nia's gaze lingered on it, sensing the faint pulse of life, clinging on but desperate for care. This was Lochlan's magic, now hers.

He had noticed the plant, too.

Shadows curled from his hand, twining gracefully around one of the water bottles Vinny had offered them and lifting it toward the thirsty plant. As the dry soil greedily absorbed the water, Nia could feel the plant's immediate relief, like a breath finally taken after too long without air.

"You caught on to that pretty fast," she murmured, grudgingly impressed.

Lochlan glanced at her, the corners of his mouth curving slightly. "Your shadows—they're magnificent. They remind me of the vines I can conjure."

His compliment sent an unexpected surge of warmth through her, but she shoved the feeling aside, focusing instead on the plant. She had the sudden urge to steal it, to bring it back to her office where she could tend to it properly. She could picture it thriving among the small collection she'd somehow accumulated over the years—plants she had, against all odds, managed to keep alive. She wasn't sure when or why she'd started collecting them.

Now, it felt almost like some kind of twisted joke from fate.

"You're taking this a lot better than I am," she said.

"I'm used to being someone's mistake." His voice was laced with quiet anger. Nia was about to ask him what he meant when the lawyer came back, his face pale.

He sat behind the desk. "I'm sorry."

Nia and Lochlan shared a glance.

"For?" he asked.

"I can't grant your annulment."

A faint ringing filled Nia's ears.

"Excuse me?" she demanded. "Why the fuck not?"

"It seems…" Vinny tugged at the collar of his shirt, the movement small but telling. "Well, I… I just can't."

Nia's jaw tightened.

"I can feel your anger." His magic must have been clawing at him, dragging every bit of her fury straight through him. Good. "Please, calm down and—

"Don't tell me to calm down. You annulled Ivy's marriage, and that devil didn't even need to be here!"

Shadows darkened the room, rising with her anger.

"That was a different situation," the lawyer said, his hands trembling. "I can't help you. I'm going to have to ask you to leave."

Nia stood so fast her chair fell and clattered to the ground behind her. This couldn't be happening. She fixed things. That was what she did. Her mind began to work, looking at all the options. Extorsion would take time; threatening would be a lot quicker.

She searched the office, looking for—

A gentle hand wrapped around her forearm.

"Come on, Nia." Lochlan's voice was cool and calm in a way that eased her anger. "I know someone who can help us."

Despite the tension in the room, his expression was all careful concern. Nia turned back to the lawyer, the tips of her writhing shadows pointing at him, each sharp as a blade. "You're going to regret this."

The second lawyer's office was nothing like what she'd expected. A gaming table covered in tiny painted figures stood in one corner, while mostly tasteful posters of half-naked people lined the walls. A mini fridge sat in one corner, stocked with more beer than water, and numerous plants thrived in the small, eclectic space.

And then there was Becket—tall with dark skin and a careless grin, his slacks and shirt rumpled like they'd spent the night on someone else's floor, or possibly like he'd just rolled out of an orgy.

She instantly liked him.

Something in her stirred, perking up like a cat scenting the air. It wasn't a conscious reaction, more instinct than intent: *You have magic,* it hummed, *but what kind?*

It was always like this with other supernaturals. Her powers stirred, too, eager to root around in his darkness, to get a feel for what lay beneath. But when he gave Lochlan's shoulder a squeeze and she caught the twitch of his lips out of the corner of her eye, she pushed down the urge.

"You just had to have all the fun without me, didn't you?" Becket said, taking a seat behind his messy desk.

"We probably have you to thank for this," Lochlan answered.

"If I'd been there, I wouldn't have stopped it." Becket held one hand by his mouth and stage-whispered. "She's freaking hot, dude."

Lochlan ran a hand over his face and Nia rolled her eyes.

"Now," Becket continued, "I don't usually deal with ruining a lovely couple's life with divorce–"

"Annulment," Lochlan cut in, his tone clipped.

Becket waved a dismissive hand. "But I don't see any reason why I can't file this and send you on your way." He glanced over the papers. "Yep, everything's in place. You sign here, Lochlan. And Nia, there."

Lochlan signed quickly and slid the papers toward Nia. She found herself hesitating. Yes, she wanted this over with as quickly as possible, but—

"I just want to say," she began softly, her fingers brushing the pen, "if there was anyone to be accidentally married to, I couldn't do better than you."

Lochlan's eyes widened as wonder flickered across his face. Caught off guard by the emotion, she quickly turned away. With a steadying breath, she signed her name.

"Now, my turn. Then we can crack open a bottle of bubbly to celebrate," said Becket.

"It's nine in the morning," Nia pointed out.

He shrugged and turned to sign the paper. The pen hovered over the blank line. Nia watched as it continued to hover, then tremble.

"What?" Becket's eyes flicked between the both of them.

"We didn't say anything," Lochlan said, frowning. "What's wrong?"

"Huh, weird." He shook his head and went to sign again. This time, Becket's hand began to shake violently. He grabbed his wrist, trying to force the pen to paper, but it wouldn't budge. The lights began to flicker as Becket shook his head. "I will not submit to you... you..."

Becket began mumbling incoherent words.

Lochlan stood as Nia gripped the arms of her chair.

Becket looked up from the papers, his eyes unfocused and nose bleeding. "Mommy, I would like some cereal," he said before his face fell to the desk with a painful thump.

"Becket!" Lochlan rushed to his friend and checked his pulse before trying to wake him with light slaps on his face.

Nia's heart pounded so violently she thought she might pass out. Memories surfaced, flashes of a time she was too young to understand: a man tied to a chair, his body straining, his mind under siege.

Her stomach turned. "That fucking asshole."

"He didn't do anything!" Lochlan's voice was harsh, commanding— and, annoyingly, kind of hot.

"Not him."

Lochlan's eyes narrowed. "Who?"

5

Lochlan

"What We Know About The Unwanted Heir."
–*THE WEEKLY HEX*

"Y ou fucking shitbag!" Nia yelled, storming into the office of Wulfric 'The Sword' Cabot—the man who governed most of the magical community. The Blade of the Goddess. The most powerful supernatural, as far as Lochlan was concerned.

And Lochlan's boss.

After Becket regained consciousness and insisted he was fine, Nia had bolted. Lochlan had chased after her, following as she ran straight out of the office, through Stella Rune, up the steep hill, past concerned regulars and supernaturals alike. Lochlan caught up just as she'd reached the Videt, the massive domed structure that sat atop a cliff overlooking the ocean. He had trailed behind Nia as she blew past the very confused— and entirely useless—security guard, then up several floors, bypassing Wulfric's elderly assistant, before barreling into the imposing office.

The room was all dark wood and towering shelves. The windows were open, letting in a sea breeze and the sound of crashing waves. Writhing shadows sent papers fluttering, a globe spinning, and a few picture frames tilting askew. Lochlan barely had time to catch his breath before Nia was across the room.

Wulfric, unnervingly calm, watched her skid to a stop before his desk. A small, knowing smile played on his lips as he smoothed his mustache, then spread his arms wide in an almost theatrical welcome.

"My lovely daughter," Wulfric declared, his tone rich with amusement. "What a joy it is to see you after all this time. Seven years, eleven months, and one day, to be exact." His gaze slid to Lochlan with a conspiratorial wink. "And who is this strapping young man with you?"

Lochlan's brows shot up as his brain scrambled to process what he'd just heard.

Daughter.

The word reverberated in his head like an echo in the tunnels beneath Stella Rune.

He had known Wulfric for years. The man had plucked him—a hurt, wide-eyed eighteen-year-old—from one path and set him on another. He'd granted the scholarship that had shaped the course of Lochlan's life; he'd been a mentor, a boss, a guiding presence Lochlan respected deeply, not just for the power he wielded, but the personal investment he'd made in Lochlan. In all this time, Wulfric had never mentioned having any family—let alone a daughter.

Now that daughter was Lochlan's accidental wife?

Well, soon-to-be ex-wife.

"I will murder you!" Nia's spat, jolting Lochlan from his thoughts.

"Patricide?" Wulfric interjected smoothly, his amusement cutting through the tension. "I'm touched."

"What did you do to those lawyers?" she growled. "Why are you interfering with the annulment?"

Wulfric ignored her and turned toward Lochlan. "I'm sorry, where are my manners. What was your name?"

Lochlan's eyes narrowed. "Lochlan, sir."

"Polite and handsome? How marvelous!" He stood and walked toward his bar cart, one he'd served Lochlan a drink from countless times. "Let us toast to your nuptials and the advantageous coupling you've found yourselves in."

"Don't act like you don't know his name," Nia spat. "You saw it when you were rooting around the minds of those lawyers."

Wulfric was a mensiter, a dream walker, and could travel through people's thoughts, regardless of how far away they were. Everyone in the magical community knew as much. What Lochlan wanted to know was why The Sword was keeping their familiarity from his daughter.

And why he'd kept the existence of his daughter a secret from Lochlan.

Wulfric cut him a look Lochlan interrupted as: *I have my reasons.*

"Wait. An advantageous marriage?" Nia looked between them. "Why would you think that?"

Wulfric leaned back, swirling the crystal decanter in his hand, silent but watchful.

Nia gasped sharply. "Oh no."

She ran a hand across her face.

"What?" Lochlan asked, his heart quickening.

"He planned this whole thing."

Lochlan's gaze jumped from Nia to Wulfric, bewildered. Why would a powerful, calculating man like Wulfric want someone like him anywhere near his daughter?

"Yes." Wulfric tilted his head, with a subtle and infuriatingly satisfied smile. "Right down to the wine."

"Fairy wine?" Nia let out an incredulous laugh, pacing the office like a furious, caged cat. "You manipulative shitbag."

Dread pooled in Lochlan's stomach. "You drugged us?"

"Don't be dramatic." Wulfric waved dismissively. "Fairy wine merely lowers inhibitions. You were fully yourselves, just more… impulsively honest." His gaze moved smoothly between them. Nia glared. Lochlan stood, mouth slack in disbelief. "I saw you two had finally noticed each other, and took the opportunity to enact my plan."

"Plan?" Nia demanded. "What do you want?"

Wulfric spread his hands in an easy, practiced gesture. "Simply for my lovely daughter to find love. To be happy." His voice was calm and confident. "To be part of my life again."

"Never," Nia snapped.

"You're here now, aren't you?"

"Under force and coercion!"

Wulfric waved lazily toward Lochlan. "There is nothing about this union you did not both willingly enter into. Force? Coercion? Oh, I think not. Even if it is for the best."

Nia scoffed. "You don't get to decide what's best for me anymore."

Her voice was ice-cold but Wulfric didn't flinch. Instead, his knowing smile deepened.

"My dear, all I've ever wanted is your safety and happiness. A life filled with love."

Nia's laugh was bitter. "Like the life you forced on my mother?"

For the first time, Wulfric's polished expression slipped.

"You may have stolen her choices from her." Nia raised her chin defiantly. "But you will not take or dictate mine."

Silence thickened between them, tense and stifling. Nia turned her glare on Lochlan, eyes narrowed as if preparing to curse him.

"Were you in on this?"

Lochlan lifted his hands, palms open in a desperate show of innocence. "Absolutely not."

She looked furious, but Lochlan could see the pain beneath her anger, and he wanted to be the one to ease her hurt.

"He was not involved," Wulfric interjected. "But don't think I didn't do my research."

"What was there to research?" Nia's gaze raked over Lochlan, as if he were an enigma she was trying to decipher. Her scrutiny triggered the part of himself that was always careful to stay unnoticed. He looked away.

"Lochlan is a son of Dover," Wulfric said, almost gleeful, "and what is it now? Third in line to that throne the regulars sit on?"

"Third?" Lochlan exclaimed.

Last he'd checked, he was tenth. Not that it mattered; the title was just symbolic. Had something happened to his family? His hand instinctively went to his pocket, fumbling for his phone. He didn't follow the royal news and made a point to stay out of it. No feeds, no updates, nothing that reminded him of a family that had never treated him like he belonged.

"There have been some... accidents," Wulfric continued, his delivery as casual as if he were conveying the week's weather forecast. "I'm sorry to say your aunts and uncles have passed."

Lochlan scrolled through the list, his stomach sinking.

Train accident.

Riding accident.

Crushed by a cow.

The explanations grew more outlandish and improbable, yet there they were, cataloged with eerie detachment. No foul play. No common thread. Just a string of bizarre incidents. Lochlan covered his mouth with one hand, trying to stifle the rising wave of panic as he paced the office.

What a fucking nightmare.

"Me being a princess wouldn't change anything," Nia said flatly. "It's just a title."

"A title is always advantageous," Wulfric replied. "It opens doors. It makes people listen. Especially in the human world."

Lochlan sank into one of the many chairs in the office, thoughts spinning wildly. A bastard. A witch. Now third in line to the throne?

His gaze flicked to Nia. She was watching him, her expression unreadable. For a moment, something passed between them—concern, or maybe just curiosity—but then it was gone. Her shoulders squared, jaw tightening as she turned on her father.

"I made a vow." Her voice cracked like a whip.

"And you made one last night, too," Wulfric replied, unshaken.

Nia's shadows lashed through the air, slamming into the bar cart and sending it crashing across the room.

"I will make you pay for this."

Wulfric shrugged. "How, dear daughter? My secrets hold no power over me. I have nothing to lose, no aspirations beyond your care and safety. Unlike you."

"Why are you doing this?" Lochlan asked.

Even to himself, his voice sounded strangely dull and devoid of emotion. This was all just too much.

"Because I can," Wulfric said to both of them. Then, to Nia, "Can you not believe I want what is best for you? Trust that I've ensured Lochlan is the best choice?"

"No!" she snapped. "There's something you want. And this won't work—it's barbaric."

"Were you not the result of a forced marriage?" Wulfric asked, maddeningly calm.

"And look how that turned out," she spat, venom in every word. But

Lochlan saw the way her eyes glistened before she looked away. "Name your price."

Wulfric raised his chin, walking to his desk with deliberate ease. He sat down, leaning back and toying with his mustache while Nia fumed, hands clenched at her sides.

Tension crackled like static in the air. Whatever their history, it had left scars deep and jagged, and Lochlan was no closer to understanding these than he had been five minutes ago.

"Fine," Wulfric said. Nia's shoulders sagged with relief. "I am certain I made the right choice, but I will give you the opportunity to change my mind. I'm feeling generous and my mood has lifted after being able to see you again."

"At what cost, Wulfric?" Lochlan knew The Sword well enough to know there would be terms.

"You must live together. You must attend five family dinners, five public events of your choosing, and five witch celebrations. If after that you can prove I made the wrong choice, I will grant you the annulment by Yule."

"You're out of your mind." Nia bristled with anger. "One of each. You'll grant the annulment by Samhain. And we won't be living together," she countered.

"You cannot prove you are incompatible if you do not give this relationship a chance. So you *will* live together. Three family dinners, two witch ceremonies, and a public event approved by me. And I will decide on Samhain."

Silence stretched between them, punctuated only by the soft crash of waves outside Wulfric's window.

"Fine." Nia sighed, clearly frustrated. "And how can we trust you to not simply decide in your own favor?"

"We can all do a promise spell at our first family dinner, which I'm so looking forward to, dear daughter."

Nia looked to Lochlan. "What are your thoughts?"

"What choice do we have?" he answered.

"There should always be a choice." She glared at her father while she said it. "Are we in agreement?"

"Yes."

They both turned to Lochlan.

"Yes," he said, because fighting it felt impossible, and some reckless part of him wanted to see what happened next.

"Lovely!" Wulfric stood and clapped his hands once. "Now if you two will excuse me, I have a meeting with someone or other. I'll have the promise spell ready for our first family dinner and will be in touch soon."

"Fine." Nia turned toward the door. "I'm going to work."

"Wait," Lochlan called, following.

She paused near Wulfric's very curious secretary, Francine. Lochlan glanced at the older witch, then inclined his head down the hall. Nia followed him to an alcove just far enough away, he hoped they wouldn't be overheard.

"I'm sorry about this."

He'd wanted a chance to be in Nia's life, but not under these terms.

She looked down at her feet and rubbed the back of her neck. "It's not your fault, so..." She glanced at Francine, then lowered her voice. "We'll be living together?"

"We'll make it work." Lochlan resisted the urge to reach out and hold her. He wanted to—desperately—but, under the circumstances, he wasn't sure how she'd receive the gesture. This was all a lot for both of them to take in. "Would you prefer your place or mine?"

"Yours," she said, quickly. "My place isn't much more than a corner of that asshat's office. I live in an apartment above Charis. Would you want to meet me there around six? I have a motorcycle, so riding with my things isn't exactly ideal."

"Okay," he said, meeting her gaze. "I'll be there at six."

Her lips twitched upward—not quite happy, but maybe relieved. Her eyes still carried the burden of what the day had thrown at her.

"Good," she murmured as a tear slipped free.

Before he could think better of it, Lochlan reached out and brushed it away with his thumb. Nia froze. Then she stepped back, wiping at her other eye with the heel of her hand.

"Good," she repeated, as she turned and left.

Lochlan stayed where he was, staring at the empty doorway as if it might offer answers. The feeling in the hall shifted subtly, and he knew without turning that Wulfric stood behind him.

He'd appeared like this many times before, usually as Lochlan worked on delicate restorations in the Videt's archives. Wulfric had often stayed longer than necessary, watching Lochlan's careful progress with almost paternal interest. They'd talked—about the pieces Lochlan handled, their history, their value—and it had been comfortable. Reassuring, even.

Now? That presence made Lochlan's stomach twist. The man he'd once respected, even admired, had orchestrated something so elaborate, so personal, so invasive, Lochlan felt like he'd never really known or understood him.

"Why are you doing this?" Lochlan asked. He didn't turn around, keeping his eyes fixed on the spot where Nia had stood.

"Because I feel it's what's best for everyone," Wulfric replied, his tone casual.

Lochlan glanced over his shoulder. "Why me?"

"Why not you?" Wulfric said. "One day, I hope you see yourself as others see you, as I've always seen you."

Lochlan moved to leave. He needed space and time to think—but Wulfric's voice stopped him.

"And Lochlan?" Wulfric said, a note of warning in his tone. "Not a word about us."

Lochlan turned, frowning as he searched Wulfric's face for some kind of explanation. "You can't possibly think I could keep this from her," he said, disbelieving.

"I expect you to," Wulfric said firmly.

"Why?"

"Because it's what's best, and what I want," Wulfric replied, his gaze unyielding. "Her knowing our connection won't help either of us."

Lochlan felt a pang of... betrayal, maybe.

"And what about what she wants?" he asked. "If you care about her, if you miss her and want her back, this doesn't feel like the way to fix things."

For a moment, Wulfric's confident exterior faltered. A faint shadow of regret passed over his face before he turned away, walking back to his office.

"It's the only way," Wulfric said, softly.

The doors closed behind him, leaving Lochlan alone with more questions than answers.

6

Nia

"The Duchess of Charity stormed out of The Sword's office today! What does it mean? Did you see her outfit? A tweed blazer with a silky dress? Swoon!" –DUTCHESSLOVER3000

Nia rested her head on a makeshift pillow of event flyers, the colorful papers crinkling beneath her cheek. They advertised a pancake breakfast to raise funds for better gear for local police dogs. But how could she focus on pancakes and pups when she'd just come face-to-face with the man she despised more than anyone?

It hadn't always been hatred her father inspired.

For the first seventeen years of her life, she'd adored him—he had been everything to her. He'd hidden her away in the grand manor that loomed in the shadow of the Videt, overlooking the sea, always claiming it was to protect her. He had said no one could know she existed, or she'd suffer the same tragic fate as her mother. Only later did she uncover the bitter truth: he'd lied about everything. Her mother's death had never been an accident.

It had been his fault.

Nia wiped her eyes against the sleeve of her jacket—or rather, Lochlan's jacket. It smelled faintly of fresh grass, lingering embers from last night's fire, and him. Not that she wanted to recognize the scent of her new husband.

Husband.

She was married, and she couldn't get unmarried unless she proved to her father that he was wrong. It should have been easy: Nia wasn't right for anyone. And she suspected Lochlan was already in a relationship with someone named Jade.

Easy.

So why did she keep revisiting the look on his face when he'd called himself a mistake? Or the way her stomach had twisted when she saw him take in the loss of so many family members? Or, worst of all, the way her heart ached when he'd wiped away her tears.

At that moment, she'd almost confided in him. It was an instinct and urge she had never felt before. She wanted to tell him all the fears that came bubbling up after seeing her father again, fears that stemmed from her mother's death and had led to her vowing to never marry. But she had six weeks to prove her father wrong, and confiding in Lochlan wouldn't help her case.

Nia's head snapped up as the foundation's double doors flew open.

Ivy stormed in, her hair and the loose fabric of her skirt billowing behind her. "Where have you been?"

Nia groaned and put her head back on the desk.

"I've been worried sick! No text, no call, no freaking cat. Nothing. I wouldn't know if you were dead or alive, if it wasn't for that damned social channel where fans follow your every move."

"Are you done?" Nia grumbled.

She heard Ivy huff, and imagined her nostrils flaring like they sometimes did.

Nia didn't lift her head, but her hand, and summoned a mess of dark flowers and leaves.

"Oh. My. Goddess!" Ivy squealed. Nia winced at the sound. "You have shared magic! You're married! I never thought it would happen. Was it that strapping man you were hanging around with all night?"

Nia whipped her head up and the room spun. She really needed to find food. And coffee. Quickly. "You saw him?"

"Nia! He was so handsome, and his hair was so dark, and his scruff…" Ivy practically swooned into a chair.

"Ivy. Why do I drag myself to those parties?"

"So I won't get in trouble or get married accidentally again."

"And what happened to me last night?"

"You—" Her blue eyes widened like saucers. She chewed on her lip for a moment. "You don't want to be married?"

Nia glared at her best friend.

"But marriage is so wonderful. You have a partner for life, you get to use their magic, not to mention the sex. And you can kiss them whenever you want."

"I have not eaten, I have not had coffee, and you were married for five minutes."

Ivy's face scrunched in annoyance. "Only because you worked so fast to get it annulled. You could have waited a few days!"

"You married a wood devil! A *wood devil*. They eat their spouses after the marriage is consummated."

"But he was so tall," Ivy said dreamily, sinking further into the chair. "And though I couldn't speak his language, he was really sweet and attentive. If he was going to eat me, I bet it would have been painless. Maybe even a teensy-bit hot."

"Please stop."

Ivy was about to continue when Eddie, one of Stella Rune's three delivery people, entered the waiting area of their office.

"Thank the goddess you ordered lunch," Nia said.

Ivy shook her head. "I didn't order anything."

Before either of them could say more, the other two delivery people—Maria and Joel—followed Eddie through the door, each carrying a bag or tray.

They all paused, staring at one another with varying levels of confusion.

"Hey, Nia," Eddie said, holding up a bag. "This is for you."

"Me?" she said, confused as he handed over the bag.

Maria stepped forward with another. "Someone's feeling generous today," she said with a smirk, handing her bag to Nia.

Joel, a glamoured wolven, was last, balancing a tray of four different cups from The Goblin Grind. "Here you go, Nia," he said with a grin. "Guess someone thinks you like variety."

"What is this?" Nia asked, staring at the tray as if it might explain itself.

"We just deliver the goods," Joel replied with a shrug, clearly enjoying the situation.

Nia and Ivy dug into the bags and unearthed Italian from Joe's, Mediterranean from Theo's, and greasy burgers from the Burger Barn. The variety only deepened the mystery. Nia's phone vibrated from where it was charging on the desk.

Unknown

I had food delivered to your office. I'm
sorry, I should have fed you sooner.

Unknown

I'm not sure what you like so I had
a few things delivered.

Unknown

This is Lochlan by the way.

"Why does it feel like you're about to cry?" Ivy asked, frowning slightly. Nia felt the familiar brush of Ivy's magic ripple between them. She probably sensed the chaos brewing in Nia's chest. "Who is it?"

Nia waved her off and began to text back.

Me

I figured. How did you
get my number?

Unknown

From the annulment paperwork.

The failed annulment your father sabotaged, he should have said.

Nia threw her phone onto her chair and grabbed the coffee that looked like her usual order from The Goblin Grind. One sip of the iced quad with orange, caramel, and cardamom, and her headache began to ease. She glared at her phone, sitting innocently on the leather. It wasn't Lochlan's fault today didn't work out. In a way, it was her fault he was caught up in this mess with her father.

And his fault she was beginning to feel better.

She sighed, grabbed her phone, and quickly typed a reply.

Me

Thank you.

7

Lochlan

"Hand-Fasted by Accident? Here's What to Do Next." –A LEGAL THREAD

L ochlan sat on a barstool, the kind that wobbled if you shifted your weight too far to one side. Gulls squawked outside of Drift, and the low murmur of conversation filled the small, nautical bar. It smelled like sea salt, fried food, and old beer. The kind of place that would soon be crowded with fishermen, tourists, and Videt staff grabbing a quick lunch.

As Lochlan stared at Nia's text, the familiar surroundings of the bar faded away.

Nia

Thank you.

He had to play it cool. Ordering lunch from three different restaurants was already pushing it—and then four coffees, just to conceal the fact there were a few things he'd noticed before the previous night. Like how she was usually holding a Goblin Grind coffee cup, or how she'd mentioned her favorite order in an interview a few months back.

Me

You're welcome.

Lochlan was married, and his wife was desperate to end it. This was, he had to admit, in keeping with the broader themes of his life. No one had wanted him—not his mother, not his family—and he would spend the next six weeks proving to Nia's father that she didn't want him, either.

Unless he did something else.

He rubbed his face, still struggling to process the whirlwind of the past twelve hours. As his beer warmed and the fish and chips cooled, a torrent of thoughts flooded his mind. An improbable number of his relatives had died in strange accidents. He was now third in line for the throne, after his brother and sister.

He still hadn't reached out to his mother. What would he say? *I'm sorry for your loss? Why didn't you tell me? Why do you hate me?*

Becket took the seat next to him with a groan, ice pack pressed firmly against his forehead, and Lochlan was thankful for the interruption.

"It's not every day you get mind-fucked by The Sword," Becket said. "Should I feel honored?"

"No," Lochlan answered immediately.

His friend slapped his back, sloshing the beer Lochlan was trying to drink.

"You got fucked the most. There was fucking, right?"

"There was not."

"Well, at least she's pretty."

"Pretty?" She was stunning. Strong. Resilient. Like a cosmo flower that could grow in almost any soil, or a daylily whose robust root system could hold back steep hills and stop erosion.

No, she was a zinnia.

"You're thinking about plants, aren't you?"

"Nia, zinnia—she's like a zinnia flower. They're vibrant colors, deepest red to softest pink, and they grow…" He trailed off, remembering a trip with his father, called in after a wildfire tore through a stretch of land. Amid the scorched earth, zinnias had already begun to bloom—bright red-orange flowers rising through the ash, their colors defiant against the blackened soil. He'd stood quietly, watching them sway in the breeze, struck by how something so vivid could thrive in such ruin.

"Make sure you tell her that when you're trying to convince her to keep you."

Lochlan blinked and stared at his friend, dumbfounded.

"Don't look at me like that," Becket said.

Lochlan had barely thought about keeping her for himself.

"Have you been poking around my present path?"

"Yes, between trying to get your marriage annulled and being mauled by The Sword, I pulled some cards, talked to my ancestors, and looked toward the stars to see where this little soiree is going."

"And?"

"Dude, I'm kidding."

Lochlan's face fell.

"But I see you're smitten and you haven't started talking shit about yourself yet," Becket continued. "You're also comparing her to flowers. You've never compared me to a flower—kind of jealous, by the way—so you're clearly not ready to give up on this. And I would probably kick you in the shin if you did."

Lochlan rubbed his face and groaned into his palms. "How can I?"

"What?"

"Keep her."

When he looked to his friend for answers, he found only annoyance on Becket's face.

"I didn't realize you were this hideous creature undeserving of love. Clearly, you can't keep her."

"Beck, please."

"You're a serious catch, and she would be stupid not to fall for you. I could seriously hurt your family for messing with your head about this stuff."

It wasn't Lochlan's entire family. His mother was cold, his sister cruel, but his brother had never wronged him. Yes, Thane had been absent when Lochlan was thrust into the role of prince, but not out of malice or disdain. He'd spent every waking moment fulfilling the duty he'd been born and groomed to perform when the time came for him to become king. He served in the military and did all he could to prevent the crown from falling, dragging a stagnant monarchy into the future by fostering the type of innovation that had turned the capital into a tech hub. Thane valued tradition; he valued growth more.

But everything had crumbled just before Lochlan's eighteenth birthday.

A year after the king died of illness, the Dover Coalition had assumed control over most of the monarchy's authority. Thane had been left to piece together what was left of a fraying monarchy stripped of power—meeting with opposition leaders, trying to steady public opinion, anything and everything a crown prince could do to uphold his family's honor and position. But their sister hadn't taken the loss with the same sense of poise and duty. In a fit of rage, she'd burned down the family greenhouse where Lochlan's father had once worked.

A phantom ache skittered across his skin, a reminder of the scars that stretched from his ankles to his knees. The burns had been terrible. But they would have been much worse if Thane hadn't been there to pull him from the fire.

Lochlan wondered what his brother was doing now. Probably out on some secret, high-tech mission, being a badass. He didn't know what Thane would think of his sudden marriage and temporary wife. But—

"It's not that," Lochlan muttered, forcing himself back to the present. "Nia's sworn off marriage. It wouldn't matter if I was the most eligible person in the world."

"What do you mean?"

"I'm not sure what happened. Something her father did. All I know is her mother died, and Nia blames it on Wulfric, and the fact that her mother was forced to marry him."

"And then he forced her to marry you?"

Becket had been brought up to speed earlier on everything that happened at Wulfric's office.

"Yes."

"Ouch."

"I know."

For a moment, neither of them spoke. Lochlan pushed his food around, calculating how much work he could put into the diaries the Videt had sent him before he'd see her again. Had she eaten yet? Did she like anything he'd picked out?

Every thought circled back to Nia. She made the world feel lighter, brighter.

"There is something…" Becket's voice broke Lochlan's thoughts, low and hoarse. His gaze was distant, as if peering through a fog. "…but it's still too hazy to see."

Lochlan watched as Becket blinked himself free of the seer trance.

"What I do know," Becket said, "is you need to be useful to her. Learn what makes her happy. My mom would kick my stepdad out if he didn't build her a barn for her chickens or grab something off the top shelf. Ladies love that shit."

Lochlan snorted. "I don't think a barn will fix this."

"Maybe not, but it's the right kind of place to start. Show her she can rely on you. That marriage isn't so bad."

The words kindled like a spark in the dark as Lochlan sat back, the gloom of doubt clearing ever so slightly. Becket was right. His mother and sister had spent years curating the idea that loneliness was Lochlan's birthright. Nia made him want more.

But if he wanted a chance to keep her, he'd have to earn it.

"What do you have to lose?" Becket said, watching him carefully.

"Nothing." Lochlan's lips twitched in the faintest hopeful smile. "Everything."

And, for the first time, both of these things felt like the truth.

DIARY ENTRY
MY EIGHTEENTH WINTER

The moon hangs high in the sky, her light casting eerie shadows on the snow below my window. But her presence holds little comfort. I can still smell the blood. My heart pounds in my chest, remembering the massacre that was my wedding only hours ago. He came for me.

A beast.

He tore through them all, even the elder who was to marry me to that monster. I had never seen such formidable magic. The raw power, the sheer brutality. And yet, beneath the horror, there was something else, something careful. Protective.

I should be terrified, and I am, but there's also a strange sense of relief washing over me. The life of misery and abuse I would have known was snatched away in a single, blood-soaked evening. I can't shake the images from my mind—his fierce incantations, the crackling energy, the devastation he wrought. But alongside those memories is the way he spoke. He stepped toward me and held out his hand, slow and certain.

"You can come with me," he said. "If that's what you want."

And for the first time in my life, I felt like I had a choice.

I don't know where this path will lead us, but for the first time in forever, I feel a spark of hope. The beast has set me free, and though the future is uncertain, I am not alone. I can even feel him now, watching over me. He will keep me safe. It is a promise I cling to, a beacon in the dark.

Nia

"Quiz Time! What Solstice Are You Most Like?"
—THE STELLA RUNE GAZETTE

Nia glanced at the clock again. Five minutes until six. She'd spent the last hour pacing and overthinking, nerves buzzing like static.

Her suitcase sat ready beside her, thrifted and well-worn, packed with essentials—toiletries, her favorite clothes, the blanket she couldn't sleep without. She could have waited upstairs in her apartment, but it had never felt quite like home. Too plain. Too practical. Ivy's place next door had life and personality, while hers just… existed.

Down here, she felt grounded. The work, the office—this was hers. Just like the tunnels that wound beneath Stella Rune, where magic moved freely and she could sit with coffee in hand, watching the world drift by.

The building itself was familiar in a way that settled her nerves. Four apartments upstairs—hers, Ivy's, a reclusive older man's, and a young artist's, who'd left paint smears along the hallway and around her doorknob. Below, the first floor held a mix of businesses that made up the heart of the block.

The corner bookstore, crammed with everything from bestsellers to dusty old tomes; the sandwich shop, where the smell of fresh bread and sizzling meat still triggered memories of her first job; the antique store, where the right eyes could spot magical glamours woven into the displays. And finally, the Charis Foundation's office—small, neat, and buzzing with quiet purpose.

This was where she belonged: in the steady rhythm of this building, this street. Here, where life made sense.

Tonight, though, even the comfort of her office couldn't settle her nerves. Any minute now, Lochlan would arrive, and she'd follow him to a home she couldn't imagine and a life she hadn't asked for. She worried about what the coming weeks held and what would happen when she saw Lochlan again. And also: who the heck was Jade?

Every way she might succeed in winning back her freedom was written on a notepad in her desk.

1. One of us is in love with someone else.

Nia knew that would never happen with her. She purposely sought out partners that screamed one night stand, so she hoped whoever this Jade was would throw a wrench in her father's plan.

Though the thought of another person holding Lochlan's affections made something shift beneath her skin. Just slightly. A faint prickle of shadows stirred at her back before the magic faded. It was probably better not to think about that.

2. They were utterly incompatible.

That felt less easy. After the initial shock of waking up married, she found herself liking Lochlan. He was calm, quiet, and not bad to look at. But that didn't mean love. That certainly didn't mean marriage. But, if she were looking for friends, he might be at the top of her prospect list.

3. *Murder.*

Murdering her father was an option. A difficult one—what with his mind-reading powers and his whole all-powerful Sword of the Goddess thing—but not impossible. She had spells. She had tricks. She just needed an opening.

As The Sword, Wulfric was the goddess's mouthpiece among supernaturals. Keeper of rituals, interpreter of signs, and self-declared authority on what counted as sacred. He didn't control everything, but the things he did were enough to make people kneel. And worse? They adored him for it.

Nia knew the truth—Wulfric came from a long line of tyrants dressed as divine keepers. Just because he wore the title convincingly didn't make him any less of a monster.

But before she could contemplate possible patricide, she had to get through her first night with Lochlan. Nia envisioned some sort of domestic torment: fighting over the remote, his dirty clothes all over the place, him using her toothbrush. Horror movie stuff.

The rumbling of a truck jolted her to her feet. She left her office and peered through the waiting area windows. Lochlan sat behind the wheel, parked in front of her motorcycle. She watched as he took a deep breath and stepped out.

When he rounded the front of the truck his eyes instantly found hers.

She walked to the door and waved awkwardly. A few too many birds fluttered around her rib cage as he stepped into the Charis space.

"Hi, Nia."

"Hi, Lochlan."

Did her voice always sound so breathless?

"So, where do we go so you can grab what you need?"

She arched a brow. "You mean besides upstairs, where I live?"

He winced. "Right. I meant to ask if you've packed."

"I have." Her tone softened just a little.

He nodded and followed her gesture to the adjoining office. When he reappeared, her beat-up suitcase looked almost comically small in his hand.

"This is it?" he asked, his voice low and even.

"Yes."

He cleared his throat, looking anywhere but at her. "Ready?"

Nia nodded, trailing after him as he carried her bag to his truck. He placed it gently in the passenger seat. She locked the office door, double-checking it out of habit, and when she turned back, he stood there, waiting. Their eyes met and a flash of memory hit her.

She was curled against his naked chest, his hand stroking her hair, laughing low in a way that made her stomach flutter.

Her cheeks burned as the memory slipped away like smoke, leaving only the heat of embarrassment and the faintest ache of longing. Fairy wine had done this: left her with gaps filled only by phantom sensations, a horny haunting that refused to leave her alone.

Lochlan shifted awkwardly and nodded toward the motorcycle parked nearby. "Yours?"

Nia followed his gaze to the bike she'd bought at eighteen—the only thing she could afford at the time. She'd built it up, cared for it, kept it running ever since. "Yeah."

"Is it safe?" He sounded curious, but there was an edge of concern beneath it.

She blinked, expecting to bristle at the question, but instead felt... almost touched. Without answering, she grabbed her helmet. "I'll follow you."

The streets of Stella Rune were alive and full of charm. The sun hung low over the ocean, casting warm light that danced across the cobblestones. People wandered in and out of shops and restaurants, chatting and laughing. Glamours hung thick in the air, cloaking the more supernatural sights—fairies dancing in the trees and wolven moving through town in their true forms—from mundane eyes.

As they rode through the historic part of town, the scenery shifted. The cobblestones grew older and more uneven, and the trees lining the streets became denser, their branches intertwining above to create a canopy that filtered the warm orange of the sky. A canal ran alongside them, its dark water catching glints of light from the lanterns posted along its banks. The hum of the motorcycle and Lochlan's truck engine filled the air as they turned onto a quiet street.

Lochlan pulled into a spot at the end, his truck coming to a smooth stop in front of a quaint townhome. The deep red bricks glowed warmly in the sunset, and its green door evoked both the comfort and vibrancy of growing things. It was charming, disarmingly so, and as Nia parked her bike behind his truck, she felt an unexpected calm settle over her.

She swung off the motorcycle, watching as Lochlan grabbed her suitcase from the truck and carried it toward the door without a word. She followed close behind, her boots clicking softly on the pavement.

Before he unlocked the door, Lochlan turned to her. "Just a warning," he said, his tone cautious, "Jade can be a handful."

Nia's eyebrows lifted. "She's here?"

Lochlan frowned. "Of course." He turned the key, pushed the door open, and stepped aside to let her enter. "Jade, I'm home."

He dropped his keys into a tray by the door, and the eager tap of claws on hardwood approached, building to a frantic rhythm with each step.

Nia braced herself as a blur of white fur and floppy ears launched itself at Lochlan with unrestrained joy. Lochlan laughed, catching the massive creature in his arms like it weighed nothing.

"I've been gone less than an hour." He hugged the dog like it was his favorite person in the world.

Nia blinked, caught off guard by the scene. The affection between them was so natural and sincere, it felt like she was intruding on something private. Her heart twisted in a way she couldn't quite name.

The dog turned its head, locking light green eyes on her from over Lochlan's shoulder. The animal began wiggling uncontrollably, and Lochlan barely had time to brace himself before he had to let go or risk getting knocked over.

"Jade, wait—"

Too late. The dog launched toward Nia, large paws landing on her hips as a cold, wet nose pressed into her stomach, sniffing her like she was smuggling contraband.

"Whoa! Okay, hi!" Nia laughed, stumbling back under the eager inspection. "Is this normal?"

She expected a quick answer, maybe a dry remark, but instead, Lochlan was silent for a beat too long. She glanced up and caught him watching—not just Jade, but her. His expression shifted too fast for her to pin it down. Hesitation, maybe?

"Not to this extent," he said.

A strange satisfaction curled in her stomach, but before she could think too much about it, Lochlan cleared his throat and straightened.

"Jade, this is Nia. Nia, this is Jade."

Nia tilted her head, scratching behind the dog's floppy ears. "Jade is a dog?"

"What else would she be?" Lochlan's brow furrowed in genuine confusion.

"I don't know, a girlfriend?"

His laughter came suddenly, warming in the space around them. It caught her off guard, and to her surprise, she found herself smiling.

"You thought I brought you home to my girlfriend?" he asked, chuckling as he shook his head.

"You didn't explain!"

"You didn't ask," he teased, his grin widening.

Nia rolled her eyes but couldn't suppress her own amusement. She scratched Jade's soft fur and muttered in a conspiratorial tone, "Well, you ruined my first plan. You were supposed to scare me away with the girlfriend act."

Jade wagged her tail furiously, eyes glinting with canine delight as if she understood every word.

"Come on, girls," Lochlan said over his shoulder, heading deeper into the house. "I'll give you a tour and then get dinner started."

Nia followed him upstairs, Jade padding alongside them. Lochlan carried her suitcase to the master bedroom, pushing the door open to reveal a simple but comfortable space. The bed was large and neatly made, the walls painted in soft, neutral tones. He set her bag on the bed and gestured to the door on the left.

"The bathroom's through there."

She nodded, her gaze lingering on the plants scattered around the room. She didn't have to touch them to feel their presence: a quiet hum of magic connected her to the vines trailing along the windowsill and the leafy ferns tucked into corners.

They moved down the hallway, Lochlan gesturing briefly to a closed door as they passed. "This is the office. I do most of my work in there."

He didn't elaborate and Nia didn't ask.

The stairs creaked softly as they descended, the air carrying the faint scent of old wood and something green and alive. The kitchen sat at the back of the house, mostly lit by soft lamps that cast a warm glow over the space. Faint music played in the background. Off to one side, a door led to the greenhouse—or so Lochlan had said—and beyond that was the backyard, though she couldn't see either from the kitchen counter.

Nia soaked in the coziness of Lochlan's home, which felt lived in and cared for. Not like her apartment, which was less a home and more a place where she occasionally dropped dead from exhaustion.

She glanced at Lochlan, who was rummaging through the fridge, pulling out ingredients with an almost surgical precision. She didn't realize she was staring until he turned, catching her mid-assessment. She looked away, hoping the dim light covered any telltale signs of appreciation.

"There's this chicken and pasta dish I was thinking about making," he said, setting a carton of cream onto the counter. "It'll be another hour, if that's okay?"

"I haven't had a home-cooked meal in…" she trailed off, searching her memory. It was bleak.

"What do you usually eat?"

He was watching her too closely, like he was absorbing every word. It made her nervous.

"Takeout," she admitted. "I'm not the best cook, and Ivy—my best friend—and I, well, we set our kitchen on fire in college. Since then…" She shrugged.

Lochlan made a thoughtful noise, then turned back to his task. "Is chicken and pasta okay?"

"Yes. I can always eat pasta, and I don't mind chicken."

He hesitated. "Is there a meat you prefer?"

"No. Chicken is fine, Lochlan."

He exhaled like she'd just settled some great internal debate. "Alright."

Nia pulled out her notepad and worked while Lochlan gathered his supplies and turned up the music before moving in practiced efficiency.

He worked quietly, the occasional sound of a knife against the cutting board or the sizzle of butter in a pan the only interruptions.

Nia tried to focus on her fundraiser notes, but when Lochlan bent down to grab something from the fridge, she lost her train of thought. Her gaze flicked up on instinct, her eyes tracing over the way his shirt pulled against his back, the way his pants clung a little too well. She forced her gaze back to her notes, but they couldn't hold her attention.

Lochlan started chopping, and she became fixated on his hands. Competent, precise, strong in a way that felt unfairly distracting.

This was going to be a problem.

She swallowed and refocused on her notes. Pancakes. She was here to plan a pancake fundraiser, not ogle the way a man handled poultry.

Jade padded over to the corner, where Lochlan filled an ornate gold bowl with kibble. The dog wagged her tail enthusiastically before digging in.

It was so normal. Too normal.

A glass of water appeared in front of Nia, sliding across the counter slowly. She blinked up at Lochlan. He didn't say anything, just watched her with an unreadable expression, waiting.

"Thanks," she murmured, wrapping her fingers around the cool glass.

"Would you like anything else? I have wine, sodas..."

He trailed off and she glanced up, catching something flicker across his face. Their eyes locked and the air between them shifted, thickened. For a moment, the kitchen quieted around them, the smallest sounds amplified—the faint clink of Nia's glass as she set it down, the slow drag of his breath, the creak of her stool as she adjusted her posture.

"No," she said finally, realizing he was waiting for her answer. "Water is fine."

She looked away, heart hammering, fingers tightening around the glass. She should have said wine. Maybe vodka. Something to dull or drown out the awareness creeping under her skin.

Jade chose that moment to shove her nose against Lochlan's leg. A slow, easy smile spread across his face as he knelt to scratch behind her ears.

Nia exhaled quietly, but her pulse refused to settle. That smile took his sharp, brooding features and softened them into something dangerously attractive.

Fantastic. Apparently, she had a thing for dog dads.

She chugged her water like it was an antidote.

Meanwhile, Lochlan moved through his cooking with infuriating grace. The scent of garlic and butter filled the air, followed by the richness of sun-dried tomatoes and heavy cream.

Nia fidgeted. It smelled too good. He looked too good.

Then he bent down to check something in the oven, and—no man should be that attractive while cooking. It was like some kind of mating ritual, a dangerous combination of skill and seduction, a strip tease disguised as dinner preparation.

He plated everything with the same casual confidence he'd shown with everything else in the kitchen, slicing her chicken before setting it in front of her.

"We can eat here at the counter," he said, nodding toward the stools. "I hardly ever use the dining room."

Nia swallowed, nodding.

And if she stared at his hands a little too long as he passed her a fork, well. That was between her and the goddess.

9

Lochlan

Lochlan watched as Nia pushed her food around her plate. He hadn't touched his, either—mostly because he was too busy wearing a hole into his jeans with his palm. He had been anxious, unable to find the nerve to talk to her, so he'd lost himself in the process of cooking.

Marry Me Chicken had always been a comfort meal, something he cooked when he needed to feel steady. He'd hoped the familiar steps would give him the balls to talk to her. Maybe some part of him had even thought the name would mean something. He was a fool.

The sound of her fork clattering against the plate broke the silence, and for a brief, embarrassing moment, he flinched.

"This is insane," she mumbled, dragging her hands down her face like she could physically wipe away reality.

Insane didn't quite cover it. He was married to his boss's daughter—a woman who, despite her local fame, had hidden her connection to The

Sword from the entire supernatural world. Lochlan had spent years looking up to this man—his mentor, his boss, the leader he'd shared drinks and long conversations with—who was now his father-in-law. And here he and Nia were, sitting in his kitchen, forced to live together by this man they both knew, for reasons neither understood.

But there was no point in saying any of that.

Instead, he reached out instinctively, wrapping his fingers lightly around her wrist. It was a stupid move—his heart reminded him of that by slamming against his ribs. But instead of pulling back she looked up, guarded eyes meeting his, and the tightness in his chest eased.

"It is insane," he said simply, his voice low.

She blinked at him, lips parting slightly like she hadn't expected him to agree. The air between them stretched thin, brittle. When her shoulders dropped a fraction, so did the tension in his.

"Are you alright? After seeing your father this morning…" He trailed off.

"No, but yes." She dragged a hand through her hair. "Six weeks… we don't know each other. At all. What if you're—"

Lochlan kept his face neutral, letting her continue, curious what she thought.

"What if I hate the way you chew? Or you're one of those people who puts the toilet paper roll on backwards?"

He felt the corner of his mouth quirk upward. "*I'm* the potential threat here?"

"Yes!" she shot back, crossing her arms, like it was the most obvious thing in the world. "Don't smile at me like that."

He tilted his head slightly, bemused.

Her cheeks flushed pale pink.

"Ugh, this whole thing is frustrating," she muttered, sinking lower in her seat.

Lochlan wanted to say he would chew however she wanted, hang the toilet paper however she liked—hell, he'd rearrange his entire house if it meant she'd give this a chance.

Not yet, you fool.

Nia's stomach growled, interrupting the moment. The unexpected sound sent an unfamiliar feeling through him—something visceral, protective. The idea of her going hungry made him bristle.

"Maybe eating will help?" he suggested.

She sighed, picked up her fork, and poked at the food once more. "It smells really good," she murmured.

His heart thumped at the compliment.

Goddess help him, he was in trouble.

The moment she took her first bite, the sound of her moan sent goosebumps skittering across his skin. He looked away, willing himself to shake off the reaction, but it clung stubbornly, settling deep.

"Ohmygoddess." The words tumbled out, garbled around her mouthful of food. "This is the best pasta I've ever had."

She shoveled in a few more bites before biting into the chicken. "How is this crispy? What magic is this?"

"Becket's mother is an amazing cook. I spent college holidays with them. And then when I got my own place... I just really enjoy cooking."

"I bet everyone loves your food."

Lochlan hesitated. "I've only cooked for Becket. And Jade, when she had a stomach bug and could only eat boiled chicken and rice."

"You're kidding." Nia looked at him, her fork stilled midair, expression faltering. The brightness in her eyes dimmed, replaced by a flicker of something dangerously close to pity.

His grip tightened around his own fork. He hadn't meant to make it sound pathetic, but now that the words were out, he realized how they sounded.

HAND-FASTING AND OTHER HAZARDS

He shrugged, aiming for casual indifference. "I don't usually cook for other people."

Silence stretched between them, heavier than before. Nia studied him, her gaze searching, as if trying to fit the pieces of him together.

"You mean to tell me," she said slowly, setting her fork down, "that you're this fantastic at cooking, and no one's taking advantage of it?"

He huffed a laugh, shaking his head. "Guess not."

"Not even a girlfriend?" She frowned.

The question caught like a hook in his ribs. He didn't look at her as he reached for his water. "No."

A beat passed. Then—

"Or…" Nia looked almost tentative. "A boyfriend?"

Lochlan blinked. "No."

"Wow." Her eyes widened, lips parting in shock or maybe revelation. "You're *chronically single*."

He choked on his drink. "I'm not—"

"Oh, this is tragic." She leaned forward, elbows on the counter, studying him like some rare, baffling discovery. "No spouse, no girlfriend, no boyfriend—hell, not even a fling that comes over for dinner?"

"Well, your father took care of the spouse thing."

Nia blinked. Then her lips thinned.

"Shit." Lochlan winced. "Sorry."

She huffed a laugh. "You're not wrong." She took a bite of food, moaning again. "He's got jokes *and* he can cook," she mumbled to herself. Then, to him, she said, "You're playing a dangerous game, Lochlan."

She smiled at him, and for a moment, he felt lighter than ever.

He didn't know how to fill the silence that followed, so he dropped his gaze to his plate and forced himself to take a bite.

Throughout the meal, he was both comforted and tormented by how much she enjoyed the food. Her soft groans of satisfaction and the little sighs she made as she ate left his thoughts scattered and his chest tight.

When she insisted on handling the cleanup, he didn't argue. Instead, he grabbed Jade's leash and headed for the door. Walking through the greenhouse, past his ducks and the tangled sprawl of plants, he slipped outside and let the cold night air hit his flushed skin, a welcome shock to his overheated system. He exhaled slowly, watching his breath curl into the darkness.

Maybe a walk would clear his head.

After finishing their nightly routines, they found themselves standing in Lochlan's bedroom, staring at the large bed as if it were an unsolvable puzzle.

"You don't have a guest bedroom?" she asked, her tone more curious than accusatory.

"No," he replied. His family wouldn't be caught dead here, and Becket's house was only a five-minute walk away, so he'd never needed to crash here. What would be the point?

"I can sleep on the couch," Lochlan offered, taking a step toward the door.

"No." Her voice was firm, cutting through the awkwardness. "No, we're adults. We can share a bed."

Share a bed.

She said it like it was simple, practical, and didn't carry the risk of unraveling him entirely.

She moved to the left side of the bed without hesitation. It shouldn't have mattered which side she picked, but the fact that she'd chosen the opposite of where he usually slept felt… deliberate. It was stupid to read into it. She—anyone, really—had a fifty percent chance of picking the right side.

Lochlan scoffed at himself, shaking his head.

"Did you just laugh?" Nia turned, one eyebrow raised.

"No," he lied, crossing his arms over his chest. "I don't laugh."

"Right." Her lips twitched. "You're very serious. Very stoic."

"Exactly."

She rolled her eyes and turned back to the bed and pulled down the covers. He watched, hyper-aware of how small she looked against the massive bed, how out of place this moment felt. He'd never shared his bed with anyone before. Not for lack of desire—he'd just never let anyone close enough.

As she settled in, he hesitated awkwardly at the edge of the mattress. His usual spot suddenly felt too intimate, too charged.

"You're overthinking it," she said without looking up, her voice softer now. "Just lie down. It's not a big deal."

Except it was. To him, at least.

Gingerly, he slid into his side of the bed, reaching over to turn off the lamp on the nightstand. The room plunged into darkness, save for the faint glow of moonlight seeping around the edges of the curtains. The silence was comfortable for all of two seconds, before a low thump and the jingle of Jade's collar filled the room.

"Oh no," he muttered, knowing what was coming.

Jade landed squarely between them, her weight sinking into the mattress like she owned the place.

"Is this normal?" Nia asked, her voice amused.

"Yes," he said flatly. "She thinks this is her bed."

Jade twisted around in an exaggerated show of getting comfortable before settling in, her head resting on Lochlan's leg.

Nia laughed. "I guess I am the one taking her spot, then. Will you share?"

Jade let out a huff.

"I'll take that as a 'yes.'"

Lochlan leaned back against the pillow as a small smile crept across his lips. The weight of Jade, the sound of Nia's quiet laugh—it all felt surreal, too close to something he hadn't let himself admit he wanted. For a long while, the room was quiet, save for the faint rustle of blankets and Jade's soft, even breaths.

"Goodnight, Nia," he said softly.

"Nigh', 'ochlan," she mumbled through a yawn, already half asleep. Within moments, her breaths evened out and the quiet rhythm of sleep filled the room.

Lochlan stared at the ceiling, his thoughts drifting and refusing to settle. He replayed the quiet moments of the evening—the sound of Nia's laughter, the way her sadness lingered in her expression—as Jade snuggled between them. It was strange, sharing his bed, his space, his life.

Ever since opening the front door for Nia, Lochlan had felt like he was balancing on the edge of something he couldn't quite name, but that he knew would either fall apart, or change everything. For now, he stayed on that edge, waiting for sleep to claim him, Nia's presence filling a space he hadn't realized was so empty before.

10

Nia

"Yes, That Love Spell Was a Mistake. No, You Can't Undo It." —THE WEEKLY HEX

Nia woke to Jade's gentle snore and the dog's solid form pressed firmly against her back. On her other side, the warm weight of a body rose and fell beneath her cheek, comforting in a way that sent a sleepy hum through her.

The scent of cedar, something clean, and something undeniably Lochlan filled her lungs. She sighed, melting further into the warmth, the faint brush of his skin and the light dusting of hair beneath her fingertips grounding her in half-conscious contentment. It was instinctual, the way her body gravitated toward his. She let herself drift there for a fleeting moment—until reality crashed over her like a bucket of cold water.

She opened her eyes and froze.

The slight movement made Lochlan shift, his arm tightening where it rested across her ribs, muscles flexing in a way that sent a pulse of awareness through her. She held her breath, panic warring with the pull of drowsy comfort.

Lochlan's breathing evened out again.

Carefully, slowly, she began to untangle herself from his embrace.

There should be medals for this kind of acrobatics, she thought, her heart pounding as she slipped from the bed without disturbing him—or Jade, who gave her a single, judgmental glance before tucking her head back down.

Nia closed the bathroom door behind her and leaned against it, ignoring the pang of guilt gnawing at her chest. Cuddling could not—would not—be allowed. Not with Lochlan. Not with *anyone.*

She glared at her reflection and muttered, "You liked that *way* too much."

Lochlan was sweet. He was kind. He was handsome in a rugged, unassuming way that made her stomach twist inconveniently. But none of that mattered. What mattered was how dangerous it felt to like him, to want to reach for him, even in sleep.

She splashed water on her face and let the cold shock her back to clarity.

She'd taken a vow years ago at eighteen, with her mother's journal clutched in shaking hands—a promise carved deep inside herself. She would never give away her freedom. Never let anyone dictate her life the way her father had done with her mother.

To Nia, marriage was a trap. And she had made it her mission to live the life her mother had been denied.

And yet...

She thought about the quiet sadness in Lochlan's voice last night, the way his loneliness seemed to linger in the corners of every room. She felt something twist painfully in her chest. Why was he so alone? How did someone like him end up here?

She shook her head, chasing the thoughts away as she dried her hands. That wasn't her problem to solve. It couldn't be. She needed to prove her father wrong, and that meant not getting close to Lochlan. It meant she couldn't like waking up in his arms, feeling so irritatingly happy and rested.

"You will not get attached," she told her reflection, sternly. "You will get out of this mess unmarried."

She repeated the mantra under her breath as she went through her morning routine, her determination fraying only slightly when the bewitching smell of coffee drifted upstairs, drawing her toward the kitchen.

Lochlan leaned against the counter with a mug in his hand. The morning light spilled across the warm brown skin of his hands and arms, highlighting broad shoulders and large biceps that flexed subtly with each sip. He spilled a little coffee, muttered a soft curse, and lifted the hem of his shirt to wipe his face like it was the most casual, unbothered thing in the world.

Nia's brain lit up with warning signals, but it was hard to heed them when faced with the blatant distraction that were his abs. They weren't chiseled or airbrushed—they were rugged, real, and undeniably him. Her eyes betrayed her, tracing the faint line from his abs to where his worn gray sweatpants hung low on his hips, barely hanging on.

Her foot missed the next step.

"Shit—fuck, ow!" she yelped as her body hit the unforgiving wood, the jarring impact knocking the wind out of her.

Lochlan was in front of her in seconds. "Nia, what happened?" he demanded, concerned.

She blinked up at him, her pride stinging almost as much as her tailbone. The words *you and your abs* hovered at the tip of her tongue. Instead, she muttered, "Just clumsy."

"Are you okay?" he asked, brow furrowed.

"I'm fine." She let him help her to her feet.

But before she could steady herself, Jade bounded down the stairs with all the enthusiasm of a dog who thought she was saving the day. Her paws landed squarely against Nia's back, pushing her into Lochlan's chest.

"Goddess help me," she grunted against his neck.

He smelled *amazing*—woodsy and clean, with just a hint of coffee— and the heat of him seeped through her clothes like he was a damn furnace. She pulled back and glanced up, locking eyes with him. His gaze was a mix of worry and something softer, edged with humor. Her head felt light, almost dizzy, and her hands twitched like they didn't know whether to steady herself or linger.

"I made coffee and breakfast." The words rumbled out of him, quiet and warm, and her treacherous brain focused on the slight flex of muscle beneath her palms.

She cleared her throat, cheeks burning. "Coffee. Good." It was all she could manage before stepping back, desperate to put some space between them.

Nia walked on unsteady legs toward the kitchen, eager to regain some semblance of composure. Lochlan handed her a steaming mug of coffee.

"Thank you." Her fingers brushed his as she took the cup, the brief contact sparking a jolt of warmth that had nothing to do with the drink.

Lochlan, ever polite, offered her a ride to work. She shook her head too quickly, the words tumbling out awkwardly. "No, I'm fine. It's a nice day and walks are good."

She could barely string a coherent thought together. The idea of being in a confined space with him when his sheer presence was making it impossible to think? What had she told herself in the shower this morning... something about not getting attached?

Nia took a hurried sip of coffee, the drink grounding her just enough for her to mumble a quick goodbye and slip out the door.

By the time Nia arrived at her building, the street was bustling with people. Hints of October were creeping in—bundles of wheat leaned against storefronts, pumpkins stacked neatly in crates, and workers carried decorations toward the town center in preparation for next week's autumn festival. Stella Rune took its fairs and celebrations seriously.

Ivy waited outside the Charis office, two Goblin Grind coffee cups in hand and a glint of mischief in her blue eyes. Nia clutched the ceramic mug that was now cold from her walk. She hadn't meant to take it. She'd just... walked out with it like some kind of mug thief.

Nia accepted the new coffee, its logo shimmering faintly on the paper cup: a goblin skull floating in black liquid, glamoured from non-magical eyes. The flavor was rich, familiar—a comfort.

But it wasn't as good as his.

Damn it.

Now she was annoyed—angry, even—that Lochlan's coffee had the audacity to rival Goblin Grind. Was it some kind of magic? Did Lochlan and the goblins have some kind of secret coffee pact? Because if so, she wanted in.

"So," Ivy said, her grin widening. She didn't budge from her spot, clearly settling in for a chat. "How was your night?"

Nia inhaled slowly through her nose, her patience already wearing thin, and brushed past the witch. "Busy," she muttered, unlocking the doors. She flipped on the lights, set the speakers to their usual morning playlist, and moved purposefully into her office. Ivy trailed behind.

"We have a case of maple syrup being dropped off at eleven," Nia began, ignoring the way Ivy was practically vibrating with impatience. "And Johanna from Peter's Diner is bringing the batter the morning of the fundraiser. She said something about not trusting us with her famous pancake recipe."

She settled behind her desk, hoping the physical barrier might discourage the inquisition.

It didn't.

"Niiiaaahhh," Ivy whined, with melodramatic despair. "I want *details.* My love life has been non-existent for so long, I'm starting to think I've been cursed."

Ivy's bottom lip pushed out in an exaggerated pout as she stomped her foot.

Nia frowned thoughtfully. Ivy could be over-the-top, but she was also stunning, sweet, and practically magnetic. She'd rarely been without a lover, or at least a date. But, now that Nia thought about it, things really had slowed down since the annulment. She filed that thought away for later—a puzzle to figure out when her business partner wasn't pestering her for gossip.

For now, she'd give in.

"Fine," Nia groaned.

Ivy squealed with glee, clapping her hands together before flopping into the chair across from Nia's desk. "Okay, spill!"

Nia pinched the bridge of her nose. "We cuddled, but it didn't mean anything," she said, trying to keep her tone dismissive. "We were sleeping. It was non-consensual cuddling."

Ivy gasped, her eyes going wide. "So he *forced* you to cuddle with him?"

"What? No!" Nia blurted, sitting up straighter. "He wouldn't force me to do anything." The words came too quickly, and she scrambled to recover. "Not that I would know that about him, or anything, but…"

Her words trailed off as the truth crept in.

She *did* know that about him.

Lochlan wasn't the kind of man who would force anything—especially not something like that. And, honestly, it hadn't been forced at all. She'd used him as a pillow, their legs tangled together like it was the most natural thing in the world.

If anything, she was at fault. He'd offered to sleep on the couch. She was the one who'd said they should share a bed, which, in retrospect, might not have been the best idea. But they could. There would just be no cuddling next time. Absolutely none.

When she snapped out of her thoughts, Ivy was smiling at her like a cat who'd cornered a particularly amusing mouse.

"Anyway," Nia said briskly, waving her hand to dismiss the topic. "I don't have other details besides the fact he's an amazing cook and his dog is adorable."

Ivy opened her mouth to reply, but Nia cut her off with a pointed look.

"We have a lot to do today."

She wanted to bury herself in work and snuff out the smoldering heat the morning with Lochlan had kindled. The warmth of his touch, the scent of him, the quiet weight of his presence—it all lingered too vividly in her mind.

Her phone dinged, jolting her from her thoughts. Her heart leapt as, for an absurd moment, she thought it might be Lochlan. But when she glanced at the screen, her pulse quickened for an entirely different reason.

One of her marks had agreed to a meeting. Tonight. A grin tugged at the corners of her mouth.

Exacting judgement on a vicious witch was exactly the distraction she needed.

II

Lochlan

"Do You Know Who's Making Your Coffee? We Sit Down With the Destroyer of Bloodlines, Natasha Gobblegrind." –THE WEEKLY HEX

Lochlan clutched a batch of cookies and a velvet envelope containing his latest project: a restored first edition book filled with fairy tales. The crisp evening air nipped at his skin as he stood outside New Chapter, but his attention was fixed on the building three doors down.

The Charis Foundation's sign hung above the door, its letters catching the golden light of the setting sun. Nia should be finishing work soon—or perhaps she'd already finished, or her work had taken her to another part of Stella Rune. Lochlan didn't know, and Nia hadn't said.

No text. No call. Nothing since she'd rushed out the door that morning.

She'd been flustered, darting out so fast she hadn't even glanced at breakfast. He told himself it didn't matter. He'd made it for her, wanted her to sit, to stay. Maybe that hadn't been a fair thing to expect. He'd hoped to recapture the gentle, unexpected comfort of eating together the previous night. But, he reminded himself, Nia hadn't asked for that.

And then, of course, she'd fallen down his stairs.

Lochlan exhaled hard and raked a hand through his hair. He hoped she was alright.

The warm, yeasty smell of the sandwich shop's bread drifted down the emptying street, mixing with the scent of his cookies. It should have been comforting, but unease twined through him instead.

He wasn't in a position to demand answers.

Still, he'd finished his restoration project for the book shop early, and dropping it off was a perfectly reasonable excuse to swing by Charis around the time Nia had finished work the day before.

Restoring books for New Chapter wasn't part of Lochlan's work at the Videt. But a few years ago, he'd stopped by and seen the aftermath of a botched repair—a stitched-up relic, barely holding together. It had bothered him enough that he'd made an offer: bring him anything delicate, and he'd fix it. He hadn't expected to keep at it. But he liked the work. The puzzle of it. The feeling of restoring something lost.

And the shop's owner and her father never turned down his baking.

Shaking off his unease, Lochlan stepped forward and pushed open the antique door. A bell chimed overhead, its cheerful tinkle as familiar as the scent of old paper wrapping around him.

Jimmy, an elderly witch with an ill-fitting toupee slightly askew, was perched at an ancient wooden table, a teacup halfway to his mouth. He squinted at Lochlan in confusion.

"It isn't Friday," his voice wavered with age and suspicion. "Right?"

Lochlan placed the box of cookies in front of him. "No, it's still Wednesday. I finished the book early for Helen."

Every Friday, like clockwork, Lochlan delivered his weekly project to Helen, Jimmy's daughter and the shop's owner. Today, she emerged from behind a beaded curtain, pushing it aside with one hand while patting the front of her overalls for her glasses with the other.

"Lochlan!" she exclaimed, her tone warm but surprised. "It isn't Friday."

"I finished early," he repeated.

Helen frowned, tilting her head. "I don't have your next book in yet—it's coming all the way from bumfuck nowhere."

"Language," Jimmy croaked through a mouthful of cookie, crumbs sprinkling the table.

Helen waved him off. "The tracking says it'll get here Thursday."

"I'll come back Friday morning to pick it up," Lochlan replied.

"With more cookies?" Jimmy asked, his eyes twinkling as he took another bite.

Helen rolled her eyes.

Lochlan managed a genuine smile as his eyes bounced between the two witches. But even as they bantered around him, his thoughts drifted back to Nia.

Lochlan said his goodbyes and stepped out of New Chapter. He took several steps down the sidewalk, then paused halfway between the bookstore and The Charis Foundation.

Nia might still be there.

Would it be crossing a line to go looking for her?

The question burned in his mind, tangled with doubts. Their arrangement was barely a day old—fragile and untested. In the little time they'd spent together, he hadn't managed to get to know her any better, really, and she hadn't made any headway in proving her father wrong.

The thought made him hesitate. Then, reluctantly, he turned to head home.

A crash shattered the quiet.

Glass. Something heavy. Loud enough to send a spike of adrenaline through him.

His gaze snapped back to The Charis Foundation and, without thinking, he broke into a run. The waiting area blurred past him, his pulse hammering in his ears as he rounded the corner to her office—

And froze.

Nia stood, her posture tense but unyielding as an enormous man loomed over her. His voice booming with anger.

"You think you're powerful? You're a fucking leech."

Blinding rage surged through Lochlan, his fists clenching at his sides. His body coiled, ready to intervene—

But Nia didn't look hurt. She didn't even look rattled. Still, when her gaze met his, he caught it—that flicker of relief. Right before her face twisted in unmistakable annoyance.

Shit.

The man thundered on, his rage unchecked. "You'll regret this, you fucking bitch."

Lochlan's fists tightened, ready to step in and—shadows slid into motion around the room. They moved with a fluid grace, wrapping around the man's limbs like living restraints, pinning his large body back against the wall with no apparent effort.

"My ride's here," Nia said with quiet authority. "So we're done. You have until next Saturday to make sure the donations go through. If not, you know what will happen."

Lochlan didn't know what this meant, but the way the man's face paled told him it wasn't an idle threat. A memory surfaced of the Mabon celebration—he'd seen her speaking to someone else who looked like they were angry, or in pain. Was this the same thing?

Was Nia *forcing* people to donate?

The man strained against the shadows binding him, his mouth twisting as if to speak, but the magic held firm. His face turned purple, eyes bulging, everything about the man seething with rage as Nia marched him through the waiting area and out onto the sidewalk before her shadows finally released him.

She locked the door behind him before turning toward Lochlan, her expression unreadable.

Part of him wanted to go to her, to pull her close, to feel her against him—whole, safe, here. The other part of him wanted to ask what the hell he'd just witnessed. Caught between the urge to comfort and the storm of questions spinning in his mind, Lochlan stayed frozen as Nia strode back into her office.

The air crackled, charged with magic, as shadows rose—twisting, coiling, righting furniture and collecting pieces of the broken picture frame Lochlan had heard fall. Nia's anger pulsed through the room with her shadows. She crossed her arms and broke the silence. "Nothing to say?"

Lochlan hesitated. There was plenty he wanted to say, but none of it would come out.

"No comment on how dangerous that was?" she continued, her voice tight with frustration. "How I'm stupid for putting myself in a situation like this?"

Yes, it had been dangerous. Reckless, even. And he hated finding her in the middle of it. But if he wanted to earn her trust, to understand her, he needed to choose his words carefully.

"Why are you even here?" she demanded. "What do you want?"

"I want—" Taking a deep breath, Lochlan ran a hand through his hair. "—to know if you've eaten."

She blinked, her anger flickering into confusion. "What?"

"Have you eaten?"

"I heard what you said." Her tone was brisk, but it lacked the ire from before.

"And?" he pressed, surprised by how calm his voice sounded.

She paused, her brows knitting together as her shadows finished their work and dissolved into the darkness of the room.

"No," she admitted. "I haven't eaten."

He nodded, the tension in his chest easing slightly. Without another word, he walked toward the entrance. Before unlocking the door, he checked the sidewalk to make sure it was clear, then opened and held it for her. Nia hesitated for a moment before stepping past him, her expression a mix of wariness and confusion. But she didn't protest.

For now, that was as much encouragement as Lochlan expected to get.

12

Nia

*"Unwanted Heir sighting! I swear he was
delivering something shady to the bookstore."*
—WOLVENLOVER₁₁₁₁

Nia tapped her pen against the white tablecloth, the rhythmic
sound at odds with the clatter of goblins cleaning up after
the morning rush at Goblin Grind.

She sat at her usual table against the outer wall, overlooking the
ocean. Heating spells kept the morning chill at bay, wrapping her in a
comfortable warmth as waves rolled lazily in the distance. Normally, this
spot brought her a sense of peace. Today, it didn't.

Lately, she'd only stopped by the to-go window, grabbing her order
before. But she had hoped that sitting here, really being here, might
settle her thoughts. She'd first stumbled upon this place as a young teen,
curiosity leading her through the tunnels beneath the town, drawn on
by the warm, sweet scent of fresh baking and the darker, richer smell of
coffee that permeated the place. From that first moment, it had felt like
hers: a quiet refuge, a place to breathe.

But even its familiar comfort wasn't enough to quiet her mind.

She was supposed to be tallying RSVPs for the next fundraiser, but all she could think about was Lochlan—specifically, what he had walked in on last night and how quiet he'd been since.

He hadn't said a word to her after they'd left her work.

Not one.

When they got home, he'd let Jade jump into his arms, giving her the kind of affection that made Nia's chest ache. Then, without so much as a glance in her direction, he'd disappeared into the backyard. She had gone upstairs for a shower, hoping the scalding water might wash away the tension clinging to her like a second skin.

By the time she came back down, he was just coming inside, carrying two plates loaded with steak, asparagus, and potatoes, all of which smelled amazing. Not a single word was exchanged as he meticulously cut up her food, poured her a glass of water, and set the meal in front of her.

They ate in silence.

When she'd thanked him, his only response had been a nod before he'd left her to finish alone. She had woken to an empty bed that morning, and an empty kitchen downstairs. The only sign of Lochlan had been a cup of fresh coffee, a beautifully arranged breakfast of sweet potato hash and fluffy eggs, with a note placed beside it.

I have an early call. -Lochlan

When Nia had left, stuffed and caffeinated, she noticed his truck parked in front of the house. She had assumed he was working from home, and had realized, abruptly, that she didn't even know what he *did* for work. It made the food in her stomach twist uneasily.

Her pen still tapping relentlessly against the table, Nia's Goblin Grind coffee sat untouched.

She was living with a complete stranger. Worse, she wasn't even trying to change that. She hadn't asked him questions, hadn't tried to make dinner last night any less awkward. She told herself it didn't matter. In six weeks, this would all be over.

That thought felt hollower now than it had just a day ago.

Her phone buzzed and she snatched it up a little too quickly, warmth creeping up her neck. Not that she was hoping it was a certain quiet, brooding, plant witch. Definitely not.

Lochlan

> Becket said he would like to talk to us about our situation, but we'd have to meet him at a work function. I can pick you up after work if you want?

Nia stared at the message, her grip tightening around her phone. Did Becket have a way to push the annulment through? Did that mean she had less than six weeks with Lochlan?

Me

Okay. Is there a dress code?

Lochlan

What you have on will be fine.

Me

How do you know what
I'm wearing?

She stared at her phone, watching the dots appear, then vanish, then reappear.

Lochlan

What you usually wear is fine. I'll pick you up at 6.

Me

Okay...

They arrived at a sprawling manor on the outskirts of Stella Rune. Grand, imposing, and a little outdated—so much mahogany and dark wood it felt like stepping into a relic of the past. Nia wasn't sure what she'd expected when Lochlan mentioned that Becket wanted them to meet him at a work event, but it wasn't this. There were too many suits. Too many fake smiles and polite, meaningless conversations.

She hated it.

All this space, all this potential, and it was being wasted on corporate events. From the decor and the stale arrangements, it was obvious no one lived here anymore. She was pretty sure it belonged to an old fae line that had been in Stella Rune since the beginning. Nia let her gaze wander over the grand foyer, the little nooks tucked here and there, the halls off which countless rooms must hide, thinking how it could all be so much more. Ivy had always dreamed of creating a space where witches who needed a home, or just a place to be themselves without constant scrutiny, could find safety and community. But it was a huge project, and though they'd both been working on the idea for years, real progress still felt just out of reach.

Nia turned to Lochlan, about to ask him if he knew who owned the place, when she remembered, with an uncomfortable jolt, that they still weren't really speaking.

Lochlan had seemed broody since he picked her up. He took a sip of his first beer—non-alcoholic, she noted—as his eyes continued to avoid hers. He wore black pleated slacks and a fitted knit polo, the soft texture and open collar doing ridiculous things for his already-unfair bone structure. No jacket, no tie. Just him, all sharp edges and furrowed brow. Did he know what he was doing, looking like that?

As they neared the bar, a cluster of well-dressed regs caught sight of them, their expressions brightening with interest; but there was no spark, no stir of recognition that came when magic encountered magic.

"Nia," Lochlan paused and nodded, "these are some of Becket's colleagues from his first firm."

One of the men leaned back with a lazy smirk, but his words were edged. "Before he left us for bigger and better things." His gaze drifted to Nia, giving her a slow, deliberate once-over.

Before she could say any of the deeply unpleasant—and doubtless accurate—things she was thinking about the man, Lochlan spoke.

"This," he cut in smoothly, "is my wife, Nia."

Someone in the group choked on their drink.

A momentary silence settled over the table.

Nia turned, arching a brow. Whispers of their marriage had been circling, but neither of them had publicly confirmed it. And her father? He hadn't reached out yet about the promise spell. She had no idea when he would, which was irritating.

"The Duchess of Charity," Lochlan added belatedly, "and a menace to society."

His expression remained impassive as he glanced at her.

Nia slowly folded her arms. "Is that so?"

One of the men coughed. Another let out a nervous laugh.

"How absurd," one of the women chimed in, playfully swatting his arm. "Stop teasing, Lochlan."

Nia resisted the urge to swat the woman's hand away as she turned toward Nia with an overly bright smile. "I read you've funded over two hundred charities and raised almost a hundred million dollars since you started. How do you do it?"

"Extortion," Lochlan cut in. Nia's stomach churned as he downed his drink in one smooth gulp, setting the empty glass down with a clink. "And I'm pretty sure she's committed murder."

Laughter erupted, light and carefree. They thought he was joking. Of course they did.

Nia felt the blood drain from her face.

She knew better.

Quiet Lochlan didn't mean happy Lochlan. It meant he'd been silently freaking out about what she'd done.

"Will you excuse me and my husband?" Nia said through clenched teeth. She grabbed Lochlan by the arm, her grip firm as she steered him away. She didn't miss the blush creeping up his cheeks.

As they walked toward an empty hallway Nia hoped would give them some privacy, she caught the first man's whisper: "I can't believe she married him. He's always been so awkward."

Nia flushed.

She sent a tendril of shadow slithering through the air, unseen, to coil around the man's arm. His drink splashed over his suit as he jerked in surprise, sputtering while the others around him erupted into startled laughter.

Satisfied, she dragged Lochlan deeper into the abandoned hallway and spun to face him. Her finger jabbed into his chest. "What the fuck was that?"

"The truth." His gaze flickered to her lips before darting away. "Wasn't it?"

This conversation wasn't going the way Nia had planned. "I thought—"

"That I wouldn't care you were putting yourself in danger?" Lochlan kept his voice low, but each word was edged with anger, frustration. "Or that I wouldn't care that you're using blackmail or entrapment or who knows what else to fund your initiatives?"

"You didn't say anything. I thought you didn't have a problem with it," Nia admitted. "Or, at least, that you accepted what you saw and that it wasn't any of your business."

His gaze locked with hers, his expression unreadable. His voice grew softer, lower as he stepped closer. "What did I see, Nia?"

She licked her lips. Nia hadn't even told Ivy how she secured donations for their charities, let alone why she did it. Still, she leaned in, meeting his intensity head-on. "What do you think you saw?"

He ignored her question. "Have you killed anyone?"

"No." The word came fast, defensive. "Why would you think that?"

"I don't know," he admitted. His hands flexed at his sides, restless. "I was so worried when I first saw you, with him. Then... it seemed like you could've ended it so quickly if you'd wanted to." His eyes searched her face, his expression intense. "Has anyone hurt you before?"

The question hit her like a punch to the chest.

She sucked in a breath and turned away, her gaze dropping to the floor as the tension built between them until it felt suffocating.

"Only once, when I was young," she admitted softly, "and too quick to act. I've learned over the years how to be safer."

Lochlan's silence gnawed at her already frayed nerves, his eyes dark and guarded. "Nia..."

"What?" she snapped, irritated at herself for how vulnerable she felt, angry they were even having this conversation. "What do you want from me? What do you want me to—"

Then his arms were wrapping around her, pulling her gently but firmly against his chest. She froze for half a beat, her breath catching as his warmth enveloped her, his breath uneven against her neck.

Slowly, tentatively, she brought her arms around him, returning the embrace.

It felt extraordinary.

Their bodies fit together as if they'd been made for this moment, and she let herself melt into him. His hands were steady and reassuring against her back, anchoring her in place. As they each pulled back, their breaths mingled in the small space between them. Lochlan didn't let her go entirely; his hands still lingered lightly on her arms as he held her gaze with an intensity that sent a shiver down her spine.

"Nothing matters more to me than your honesty. And your safety. I need you to trust me enough to tell me if you're in trouble, or if there's anything you need."

His words struck something deep within her, loosening the tension in her chest.

Her gaze locked with his, the intensity in his light brown eyes and the determination in his expression made her heart thud harder, her breath catching in response.

"I want you to swear," he whispered, gruffly, but before he'd even finished she heard herself blurting out—

"Yes. Yes, I'll tell you."

He bit his lip, like there was more he wanted to say, but was holding back. Her gaze caught and lingered on his mouth, wondering if he looked at her lips with the same hunger she felt stirring, or if it was just her own desperation. Warmth spread through her chest as they drew closer, curling low in her stomach as she realized she was about to find out what it was like to kiss—

"There you two are."

Becket appeared in the hallway entrance, grinning mischievously.

Reluctantly, Nia stepped back and smoothed her clothes, trying to ground herself, while Lochlan rubbed the back of his neck.

"Becket, you said you had news?" Nia asked.

"Did I?" he replied, his gaze flicking between them like he was enjoying a private joke.

Nia glanced at Lochlan, who looked equally confused, his brow furrowed as he stared back at Becket.

"About the annulment," she pressed, a knot of curiosity and apprehension in her chest.

"Oh, that," Becket said casually, his smile widening just enough to make her eyes narrow. "I've checked with all the other lawyers who are also witches—there aren't too many of us in Stella Rune—and asked their opinion on the situation. Anonymously, of course."

"And?" Lochlan pressed.

"And, so far, they think more or less the same thing I do."

"Which is?" Nia asked, exasperated.

"That there's nothing we can do, and you're going to have to get The Sword to grant the annulment."

"Becket," Lochlan pinched the bridge of his nose and said, with forced calm, "we needed to come here for you to tell us this?"

"Oh, no. I just wanted to see how you two were doing."

Nia glanced at Lochlan, whose face mirrored her own annoyance.

"Great. Thanks." Nia repressed the urge to kick something. Specifically, something tall and Becket-shaped. "We'd figured that much out ourselves."

Taking a steadying breath, Nia walked away before she did something to Becket she—or, more likely, Lochlan—might regret. As she headed toward the bathroom, Nia caught Lochlan's low curse followed by Becket's soft chuckle. Her jaw tightened.

Becket had officially made it onto her shit list.

DIARY ENTRY
MY EIGHTEENTH AUTUMN

I can always tell when it's him. His steps have a rhythm I know all too well. Steady. Sure. My own heart always stumbles at his approach.

Tonight I met him at the doorway. I wasn't afraid of him. I was afraid of what might happen if I let him in.

Nearly a year has passed since he brought me here. I've been given space to heal, an entire wing of the manor. But this solitude has sharpened my curiosity. I've listened at doorways, lingered in shadowed halls.

Supernaturals have come to see him. Strange, powerful beings who speak in riddles or poetry. The fae queen, with a lilting voice I could listen to forever. A forest lord, more bark than skin. Even humans, bold and curious, who know magic lives in Stella Rune.

None of them believed him. Not about what he wanted. Not about what he imagined this town could become. A haven. A place where humans and supernaturals might live side by side without hiding or harm.

I didn't believe it either, not at first. His bloodline is full of monsters. Usurpers who wanted to rule and keep humans beneath them.

He stood in front of me tonight, only moments ago, perfectly still.

"Are you well?"

I nodded.

"You look stronger," he said, and there was warmth in his voice that matched the heat in my cheeks. When he added, "Good," my knees nearly buckled.

"I've come to give you news. The Videt elders are gone." I flinched as memories flashed, harsh and unwanted. He saw it in my face, because he added, "I considered blood. It would've been simpler. But I can't build a better world from bones. So I found others. New leaders. Ones who understand that power is a responsibility, not a right." He paused. "They're not perfect. But I will keep watch."

"And if they fail?" I asked.

His mouth curved. Not quite a smile. "Then I'll find others. Again and again, until this place becomes something worth belonging to."

There was steel in his words. But also hope.

I didn't know what to say, so I said nothing at all. I watched him instead. The way he held himself, tired but resolute: a man carrying the weight of a broken legacy and refusing to let it crush him.

I wanted to believe him. I think I did, even then. But belief is fragile, and I've spent so long trapped in fear that I don't know how to hold onto it.

Still, as he turned to leave, I felt the faintest flicker of something unfamiliar. Hope.

It will take time to grow. But it's here. Sparked by the beast who is already more than that to me, though I am afraid to admit it. Even to myself.

13

Lochlan

"Pancakes: The New Aphrodisiac."
–THE STELLA RUNE GAZETTE

Lochlan stood at the edge of Third Street, watching the crowd weave between vendor tables and clusters of cops with their canine companions. Nearly everyone held a plate stacked with pancakes, fruit, and breakfast sausage, a delicious spread served up for The Charis Foundation's inaugural fundraiser for police dogs. The event had drawn families, couples, and a ridiculous number of dogs happily weaving through the sea of legs. Strands of orange and gold leaves decorated lamp posts, and the scent of maple syrup clung to the crisp air, making it feel like October had arrived early.

He would've brought Jade, but she didn't have the patience for this kind of chaos. Honestly, neither did he.

Nia stood by one of the large portable griddles, her black shirt speckled with splatters of pancake batter—a streak of the same marked her cheek—as she smiled and talked animatedly with a mother of three. The youngest, a little girl with wild curls and a syrup-sticky face, tugged at

Nia's skirt. Lochlan watched as she bent down, giving the child her full attention, nodding thoughtfully.

Nia's expression shifted into something playful and, with a quick glance over her shoulder, she opened her hand to reveal a small cluster of deep purple flowers. Their five-petaled shape mimicked a desert rose. The little girl's eyes widened with wonder, flickering from the flowers to Nia's face, before breaking into a delighted, gap-toothed grin.

"Just a little magic trick," Nia murmured.

Lochlan heard her as though she'd spoken directly to him, though he realized belatedly he'd stepped closer. With so many regulars around, magic had to be used discretely, but the joy radiating from the child in that small moment was pure and unbridled.

"So cool!" the little girl exclaimed, clutching the flowers as she skipped back to her mother and siblings.

Lochlan's chest tightened. His father had used magic the same way— conjuring a flower in his palm, holding it out with a quiet smile.

Tell me its properties, he would say. *What medicines could it make? What spells might it strengthen?*

On his loneliest nights, Lochlan would summon a flower in his palm, reciting its properties into the empty room, pretending his father was still there. Now, watching Nia wield the same magic through their bond, he felt a bittersweet pang.

"Lochlan?" Nia's voice pulled him back. He exhaled sharply, shaking off the memory as her face came into focus.

He cleared his throat. "You picked that up easily."

She glanced down at her palm, a blush creeping across her cheeks. "I guess I did," she said, a trace of pride in her voice. "What're you doing here?"

"How could I miss it?"

"We haven't done the promise spell with my father yet," she warned. "It won't count."

"I just came to see you, and to see how well the hard work you've put into this turned out."

For the briefest moment, her eyes met his. "Ivy did most of it."

Lochlan knew better. He'd heard her talking in her sleep about lists and RSVPs, seen the open notebook filled with painstaking calculations to ensure they sold enough tickets to cover the cost of K9 care and safety equipment. She'd poured her heart into this fundraiser.

Before he could say any of this, a pale blonde woman bounded over, her energy bright and uncontained. "Hi!" She extended a delicate hand. "I'm Ivy, the other half of Charis."

He felt himself return her infectious smile. "It's nice to meet you. I'm Lochlan."

Ivy giggled. Beside her, Nia let out an exaggerated sigh, rolling her eyes.

"We've met before," Ivy said with a playful lilt. "But, from what I hear, you were pretty deep into the fairy wine at the time."

Lochlan's brow furrowed. He wished he could remember—not because he doubted Ivy, but because he'd been fearless that night. Free. He wanted to know what it had felt like to be this version of himself.

"Anyway," Ivy continued, breezily, "I'm so happy you came. We could use an extra set of hands. Johanna—the owner of Peter's Diner—just ran off to grab more batter. The turnout has been even bigger than we expected."

"No, he doesn't need to—" Nia started, but Lochlan cut her off before she could finish.

"I'd love to help." He liked cooking. And he wanted to be near her.

Instead of heading to the empty griddle, he stepped up beside her. Their arms brushed as he reached for a spatula.

She didn't say anything, but he caught the subtle hitch in her breath. *Don't be thick. Say something. Anything.*

"How's your ass?" he asked, before his brain could catch up with his mouth.

Nia froze, her pancake hovering mid-air. She gave him a look. "You just jumped straight to butt stuff, huh?"

"I meant... after you fell. On the stairs." He winced. "I've been worried but didn't know how to ask, and now I've made it weird."

"It was already weird," she said, grinning.

They fell into a rhythm, handing plates across the griddle and keeping up with the steady line of people waiting.

"My butt is fine, by the way," Nia said. "Did you do something to the stairs? I don't remember them being carpeted."

Lochlan's face heated. He had installed it yesterday, telling himself it was for Jade. She wasn't getting any younger. That was true. But it wasn't the whole reason, and he didn't know how to say the rest.

Before he could answer, Nia swore as smoke curled off a pancake. It wasn't the first to catch fire.

"You're not very experienced at this, are you?" he asked, trying to keep his tone light.

"Just because I can't craft edible flowers and puppy dogs from batter like you," she said, waving her spatula toward his side of the griddle after she'd removed the scorched pancake, "doesn't mean I'm not needed."

"You're definitely needed." He stepped closer, guiding her toward the tray of chocolate chips and blueberries, his hand lingering on her back. She didn't move away. The scent of her filled his head—smokey vanilla, amber, and maple syrup. His voice came out low and rough. "But how about you take toppings, and I'll handle the pancakes."

Nia's breath whooshed out in a surprised laugh, her cheeks flushed with a heat Lochlan hoped he'd caused, though it might just have been the griddle.

"Are you trying to fire me from my own fundraiser?" She sounded bemused.

"Not firing, just… reassigning." Nia had many talents, but cooking clearly wasn't one of them. "To a role where you're not a danger to yourself. Or anyone's breakfast," he said with a grin before turning back to the griddle.

Lochlan threw himself into the task of making pancakes, crafting them into flowers, cats, and dogs that earned delighted giggles from the children crowding around. But as hard as he tried to focus, his attention kept drifting to Nia, working too close beside him. It was a test of restraint he hadn't been remotely prepared for. Every accidental brush of her arm, every fleeting touch of her hand sent a pulse of heat through him. His thoughts wandered to the night before—and what might have happened if Becket hadn't, well, been Becket.

Nia leaned behind him to grab a clean cloth, brushing against his back in a fleeting, maddening caress that made him fumble the spatula. He bit the inside of his cheek, desperately willing his body to behave—the last thing he needed was to flip pancakes while battling a very inconvenient, very obvious problem. Divine intervention would be nice right about now. Or, at the very least, an apron.

Intervention did come—just not in the form Lochlan had hoped for.

A weary-looking woman waddled up, hauling an industrial-sized bucket, her presence dousing the fire kindling between him and Nia.

"I brought more batter," the woman announced gruffly.

"Thanks, Johanna, you're the best." Nia pried off the bucket's lid and used it to fan herself.

Johanna grunted in response before shuffling off toward the fruit station, muttering something about strawberries.

Moments later, Ivy appeared, her arms full of empty batter dispensers. "I'll fill the bottles," she said brightly. Before anyone could protest, the batter began pouring itself neatly into the dispensers, as if guided by an invisible hand.

Nia gasped, grabbing the bucket. "Don't use magic! There are too many people. We don't want to piss off Aurelia."

Aurelia, the eraser witch of Stella Rune, was a name that could silence even the boldest witches. Her job was to clean up magical slip-ups before they caused real trouble—wiping memories if necessary, issuing fines, and in more serious cases, handing out jail time. Lochlan had never met her, and had no intention of doing so. He'd seen her once wag a finger at a werewolf twice her size. By the time she was done, the wolf had looked like a scolded puppy.

"Oh, please," Ivy scoffed, trying to wrestle the bucket back. The batter sloshed dangerously. "No one's paying attention. They're too busy wondering if you and your husband are about to make out."

Nia's face went red as she yanked the bucket back, her voice low and sharp. "Shut up."

"Admit it!" Ivy teased, her grin wide and unapologetic.

Lochlan stepped in as the batter swayed dangerously close to the rim. "Easy there," he cautioned, hands outstretched—

But he was too late.

A tidal wave of batter surged over the edge, drenching him and Nia in thick, sticky streaks. Somewhere in the background, Johanna let loose a string of muttered curses, the kind usually reserved for particularly bad burns—magical and otherwise.

"Oops," Ivy chirped, not even attempting to hide her glee. "I guess you two better go get cleaned up."

Lochlan turned to Nia. The left side of her hair was plastered with beige goo, dripping onto her equally drenched clothes. She looked like she'd been caught in a batter storm. He glanced down at himself—his chest and lap were soaked, the cold batter seeping through the fabric and clinging uncomfortably to his skin.

When he glanced up, Nia's eyes were glistening with barely contained laughter.

"Come on," she murmured, grabbing his hand and pulling him along behind her. They wove through the thinning crowd toward her building, stopping at a door labeled *Private Apartments*. "We can use my place," she said, swiping her key. "I need to rinse my hair. And I might have a shirt you can borrow."

They climbed the stairs in silence, the tension between them building with each step.

The inside of her apartment was... mostly empty space. She gestured toward the kitchen before heading for a nearby closet, rummaging around for a towel and a shirt.

"Here, this should do," she said, handing him a bundle of cloth. "I'm going to rinse off and change."

Lochlan nodded, his ears buzzing as he tried not to think about the fact that she was about to be naked in the next room. He clutched the towel and shirt and reminded himself of his plan—to take things slow, to show her that he was worthy of her trust. Memories of what it had felt like to have her in his arms flickered at the edges of his mind, tempting him, testing him.

It took everything he had to keep his thoughts in check.

Lochlan wandered the kitchen, searching for anything—*anything*—to distract himself with. He forced his attention onto the little details of the space, hoping to latch onto something, some glimpse of her. But there was nothing. The apartment felt functional but bare, almost like a dormitory or hotel room: a place to eat and sleep.

It didn't feel like Nia.

The sound of running water from the bathroom made his pulse quicken. He clenched his jaw, dragged himself back to the task at hand and began stripping off his soiled shirt and wiping the sticky batter off his pants. Before he'd finished, Nia reappeared in the bathroom doorway, her damp hair clinging to her shoulders.

She froze mid-step, her eyes widening slightly as she took in his still-shirtless body.

"Shit," he muttered, yanking the borrowed shirt over his head. It was ridiculously small; the hem barely grazed his belly button, and the sleeves strained against his arms. Across his chest, a large pink flag with bold SC lettering stretched wide. Stella College's logo warped with every breath he took.

Nia let out a disarming laugh. She stepped closer, her eyes bright as she grabbed the discarded towel. "You still have batter on you," she murmured, holding the cloth up in silent question.

Lochlan nodded, jaw tight, the words catching somewhere between his chest and tongue.

She reached up, dabbing gently at his cheek, wiping away stray streaks. Her touch was light, hesitant, but it undid him all the same. He leaned into her hand without meaning to, instinct chasing the warmth of her palm.

Flashes of a bonfire and the memory of his hands gripping her skin surged through his mind—dangerous and all-consuming. He shoved them down with a slow, forceful breath, focusing instead on the curve of her lips, the scattering of freckles across her nose, the way her damp lashes framed her eyes.

"I'm sorry about the mess back there." Nia reached up to wipe his hair. Her voice was quiet enough to make him lean in without thinking.

The motion brought her chest against his, and Lochlan's grip on the counter tightened, his fingers digging into the wood. Every nerve in his body screamed at him to close the space between them, but he forced himself to stay still, the tension winding tighter with every passing second.

He cleared his throat, his voice rough as he said, "Are all your fundraisers like that?"

Nia kept running the towel over his skin, even though he was sure there couldn't be any batter left. When her hand swept over his lower stomach, he sucked in sharply, heat pooling low in his abdomen.

"One time," she began, her voice light, "Ivy convinced the local fire fighters to pose with kittens for a calendar shoot. We set it all up in the middle of the street—fires, hoses, oil. The works." Her lips curved into a smile, and Lochlan felt himself mirroring it.

"Small groups of people stopped to watch, of course—how could they not?" she continued, glancing up at him, a faint flush still lingering on her cheeks.

He nodded, forcing himself to focus on her words instead of the way their toes touched, or how the subtle brush of her fingers against his skin was making it very, very hard to think.

"Well," she said, her tone turning conspiratorial, "Beatrice—she lives across the street—decided to bring her famous lemonade and flirt with a couple of the fire fighters. Her husband, Hank, wasn't having it. He thought grabbing one of the hoses and breaking them up was the best plan."

Lochlan raised a brow. "How did that go?"

Nia shook her head and laughed. "Hank's about seventy and smaller than Ivy. When he turned the hose on, the pressure sent it flying, and he held on for dear life. It was like... I don't know, some kind of hose rodeo. Beatrice got completely soaked, one of the businesses had water damage, and now—" Her grin widened. "—we're banned from hosting shirtless photo shoots in the square."

He wished he could have been there to see it himself. He was realizing how much of life in Stella Rune he'd been missing out on. From now on, he wanted to be there—for all of it.

And for her.

"Lochlan?" Nia's voice was soft but threaded with urgency as she leaned against him, her warm hands resting lightly on his chest.

His breath hitched as he met her gaze. Dark, liquid eyes and parted lips beckoned him closer. Oh, goddess. He told himself he needed to hold back. He needed to be patient.

He needed to kiss her.

Lochlan leaned in slowly, her breath a soft caress against his lips. His hand rose to brush against her cheek and—

A crash shattered the moment.

Lochlan jumped and spun on instinct, his arm moving to pull Nia behind him, bracing for the threat. A thief? A demon? A—

Cat.

A massive white Maine Coon sat amidst shards of glass, lazily licking its paw as if it hadn't just barreled through the window. The feline's gold collar glinted in the light, a delicate scroll dangling from it.

Nia let out a slow breath and stepped around Lochlan to crouch beside the oversized menace. She stroked its head with affection. The cat leaned into her touch, utterly unbothered.

She plucked the scroll from its collar, saw the handwriting, and sighed. "Ass hat," she muttered, sounding irritated and exasperated. The warmth and tension that had been building between them bled away, until it felt like it had never existed.

The cat stretched, turned in an elegant circle, and sauntered off. As it slipped out of sight, the shattered window began to reassemble. Shards rose and slotted back into place with quiet, effortless magic.

Nia handed him the scroll, her expression unreadable. "It's Wulfric," she said flatly. "He's summoned us for dinner tomorrow."

14

Nia

*"A Prince Half Royal Reg: What This Match
Means for the Supernatural Community."*
–THE WEEKLY HEX

Wulfric's manor loomed dark and foreboding against
the dimming sky, its black walls and spires casting
long, jagged shadows over the surrounding grounds.
Gargoyles perched on every corner, their stony eyes tracking Nia and
Lochlan's every move. As they climbed the staircase, one gargoyle's head
gave a stiff swivel before bowing slightly.

Nia lifted a hand in a casual wave. "Hi, Larry."

Beside her, Lochlan made a sound somewhere between amusement
and irritation. "You would charm a statue."

She shrugged, suppressing a smile. "Larry and I go way back."

"Should I be jealous?" Lochlan asked.

Nia smirked. "Depends. He's very reliable. Always watched out for me."

Lochlan eyed the gargoyle as if Larry had become competition.

The manor's massive purple doors groaned open, revealing an

expressionless butler Nia had never seen before, who stared at them for an uncomfortably long time before turning wordlessly and striding into the house.

"I guess we follow him?" Lochlan murmured, warily.

"I guess so."

Before they crossed the threshold, Lochlan slipped his fingers between hers, the sensation jarring and unfamiliar. Holding hands. They were holding hands. She'd done this as a child, but not since, and never like this. She told herself it was just the effect the house had on them both— the way it swallowed light, how the air felt thick with ghosts of the past. The connection was practical, grounding, and nothing more.

The manor's interior was a labyrinth of dark and opulent furniture, shadowy corners, and an atmosphere that seemed to breathe. Each step echoed ominously.

Looking at it now, she couldn't understand how she'd once thought this place was magical. The memory of her childhood wonder felt distant and distorted; the warmth she'd once believed in had never been real, only a carefully constructed illusion.

She had been hidden here, a secret tucked away, told it was for her own protection. *Bad people don't like the choices I've made,* her father had said. *That's why your mother died.*

She had believed him.

Until she turned eighteen and found the diary, tucked between forgotten tomes in the library. The delicate scrawl, the ink smudged in places from tears. The horror in those last pages. Her mother had been forced to marry Wulfric. His family had been cruel. She had wanted to escape, but never had the chance.

Nia had confronted him.

It was my fault, he'd admitted. *I couldn't keep her safe.*

She had walked away then. Dropped her full name. Enrolled in college under a new one. Found work at a sandwich shop, and built a life of her own. Now, after all these years, she was back because her father was once again trying to take what wasn't his—only this time, it was her freedom on the line.

They followed Wulfric's butler in silence, his stiff movements giving no indication of where they were going or what awaited them. Lochlan held Nia's hand until they reached the attic door. There, with quiet reluctance, she let go.

The door creaked open and they entered the shadowy expanse illuminated here and there by the warm orange glow of the setting sun streaming through grimy windows. The beams hanging over the large room were covered in cobwebs, and the walls were lined with shelves sagging under the weight of old tomes, dusty scrolls, and jars filled with mysterious substances that shimmered softly in the dim light.

Amid the curious and eerie items stood one pristine shelf. Not a speck of dust could be found on the wood, or the three stuffed animals sitting in a neat row. Their shiny button eyes gazed innocently but intently, as if guarding the secrets of the attic.

"Are those yours?" Lochlan asked, pointing toward the rat, dog, and an orange cat plushie on the shelf next to the thirteen books on necromancy.

"No."

They were her father's.

He stood in the center of the room, glowing lines tracing intricate patterns on the floor, all leading to the large ornate altar where he worked. Chopped herbs and other ingredients lay scattered across its surface, evidence of his preparation.

"My lovely daughter and son-in-law," Wulfric said, eyeing them over the rim of his half-moon glasses.

Nia rolled her eyes. "Let's just get on with it."

They stepped up to the altar, and she scanned the ingredients neatly ordered in a row.

Mugwort—to open the mind. Bleeding Heart—for love. Peppermint—for pure thoughts. And… Honeysuckle?

She frowned, glancing at her father. "Honeysuckle?"

"To sweeten the spell," he replied smoothly.

Nia made a vague sound of acknowledgment, already moving on. The mugwort gave her pause. Magic came from the witch, but herbs and crystals helped steer it. And mugwort—that could cloud your judgment. Exactly what Wulfric would be hoping for.

Verbena, lemongrass, rose petals, and there: aspen.

"Lochlan is curious about your collection on necromancy," she said nonchalantly.

He gave her a curious look but recovered quickly. "Yes, I haven't seen such an extensive collection."

Wulfric took the bait immediately, launching into a detailed account of how he had acquired all thirteen volumes. As he spoke, absorbed in his own self-importance, Nia made her move. With practiced ease, she dumped the mugwort beneath the altar and replaced it with an equal amount of aspen in the gold dish. Cleaner. Safer. Less likely to mess with their heads.

Satisfied, she turned her attention to the spell her father had been preparing. She skimmed the words and scoffed.

Lochlan turned, abandoning his conversation with Wulfric to join her.

Behind them, several thick tomes slipped from a shelf and hit the floor with a dull thud. Wulfric cursed softly and moved to retrieve them, grumbling about "poorly enchanted bindings" as he began to rearrange the stack.

"'Open the mind to seal your fate. Promises to keep and love to wake,'" she read, her tone dry.

This wasn't a promise spell—it was a love spell.

Lochlan leaned in, his warmth pressing against her back. She let herself sink into him for the briefest moment, the solid presence of him an unexpected comfort. But then reality pulled her upright again. With a promise spell looming, and her father's doubts hanging over them, she couldn't afford to let herself get caught in something she might not be able to escape.

She steeled herself and shifted away.

"'Fate' and 'wake' don't even rhyme," Lochlan muttered behind her, voice laced with quiet skepticism.

Rhyme and rhythm matters, she thought, grabbing the ink pot and quill. *Sloppy words make sloppy spells. Everyone knows that.*

She cast Lochlan a sideways glance, the corner of her mouth twitching despite herself.

"What if it starts with 'Light to flame'?" Lochlan suggested, his voice thoughtful. "We could each light a candle during the spell."

She glanced up, considering. "Yes. Light to flame, seals the... bargain? Pact?"

"Deal." Lochlan tapped the table. "Light to flame, seals the deal."

Her lips twitched. "I'll allow it."

"What about 'Bound by truth'... no, that's not it," he mused.

"No, it's perfect," she said, already writing. *Bound by truth, our hearts reveal.* "Because we're proving what's in our hearts."

Lochlan hesitated, then nodded. "What's next?"

She tapped the quill against her lip. "Right are our actions—"

"And we win this fight?" Lochlan finished.

Nia tilted her head. "I was going to say something about honor, but I think I like yours better."

Lochlan's grin was small but proud, and she couldn't help returning it.

"And since we started with light, let's finish with it," she added, scribbling the last line. "The moon will be close to full on Samhain, so how about... 'Prove our fate under the moon's light.'"

"Well, well, well," Wulfric drawled, making them both jump. Nia had completely forgotten he was still in the room. "I'm glad to see you two working so well together."

"It's just a simple spell," Nia replied, though the words tasted bitter on her tongue as she said them. Diminishing the moment they'd just shared felt like swallowing coffin nails.

Lochlan cleared his throat and stepped back, busying himself with the candles. Nia turned away, grabbing the mortar and pestle and adding the first herb—her swapped aspen. She had never created or worked on a spell with anyone before. She'd have expected it to be tedious, frustrating—a chore to tolerate. But instead, it felt like breathing fresh air, like fun. It shouldn't have been fun.

Not with the husband she was trying to leave.

Grinding the herb into fine pieces, she forced her thoughts elsewhere as the rhythmic motion of the pestle anchored her. She didn't want to be married. Her grip tightened as her thoughts drifted to her mother—the woman with whom she shared the same magic.

The woman who had died after giving birth to her.

Whether it had been an accident or something more sinister, like her father claimed, Nia didn't know.

That was the reason he'd kept her hidden for so long. Or, at least, that was what he had wanted her to believe, whispering stories of unseen enemies, of the dangers lurking beyond their walls. But a part of her had always wondered: was it truly about keeping her safe?

Or had it been about keeping her under control? She remembered a passage from her mother's journal.

I must escape before they take me—before they claim my power and add it to their own. The Cabots have always coveted the magic in my blood. They want to control it. Shape it. Breed my magic into their bloodline so its power will pass to their heirs.

But I have no one to turn to, no one willing to help me flee. My grandfather won't protect me.

He has sold me to save himself.

Her mother hadn't escaped. And Nia couldn't fathom the fear and loneliness she must have felt in the days leading up to her death. Reading those words had changed everything. She had sworn she would never end up like her mother—never marry, never let anyone dictate her fate.

Nia added the second ingredient, bleeding heart, grinding it with the aspen, its petals stretching and tearing against the rougher herb. Then came the peppermint—for pure thoughts, for promises. She had made so many promises—to herself, to her mother's memory. Vows to be stronger, to undo the damage of the past. Yet, here she was, bound to a man she barely knew.

But not for long.

Finally, she added the honeysuckle. The sweet scent curled around her, tugging her back to that morning in the field—waking up beside him. A man nothing like what she'd feared. Lochlan was kind, gentle, attentive.

But promises were still promises.

And she wouldn't break them, not even for him.

She thought about her freedom as she weaved a never-ending symbol around the candles with the crushed herbs, but the freedom she had always been so desperate for didn't taste sweet. The idea of being alone became more bitter with each moment she spent with Lochlan.

As she finished her work and gazed back at him, the low light cast shadows across his features, highlighting the gentle furrow of his brow and quiet concern etched in his face.

He was worried about her.

Nia felt a pang of guilt. She'd been so focused on her own internal struggle that she hadn't considered how all of this might affect him. Shame washed over her. He was a stranger, yes, but he was kind and cared for her in a way she hadn't anticipated. She realized she hadn't treated him the same way.

"Step into the circle," Wulfric said from the altar. Lochlan and Nia complied, each taking a spot near him. "Are you both ready?"

They each nodded as Lochlan's fingers brushed her knuckles. It brought her a small comfort amidst the dark attic and the presence of the man she despised above all else. Her father began speaking the words of the spell. With the first line, one candle lit on its own.

"Light to flame seals the deal.

Bound by truth, our hearts reveal.

Right are our actions, and we win this fight.

Prove our fate under the moon's light."

The air shimmered with magic, the lines on the floor pulsing in rhythm with Wulfric's words. Lochlan began speaking the spell and the second candle lit. With each word, the power of the spell weighed more heavily on Nia's shoulders. When he finished, she grabbed his hand, anchoring herself to him.

"Light to flame..." she hesitated, and he squeezed her hand in encouragement. "...seals the deal." The last candle lit. "Bound by truth, our hearts reveal. Right are our actions, and we win this fight. Prove our fate under the moon's light."

The intricate designs on the floor pulsed brightly before dimming to a soft glow.

"By these flames, your bond is forged. May your actions prove your worth, and your fates be sealed under the moon's watchful gaze," her father said.

It felt like a curse. This wasn't part of the spell, or their agreement. Fury flushed over Nia as she opened her mouth to spit an insult at him, but before she could—

"Now, who wants burgers?"

15

Nia

"Autumn Festival in Full Swing! We Have Your Itinerary." –THE STELLA RUNE GAZETTE

The windows of the Charis Foundation framed the decorated square, where October had settled in fully, bringing with it the autumn festival. Garlands of dried corn husks and bright orange marigolds draped over vendor stalls, and carved pumpkins lined the walkways, their flickering candlelight dancing against the cobblestones. Through the glass, Nia could hear the bustle of people weaving through the market, the faint murmur of laughter and music drifting from outside.

She was inside, hoping the couch would swallow her whole.

They bought it secondhand and years of use had worn it into something impossibly squishy and soft. She and Ivy had spent countless hours on this couch—holding hands with people in need, sharing exhausted glances after long nights of chasing down funding, even dozing off in the early hours of morning when work had stretched on too long.

And now? Nia wished it would just pull her under entirely.

Coward.

She was a coward.

Usually, she got things done. Kicked ass and took names. She didn't hide, certainly not from a handsome plant witch just because she couldn't wrangle her creeping affection for him. She'd begun to lose control three nights ago, in her father's attic. Now she was questioning the one thing that had guided her for years: the belief that marriage was a trap, that losing yourself in someone else was dangerous. Since the promise spell, she'd been hiding—leaving the house early, working late, spending as little time as possible with Lochlan for fear of what might happen if she let herself stay. If she really, truly lived with him the way her father had intended.

The town bells chimed six times and Nia pressed the pillow over her head.

Jade probably had her head in her food bowl now and Lochlan would be prepping dinner. But she was here, hiding, instead of enjoying his company and the delicious food she knew he was still making for her, even though she hadn't eaten anything he'd cooked the last three days.

Nia groaned as Ivy dropped onto the couch, picking up Nia's legs with a huff and setting them on her lap.

"Why are you still here?" Ivy asked. "Lochlan is probably worried you aren't home yet."

He probably was, because he cared, and it was utterly annoying.

Ivy tsked. "You could be cursed like me, but no, you have a husband. And this is how you act?"

"Shut up," Nia's voice was muffled by the pillow. She threw it to the side. "You are not cursed, you're just bad at picking partners."

It came out harsh and Nia winced. She wasn't mad at Ivy.

"Sorry."

Ivy didn't look hurt, just thoughtful as she flipped her white blonde hair over her shoulder. "It's fine, you can make it up to me. And you're probably right. I have a date tonight with a reg."

That got Nia's attention. She bolted upright, staring at her friend with wide eyes. "A regular? Good luck."

"Why does everyone say that?" Ivy rolled her eyes. "He's nice, okay? Funny. Has biceps bigger than my head. It's not *impossible.*"

"It's not impossible," Nia agreed, cautiously, "but it's not easy."

Regulars and supernaturals mingled all the time, but it was never simple. It always started with deceit—the supernatural hiding their true nature for as long as possible. And if things got serious, the real work began. Elders and the Videt would get involved, running background checks, conducting interviews, even requiring presentations and studies. It was a lot.

Something nagged at her. Ivy stared at her with an expectant smirk until Nia finally realized—

"Wait. *Make it up to you?* How?"

"By coming with me."

"Like a chaperone?"

"No," Ivy said, grinning wider. "You and Lochlan. A double date."

"No way. Not happening—"

Before she could finish, Lochlan burst into Charis, his hair wild, eyes wide, looking frantic.

Ivy giggled, drawing his attention immediately.

"I may have texted him from your phone about an emergency," Ivy stage whispered.

"What happened?" Lochlan's breath came fast, shoulders rising as his gaze darted between them. When his eyes settled on Nia, her heart clenched. "Nia?"

There it was—*feelings.* Big, messy, gushy ones for this man who looked at her with so much worry over whatever nonsense Ivy texted him.

They'd known each other for a week, yet he was ready to drop everything and rush to her side.

Nia drank him in: wild hair, dark eyes, the concern etched across his face. She'd been avoiding him for days, wasting hours in the tunnels, grasping at any excuse to stay away. But there was no avoiding him now. They stared at each other, the space between them thick with unspoken words.

"Whoa," Ivy said, slicing through the tension like a blade. "You two, I swear." She fanned herself dramatically before turning to Lochlan. "What happened is that I need you two to go on a double date with me."

Nia barely had time to process the shift before Lochlan blinked, his concern giving way to confusion. "No one is hurt?"

"I'm hurt!" Ivy whined.

"What's wrong?" he asked, baffled as he studied her with genuine worry.

Nia rolled her eyes. Ivy fed on chaos, could sense it like a pulse in the air, and right now, she was practically buzzing with it. No doubt she could feel the tangled mess between Nia and Lochlan, and was enjoying every second of it.

"I'm lonely and sad and no one wants to be with me!" Ivy wailed, throwing her arms up.

"She thinks she's cursed," Nia deadpanned.

"I am cursed!" Ivy insisted.

Lochlan let out a long breath and dragged a hand over his forehead, like this entire conversation had physically drained him. "Okay," he said roughly. "Okay, that's fine. You said a double date?"

"You'll go?" Ivy asked, practically bouncing with excitement.

"Of course," Lochlan replied, his attention turning back to Nia. The energy between them shifted, quieter, gentler. "Whatever you need."

Nia's stomach twisted. She wasn't sure if it was guilt, gratitude, or something more dangerous. She managed a small nod, but her mind raced. *What did she need?* The answer should have been simple: escape, distance, an end to this charade. Instead, all she could think about was him.

And how he was making her question every promise she'd ever made to herself.

Rosé & Reverie was designed to evoke romance: soft lighting, plush seating, and an air of quiet intimacy woven into every detail. The love witch who owned it had laced the space with magic, a subtle enchantment humming beneath the surface. Regs couldn't identify magic the way witches could, but they could still feel it: the glow, the ambiance, the way everything seemed to slow, like the night itself was leaning in to listen.

None of that was enough to make Nia forget she'd been bamboozled by Ivy and fist-bumped by her tardy date, Daniel.

The juggernaut was clad in a cutoff shirt, in freaking autumn. He chewed loudly on a piece of bread, the rest of the loaf held hostage behind one meaty arm.

Every aggressive bite made Nia's eye twitch.

She didn't even want to read him. But her magic moved on instinct when it came to protecting the only person she loved. Sweet, sunshine-hearted Ivy clearly didn't see the warning signs flashing in human form across the table. So Nia reached. Just a brush against the darker parts of him: the quiet places most people tried to hide.

She instantly hated him.

No regret. No fear. Just ego, loud and hollow. Daniel's darkness wasn't born from suffering, but entitlement.

Lochlan's hand gently wrapped around hers. Only then did Nia realize she was gripping her fork like a weapon. She blinked, stealing a glance at him as she let out a slow, measured breath and eased her grip.

"So, Daniel," Lochlan began.

"Big D," Daniel interrupted, mouth still full of bread.

Lochlan remained patient. "I'd rather not call you that."

"But it's true. I'm Big D." Daniel's pecs flexed under his shirt as he winked at Ivy then turned back to Lochlan. "Bigger than you."

This was a ridiculous thing to say on what was supposed to be a double date. Nia nearly bent her fork in half. Lochlan didn't so much as blink. "So, what do you do for work?" he asked, as if Daniel wasn't embarrassing himself.

"I'm in supplement sales." He curled an arm to show off an unnaturally large bicep. This, Nia realized, must be why he was wearing a cut-off.

"And is that rewarding?" she asked.

A sharp pain shot up her leg and Nia gasped, glaring at Ivy across the table. The witch had kicked her! Over this buffoon?

"Super rewarding," Daniel went on, oblivious. "I lead a team that sells this *magic pill*." His thick fingers made air quotes. "It says it helps people lose like, fifteen pounds in a week. Dummies fall for it all the time."

Nia kicked Ivy this time. How dare she subject them all to this ass hat.

Unaware of the silent battle beneath the table, Daniel continued. "I mean, we can't all be filatherapists."

Nia's brain melted as she realized Daniel meant philanthropists.

Through tight lips, she said, "*I mean,* you can, actually. We have a volunteer event this weekend—harvesting from community gardens around the area to feed anyone who could use a little extra help. Ivy worked on this all year. I'll get you all signed up, and you'll be well on your way to becoming a *filatherapist.*"

Daniel laughed, throwing his head back with half-chewed bread on full display. "Digging around in the dirt on a Saturday? I'll pass. But if you want to hit the gym, or get in another kind of workout—" He smirked at Ivy. "—then I'm your guy."

Nia found herself gripping her utensil again. She was going to kill Daniel. Possibly with a fork, in front of an entire restaurant of canoodling couples. The community garden harvest was Ivy's passion project, one she poured her heart into because she grew up never knowing where her next meal would come from.

"I can't wait to dig into the gardens Ivy helped create," Lochlan said, his steady voice cutting through the tension. "I understand one community garden can feed three hundred people. All the gardens Ivy has been involved with will provide enough food to support not just those in Stella Rune, but the surrounding towns as well. It's incredible."

Nia was speechless. She glanced toward Ivy and saw a blush creep across her cheeks. Nia could kiss Lochlan for bringing this tiny bit of joy to the otherwise irredeemable encounter.

Then Daniel opened his mouth.

"Yeah, gardening sounds about right for you," he said with another smirk. "Bet you've never lifted anything heavier than a book."

"Say one more thing about him," Nia murmured under her breath, "and I will gut you where you sit." Her shadows stirred, uncoiling like restless serpents, creeping along the wooden floor of the restaurant. It would be quick. No one would know. She'd drag him under the table and strangle him and—

A warm spark flared through her magic. Lochlan's shadows entwined with hers, curling around them like a soft tether. The caress echoed across her skin, soothing her rage. Suddenly, she didn't feel quite so murdery.

Nia glanced toward Lochlan. He gave a subtle shake of his head and she decided to stand down.

The server came with their main course and Nia pushed her food around her plate, her appetite long gone. She couldn't eat—not with Ivy looking like she wanted to melt into the floor and Lochlan trying to keep the peace as Daniel droned on about this party or that supplement or this workout. At one point, she caught Lochlan checking his phone; she didn't blame him. If she thought there was an escape that wouldn't leave Ivy alone with *Big D,* she'd take it in a heartbeat.

Across the table, Daniel shoveled the last bite of his steak into his mouth. His eyes landed on Ivy's plate. "If you're not going to eat that—"

"Oh, um, I might..."

Without waiting for Ivy's answer, he dragged it across the table and began plowing through her untouched pasta. Ivy looked uncomfortable and even a little worried. As irritated as Nia was with her for dragging Lochlan and her into this, she hated seeing Ivy like that.

When Daniel's gaze shifted toward Nia's plate, she stiffened. She met his gaze head-on, daring him to try.

"Don't even think about it," Lochlan said, low and commanding.

But Nia wanted Daniel to think about it. *Let him try,* she thought. She'd spent the past half hour conjuring increasingly creative—and satisfying—ways to stab him with her fork.

The server approached, smiling brightly, oblivious to the tension simmering at the table. "Would anyone care for dessert?"

Before Nia could respond, Lochlan raised a hand. "Just the checks, please," he said with his usual politeness, though the edge in his voice was unmistakable.

Daniel shoved his chair back with a loud screech, making everyone wince. "Bathroom," he grunted, disappearing without another word.

Nia threw her napkin onto her plate. "Well, that was torture."

Ivy looked like she was about to cry. "He really didn't seem this awful when he asked me out, but... he is. Isn't he? I really am cursed!" She buried her face in her hands. "How do I get rid of him?"

Nia could think of several ways, all of which were satisfyingly violent, and none of which were particularly feasible in a restaurant full of witnesses. She was searching for something reassuring to say to Ivy instead, when she caught sight of a familiar figure weaving through the restaurant.

"Becket?" she said, surprised.

"Well, look at this," he drawled with an easy grin. "If it isn't my favorite witch and her husband-slash-my-best-friend."

At the sound of Becket's voice, Ivy's head popped up, her wide eyes blinking at the stranger.

"What are you doing here?" Nia crossed her arms tightly over her chest. Her suspicions had her skipping introductions.

She hadn't seen Becket since the lawyer's networking event—since *that moment* in the hallway. She could still feel the warmth of Lochlan's arms, the soft rasp of his breath against her neck, and the hollow ache as they'd pulled apart when Becket appeared.

He stood before them, grinning, like he'd orchestrated this moment, too.

"I was grabbing a drink before heading to the autumn festival," Becket said casually.

Nia's gaze flicked to Lochlan, then back to Becket, her eyes narrowing. "Alone?"

Becket sighed dramatically, pressing a hand to his chest. "I can't help it if a certain gorgeous redhead has monopolized all the time of my one and only friend."

Nia raised an eyebrow, unimpressed.

"It's fine," Becket continued with a shrug, clearly undeterred. "I figured the autumn festival would be fun, even if I'm going solo—maybe it'll distract me from my loneliness."

"Oh no," Ivy piped up, her breathy tone edged with concern. "You can't go alone. That's not how it's done."

Their eyes met and Becket extended his hand.

"I'm Lochlan's best friend, Becket." He took Ivy's hand gently and brought her knuckles to his lips, brushing them lightly. "Though, sadly, he hasn't named me after a flower yet."

Ivy tilted her head, studying him with quiet but intent curiosity. Lochlan rolled his eyes. "Becket, this is Ivy," he said, his tone long-suffering, "Nia's best friend and business partner."

Becket's gaze remained locked on Ivy as his smile turned softer, more sincere. "Ivy suits you perfectly."

Nia watched the prettiest pink spread across her cheeks.

"It looks like you three are all finished with dinner," Becket continued, leaning back with an easy air. "Maybe you could join me?"

Ivy hesitated, her eyes flitting to the bathroom door.

Lochlan and Nia spoke at once.

"I'll take care of the checks," he said, rising.

"I'll go take care of…" Nia's voice trailed off as she glared at the bathrooms.

"Why don't you three head out front?" Lochlan suggested, following her gaze. "I'll handle things here."

Nia hesitated, her instincts telling her to stay and see things through herself. But Lochlan was calm and exuded quiet confidence, and she did want to keep an eye on Ivy.

She exhaled softly and turned, allowing Becket to guide her and Ivy outside.

The autumn festival spilled onto the streets, its decorations extending beyond the square. Twinkling lanterns hung from the lamp posts, their golden glow casting warm pools of light on the cobblestones. Bundles of dried wheat and pumpkins lined the storefronts and the crisp night air carried the scents of cinnamon and cider.

Still, despite the festive atmosphere, the unpleasant tension from dinner clung stubbornly to Nia. Becket filled the silence with easy small talk, his tone light and teasing, but she didn't hear a word. Her thoughts were back in the restaurant. She was the one who always handled things—cleaned up the messes, dealt with the bad guys.

Why was it so hard to let someone else take responsibility?

Arms crossed tightly over her chest, she muttered something vague to Becket, ignored a questioning glance from Ivy, and turned back to the restaurant. The dining room was nearly empty now, and their table abandoned. Nia's eyes scanned the space until they landed on the hallway where the bathrooms were. With quick steps she headed toward it, but slowed as she realized the air felt odd, different: heavy with a kind of magic that had nothing to do with the glow of romantic warmth.

She rounded the corner and froze.

Daniel stood against the wall, all smugness gone and replaced by an unease that bordered on panic. An angry rash spread across his skin in vivid streaks as ropes of ivy and shadows curled around his arms and chest. The tendrils pulsed faintly, alive with magic, their movements glamoured so he wouldn't notice.

Lochlan stood before him.

"I don't care what videos you saw of Ivy. That doesn't make her yours, and it sure as hell doesn't mean she owes you anything." His voice was measured, each word sure and controlled, like his magic. "You're going to delete her number. You're never going to contact her again."

Nia's breath hitched. She'd seen Lochlan use magic before, but never like this. The shadows and vines obeyed him with seemingly effortless precision, subtle enough to stay hidden but potent enough to make her pulse race.

Goddess, it was hot.

Daniel gazed at Lochlan, his confusion replaced with uneasy fear.

Lochlan looked at the rash, then met his eyes. "You should go home, Daniel. Before that spreads any further."

Daniel glanced down to the angry red welts creeping along his arms. With a strangled noise, he scrambled away and pushed through the door at the end of the hall without a backward glance.

Lochlan turned to leave, mild annoyance written across his face, but when his eyes landed on Nia his expression shifted—relief, first, then something more guarded.

"You took care of things," she said. It wasn't a question.

"Of course." He sounded wary but matter-of-fact.

Nia's jumbled thoughts suddenly clicked into place. Lochlan showing up to the date. Checking his phone at the table. Becket's sudden arrival. Lochlan quietly taking care of the checks. Becket taking Ivy to the festival. Lochlan taking care of the ass hat.

Taking care of her.

Oh no.

No, no, no.

There was a mess of warm feelings rolling around her rib cage, sticky and unavoidable. And worse—a mess of heat creeping across her skin, pooling low in her belly. She was getting all worked up over being cared for.

Oh, goddess help her.

Lochlan's voice pulled her from her spiral. "Ready for the autumn festival?" His eyes held hers. "There's a chance we can still turn tonight around for Ivy."

Nia swallowed hard. Her pulse skipped as she nodded quickly and managed, a little breathlessly: "Yeah. Okay."

Lochlan's lips quirked in a faint smile, and she prayed he couldn't see the war going on inside her. He held out a hand. After a heartbeat of consideration, she slipped her fingers into his, and they walked into the cool night together.

16

Lochlan

"Who is in charge of the fairies? They are getting out of control!" —PRINCES&PIES444

The town center looked like it had tumbled straight out of a postcard. Strands of fairy lights crisscrossed the streets, while lamp posts were wrapped in wheat stalks and autumn garlands. Booths selling handmade crafts and steaming drinks dotted the sidewalks, and a Ferris wheel creaked merrily in the background. Pumpkins and gourds filled every available nook, and the air was thick with the scents of caramel and apple cider. Even the park had been transformed into a golden maze of corn stalks, where breathless couples emerged, cheeks flushed and grins triumphant.

Lochlan smiled, thinking of the wonderful turn their terrible evening had taken. They'd survived the dreadful double date, his best friend was here cracking jokes with Ivy—who no longer looked pale and miserable—and Nia was tucked under his arm.

This moment felt like a spell strong enough to overpower the unraveling of their marriage.

"Where to first? Food?" Becket asked, already scanning the booths like a man on a mission. "Oh, wait, you just came from dinner."

"I don't think any of us actually ate," Lochlan said dryly, earning a soft snort from Ivy.

"How about rides?" she suggested, bouncing on her toes, clearly eager to leave the double date disaster far behind.

"The Chaos Cyclone?" Becket offered with a mischievous glint in his eye.

Lochlan groaned, his stomach lurching at the very thought. "You've got to be kidding me. I hate rides that spin."

Ignoring his protest, the group headed toward the twirling monstrosity. The ride towered above them, all screeching bolts and whining metal, the structure swaying precariously with every gust of wind. Just watching it was enough to make Lochlan queasy. The line wasn't long—not nearly long enough for him to summon the nerve to get in one of those rickety, swaying carts. Lochlan scanned the ride's dizzying motion, searching in vain for an escape route.

He swallowed hard.

"You know what?" Nia suddenly said, rubbing her chest. "The wine I had isn't sitting right. Maybe I shouldn't risk it. Loch, can you sit this one out with me?"

Lochlan blinked at her, relief sweeping through him like a tidal wave. "Of—of course. No problem at all."

"We'll see you when we get off!" Ivy brimmed with excitement as she tugged Becket toward the waiting cart.

Becket glanced over his shoulder, his grin turning wicked. "You're missing out, Lochlan," he teased, but his expression softened when his gaze flicked to Ivy.

As Ivy and Becket climbed into the swaying cart, Lochlan exhaled and turned to Nia. She was already smirking.

"Thank you," he said as they walked toward the exit, stopping near the metal gate.

"I should be thanking you," she replied, bumping her shoulder playfully into his arm.

"For what?"

"Oh, I don't know," she said, her voice light and teasing. "I'm pretty sure you're the reason Becket just happened to show up at the restaurant. You kept me from stabbing anyone with a fork, paid for dinner, and—oh, let's not forget—got rid of Daniel."

Lochlan's mouth opened to respond, but no words came. His face grew uncomfortably warm as he managed a small, bashful smile.

Nia bumped him again, her laughter as light as the breeze that ruffled her hair. Together, they watched the Chaos Cyclone spin wildly, its colorful blur whipping against the night sky. The sight should have made his stomach churn, but it didn't. Instead, he felt weightless—like he might float away.

After a few minutes, Ivy and Becket made their way over, Ivy's hair tousled and both of their faces lit with wide smiles. Becket leaned in to say something to Ivy, making her laugh, bright and unrestrained. But it wasn't Ivy's reaction that caught Lochlan's attention—it was the way Becket looked at her.

His friend was looking at Ivy the same way he probably looked at Nia.

The thought unsettled Lochlan. Becket had always been like a wildflower—impossible to pin down, thriving only where the soil was loose and the roots could run shallow. He wasn't the kind of person to take root and grow alongside someone else. And yet, he watched Ivy like she was sunlight—something vital he was leaning toward without realizing it.

"That was amazing!" she exclaimed, throwing her arms around Nia. "Where to next?"

"I'm starved," Nia declared dramatically, clutching her stomach.

Ivy tilted her head, eyebrows knitting together. "I thought your stomach was bothering you?"

Lochlan watched as Nia feigned a pout, her expression so exaggerated it wasn't even close to convincing. Ivy laughed, nudging her with an elbow. "If you were scared, you could've just said so."

Nia scoffed, rolling her eyes. "If I don't get an apple cider donut in my hand soon, something bad might happen."

"We wouldn't want that." Lochlan's gaze scanned the booths. "The donut cart's five stalls away."

When he looked back, Nia was watching him, her expression unreadable. Not quite surprise—something closer to wonder.

Their eyes met. He held her stare, waiting, until she glanced away biting her lip.

Ivy grabbed Becket's sleeve and tugged him away. "Come on, let's give them a moment before they combust."

"Can you not do that?" Nia huffed.

Lochlan raised an eyebrow. "Do what?"

She gestured vaguely at him. "Make it hard for me to stick to my plan. It's like you're doing it on purpose, but I know you aren't."

"I'm not," he admitted, frowning thoughtfully. "I don't know what I'm doing."

"That makes it even worse." Nia sighed and pulled her hair up, fingers combing through it in frustration.

Lochlan reached into his pocket and handed her a hair tie.

She closed her eyes for a beat, as if gathering patience—or courage—but her lips twitched as she took it from him, quickly securing her hair into a pony.

"You need to stop this," she muttered.

"When you tell me what I'm doing, we can talk about that." Lochlan caught her hand and tugged her toward the donut cart. "For now, I think you're hungry. And if I don't get you a donut soon, bad things will happen. Remember?"

With food and drinks in hand—Nia's beloved donut included—they wandered between the small artisan booths. Handmade pottery, cozy autumn crafts, and scented candles tempted passersby, the crisp air filled with the scent of spice and smoke.

Their group stopped outside a fortune-teller's booth, its rich purple-and-gold banner catching Ivy's eye.

"Oh my goddess," Ivy breathed. "I haven't had my cards read in forever!"

"Any time you want, pixie, I'll read your cards," Becket said with a wink, but as his eyes traced the intricate artwork on the banner he froze. Lochlan watched recognition flicker across his friend's face and his own stomach sank. He knew that design. The careful swirls of ink, the vivid lines—he'd seen those exact doodles in old notebooks, scrawled in the margins of one of Zora's journals.

Becket had four sisters, but only Zora shared his gift. Their father, a seer himself, had disappeared long ago, leaving behind a void that had shaped Becket and his sister in ways they rarely spoke about. Though their mother had remarried and brought two more daughters into their family, the shadow of their father's absence lingered.

Ivy tried to tug the group toward the booth, her excitement contagious. Nia followed with a small laugh, but Becket didn't move.

"You two go on," Lochlan said, keeping his tone light as he stepped closer to Becket. "We'll wait here." He gestured casually toward the booth. "I don't cheat on my own seer."

Ivy giggled, easily distracted by the thought of a reading. Nia, however, glanced back at Lochlan, her brow furrowed. He gave her a small nod, hoping she wouldn't question it. After a brief hesitation, she let Ivy pull her toward the purple-and-gold drapes.

As soon as they disappeared behind the curtain, Lochlan turned to Becket. "How long has it been?"

Becket's easy grin slipped and he ran a hand through his hair. "Fourteen months, maybe. Not that anyone's counting."

Lochlan crossed his arms. "What happened this time?"

"The usual." Becket let out a low chuckle, but there was no humor in it. "We had words. I told her she was reckless, that she needed to stop running off to every small-town carnival or pop-up fair like it was her life's calling. She told me I needed to stop projecting my shit onto her and figure out my own mess." He shrugged. "She's not wrong."

"You think that's why she hasn't called?" Lochlan asked, his tone carefully neutral.

Becket shoved his hands into his pockets. "Nah, that's on me. I let her leave and didn't say a damn thing after. Figured she'd be better off without my overprotective crap. Zora's got enough to deal with without me breathing down her neck."

Lochlan studied his friend. "She's your sister. You think she's not waiting for you to fix this?"

Becket's crooked grin didn't reach his eyes. "What's there to fix? I'm a hypocrite, Lochlan. I've got my own commitment issues, but hers are too much for me to handle? It's stupid, I know." He let out a long breath. "Anyway, I've got no business telling her what to do, playing big brother when it suits me, and ignoring my own advice. She deserves better."

"You're still her brother." Lochlan shook his head. "Say something tonight. You might not get another chance."

Becket grumbled something noncommittal under his breath.

"And it could be worse," Lochlan pointed out. "You could have a sister who enjoys setting things on fire."

Becket shot him a look. "Way to be depressing."

"Just offering perspective," Lochlan said, his gaze wandering past Becket, toward the swirling crowds beyond the festival, as his thoughts drifted.

He and Becket had always understood each other in ways that didn't need words. The pain of missing parents. The burden of being left behind. But where Becket still had a sister to fight for, Lochlan had spent years pretending he didn't care that his own siblings never fought for him. And he'd been good at it.

He still was.

Lochlan opened his mouth to say something else, but before the words could form, Ivy emerged from the booth. She avoided their eyes, her brightness dimmed and her brows knit as she stared at the ground.

Lochlan stepped forward, concerned. "What's wrong?"

"What? Oh. Nothing." Ivy blinked and forced a laugh, waving off his question. "Everything's fine. She's just doing Nia's reading now."

Becket's expression shifted, his earlier emotions slipping away in an instant. He stepped closer to Ivy with a smile that managed to be both reassuring and mischievous. "How about I go win you the biggest stuffed bear in the area?"

Ivy's face lit up, regaining some of its usual warmth. "You're on," she said, already pulling him toward the game booths.

Lochlan watched them go, worry lingering as he glanced back at Zora's seer booth. Nia was still inside.

He couldn't shake the feeling that something wasn't right.

17

Nia

"How to Know If Your Seer Is a Fake."
—A PAGANS BLOG

The tent's interior was dimly lit, bathed in the warm glow of candlelight. Rich purple drapes hung from the low ceiling, their embroidered patterns shimmering faintly. The air was thick with the scent of sandalwood and something herbal—sage, maybe. A table stood at the center, draped in deep crimson cloth, a black velvet pouch resting at its edge.

Nia hesitated as Ivy slipped out of the tent, torn between following her to make sure she was alright, and staying put to hear what her own future might hold. The seer before her—Zora—had a presence that, in the end, pinned her in place.

Ivy's reading had uncovered some shadow-work to be done, an introspection Nia knew her friend wasn't prepared to deal with yet. Oh, and that she wasn't ready for love, but when the time came, it would be something extraordinary. Ivy was a hopeless romantic with very little patience.

She's going to hate that, Nia thought.

Zora shuffled her deck, deliberate and unrushed. Her resemblance to Becket was impossible to miss—the same sharp cheekbones, the same rich brown skin, the same chestnut eyes—and the same gift.

Sister, Nia assumed. Still, where Becket carried himself with a casual, devil-may-care attitude, Zora's energy was unwavering and intense, as if she could see straight through Nia to the parts she kept hidden. Zora fanned out the cards, flipped one over, and placed it firmly on the table.

A single gold cup stood alone on the card.

"Your friend isn't ready for love," she said, her tone matter-of-fact. Her fingers hovered over the next card before she glanced up. "But the Ace of Cups speaks to new beginnings. Love, joy, deep connection. This says you're just finding yours."

Nia blinked, her chest tightening. "My what?"

"Your love." Zora flipped another card, her brows drawing together in a deep crease. A woman sat before a set of scales, one arm raised as if to tip the balance. The card landed upside down. Zora's brow creased. "Well, that's... not good."

"What's worse than love?" Nia asked, her tone light even as unease twisted in her gut. The thought didn't sit right. The night had been full of laughter, of shared glances and lingering touches with Lochlan. Every time their shoulders brushed, she'd found herself leaning in instead of pulling away. But now Zora's reading weighed on her.

The seer rolled her eyes, her voice tinged with exasperation as she tapped on the second card. "Who did you piss off?"

"You'll have to be more specific." Nia leaned back, crossing her arms. "This week? This year? Today?"

"Justice reversed," Zora said. "It means something is off. Consequences are coming. And you don't get to decide when."

Zora sucked in a sharp breath as she flipped another card: a woman laying before the oceans, ten swords impaling her from head to foot.

Her head shook slightly as she gathered up the deck. Without a word, she set this aside and pulled out another deck, shuffled it briskly, and flipped the top card.

The same card, albeit with different and more faded artwork stared back at them.

Zora's expression tightened as she tried yet another deck.

Again, the same card appeared.

"I didn't know you did magic tricks, too," Nia said, her unease bubbling into forced humor.

"This isn't funny," Zora snapped.

"What is it?" Nia asked, feeling defensive.

Zora set the deck down, her lips thin. "Someone hunts you."

Nia exhaled slowly, her lips quirking into a small, sardonic smile. "Not surprised."

"I don't think you understand," Zora said, leaning forward.

"Trust me, I understand," Nia said, brushing off the tension with a shrug. She'd spent most of her life hidden from the people who wanted her father dead—the same ones who ran his car off the road and killed her mother while she was still in the womb. The Anti-Glamour Coalition believed magic should rule and humans should kneel. They saw her father's rise as a betrayal. After the crash, he'd told everyone she had died, too. But the threats never stopped. And Nia? The moment she'd gotten a taste of freedom, she ran straight toward danger. Again and again.

Nothing had ever happened that she couldn't handle.

"Been there, done that. I'll be fine."

Zora's expression darkened. "Not now. Not when you have so much to lose."

Before Nia could respond, a chime cut through the tension. Zora pulled out her phone and flipped it over, sighing as she silenced the alarm.

"Time's up," she said briskly, the edge in her tone softening to something closer to detachment. "That'll be fifty for the both of you."

Nia rose to her feet, frowning skeptically at Zora before pulling out the cash.

"I like your brother better," Nia said flatly.

Zora didn't flinch. She looked at Nia with a faintly curious expression and said, "You're pretty powerful. I didn't feel your magic."

Nia smiled, cool and humorless. "I didn't use magic. You just confirmed what I already suspected."

As she turned to leave, her magic caught a flicker of regret curling in the shadows of the tent, a tangible weight that tugged at the air around Zora. Nia's magic stirred instinctively, coiling at the edges of her awareness, itching to probe those regrets and wield them like a weapon. But she didn't.

Before Nia could push through the tent flaps, Zora called after her. "Don't let Lochlan get hurt. He's one of the good ones."

Freaking seers.

Nia stepped out into the crisp night air, letting the briny breeze chase away the scent of incense and candle wax.

Lochlan stood just outside, his face brightening the moment he saw her. Without hesitation, she went to him, and his arms opened to catch her.

"Everything okay?" he murmured against her hair.

She let herself lean into him, drawing strength from the way he held her. "Nothing I can't handle."

"Good."

That was one of the things she loved about him—he didn't press, not because he didn't care, but because he chose to trust her.

Love.

What a silly word.

"Let's find Becket and Ivy." He pulled back just enough to look down at her, though he didn't let go. "I'm worried he's spending all his money trying to win her a bear. The man has horrible timing and worse coordination."

They strolled toward the row of game booths, and sure enough, Becket was at one of them, winding up for another throw. A baseball flew from his hand, veering wildly off course and missing the metal milk jugs by a mile.

The booth attendant, a wiry glamoured vampire with a red-and-white striped vest and an exaggerated mustache, smirked. "Ladies and gentlemen, behold! The rare and mystical curveball of disappointment!" He waved his hand theatrically toward the fallen ball.

Ivy doubled over, tears streaming from her eyes as she laughed uncontrollably. Becket, unfazed, slapped more money onto the counter.

"This time," Becket muttered, narrowing his eyes at the milk jugs.

When he threw again, the ball wavered in the air, teetering off course before righting itself and smashing into the jugs with a satisfying clatter. The booth attendant raised an eyebrow, but Ivy squealed with delight, jumping up and down as the man reluctantly handed her a large purple teddy bear.

"You did it!" Ivy exclaimed, hugging the bear.

Becket blinked, clearly as shocked as the booth attendant. "Of course I did it," he said, recovering quickly. "Pure skill."

Lochlan straightened as Aurelia Shade, the eraser witch of Stella Rune, stormed past, chasing a few fairies who were hiccupping with laughter as they bobbed through the air. They were glamoured from non-magical eyes, but that didn't mean the chaos they left behind would go unnoticed.

Once the terrifying witch was out of sight, Nia leaned in, her voice low and conspiratorial. "That's cheating."

"Would you call it cheating if I won you that one?" he asked, pointing to the largest prize on display: a colossal bear that towered over the rest of the plush animals.

"No," she admitted, picturing Jade's excited prancing when they brought it home. Nia smiled. "No, I wouldn't."

18

Nia

"Your Guide to Supernatural Compatibility."
–THE STELLA RUNE GAZETTE

Nia stepped into the townhouse, exhaustion draped like a blanket over her shoulders. Behind her, Lochlan locked up just before Jade barreled into him. He caught the large dog with ease, and her tail thumped lazily. Summoning what little energy she had left, Nia went up on her toes and pressed a kiss to Jade's forehead. The dog huffed contentedly, her tail wagging harder.

"Someone's spoiled," Nia murmured.

Lochlan smirked, his closeness sending a quiet hum through the air between them. "She's not the only one."

Nia's gaze dropped to the enormous stuffed bear that was almost as big as Jade, cradled in her arms, then rose to meet Lochlan's. His eyes were warm and entirely too knowing, like he could see every thought flickering through her head.

The moment lingered, faintly charged.

He was catching her off guard again—he'd been doing it all night.

And she had been avoiding this man? The one who made sure she ate, who gave her what she needed before she even thought to ask? The one who somehow managed to make carnival games look... hot?

Her face flushed, and she quickly stepped back, shrugging off her leather jacket. It fell carelessly onto the armchair as she made her way to the couch, flopping onto it with a sigh. The oversized bear Lochlan had won cushioned her fall, its soft fur enveloping her as she sank into the plushness.

Behind her, Lochlan's voice rumbled low as he set Jade down, the door opening and closing softly as he let her out into the yard, and for a moment, Nia let herself relax into the bear's warmth. She must have drifted off, because the next thing she knew, Jade's tongue was on her cheek, wet and insistent.

Groaning, Nia opened her eyes to see Lochlan leaning against the doorway, his sleeves rolled up and his gaze steady. The sight sent a flicker of hunger through her—one she was too tired to fight. Maybe she was too tired to fight her feelings, too.

"Would you like to shower first?" he asked.

"Shower?" She cleared her throat, quickly pushing aside the unhelpful thought of him naked under the water. "No, go ahead. I'll wash the night off after I decompress with Jade."

Their eyes met for a moment, Nia's chest tightening with every heartbeat, until Lochlan nodded and turned. Her gaze trailing over the lines of his broad shoulders down to the curve of his ass as he walked down the hall and disappeared up the stairs.

Making a soft and embarrassingly desperate sound, Nia dropped back onto the couch. The dog licked her cheek once more, then flopped down with a yawn.

"What am I going to do about your dad?" she murmured, running her fingers through Jade's fur.

The dog fixed her with what could only be described as a judgmental stare.

Nia gave Jade a small smile and scratched her head. "Yeah, I don't know either."

And what was she going to do about *her* dad?

Her feelings for Lochlan were becoming harder to ignore, and after tonight, all she wanted was to jump his bones and thank him in ways words couldn't manage. But these feelings didn't mean marriage, she told herself, firmly.

She just didn't believe it the way she had a few days ago.

The sweet scent of apple cider clung to the plush bear, filling her senses as sleep pulled her under. Jade's warm fur was the only pillow she needed. Then—

A voice slipped through the haze of sleep, cold, sharp, and far too familiar.

"Why are you sleeping on the couch?"

Pressure crushed against her chest and—

She floated into existence.

The living room pulsed faintly with a purple hue, the atmosphere wrong—heavy, distorted. Nia sat up, the air around her shifting like a slow, rhythmic heartbeat.

No. No. No.

She knew this place: she was in the astral plane, the place her father loved to hunt. A memory slammed into her, unbidden.

The attic, candles flickering in a perfect circle. Her father sitting cross-legged in the center, eyes milky white, lips moving in a soundless chant. The room's energy dense and oppressive, pressing against her lungs. Her father finally coming back to himself, looking at her like this wasn't scary for a child to see. "I'm watching our enemies," he said calmly. "The ones who believe magic should rule out in the open. The ones who would tear down everything we've built." His voice dropped to a whisper. *"Making sure no one gets too close."*

Nia swallowed hard, pulse pounding in her throat. She turned her head and her breath hitched.

Her own body lay curled on the couch, Jade no longer resting at her side. The dog stood rigid, her gaze locked onto the space just behind Nia. A low, warning growl rumbled in her chest.

Nia turned slowly. And there he was, floating like a nightmare, his presence suffocating the room.

Her father.

"I'll ask again, daughter," Wulfric said, his voice low and dangerous. "Why are you sleeping on the couch?"

Nia stiffened, trying to keep her breathing steady. "How did you get into my head? I have things in place to stop this."

"Your guards fell. I took that as an invitation," he said, almost gently. Then his voice cooled. "But the one who let you end up like that, on a couch, unshielded, should be ashamed."

Her father's fury was a force she had only witnessed a handful of times, and never directed at her. He thought Lochlan had forced her here, and she didn't correct him. Not because it was true. Not because she was afraid. But because saying so meant acknowledging how much of her heart was already his, and that scared her more than her father ever could.

"Where I sleep is none of your concern," Nia replied, trying to keep her voice steady. "I'm here because of you."

She loved it here—being in Lochlan's home, surrounded by his quiet care—but she couldn't admit that to her father.

"You don't even have a blanket," Wulfric muttered, his form turning as he rubbed his face in frustration.

Jade's growl deepened, her stance stiff and protective.

"I'll do something about this," Wulfric declared.

"Stay out of it!" Nia snapped. "Stay out of my life!"

He turned back to her, his expression softening in a way she didn't trust. He sounded sincere when he said, "I just want what's best for you."

But she didn't believe him.

"It's my right to decide what that is," she said, her resolve hardening. "Let me choose Lochlan on my own."

The words slipped out before she could stop them. Her chest tightened as Wulfric's brows lifted, his expression shifting—not with anger, but something far worse.

Curiosity.

"Well, well," he murmured, amused. A knowing smile curved his lips. "Let's do dinner Sunday. We have much to discuss."

Then he vanished, leaving her stranded on the plane, the purple haze thickening for a moment before fading. Nia exhaled shakily, forcing herself to focus. She had been astral projecting since she was young— finding her way back to her body was second nature.

Before she could settle, though, she noticed Jade approach her sleeping form, her growl dissipating as she nudged Nia's face with her nose.

"Leave her," Lochlan's voice murmured, gentle but firm enough to stop the dog.

Nia's astral form stilled as she watched Lochlan move closer, shirtless and wearing only sweatpants. For a moment, the sight of him was enough to obliterate every thought of her father. She would deal with Wulfric and his meddling tomorrow.

Right now, there was only Lochlan.

He crouched beside her sleeping body, his expression soft in the dim light. Slowly, he reached out and brushed a strand of hair from her face, his fingers lingering against her temple. His touch was maddeningly gentle, like he thought she might shatter if he wasn't careful.

Her sleeping form shifted slightly under his touch, her lips parting faintly as he traced the edge of her cheek. The look in his eyes was one she was getting used to—quiet wonder.

He gazed at her, his expression still and focused in a way that tugged low in her stomach. By the time Lochlan slid his arms under her and lifted her off the couch, she'd forgotten about Wulfric entirely. She drifted back into her body halfway up the stairs, the familiar weight of her limbs settling in sync with Lochlan's steady movements. His clean, earthy scent filled her senses, and she couldn't resist nuzzling against his chest, letting out a soft, contented sigh.

The sound made him stiffen, his breath catching.

"I can put you down, if you prefer," he murmured, his voice low and rough.

"And miss out on being carried like Jade?" she teased, her arms looping lazily around his neck. "Not a chance."

A soft laugh rumbled in his chest as he carried her into his bedroom, the sound pulling at the edges of her self-control in all the wrong ways.

"Too tired to clean up?"

"No," she said softly. Leaning up, she kissed his cheek. "Thank you for today."

For a moment, he held her tighter, his arms reluctant to let her go. Then, slowly, he set her feet on the ground. Nia stepped toward the adjoining bathroom, pausing to glance back at him.

His eyes were on her, dark and restrained, but the heat in his gaze was unmistakable.

The tension sent a ripple through her, made her wonder what would happen if he let go of that restraint. If she asked him to.

She finally felt unafraid to admit to herself that she liked that look— the way it made her feel like anything was possible.

Her gaze traveled to and then lingered on the faint outline in his sweatpants. For once, she decided not to hold back. "Did carrying me get that going," she asked, nodding to the bulge in his pants, "or the idea of me naked on the other side of the door?"

Lochlan hesitated. He didn't look away or ashamed, didn't pretend she had no effect on him—but the intensity of a moment ago yielded to something deeper, gentler, but still heated.

"All of you, Nia." His lips quirked into a small smile. "Even the parts you think no one can see or reach."

Nia's breath caught.

She hadn't expected him to be so... honest. Part of her wanted to return that honesty. Another part was too afraid of what might happen if she did.

Heart pounding, she backed into the bathroom, the door clicking shut. She rested her forehead on the cool, smooth wood of the door.

All of you.

The words looped in her mind as she turned on the water, stepping under the spray before it had time to warm.

Even the parts you think no one can see or reach.

She was sure she washed her body, her face, maybe even brushed her teeth, but it was all a blur. His words lingered, filling and tangling in every corner of her mind.

By the time she climbed into bed, the room was dark, the air still.

Lochlan's arm reached for her instinctively, gently pulling her against him. His warmth enveloped her, and she let herself relax into him as his breathing slowed and deepened with sleep.

All of you.

The echo of his voice was the last thing she thought of before sleep pulled her under.

19

Lochlan

"An Uptick in Stray Cats - What to Do."
–THE STELLA RUNE GAZETTE

L ochlan woke to the insistent smack of a paw against his cheek. A feline menace, sleek and smug, sat perched on his chest. The glowing green eyes of one of Stella Rune's delivery beasts locked on his, seeming to say *get up.*

It smacked him again. With a soft groan, Lochlan retrieved the scroll that dangled from its gold collar, sealed with the unmistakable sigil of the archives. "You couldn't have waited an hour?" he muttered.

The cat snorted—a sound he was fairly certain wasn't natural—and leapt off the bed, disappearing into the shadows.

Lochlan glanced down at Nia. She was still asleep, her face soft and a small smile on her lips. He hated leaving, but he had to see what the summons was about. Sliding carefully out of her embrace and the covers, he broke the scroll's seal and unrolled it.

The message was brief, but urgent: an ancient tome had arrived at the

Videt in a state of rapid decay. If he didn't come immediately, centuries of history could be lost forever.

Sighing, he dressed quickly in a dark sweater and jeans, moving quietly around the room. In the kitchen, he made coffee, pouring it into a metal travel mug and leaving it on the counter with a note:

For whenever you wake up.

Sliding his bag over his shoulder, Lochlan stepped outside and rounded the corner, heading toward one of the discreet entrances to the tunnels beneath Stella Rune.

He hated the tunnels.

The cold, unyielding stone reminded him too much of Dover—the places he'd been forced to hide, the narrow spaces he'd sought out and run to, just to get away from his sister. She had been cruel, whispering barbs where no one else could hear: *No one wants you. Your dad was happy to die just to get away from you. You'll never be one of us.* When no one was looking, she'd poked him. Pinched him. Kicked him. And when he'd tried to speak up, he had been the one scolded—called a liar, an attention-seeker. So he had kept his distance, hiding in the greenhouse or locking himself in his room, the only two places that felt safe.

Until she took the greenhouse away from him, too.

The hidden shops and cafés run by supernaturals along some stretches of the tunnels brought a touch of life to the dank space, but it wasn't enough to distract Lochlan from the memories that haunted him. Still, the tunnels were the most efficient way to reach the Videt. A pair of witches passed by, arms linked, their laughter echoing off the stone as they ducked into the messenger-cat office, its window filled with felines of various sizes and colors snoozing peacefully. Nearby, a troll hummed softly from his perch outside a barbershop, patiently waiting his turn while, inside, a rune-carved razor floated steadily along a customer's jaw.

The Videt soon came into view: its imposing, carved facade loomed up, a testament to centuries of history.

The entrance opened into a grand, arched corridor that led into the archives—a labyrinth of knowledge, meticulously organized and enchanted to preserve its trove. The Videt archives were a reflection of Lochlan's work, and of his solitude. They suited him.

Or, *had* suited him.

After the brightness of Nia's company, he wasn't so sure anymore.

Lochlan made his way through the entrance hall and down to the heavily secured chamber that housed the oldest and most fragile artifacts. The temperature dropped noticeably as he stepped inside, a chill that seeped into his bones.

"Speaking of old things," he muttered under his breath as his gaze landed on Wulfric, who stood like a sentinel in the center of the room.

"How could you?"

Lochlan froze, at once wary and exasperated. "I assume there's not actually a tome that needs my immediate attention?"

"And I assume you care more about your precious work than my daughter," Wulfric shot back, scathing.

Lochlan's mind raced, replaying every moment he and Nia had shared, searching for anything that could've justified Wulfric's words. Nothing came to mind.

"What are you talking about?"

"I found my daughter sleeping on your couch last night," Wulfric snapped, his voice echoing off the chamber's cold walls.

"What?" Lochlan blinked, completely thrown. "When?"

"What does it matter?" Wulfric growled. "I trusted you, thought you were the one she needed!"

"Maybe I am." Lochlan squared his shoulders. "But that decision isn't yours to make."

Wulfric narrowed his eyes, his voice dropping into cool calculation. "I know my daughter. I know you. This will benefit you both—if you weren't intent on ruining it."

Lochlan's temper flared. "If you're not careful, Wulfric, you'll be the one who ruins it."

He scoffed, turning abruptly and pacing a few steps away. "Is she well?"

"Why don't you ask her yourself?" Lochlan said, his tone harsher than he intended.

Wulfric's answer was surprisingly subdued. "She wouldn't tell me."

Lochlan couldn't blame her. But, despite his own frustration, he could see the genuine concern in Wulfric's face. "She wasn't sleeping on my couch," he explained. "She fell asleep there while I was showering. I carried her to bed, and that's where she was when I left her this morning."

Wulfric's posture softened with relief. "Does she love you yet?"

The question landed like a blow. Lochlan blinked. "Of course not," he said, quietly. "It's been less than two weeks."

"Do you love her?"

The silence that followed felt as oppressive as the stone walls around them. What could Lochlan say? He cared for her deeply. Immensely. But love?

He didn't know.

Whatever he felt for Nia was real, and he wasn't ready to let go of it. But that wasn't for Wulfric to dictate.

The Sword tilted his head, studying Lochlan for a long moment. "Right," he said, his tone unreadable. "I see."

Lochlan opened his mouth to respond, but something brushed the edge of his thoughts—a faint, unwelcome intrusion, like fingers pressing between his brain and skull.

"Get out of my head," Lochlan growled.

"Let me help you," Wulfric insisted, calmly.

"No," Lochlan shot back.

Wulfric's expression darkened, his patience wearing thin. "You have a month." The words sliced through the quiet room like a blade. "If she doesn't choose you by then, you're done here. And I'll make sure you're done everywhere. Stella Rune, the Videt—all of it."

The threat struck Lochlan's chest like a physical blow.

Wulfric had always been calculating, but never this ruthless or blatant. Lochlan had heard the stories, of course—the way The Sword dealt with obstacles, the quiet but undeniable force he exerted over those who crossed him. But seeing it, feeling it directed at him, was something else entirely.

Lochlan forced himself to breathe, to control the anger building in his gut. "What do you really want from this?" he asked, his voice measured. "Why me?"

Wulfric's expression remained unreadable. "Finish the diaries," he said simply. "You'll find out."

Lochlan stiffened.

His current at-home project was a set of diaries sent from the Videt. This was nothing unusual. He received assignments like that all the time.

Inventory: *Set of diaries from a since-passed witch.* Damage: *Unknown.* Restoration Status: *Important.*

Sometimes, Wulfric took a hands-on approach, not to help, but to hover. If a particular book or scroll mattered to him, he would check in, ask for updates, and make his presence known. But not with these. They had arrived with nothing but the standard paperwork, slipped in among other restoration jobs, like they were just another project.

Wulfric had never mentioned an interest in them until now.

"What does that even mean?" Lochlan's fists clenched at his sides. "And if you get rid of me, who exactly is going to repair your precious books?"

Something flickered in Wulfric's gaze. Not anger, or even irritation. Pride.

"There's a lot on the line," he admitted, regaining some of his usual composure. "Your second dinner is Sunday. And I expect you both at the full moon celebration."

With that, Wulfric turned and strode out of the chamber, his footsteps ringing in the empty space, each one a reminder of the ultimatum he'd just laid down.

DIARY ENTRY
MY TWENTIETH SPRING

He brought me to the heart of it today. The Videt. The place that haunted my dreams for years, its name a shadow over my life. But it wasn't what I expected. The darkness I feared was gone, replaced by... hope.

I stepped into a room with a round table at its center and chalkboards lining the walls, each filled with diagrams and spell work. None held depictions of weapons or control spells, but tools of protection instead: barriers meant to keep humans safe, spells to ease tensions, plans to build peace. Around the table sat witches, wolven, goblins, vampires, fae, and even a few wood devils. They were talking and listening in turn, offering solutions instead of threats.

For years, I believed the Videt wielded a power meant only to rule and control, to crush anyone without power. But now, it's becoming something else something better.

I turned to him, my chest so full I thought I might burst. He had done this, quietly and steadily, while I was too afraid to believe it could ever change.

And all that time, he'd kept his distance. Never touching me, not even when I wanted him to, needed him to.

In that moment, I could hold back no longer. I reached for him, hand shaking as I touched his chest. When he didn't pull away, I stood on my toes and kissed him. It wasn't soft or hesitant, but filled with everything I'd buried. Grief. Hope. Love.

For a moment, he froze, and I thought perhaps I'd imagined everything between us.

Then he kissed me back, fierce and unrelenting, like he'd been waiting and wanting just as long as I had.

When we broke apart, I couldn't look at him. But he cupped my face gently, guiding my eyes upward until they met his. "You'll never need to be afraid here again." His voice was rough and filled with something deeper than promise. "Not while I still draw breath. Not while this place answers to me."

20

Lochlan

"What the Stars Say Today - Venus Is Up to No Good, Wear Protection!" –A PAGANS BLOG

Lochlan rushed home after the encounter with Wulfric, hoping to find Nia still in bed. But all that was left for him was her handwriting on his own note.

You make such good coffee, N xx

Between Nia, her father, and those insistent x's, he couldn't focus.

Filled with plants and tools essential for repairing old tomes and manuscripts, Lochlan's office held the soothing scents of soil, old paper, and the subtle fragrances of the flowers he tended. But the familiar surroundings did nothing to help him find peace. His fingers traced the recently repaired page. He'd only managed to finish one in the past few hours, a number that should have been four or five or six.

Lochlan knew he should keep working, but his mind was elsewhere, replaying recent moments with Nia.

"Did carrying me get that going," she'd teased, her eyes dragging deliberately over him, leaving a desperate want in their wake. *"Or the thought of me naked on the other side of the wall?"*

The memory of her voice, low and rough, curled in his chest like smoke. But it wasn't just the fire twisting through him that pulled his thoughts from his work. Hunger churned low in his body, yes—but it wasn't just that.

He wanted more.

He wanted to know Nia's thoughts and her fears, wanted to see her quiet smiles in the mornings. He wanted to hear the way her laugh sounded like it was breaking free from her, untamed and unstoppable. He wanted every piece of her she'd ever been afraid to give anyone else. And he wanted her to want that from him, too. Not just teasing barbs or fleeting touches—he wanted something real and whole.

If Nia didn't want the same thing, could he give in to the desire burning between them, knowing it was only for a moment?

The sound of someone at the front door pulled Lochlan from his thoughts. It was strange; no one from work should be delivering new projects to him, and this set of diaries still had weeks of work left. Jade left her spot next to his chair and began scratching at the door, eager to get out. Lochlan's heart skipped a beat.

Maybe Nia was back from wherever she'd gone.

As soon as he opened the door, Jade hurried down the stairs. He shut it again before following her, moving silently as hesitation gripped him. At the bottom, he paused, heart pounding as he peered into the kitchen.

Nia was there, rummaging through a few shopping bags, her movements brisk and efficient. Two Goblin Grind cups sat on the counter, their rich smell mingling with the scent of fresh pastries. He watched her, wondering what she was doing.

And how to move forward after the previous night.

She greeted Jade warmly and took off her collar, which was strange. Then Nia pulled out three large candles from a bag and did something with them he couldn't quite see. When she placed one in a holder, he noticed his name carved into the black wax.

His feet started moving before his mind could catch up.

"What is this?" Lochlan picked up the candle, his name flickering against the wax as he turned it in his hands. He nodded to the bags on the counter. "All of this?"

Nia sighed and handed him a coffee. As their fingers grazed, a warm echo thrummed under his skin.

"Last night, my father wormed his way into my mind, bypassing all the protective spells I'd cast against him. Freaking jerk."

Lochlan's grip tightened on the cup. "And you didn't want to tell me?"

"I was going to handle it. I *am* handling it."

He stepped closer, his arm brushing hers as he carefully put back the candle with *Lochlan* on it. Instead of pulling away, he lingered, letting her scent wrap around him, dark and intoxicating.

"And what does handling it look like?"

Nia didn't move, and the way her fingers curled slightly, the way her magic rippled—just the tiniest bit—told Lochlan he had the same effect on Nia that she did on him.

A flush crept over Nia's cheeks as she nodded across the room, to where her shadows glided over the space. Lochlan watched them for a moment, mesmerized by their eerie grace, before Nia's voice pulled him back.

"There's a spell in my mom's journal." Her shadows stilled as she turned back to the island and opened the diary she'd left there. Lochlan stepped in beside her, close enough to read over her shoulder. Nia flipped the pages with careful fingers. "She created it to protect herself from my father's dark magic."

Lochlan glanced down at the intricate spell beside her, below which was a footnote.

Dream walkers. Known for their ability to crawl into minds across any distance. A talent rooted in the Cabot line. Foul witches with one purpose: control. I may not be able to stop this marriage, but I can protect my mind from my betrothed.

A chill raced down his spine as recognition struck.

The handwriting was unmistakably familiar: he'd been staring at it all morning. The last part of his conversation with Wulfric echoed, harsh and haunting.

What do you really want from this?

Finish the diaries. You'll find out.

The diaries he was working on were hers—Nia's mother. The ones in his office had been ruined, painstakingly pieced back together with magic. But this one was untouched. Pristine. An earlier diary, maybe, one that had somehow survived while the rest had been destroyed.

His stomach twisted.

Shit.

Lochlan swallowed hard, pulse hammering in his ears. Wulfric had made it clear Nia couldn't know about Lochlan's work with The Sword. Which meant he couldn't tell her what he was restoring without risking everything. His job. His life. His chance with her.

Lochlan hated it.

He would never choose to keep any of this from Nia, but he didn't feel like he had a choice. Wulfric had handed him the last words of her mother. Somehow, buried in those pages, was the answer to why he'd forced this marriage on both of them.

And Lochlan couldn't tell her.

Heart still thrumming, he forced his expression to remain neutral. Maybe if he finished the journals and learned what Wulfric wanted, then he could give them to her; maybe it wouldn't matter that he'd kept them a secret. Either way, this wasn't a problem he could solve now.

Lochlan willed his pulse to steady as Nia turned, curious.

"What is it?"

"Nothing," he said, a little too quickly.

Nothing but a secret that could ruin everything.

Nia arched a brow, unconvinced. "You can help if you want."

Lochlan stepped closer, drawn to her warmth despite the tension coiling in his gut.

"I'd like that."

He needed the distraction, the closeness—needed to keep himself from spiraling. Lochlan moved past her, focusing on the diary.

With the labeled herbs beside him, he began laying out the spell: sprinkling dried lavender and bay leaves across the counter they usually used for meals, then crushing juniper berries between his fingers and shaping the rune from the diary with the berry's dust.

The symbol combined protection and veil, forming an eye with an arrow at its center. As he worked, the earthy aroma of mugwort rose into the air, blending with the sweetly sharp scent of star anise.

When everything was ready, his attention snagged on a small brown paper bag sitting on the counter. It was suspicious, out of place.

Nia reached for it and withdrew two gold rings. She hesitated, holding them out as if unsure how they'd be received.

"This feels awkward," she admitted.

"Why rings?" Lochlan asked, his tone carefully neutral, though a thought flickered unbidden through his mind: *They were married. They should already have rings.*

"Necklaces get lost, bracelets break, and I saw these in a store." She stepped closer, the rings catching the soft candlelight. "This one has honeysuckle blossoms on it. You were looking at a bush full of them when I first saw you, and it just felt... serendipitous."

He stared at her, then at the rings, Lochlan's chest tightened with the ache of wanting something she didn't.

"The spell requires tokens you can hold close to you," she continued. "Jade has her collar, and we can have these."

She placed the rings gently in his open hand, her fingers brushing his palm.

Lochlan's ring, the metal cool and smooth against his skin, did in fact have a honeysuckle signet delicately etched into its surface. Hers was a thin golden band with black stones surrounding an opal at its center, the gem's colors subtly shifting and shimmering in the candlelight.

Nia grabbed the diary and Jade's collar and inscribed the remaining candles, the first with Jade's name, the other with hers, then added runes to all three—ancient symbols for hiding and protection.

"In the center, we'll place the items," she said quietly, her mother's diary open in her hands as Lochlan placed their rings next to Jade's collar on the counter.

The air in the room shifted, charged with a sense of something sacred, as though the space had been transformed. Melancholy seemed to wash over Nia as she traced her finger along the worn page. Now that he knew what it was, Lochlan realized she'd always had the diary with her, hidden among her things, tucked in her purse.

"My mom created this spell specifically to protect against the magic that runs in my father's bloodline. We need to pour our energy into this, focus on our intent to protect ourselves and Jade. The spell will not only shield us, but also hide us from my father's magical sight, whether in person, dreams, or on the astral plane, as long as we wear the tokens."

She closed her eyes and took a deep breath, then let it out slowly. The air thickened with magic: a tangible force crackled around them. Nia's shadows grew denser, wrapping around the spell's components with eerie precision. Lochlan focused on the candles, their flames flickering but holding. The rings and collar glowed softly, pulling energy from both of them.

Most witches could channel raw power into shared spells, but doing it well meant syncing intent. Trusting the other person. Lochlan hadn't expected it to come this easily with Nia. Magic pulsed outward in a quiet wave, brushing over his skin like warm wind. A shimmer rolled along the walls, too faint to see clearly—but it felt like a lock clicking into place.

Nia's voice grew stronger, each word read from her mother's diary spoken with purpose, each movement filled with focus. Lochlan felt the magic intertwine with his own energy, strengthening the shield they were creating. As she uttered the final words, the air shifted again: the room felt lighter, and the candlelight softer. The rings and Jade's collar hummed with quiet power, infused with the protective magic he and Nia had woven together.

She took a deep breath, the tension in her shoulders easing as she reached for Jade's collar. The dog waited patiently as the collar was placed around her neck. Lochlan and Nia reached for the rings, their hands brushing awkwardly as Nia took them both then held them out.

"Oops," Nia said with a sheepish smile. "Here."

Lochlan hesitated. Instead of taking the signet ring, he picked up the thin band, the opal reflecting the candle light as he took Nia's other hand in his and slid it onto her middle finger. She glanced up at him. Then, her hands trembling slightly, she took his hand and slipped the signet ring onto his finger.

His pulse tripped as Nia's fingers lingered, her grip warm and steady as her gaze flicked to his again—uncertain, searching.

"Fuck it," she muttered under her breath as she pulled him to her and pressed her lips to his.

The kiss was quick and reckless, her lips gone almost as soon as Lochlan realized they were there. She pulled away looking startled, maybe even a little scared, but beneath this—

Excitement.

The corner of her lips twitched into the barest, breathless smile.

With sudden clarity and need, Lochlan realized *fuck it* was exactly right. He closed the distance and kissed her, longer, deeper.

Kissing Nia wasn't like breathing; it was like drowning in fairy wine. Each touch pulled him deeper into a sea of desire. Every brush of her soft lips made him want more. Endless possibilities flashed through his mind. Kissing her good morning. Kissing her goodnight. Kissing her because he damn well felt like it.

She let out a sharp breath as he gripped the back of her thighs and lifted her onto the counter. Nia pulled him closer, tighter, drawing him in to the space between her legs.

He ran his fingers through her hair, tilting her head so he could kiss her deeper but slower. He needed to be careful, to grasp for control after her little excited gasp made him feel different, dangerous. Being with Nia made Lochlan feel alive: like he was finally waking up from a long, dull dream. She ignited something fierce and primal that yearned to protect, possess, and care for her with a passion he never knew he had.

But he still didn't know what she wanted, or what she was willing to give.

He pulled back, breathing heavily, his forehead resting against hers. Her breathy laugh calmed the turmoil churning inside him—maybe they could do this together, carefully, one step at a time. Maybe this raw connection could be the beginning of something real.

He didn't want to rush, not if it meant risking their chance at having this and more.

"Right," Nia said, her voice and breath unsteady. "Wow. Okay." She let out a shaky laugh, brushing her hair back. "So, that's what it's like."

"What?"

"Kissing you," she said, simply. For once, she didn't sound guarded, or like she was worried about maintaining the upper hand.

"That bad?"

He meant it as a joke, but the words came out rougher, hungrier than he intended.

Her lips curved into a slow, wicked smile, her thighs tightening around his hips just enough to make his vision blur at the edges. "If you could feel my underwear right now, you'd know it wasn't bad at all."

That hit him like a freight train. The restraint he'd been clinging to began to slip through his fingers. His forehead pressed to hers as his voice dropped. "If we go that far, it's going to get hard to prove to your father he was wrong about us."

He felt her stiffen in his arms, and for a fleeting second, he wondered if he'd pushed too far—or not far enough. Lochlan exhaled and forced himself to step back and put space between them before he forgot why he needed to. Her lips were swollen from their kiss, her cheeks flushed.

Walking away from her in that moment was the hardest thing he'd done in years.

"Think about it, Nia." His voice was carefully steady even as his resolve wavered. "Because I think we both need to. We may want this. But you want other things, too."

He turned before he could see her reaction. The sound of her ragged breath haunted him as he slipped out of the room, every step away from her feeling heavier than the last.

21

Nia

"Spend a Day With The Sword!"
–THE WEEKLY HEX

The gloom of Wulfric's manor suited Nia's mood. She followed the butler into the parlor, her steps stiff, her mind an irritating jumble of thoughts. The room was all dark wood and heavy drapes, as if someone had decorated with the explicit goal of blocking out joy.

Lochlan walked just behind her, close enough that she could feel his presence without turning around. Too close. His fingers brushed hers— barely a whisper of contact—and her pulse kicked up, traitorous and immediate.

"Think about it, Nia. Because I think we both should."

She had thought about it, and all that came to mind was the memory of how his mouth felt against hers.

She chose a lone armchair, the back stiff and uncomfortable, far away from any other chair.

The butler cleared his throat. "What can I get you to drink?"

"Peach Aperol spritz with an Eye of Newt twist," she said, the words slipping out before she could stop herself.

The butler blinked, unimpressed. "Peach is out of season."

Of course, it was autumn. She slumped back in her seat, regretting the attempt at humor. Before she could muster a proper response, Lochlan's calm voice cut in.

"She'll have a blood orange martini, and I'll take a bourbon on the rocks."

Her head snapped toward him. He wasn't even looking at her, just casually inspecting a dark painting on the wall like he hadn't just rattled off her favorite drink without hesitation.

It arrived a moment later, the vibrant orange liquid catching the light as the butler placed it beside her. She picked it up, fingers curling tightly around the delicate stem, and took a long sip. The bright, tart sweetness hit her tongue, offering a momentary reprieve from the storm of thoughts.

Across the room, Lochlan raised his bourbon in a silent toast, his gaze unreadable. She didn't return the gesture, keeping her eyes fixed on the rim of her glass instead—but her heart betrayed her, hammering harder with every passing second.

He hadn't made a single move since the kiss.

Their conversations had dwindled to almost nothing, aside from the single text he'd sent to let her know about her father's dinner and the full moon celebration. She had been so caught up in the spell—and the kiss—she'd forgotten to tell him she already knew about dinner. Not about the celebration, but still. Now it felt like Lochlan was taking every opportunity to prove how maddeningly suitable a husband he was, always knowing the right thing to say, the right thing to do.

It wasn't helping her case.

Not at all.

She'd wanted so badly to prove her father wrong about Lochlan. But how could she do that when he was making it impossible for her to believe her own reservations and doubts? Her grip on the glass tightened. She was in so much trouble.

Just as she finished her drink—two gulps, entirely undignified—the butler returned with her father.

"I apologize for my tardiness," Wulfric announced, arms spread in a theatrical gesture. "Dinner is ready."

Lochlan rose, his movements easy and fluid. Nia shot up from her chair, hastily following as her father strode ahead, clearly pleased to be the center of attention.

The formal dining room was grand in the most suffocating way, with its vaulted ceiling and looming portraits of long-dead ancestors staring down disapprovingly. The butler pulled out a chair for her father at the head of the table, while Lochlan, to her surprise, stepped in smoothly to pull out the chair at the opposite end—for her.

Nia hesitated, her gaze darting to him. His expression was calm and perfectly neutral. Huffing softly under her breath, she sat, the rustle of her skirt breaking the tense silence.

As she adjusted in her seat, Lochlan stepped closer, his hands brushing the back of the chair as he scooted her in. His fingers moved to her ponytail, freeing it in one gentle motion from where it had caught between her back and the chair.

The touch was fleeting, but goosebumps erupted down her neck and shoulders, trailing all the way to her fingertips. Her thighs clenched involuntarily as heat bloomed low in her stomach, entirely unwelcome and distracting.

She turned, her eyes narrowing, but he gave nothing away. No heated gaze, no glint of amusement, no conspiratorial smile—nothing to suggest he'd done it on purpose or had any idea the effect it had on her.

It was infuriating how unaffected he seemed, and even more infuriating how little it took to upset her composure.

The butler returned, carrying the first course.

"How did the Feeding Families Harvest go yesterday?" her father asked, his gaze pinning Nia as salads were placed before them.

Her fork froze halfway between her plate and her mouth. Of course he knew about the harvest—it had been all over the media. But hearing him ask about something so directly tied to her work made her stomach twist uncomfortably.

"Fine," she said quickly, before her voice could betray her emotions.

"It was incredible," Lochlan added. "Over fifty-three hundred pounds of fruits, vegetables, and tubers were distributed to food pantries across the area. Ivy told me over a hundred volunteers showed up to help."

Nia stabbed at her salad, pushing the greens around without eating. Ivy had been in charge of the east side of Stella Rune, where Lochlan had been stationed. Nia hadn't worked up the nerve to tell him she wanted him on *her* side.

She hadn't been able to find the courage to bring up the kiss, either.

"I'm pleased," Wulfric said, his tone approving. "You should be proud, Pyronia."

Her full first name sounded so strange, now—almost like it belonged to another person.

"It was all Ivy," Nia replied, her voice clipped as she shoved a too-large bite of salad into her mouth.

Lochlan shifted, and his knee brushed hers beneath the table. The contact was brief, almost incidental, but it sent a jolt through her that she couldn't ignore.

Her throat tightened.

She knew it was an accident, that he didn't even realize what he'd done. But her body betrayed her, heat pooling low and sudden as memories of him—pressed between her legs, his lips claiming hers—rushed to the forefront of her mind.

She took a quick sip of water, desperate to cool the flush creeping up her neck.

The plates were cleared, leaving behind an awkward silence that clung to the room like a damp fog. Wulfric seemed entirely comfortable in it, feeding off the tension he'd created by forcing this marriage. Nia shifted in her seat, her appetite fading under the weight of his amusement.

Finally, the main course arrived. But before she could reach for her fork, Lochlan took her plate. If they were in the privacy of his home, this would have been normal—something she liked—but here, under her father's watchful gaze, it felt like a spotlight had been trained on them. She didn't want Wulfric to see just how attentive Lochlan usually was.

"What are you doing?" she whispered, her voice sharp.

"What I al—" Lochlan began, but before he could finish, she grabbed the plate back.

Their hands touched, and the sudden jolt of contact threw her off balance. The plate slipped from her grip, clattering to the table, knocking over her glass and sending a stream of water splashing across both of them.

"Oh, for goddess's sake!" Nia yelped, snatching her napkin.

Lochlan moved just as quickly, grabbing his own napkin and dropping to the ground to help. Their hands collided over the spill, fumbling awkwardly as they both tried to blot up the water.

"It's fine," Nia muttered, wrestling the napkin from him.

"Just hold still," Lochlan said, his tone calm and steady as his hand moved to her lap. He blotted at the water that had soaked through the fabric of her skirt, utterly unfazed by the chaos.

Her breath caught.

Her body stiffened as heat rushed through her veins, spreading like wildfire. She couldn't decide if she wanted to shove him away or pull him closer, but before she could do either, she bolted to her feet.

Lochlan froze, still kneeling on the floor in front of her, napkin in hand, his face a mix of embarrassment and—

Her father clapped his hands once, the sound sharp and commanding. Instantly, the tablecloth dried, their clothes were crisp, and the glasses were refilled as if nothing had happened.

"Why didn't you do that in the first place?" Nia rounded on him, her cheeks burning.

"And miss *this*?" Wulfric gestured broadly between her and Lochlan, his expression smug. "Not a chance, daughter."

Nia shot him a glare but said nothing, lowering herself back into her seat with a decisive thud. She scooted in before Lochlan could even think about helping.

Dinner passed in a haze. She barely tasted the food. Her attention was tethered to Lochlan, every movement amplified: the scrape of his fork, the quiet clink of his glass, the brush of his fingers along the table's edge. Her chest tightened with every passing second. It was maddening, the way his presence seemed to expand, filling the room until it left no space for anything else.

Across the table, Wulfric's gaze darted between them, a gleam of triumph flickering in his eyes.

"I'll leave you to finish," he announced suddenly, pushing back his chair. "There's a call I must attend to."

Without waiting for a response, he strode out, his satisfaction palpable.

The moment he was gone, the atmosphere shifted. The lighting softened, shadows pooled in the corners of the room, and a low, seductive melody drifted from unseen speakers. The air felt heavier somehow, tinged with something unspoken and electric.

Nia's pulse stumbled. Of course her father had planned this.

She cleared her throat, pushing back her chair abruptly. "I'm just going to…" She gestured vaguely toward the hallway, not even finishing the thought as she rose and hurried out.

Cool air greeted her in the corridor, soothing her overstimulated senses. She made her way deeper into the house, past the staircase and several closets. She needed space, needed to breathe—and figure out what she was going to do.

With trembling hands, she pulled a vial of black salt from the deep pockets of her skirt and scattered it across the stone floor. Whispering urgently, she said:

"Darkness wrap and keep me sound,

Let no one in, let none around.

Stay alert, stay sharp, stay true—

And you will know just what to do."

The spell hummed faintly, the shadows thickening around her and offering a moment of reprieve from prying eyes. She felt safe here, cocooned in her own magic.

Until Lochlan stepped through the barrier.

The faint ripple of her wards shivered, but didn't push him back, didn't sound any alarms. Her breath caught as she realized her magic didn't even try to stop him—how traitorous. Maybe it recognized him. Maybe being magically married meant he got a free pass.

"What's wrong?" Lochlan asked, his voice gentle yet urgent as his eyes searched her face.

Her cheeks flushed hot, and she grabbed his arm, shoving him toward a nearby door—a small closet beneath the stairs. The space was cramped, and the only light came from a stained-glass window and candles that lit automatically, but she didn't care.

She kissed him, fierce and unrelenting, her hands fisting in the fabric of his shirt. For a moment, he kissed her back, just as fervent. But then he pulled away, too soon, leaving her groaning in protest.

"I can't stop this," she said, her voice shaky, her forehead resting against his.

"What about your father?" he asked, his tone measured but tight.

"Mood killer," she muttered, her lips brushing his as she spoke.

"I just need to know the rules," Lochlan said, his hands gently running down her arms.

"Why do there need to be rules?" She tried to hide the whine from her voice, but she felt desperate.

"Because I need them with you," he said, his voice low and steady. "I need to know what you're thinking, what you're feeling. What's allowed. What's not."

She exhaled sharply, her hands gripping his shirt tighter. "I feel like I need to kiss you."

"Why?"

His question caught her off guard, her chest tightening at the vulnerability in his tone. "Now you're the mood killer," she said, trying to deflect.

"Am I?" His voice was calm but insistent, his gaze unwavering in the dark. "Why, Nia?"

"Because I like you," she admitted, her words tumbling out in a rush. "Because I can't stop thinking about you, or that kiss, or the way you treat me. I need more, but…"

"But what?"

"But I can't let him win." Her voice wavered. "I can't be married. But I want you."

She saw the struggle in his eyes, the war he was waging within himself, and for a moment, she thought she'd lost him. Desperation clawed at her chest, and she offered more.

"No one has to know."

"I'll know." His voice was strained, and she hated herself for being the one who put that look on his face.

"What if... we fake it?"

"I can't fake this," he said softly, fingers brushing the small of her back, grazing just above her ass.

"I know," she said quickly, her words nearly tripping over each other. "But publicly. What if we prove him wrong in public, but behind closed doors we let things... grow?"

His brows furrowed, jaw tightening. "So you want to lie?"

"Just to him," she said, her voice softening. "To you? No. Never."

Something flickered across his face, too fast for her to read, and her heart sank again.

She pressed on, her voice trembling with sincerity. "I'll be honest with you. I will try, but please, let me have this fight with my father. I won't have it with you. I can't... I don't want to fight this."

"Then we won't," Lochlan said, his voice low and certain.

He leaned in, his lips claiming hers.

This kiss was nothing like the first—no hesitation, no restraint. His hands slid down her body with a purpose that left her breathless, his fingers gripping her hips as if to anchor her to him. Her skirt bunched under his touch, and when his warm palms met her bare skin, it was as though he ignited something raw and wild within her.

A sound escaped her, somewhere between a moan and a gasp, as her body pressed closer, her hips moving instinctively against his lap. His responding groan was guttural, primal, a sound that sent a shiver racing down her spine. She tangled her hands in his hair, pulling him deeper, harder, desperate to feel more of him, as if the sheer force of his presence could fill the aching void inside her.

His lips left hers only to blaze a trail down her neck, each kiss and nip leaving her trembling, her head tipping back to grant him access. Every inch of her skin felt alive, hypersensitive, the friction of his touch as intoxicating as it was maddening.

It was bliss. It was torture. She didn't know where he ended and she began, didn't care, until—

Her shadows snapped.

A sharp, magical pulse thrummed through the air, vibrating in the tight confines of the closet. It was a warning, insistent and unmistakable, and it hit her like a cold splash of water.

Her heart stuttered as reality crashed back in.

"Wait," she gasped, shoving Lochlan away with a force that surprised even her.

He stumbled back, his breathing ragged, his expression a mix of shock and hurt. The trace of pain in his eyes twisted something deep inside her, and for a moment, her fingers twitched with the need to pull him close again, to undo what she had just done.

But the shadows pulsed a second time, dragging her back to the danger she had momentarily forgotten. Someone was passing through the magical barrier she'd created.

"I think my father's coming," Nia whispered, panic edging her voice.

Her hands flew to smooth down her hair, trembling as she scrambled for anything—anything—to make it seem like she hadn't just been tangled up with Lochlan and seconds away from dry humping him in a closet under the stairs in her childhood home. The charged air between them felt suffocating, a storm of tension and heat that made it impossible to think.

"I'm sorry," she muttered, her fingers twitching as she reached for her magic. "Skin of mine, break and burn, welt and writhe—"

She didn't even need to finish the words. A pulse of energy swept over her skin like a flash of heat, followed by an agonizing itch. Red welts erupted across her arms, her neck, and even along her collarbone, angry and raw, as if her very body was rebelling against her. The hives burned and prickled.

"Nia, no." Lochlan's voice was low, horrified. He stared at her, his expression twisted with worry. "What are you doing to yourself?"

Before she could answer, the closet door swung open.

Wulfric stood there, his appraising gaze sweeping the space. His eyes lingered on Lochlan's disheveled state, the flush still visible on his cheeks, and the tension crackling in the air between them. Finally, his focus shifted to the welts marring Nia's skin.

"See?" Nia snapped, turning her glare on Lochlan. "I'm allergic..." Her voice caught, and she couldn't bring herself to say *allergic to you.* She stomped her foot instead, her frustration bubbling over. "That's why I came in here—to get away!"

She rounded on her father, glaring. "And now you're here too!" Her arms flailed as she gestured between the two men, her emotions spiraling out of control.

Wulfric's amused expression faltered, replaced by concern. His voice softened, though it remained firm. "Nia, you need a healer."

"What I need," she bit out, shoving past them and storming out of the closet, "is space. From both of you!"

Her footsteps echoed down the hallway as she marched away, her skin still burning with the magic of the jinx. She didn't look back. She couldn't.

She stormed through the house, her skirt swishing angrily behind her. The front door creaked as she stepped onto the porch, the fresh night air washing over her like a salve. Folding her arms, she leaned against the railing, staring out at the expanse of yard, and waited.

It was only a minute or two before Lochlan appeared. His steps were hurried as he pushed through the door, the faint flush of concern still visible on his face. Nia didn't meet his gaze as she muttered the counter-spell under her breath: "Skin of mine, heal and calm. Burn no more, soothe and balm."

The relief was instantaneous. The welts faded away, leaving her skin cool and smooth, though a dull ache lingered where they'd been. She exhaled softly, and Lochlan mirrored her, letting loose a relieved sigh.

For a moment, neither of them spoke. Then, without looking at him, she reached out, letting her pinky brush against his.

"Want to get coffee?" she asked quietly.

22

Nia

"We Have Your October Stella Rune Itinerary!"
—THE STELLA RUNE GAZETTE

Nia loved the tunnels under Stella Rune. Some parts were narrow, barely wide enough for two people to pass through, but then they would open into wide expanses that held cafes and magical stores. She inhaled deeply, taking in the scent of saltwater, ancient stone, and a lingering trace of magic. The tunnels had started as sea caves, and over centuries were shaped and expanded by supernaturals into the winding network now hidden beneath the town.

She glanced over at Lochlan, noticing the way his shoulders had tensed.

"What's wrong?" Nia asked. "I told you, I'm fine." She tugged up her sleeve, revealing clear skin where the angry welts had been. "See? No lasting damage."

Lochlan's frown deepened as he kept his gaze ahead. "You shouldn't have done that to yourself," he muttered.

Nia's smile turned faintly apologetic. "It was the first thing I could think of to throw my father off. It worked, didn't it?" She gave a weak shrug.

"That doesn't mean it was necessary," Lochlan said.

She bit back a retort, reminding herself he wasn't wrong. He'd been grumpy about the whole ordeal—the spell and the hives—but so far, he hadn't brought up the kiss. Her skin heated.

"What is it, then?"

"I hate the tunnels."

Lochlan didn't seem like someone who hated things, not without a reason, at least. She almost asked why, but his furrowed brow made her hesitate.

Her lips curved slightly as she posed a different question. "What about the ocean?"

"We're underground." He arched an eyebrow.

She took his hand and led him into one of the darker nooks, where the glow-spells barely held, their waning magic little more than a warm but dim flicker.

"Nia…" Lochlan's voice carried a note of hesitation, almost a warning.

She turned back to him, his expression wary and uncertain, half-hidden in shadow. Then she leaned in and kissed him, quickly, her lips brushing his. She resisted the urge to linger, to lose herself in the kiss, as she whispered against his lips: "Trust me."

He held her gaze for a moment before squeezing her hand once—a silent agreement.

She continued forward, leading him deeper down the path. A few minutes later, the orange glow of sunset spilled through a wide opening. Fresh, salty air rushed in, and she glanced at Lochlan just in time to see him blink, his eyes adjusting to the sudden change in light.

His guarded expression softened. Nia felt a gentle swell of delight and relief.

"This," she said, gesturing to the open alcove, "is my favorite place in all of Stella Rune."

Lochlan followed her gaze, taking in the scene: a few wooden tables draped in white tablecloths, goblins bustling behind the counter along one side of the alcove, pulling shots of espresso and crafting pastries with brisk efficiency.

His brows rose. "The Goblin Grind?"

"The Goblin Grind," she confirmed. "Everyone's been to the takeout window in the tunnels, but this spot? This is special."

Lochlan stepped into the tiny café, scanning the space with a mixture of curiosity and disbelief. "How does no one see this?"

Nia pointed upward, her gaze following the jagged silhouette of the cliff above them. "That's where the Astrarium is—the star-watching witches study the skies from up there. It blocks the view from above." She turned back to him, grinning. "And Natasha has special sound wards in place, so we can't be heard."

"Natasha?" Lochlan asked, his curiosity clearly piqued.

A shrill, accusatory voice cut through the air. "Nia the Damned has returned! And where, child, have you been?"

Nia turned to Natasha, a green-skinned goblin standing on the counter, brandishing an oversized wooden mixing spoon like a weapon.

Nia laughed and went to hug the goblin, her head swallowed by Natasha's ample chest. She inhaled the comforting scent of coffee and sugar.

"Hi, Tashy," she said, her voice muffled.

"Answer me," Natasha demanded, her arms squeezing tighter around her neck.

Nia hesitated. "Well, you see…"

"I knew it!" Natasha sniffed her hair and huffed, pushing Nia to arm's length to glare at her. "You've found one of those fancy coffee places upstairs, haven't you?"

Upstairs is what Natasha called the main streets of Stella Rune. Nia shook her head, her smile widening. "No, I found a Lochlan who makes coffee to rival yours."

Natasha's eyes widened, and she raised the spoon high. "Where is he? I must battle him and reclaim my crown!"

Nia laughed and pointed toward the entrance. "I brought him." She gestured at Lochlan, who still lingered at the shop's entrance. The golden light of the sunset glowed on his skin, and for a moment, her breathe caught.

Natasha huffed and glared at him. Lochlan's face flushed under the intensity of her scrutiny.

"He yours?" Natasha stage-whispered.

Nia hesitated, a surprising flicker of possessiveness curling in her chest.

"Come in, Lochlan," Natasha called, waving him in with her spoon without waiting for Nia's reply. "Tell me what you do to make your coffee better than mine."

Lochlan glanced at Nia. She gave him a small nod.

"I use caramel sauce instead of the usual syrup," he said, clearing his throat.

Natasha hummed, suspicious.

"I add the cardamom in when making the orange syrup," he continued. "And osmanthus flowers. I steep them into the syrup and sprinkle a sugared version on top."

"Devilwood?" she asked, narrowing her eyes.

"Yes. Osmanthus is sometimes called devilwood. It adds a little tension on the back end."

"You sneaky little witch," Natasha said, sounding scandalized and delighted. "Where are you from?"

"Dover, madam," Lochlan said, bowing his head slightly.

Natasha's cheeks flushed a deep green, the skin around her eyes crinkling. She sniffed the air, her gaze sharpening. "There's royal blood in your veins. Our kind used to feast on your ancestors."

Lochlan choked out a laugh, his eyes meeting Natasha's with a hint of challenge. "I hope you take coin instead of blood these days."

Natasha grinned, her eyes brightening. "I like you," she said, her tone approving. She swept toward the espresso bar, spoon aloft like a scepter, muttering something about herb witches and nice asses. "Now sit, sit. I'll make you two drinks and grab you pastries."

Nia led Lochlan to a table against the outer wall, overlooking the ocean. The heating spells kept them warm, allowing them to comfortably enjoy the breathtaking view.

Lochlan settled into his chair, glancing out at the ocean before turning his gaze back to Nia. "Have you been coming here long?"

Nia nodded. "Since I was thirteen or so. It was hard growing up as an only child in a big, empty house. As a teen? I was horrible." She shook her head, remembering Wulfric trying to wrangle her. "I got curious after hearing whispers about the tunnels under the town, so one day, I decided to go hunting for them. It was scary. And amazing."

"Scary?" Lochlan asked, his brows drawing together.

She let out a slow breath, ready to let him in on this part of her past. She thought she would need to build up the courage, but it was already there, waiting.

"It took me a while to piece together why my life was the way it was," she admitted. "My father told people I'd died in childbirth—after The Anti-Glamour Coalition orchestrated my mother's death. And then he kept me hidden. I never left the manor grounds."

Lochlan's jaw tensed. "I'm so sorry."

Nia hesitated. "Thank you."

"So... no one knows?"

"You. Ivy. I'm assuming Becket." She smiled faintly. "I had healers and tutors, but either my father wiped their memories, or they're too scared to tell anyone who I am."

Lochlan studied her for a moment, his face unreadable. There was a lot he wasn't saying, and she could feel the unspoken thoughts hanging in the air between them.

Before he could find the words, a different goblin approached, carrying a large tray over his head. On it were two steaming mochas and a plate of fluffy pastries.

"Thank you, Albert," Nia said warmly.

Albert gave her a sharp-toothed grin, but when his gaze flicked to Lochlan, his eyes narrowed in warning. Lochlan offered a polite nod and Albert huffed before disappearing back inside.

Lochlan lifted his mocha in a small toast. "Am I safe here?" he asked, a playful glint in his eyes.

Nia laughed softly. "Yes. It's very safe. This is my table." She lifted the edge of the white tablecloth, revealing intricate runes etched into the wooden surface, ones she'd carved herself. "No one can hear us, and if anyone looks at us, they'll forget we were here. Except the goblins, of course."

Lochlan sipped his drink. "Is this a place where you come to spy?"

Nia shook her head. "No, it's a place where I hide."

Lochlan's gaze softened, a hint of nostalgia in his eyes. "I had a place like that, once."

Nia tilted her head, curiosity piqued. "You don't talk about Dover much."

"Too many bad memories," Lochlan said, looking away.

Nia reached across the table, her fingers brushing his. "And the tunnels remind you of them?" she guessed.

Lochlan turned, his eyes searching hers before his expression softened. "Not this place," he said, with a small, sad smile. "The tunnels themselves. But there's clearly a lot I haven't seen. Maybe you can show me more, and they won't remind me so much of the castle."

Nia smiled, her heart warming. "Of course." She squeezed his hand, and he took hers, pressing a soft kiss to her knuckles.

A giggle echoed from the back, and Nia shot a playful stream of shadows toward Natasha, who peeked out from behind the espresso bar, laughing as she dodged. "Behave, you two!"

"See?" Nia shook her head, smiling. "Perfectly safe."

They finished their pastries in comfortable silence, the warmth of the moment wrapping around them like a blanket.

"So," Lochlan said, finally, "tomorrow is the full moon celebration. How do you want to handle it?"

Nia exhaled, her eyes narrowing thoughtfully. "I doubt my father will have time for us—he'll be too busy preening like a peacock." She'd seen the photos the media captured at every public event, The Sword surrounded by fawning supernaturals, basking in their attention.

"Besides," she added, "he wouldn't dare out me as his daughter. We can fly under the radar, make our rounds, act like we barely tolerate each other, then leave."

Pretending was the only way to win against her father.

So why did it feel like she was setting herself up for failure?

The thought of keeping Lochlan at arm's length in public while allowing herself to fall for him in private sent a ripple of unease through her. Could she really separate the two? Was she a good enough actress to convince others he meant nothing, when really he was beginning to mean so much?

Lochlan frowned. "I don't know that I can hide how I feel about you."

Nia's breath hitched. Her instinct was to deflect, to downplay—because acknowledging it felt dangerous. She hesitated.

"Then I'll just get myself kicked out," she said, smirking.

"You go, I go. " Lochlan's lips twitched. "How?"

"The Videt has a strict no-nudity policy. Feel like getting naked in public again?"

"It can only get easier with practice." His confident tone didn't quite match the uneasy look in his eyes, but Nia smiled anyway.

"We'll figure it out."

Lochlan studied her, his expression unreadable. Then he reached over, his hand closing over hers.

Nia's gaze lingered on their joined hands, her mind spinning in a thousand directions. Balancing the tentative pull of a relationship with Lochlan against the counter-weight of her battle with her father felt impossible, like standing on a tightrope over the roaring ocean. She'd never let herself want like this, never been in any real relationship before. And now the thought of hiding it—even for a purpose she believed in—made her chest ache. Could she win against her father while still exploring what this could become? Could she let herself be vulnerable with Lochlan while pretending to be indifferent in front of everyone else?

She didn't know.

But for now, she let the quiet warmth of his touch settle her, a small reminder that even if the road ahead was tangled and uncertain, she wasn't walking it alone. They would find their way through tomorrow night together.

And when in doubt, cause chaos.

DIARY ENTRY
MY TWENTY-FIRST AUTUMN

I never thought I would love a place made of stone and shadow.

The tunnels beneath Stella Rune were meant to be a refuge, a place for supernaturals to move freely without fear of being seen. But to me, they are more than that. They are camouflage. Down here, I exist without expectation. No one knows my name, my history, my fears, my dreams. In that anonymity, I have found something unexpected.

Community.

For so long, I was raised to be a wife, to breed, to serve—until the beast plucked me from that path. And down here, with the damp air cool against my skin and the lanterns casting soft, flickering light, I feel alive. I feel myself transforming.

I've wandered alone for hours at times, tracing the etched runes along the walls, letting my fingers skim over centuries of secrets. I've sat in shops, listened to people's stories, heard their histories, discovered how they live. I've learned what life is like—and how to live it myself.

And if I don't come home after some time, he will find me. I've made it my game.

He is too careful with me. Too cautious. And I want him to feel as free as I do.

So I run, and hide, and wait.

Tonight, I hid on a secret ledge over the water, the salt in the air so thick, I could taste it. I let my feet dangle above the endless ocean, the dark waves stretching into forever. It reminded me of my powers—vast and unknowable, a darkness that saw all and held everything within it.

He found me easily, as he always does. He sat beside me without a word, the weight of his presence familiar, steady.

At first, I could feel the frustration rolling off of him, though little by little, it faded. Being with me appeared to calm him, and I was happy to be that for him. But I wanted more. So much more.

Finally, I spoke. "Do you ever wonder what your life would have been like if you hadn't taken me that night? If you hadn't destroyed them all?"

He was quiet for so long I thought he wouldn't answer. Then, his voice came, rough but certain. "No."

I turned to him. He was already watching me, his expression raw and unguarded.

"No?" I repeated, my chest tight.

His lips quirked, but there was no amusement in his expression. "There is no life—no path, no version of this world—where I would have left you there."

Something in me broke open then, and before I could second-guess myself, I reached for him. He stilled as my fingers brushed along his jaw, but he didn't pull away. So I took more, shifting until I straddled him, my knees pressing into the stone on either side of his hips.

He said my name, over and over.

Luna, Luna, Luna.

That moment was everything. Every beginning and every end. It was too much. And it will never be enough.

I am his moon. And he is my wolf.

23

Nia

"It's a Full Moon - What It Says for Your Sign."
—A PAGANS BLOG

Nia stepped into the ballroom of the Videt and immediately regretted it.

The space was breathtaking—a towering monument to magic, history, and power. Ornate marble floors gleamed beneath enchanted chandeliers, their flickering light stretching up to vaulted ceilings so high they disappeared into shadow. Stained glass windows depicting legendary supernaturals lined the walls, the moonlight spilling through them in fractured rainbows.

She hated it here.

The Videt had started as a sanctuary for non-humans, created generations after the founder of Stella Rune passed. And for a long time, it stayed that way—safe, hidden, sacred. But peace makes some people restless. Over time, the ambitious crept in, and there were always those who believed magic shouldn't stay hidden, who wanted more. The Anti-

Glamour Coalition rose from that unrest, and at the head of it were Nia's ancestors, the Cabots.

Eventually, they had gained control of the Videt. The history books called it a shift in leadership, a political realignment. The Cabot family had ruled for generations, wielding their mind-walking magic to "commune" with the goddess—also known as the Mother. Supposedly, she whispered through them, guiding their every decision.

Then her father had taken over.

Now the Videt was part museum, part sacred site, part supernatural capital, where laws were upheld, magic was studied, and her father played at being the goddess's chosen voice. Nia wanted nothing to do with any of it. She had cut the Cabot name from her identity the way her ancestors once cut down anyone who challenged the goddess's will.

So, yeah. No, thank you.

She never attended the Videt's celebrations. The ones held in parks, or by the water, or tucked in the warmth of someone's home were far better. But tonight, she had no choice.

Nia scanned the room. Witches she recognized by the subtle hum of their magic, fae were easy to spot, with their gorgeous ears and dazzling clothes, and several wolven who'd ditched glamour for full fur and fangs wove through the crowd. A few other supernaturals mingled at the edges: glowing, floating, or otherwise defying physics, all of them buzzing beneath the soft strain of music. Three guards stood along the perimeter, watching. She knew why they were here. They weren't protecting the guests.

They were here for The Sword.

As a child, she'd seen guards stationed outside the manor, their presence a silent warning. She saw them again, later, as an adult, when she'd spied on her father out of morbid curiosity. The guards had never made sense to her.

They hadn't saved her mother.

And her father didn't need saving.

A warm brush against her fingers broke through her rogue thoughts. Lochlan. The touch was fleeting—just a whisper of contact before he turned and walked away toward the bar. She watched him go, her fingers twitching with the urge to reach for him.

But that wasn't part of the plan.

There were only four weeks until Samhain. She inhaled slowly, steadying herself. Their plan was simple: one drink, one lap around the room, be seen, and leave. Then they'd go home to Jade, where Nia could finally breathe—and maybe let her guard down enough to face whatever this thing with Lochlan was, without the weight of expectations pressing in from all sides.

And, if anything went wrong, they could always get naked.

A ripple of gasps and whispers tore through the crowd, pulling her attention to the stage at the far end of the ballroom.

Her father entered, arms spread wide, commanding the room with ease.

A bitter pang shot through her—resentment, frustration, and, if she was honest, a flicker of fear. Nia had never seen the monster her mother described in her journal, but she knew it was there, lurking beneath the polished facade of The Sword of the Goddess.

Lochlan returned, handing her a drink, his careful distance a silent reminder.

"Your father is here," he murmured.

She tightened her grip around the glass. "Get ready to strip."

Lochlan huffed a quiet laugh, but the tension in his shoulders didn't ease.

Nia thought Wulfric would only give her a passing glance, confirming she was here before moving on to his adoring fans. For eighteen years, she hadn't existed to anyone but him. A secret. A ghost. Now the wider world knew her as someone else, someone he'd have no reason to give any particular attention to.

But as Wulfric's gaze found and held hers, Nia tensed.

The room seemed to freeze.

Oh, no. No, no, no.

"You said he wouldn't out you as his daughter," Lochlan murmured.

"He wouldn't." But as Wulfric's sharp eyes remained locked on hers, amusement glinting in their depths, a sick realization settled in. *He's going to do it.*

The energy in the room shifted—eyes bouncing between Wulfric and Nia, speculation blooming like wildfire.

Lochlan stepped closer. "Now doesn't seem like the right time for the whole supernatural community to find out."

Nia shot him a look. "You think?"

Before Lochlan could respond, Wulfric's voice boomed through the room, magically amplified. "My beloved supernaturals!"

A dramatic pause.

Nia's stomach dropped.

"Tonight, we celebrate our Mother moon in her full glory! And, in honor of this blessed night, I am delighted to introduce you to my daughter."

The lights dimmed. Nia's fingers tightened around her glass, knuckles turning white as a hazy blue glow bloomed around her, casting her in a spotlight. She blinked rapidly, trying to process the absurdity of the moment. The glow expanded—widening to include Lochlan.

He gave her a sidelong glance. "What the fuck," he cursed under his breath.

"And her charming husband," Wulfric continued, his smile almost audible. He waved his hands as if summoning applause.

Two guards in sleek suits materialized, gesturing for them to step forward.

Lochlan sighed, bumping into Nia as they were ushered forward. "Do I start taking my clothes off now?"

"I don't know if it'll help," she muttered as they were ushered onto the stage.

A few people whispered her name. Others openly stared. Nia's pulse pounded in her ears as she struggled to process the moment—what to do, where to look. Every instinct screamed at her to run, but she forced herself to keep her chin high, a tight smile on her lips.

She knew these people. She'd worked beside them, helped them; now they were looking at her like she was something new, someone they didn't know.

Her focus narrowed to Wulfric.

"You all know the Duchess of Charity," he proclaimed, standing before the crowd, soaking up the attention like some photosynthesizing plant. "But now, I would like you to also know her as my daughter."

The murmur of the crowd swelled, rippling outward in waves of shock and curiosity. Wulfric let it build, basking in the reaction before continuing, his voice smooth, practiced. "For years, I kept her hidden, fearing I would lose her as I lost her mother. But tonight, we no longer hide."

Nia's stomach twisted. No longer hide? She didn't like the sound of that.

"She has grown into someone extraordinary, without my name, my aid, or my influence." He turned to her. "Yet here she stands, a force in her own right. And beside her—" His eyes flicked to Lochlan. "—her husband, with deep roots in the regulars' world."

Lochlan cursed under his breath as understanding sank like a stone in Nia's gut. She saw it now: the threads of his plan weaving together. This wasn't about claiming her. It was about Wulfric using her and Lochlan for some political purpose.

The fucker.

Wulfric's voice rang through the ballroom, his smile practically glowing with satisfaction. "The union of Pyronia Cabot and Prince Lochlan of Dover is just the beginning—a happy omen of what's to come. But enough from me," Wulfric declared. "Tonight is a celebration! Let us dance, let us revel, and when the Mother's light reaches her peak, my daughter will honor her fullness by awakening the Lunaflor."

The room murmured in approval as the lights dimmed and the music swelled. Nia barely had time to process what the hell had just happened before an elder appeared at her side. She took several steps away, eyes locked onto her father. Her blood boiled. This whole moment was orchestrated. Just like her marriage. Just like so many other aspects of her life.

"How dare you," she hissed under her breath.

Wulfric's expression didn't falter. "I dare to do whatever I please, so long as it ensures a bright and prosperous future for us all, Pyronia Cabot."

Her jaw clenched at the name given to her at birth, which she'd cut away like a rotting limb. She shoved the anger down, focusing on what mattered. "What are you after?"

Wulfric ignored the question entirely. "Elder Patrick will prepare you for the blessing of the flower." Then, with a saccharine smile, "Would you like your doting husband by your side as you prepare?"

Internally, yes. Goddess, yes. Her mind was buzzing, her skin felt too tight, and her heart was hammering out of rhythm. He had just outed her to the entire supernatural world. Everyone would have questions— about her, about her work, about whether she'd built it all herself, or if her success had been his all along.

She'd hated being a secret. But she'd realized and accepted that severing ties from Wulfric meant cutting herself free from more than him—it meant cutting herself free from a lineage of monsters, a heritage of corruption.

Before she could form these words, Lochlan stepped in. "Nia may not want me by her side," he said, voice steady, "though I would prefer to be with her."

Goddess, she needed him right now. But she couldn't let it show. "Fine."

Wulfric gave a pleased smile—like this was all going exactly as intended—then stepped off the stage. She could hear the crowd murmuring, exclaiming, congratulating him.

The stage curtains swept shut and mercifully blocked out the crowd.

Elder Patrick's attention shifted between them—first to Lochlan, who looked concerned, and then Nia, who probably looked like she was about to set the entire damn place on fire.

"Prince Lochlan," Patrick said smoothly. "Pyronia Cabot."

"Nia," she corrected flatly.

He nodded once. "Blessed full moon to the both of you."

She glared at him. Right. Blessed full moon, sure.

"We have less than a half hour to prepare you," Patrick continued.

"Prepare me?" Nia repeated, anxiety flaring. She'd never been to one of these celebrations and had no idea what he was talking about.

"Oh, yes. There are several steps."

"What the fuck." She almost stomped her foot. "What the actual fuck. One drink, one lap, and then leave—" she rattled off, like reciting the original plan might somehow show her a path to reverse the disaster unfolding around her. "—get naked?"

Maybe that really wasn't such a bad idea.

Elder Patrick barely looked fazed. "Prince Lochlan," he said instead, turning toward him.

"Elder Patrick, sir," Lochlan replied. "Is there someplace we could— have a moment? This is a lot for Nia."

Patrick raised an unimpressed brow. "Clearly."

But he nodded and gestured for them to follow. They stepped down a narrow set of stairs behind the stage. As they went, Nia's eyes caught on a door behind the stage marked with bold letters—EXIT.

It practically sang to her.

But Patrick kept walking. Past the exit. Past freedom. Until they reached a small, dimly lit room. "I'll give you a few minutes while I gather the supplies," he said before stepping out and closing the door behind him.

The second he was gone, Nia dragged her hands down her face and groaned.

Her mind spun—too fast, too loud. Her father had outed her. The world knew. There was no undoing it. No disappearing into the tunnels, no slipping away into the life she had built for herself. This was happening. And though she longed to escape, she knew leaving now wouldn't change anything. Her breath grew shallow. She was breathing too fast, too often, too—

"Look at me."

Lochlan's hands landed gently on her shoulders, steadying her.

The moment their eyes met, he brushed his fingers lightly against her cheek. She leaned into his hand, chasing the contact, grounding herself in it. She inhaled slowly, filling her lungs with something other than panic.

"None of this changes who you are," Lochlan said, calm and sure. "Who you've become."

Her chest ached, but she nodded.

"You can do the spell," he continued. "Then we'll leave. One witch event down, and we'll figure out the rest together, on our own."

Her fingers curled into his sleeve. "But—"

A knock cut her off. She tensed.

Lochlan sighed. "That was hardly a moment." He gave her hand a final squeeze. "You do the spell. We leave."

Then, before she could argue, he pressed a quick kiss to her forehead.

She exhaled, steeled herself, and pulled the door open—to find Wulfric and Elder Patrick waiting on the other side.

"Well, well, well," Wulfric drawled, eyes gleaming with amusement. "I swear, I'm always finding you two in a closet."

Nia's vision reddened. She barely registered him turning on his heel and walking away before her body moved, storming after him. But Elder Patrick blocked her path, his expression as impassive as ever as he gestured the opposite direction. "This way."

Grinding her teeth, Nia let herself be led back toward the stage.

At its center, a circular stone platform lifted and slid apart with soundless precision. From within, the Lunaflor began to rise. The massive plant sat in an ornate pot, its thick, pale vines draping over the edges like frozen tendrils. Dormant petals—silver-white and smooth as porcelain—gleamed faintly under the full moonlight now spilling through the open dome in the ceiling overhead.

Elder Patrick stood beside her, his voice steady and clear. "When the moon reaches its peak, you will take the blessed mirror your father gives you and direct its light into the second, larger mirror across from you, there."

Nia hadn't even noticed the mirrors before, standing like sentries around the platform.

"And then?"

Patrick gave her a patient smile and handed her a piece of parchment.

"You speak the invocation—'*Moonlight eternal, sacred and true, awaken the petals, magic renew. By silver's glow and goddess's light, let the bloom rise to celestial height.*' As you recite, you will reach inside yourself and pull a seed of your magic as an offering to the goddess and the flower. This energy will wake it, and the petals will unfurl."

Nia took the parchment with trembling fingers. The words blurred. She blinked hard, once, twice—nothing. Her mind refused to catch up.

"And then I can go home?"

"Yes, my dear." Patrick inclined his head. "You will be done."

It sounded simple. Mirror, light, magic, home. But as Patrick stepped back and led Lochlan away, the pressure of it all—the supernatural community's expectations, her father's reveal and manipulation, her role in the ceremony—made it suddenly feel like she couldn't breathe. With a wave of Patrick's hands, the curtains swept open, the lights dimmed, and the world narrowed to just her and the moon.

Her father approached, exuding serene authority as he handed her a small mirror with a bow. "Blessed full moon, daughter."

Around her, the gathered supernaturals echoed the words in eerie unison: "Blessed full moon."

The sound reminded her everyone was watching as her father turned away, disappearing into the shadows as Elder Patrick cleared his throat expectantly. The mirror felt heavier than it should, its cool surface pressing into her palms as if it carried the weight of a thousand moons. Her legs were stiff as she shuffled into position, her eyes finding the mirror she was meant to direct the moonlight toward. The air felt thick, watchful, laden with unspoken expectation.

Mirror, light, magic, go home.

But her father's spectacle was all she could see. Her mother's journal told the true story: a tale of fear and desperation. Marrying Wulfric had cost her everything—her freedom, her life. She thought about that last entry, one she'd read countless times.

This may be the last time I write my own words.

It's hard to think past my labored breaths. The damned dress they forced me into has hundreds of buttons. Each one felt like a lock closing.

They call him The Sword. The new Cabot heir. A man I've never met, only heard stories about. They say he is ruthless, powerful, obsessed with legacy—and that he'll lead the witches out of hiding and into power.

This marriage is a cage meant to contain me and my magic, a transaction meant to bind my family's power and position to his.

No one is coming to stop it. Maybe my mother would have tried, but she's gone. I'm alone.

And I am afraid.

Now Nia stood in full view, a pawn in the same game her father was still playing. The realization woke something deep inside as her magic stirred, keen and restless.

Just do this and go home.

"Moonlight eternal, sacred and true—" Nia began to read. But the words didn't carry the usual lilt of her spell work. There was no rhythm, no flow; they were just hollow syllables forced past clenched teeth. "—awaken the petals, magic renew." She reached for a seed of magic, just a drop, just enough to coax the flower awake. "By silver's glow and goddess's light, let the bloom rise to celestial height."

But instead of a drop, a torrent of her magic rushed free, flooding from Nia before she could stop it. Moonlight struck the small mirror she held, the light mingling with her power as it ricocheted between the mirrors before cascading into the dormant flower.

Gasps echoed around her as the Lunaflor rocked and swayed under the force.

She felt it wake.

Raw, erratic power rushed through her, tangling with her own magic as the Lunaflor shuddered, its dormant petals beginning to unfurl.

Murmurs rippled through the crowd as the flower came alive, blooming into a stunning opalescent masterpiece. Its petals shimmered under the moonlight, shifting in hues of silver, blue, and pink. For a brief moment, awe filled the room as the sheer beauty of the flower held everyone spellbound. Then—

A low, drawn-out creak that made the hair on Nia's arms stand on end.

From the base of the flower, vines began to snake outward, glossy and as thick as her arm, growing with unsettling speed. They curled and twisted, spreading across the stage, their leaves gleaming like polished emeralds. The thrill of the flower's bloom was gone, replaced by the crushing realization the plant wasn't just waking—it was exploding.

The mirror slipped from Nia's hands, landing with a dull thud mere inches from where the closest creeping vine had already reached.

"Oh, fuck."

24

Lochlan

"It's a Full Moon - What It Says for Your
Supernatural Affinity." –THE WEEKLY HEX

C haos erupted.

The room's awe turned to unease as vines grew, creaking and rustling, spreading outward from the Lunaflor with unnatural speed. The bloom itself swelled to ten times its original size, its gleaming petals casting ghostly reflections under the moonlight. Wild vines snaked up the walls and across the floor, spilling onto the stage and into the crowd. People screamed, scrambling to escape as smaller flowers burst open along the twisting greenery, releasing shimmering clouds of pollen into the air.

The silvery dust hit quickly and powerfully.

Witches and supernaturals coughed, sneezed, and choked. Some staggered, eyes glassy from the pollen, while others lashed out. Shields flared as witches shouted spells. Fae summoned blades, slicing through vines. Wolven snapped and tore with teeth and claws.

Lochlan froze, his mind momentarily blank before instinct took over.

He ran for Nia, putting an arm around her middle, pulling her toward the edge of the stage and away from the chaos. She stumbled into him, her wide eyes locked on the Lunaflor, as if she couldn't quite believe what she'd done.

She clung to his arms, the tension in her body telling him she wasn't far from snapping.

"What do we do?" she yelled, her voice barely carrying over the cacophony of sounds—the creaking vines, the popping sound of smaller blooms bursting into clouds of dust, the shrieks and shouts of the panicked crowd.

Lochlan shook his head, thoughts racing. He'd spent his life studying plants. There had to be something he could use.

"A freezing spell?" she asked, desperate.

Lochlan scanned the room. Wulfric was being dragged away by his guards, his carefully curated mask of confidence cracking as his eyes darted to Nia.

"Ice shards might do as much harm than good!" Lochlan shouted back.

Before either of them could try anything, a rogue vine lashed out toward a man struggling to shield himself. A stream of shadows whipped from Nia's hands, slicing cleanly through the vine before it could wrap around the man's legs.

"It feels alive," she said, her voice tinged with wonder and dread. "And wild. Not mean—just excited. Like it doesn't know what to do with so much freedom."

As Lochlan took in the writhing vines, an idea hit him. Nia turned to him with the same wide-eyed understanding and they spoke at the same time.

"A sleeping spell."

Nia fell to her knees, ripping open pockets and pouches hidden in her skirt. Vials and tins spilled onto the stage, clinking and rolling in all directions as she frantically rifled through them.

"Mugwort, no. Black salt, no. Peppermint—goddess, no. Oakmoss... why do I even have this?" Her hands trembled as she picked through her supplies, her voice growing more panicked. "I—I have nothing!"

"Moon moss," Lochlan said firmly, kneeling beside her.

Nia snapped her head toward him, disbelief flashing in her eyes. "Moon moss? Is that a thing?"

"It is," he said, his voice steady despite the chaos around them. "It just has to be made. Now, do a protection spell, love. Quickly."

Love.

The endearment slipped out naturally, effortlessly, as if it had always been there, waiting for its moment.

Nia stared at him for half a second, panic flickering over her face, before she nodded and pressed her hands into the spilled salt, whispering the words of a spell. A translucent dome formed around them, vibrating faintly, the salt glowing softly as her magic went to work.

Vines and pollen struck their wards, but they held. The once-chaotic ballroom was eerily empty now—no longer did the Lunaflor have supernaturals to toy with. They had all fled, leaving Lochlan and Nia alone amid the creeping vines and shimmering flowers.

Lochlan grabbed a handkerchief from his pocket and tied it around his face to protect himself from what the moss would become. He lifted the withered clump into the moonlight, his lips moving in steady, whispered repetition:

"Mother, bless this moss with your light,

Let it guide those needing restful sleep at night."

He said it three more times, pouring his magic into the spell, grounding himself in the words. Slowly, the moss began to change. Its veiny green leaves brightened, their color bleeding away as they turned a spectacular silver, shimmering like the moon itself.

"Cover me," Lochlan said, eyeing the Lunaflor.

"What?!" Nia whipped her head toward him.

But he didn't have time to explain. Lochlan stepped out of the protective circle and sprinted toward the massive bloom at the heart of the chaos.

"Lochlan!" Nia shouted, panicked. But he didn't look back.

The vines reacted instantly. They lashed out, snapping toward him like living whips. He ducked the first, vaulted over another, and barely managed to twist out of the way as a third coil slammed into the stage where he'd just been. Pollen exploded around him in a glittering burst, coating his skin, making his eyes water. His vision blurred as vines closed in. One caught his ankle and yanked. Lochlan hit the ground hard, slamming the breath from his chest. Before the others could take advantage of his stumble, shadows lashed through the air. Nia's power surged, wild and unrelenting as she carved through the attacking vines, clearing his path.

Still, more vines kept coming.

Nia's voice rang out over the chaos. "Move, Loch!"

Pushing himself up, he staggered forward, forcing his burning lungs to keep pace. The stage was a battlefield of twisting greenery and ruptured wood, forcing him to weave around broken beams and thick, grasping vines. It wasn't far, but the Lunaflor had claimed the stage entirely, its roots anchoring deep, its enormous petals shifting like the flower was breathing.

At last, he reached the base of the monstrous bloom, chest heaving, skin slick with sweat and pollen. He shoved a hand into his pocket, fingers closing around the moon moss. It was warm now, pulsing with energy. He rubbed it between his palms, grinding it into a fine dust.

He tossed it upward, letting the powder scatter across the Lunaflor. The moss shimmered faintly as it fell, settling into the vines and blooms.

The air shifted.

The plant seemed to hesitate, its movements slowing, its energy dimming. The vines ceased their writhing, and the pollen's shimmer faded to dull specks. A peaceful stillness crept over the ballroom and stage, blanketing the room as the Lunaflor calmed, then slumbered.

Lochlan stood there for a moment, removing the cloth from his face and catching his breath. He turned slowly, taking in the transformed space. Vines still clung to the walls and ceiling, draped over tables and chairs, but their movements were gentle and almost imperceptible now. The flowers blooming among them were breathtaking—silver and pink, their petals glowing softly in the moonlight.

Lochlan looked back, searching for Nia. Her expression was grim as she took in the vines draped across the room and the pollen still lingering in the air. She turned and her gaze met his. A flicker of anger crossed her face.

"Nia?"

The ballroom doors slammed open and Wulfric strode in, his guards trailing behind him, struggling to keep pace. His steps were hurried, almost frantic, as his eyes scanned the room before locking on Nia.

Lochlan recognized the tightness in Wulfric's jaw, the fear in his gaze as it darted over the remains of the chaos. Concern etched faint lines into his otherwise polished expression.

But Nia didn't seem to see these same things.

Before Wulfric could even utter a word, she stepped forward. "Next time, you will ask my permission." Her tone was cold and furious. "Don't ever again try to force me to perform magic."

Her words echoed through the empty space as she stormed out of the ballroom.

Lochlan hesitated only a moment before following her, his boots crunching softly over fallen petals and debris. He didn't speak as he trailed her through the corridors, past fleeing guests, and all the way to his truck waiting outside.

"Nia, wait," Lochlan called as he hurried to catch up.

She stopped abruptly by the driver's side door, spinning to face him. Her cheeks were flushed, her hair wild, and her eyes roved over him, scanning him from head to toe.

"Don't scare me like that," she snapped.

He blinked, utterly confused. "What?"

She yanked open the door and climbed into the driver's seat, her fingers gripping the wheel like it was the only thing tethering her to reality. Lochlan jogged around to the passenger side, barely managing to get in before the engine roared to life. The door slammed shut beside him as the force of Nia hitting the accelerator and peeling out of the lot, tires squealing against the gravel, threw him back against the seat.

"Leaving the protection circle," she muttered, her knuckles white on the wheel.

"Where are we going?" he asked, glancing around as the thick trees lining the road began to thin out. They drove in silence for several more minutes before Nia steered the truck into the lot of a park at the bottom of the hill.

She turned off the engine, the sudden silence deafening after the chaos of the night.

Lochlan barely had a moment to gather his thoughts before Nia shifted across the console and climbed into his lap.

"Nia—"

"Don't," she murmured, cutting him off. Her hands gripped his shoulders, fingers tight like she was holding on for balance—no, for control. Her breath was uneven, her lips brushing his in a way that felt almost frantic.

"I messed up," she whispered. "I lost control. All those people. I could have hurt them... and you." She swallowed hard, shaking her head like she couldn't say the rest. "I just—" The words tumbled out, raw and unfiltered, as if she wasn't speaking to him so much as trying to outrun her own thoughts. "—I need to feel something else. Anything else."

Her mouth crashed into his, desperate, insistent, her hands sliding beneath his jacket, lifting his shirt so her nails could scrape across his skin.

A shiver ran through him, but he didn't pull her closer—not yet.

"I hate how tonight went." Her hands fisted in his shirt, her forehead pressing to his like she was trying to steady herself. "I don't want to be angry right now." Another kiss, deep and urgent, like she could drown out the pain with him. "Please, Loch. I just... I need you."

Lochlan's breath hitched, his hands settling on her waist. She was unraveling in his arms, and he felt it—the ache of her fear and pain, the way she was trying to replace one feeling with another.

Her fingers twisted in his collar, pulling him closer, her hips rolling against him.

She kissed him again, tasting of desperation, of magic, of something so much deeper than the moment. Lochlan wanted her, wanted to lose himself in her—

But not like this.

Not when she was trying to disappear inside him, to hide in the heat between them.

"Please," she begged, her voice thick with urgency. Her fingers framed his jaw, her mouth moving against his like she could will away all that she was feeling. "You're so hard," she whispered, rolling her hips again, chasing friction. "I need you."

A sound rumbled deep inside him, primal and unbidden.

"I'm here for you," he said, his tone rough and clipped with restraint. "But clothes stay on."

She whined softly, but her legs widened, pressing herself so firmly against his lap that his vision flashed white. He was going to come in seconds, and he couldn't find the nerve to care. She was sexy and stunning and Lochlan wanted to be lost in her as much as she seemed lost in the moment. If this was what she needed, he'd give it to her— without letting things go too far.

His hands moved under her skirt, gripping her ass and guiding her movements, amplifying the friction that had her gasping.

"Chase that feeling, love," he murmured. "Use me all you want."

He was so hard it bordered on painful, the pressure dizzying. As her hips rocked into his, their bodies aligned just enough for him to slip partially free from the grip of his waistband.

Her eyes fluttered closed, breath catching. He swore he could feel her heat through the damp fabric, the tip of him exposed and pressing against it, straining for more.

"Loch," she moaned, her rhythm faltering as tension built in her body.

He gripped the back of her head with one hand, firm but careful, anchoring her. His other hand slid up her thigh, finding the swell of her. His thumb pressed against her through the damp fabric, moving in slow, deliberate circles.

"Let me have it," he rasped, his voice ragged and thick. "Make a mess of me."

"Fuck-fuck-fuck," she panted roughly against his mouth, her body jerking as waves of pleasure crashed through her.

Lochlan braced his feet against the floor of the truck, his own release surging violently through him, spilling hot against his stomach, pressed between him and her.

Nia let out a breathless sigh, rolling her hips again, teasing him until he groaned and gripped her firmly, stilling her movements. The overstimulation made him shudder, and she seemed to relish it, her smile soft and satisfied.

Their gazes met, and for a moment, the world seemed to fade, leaving only the quiet intimacy between them. Soft smiles lingered as the aftershocks ebbed, heat and tension giving way to hazy warmth.

A sharp knock shattered the moment.

Rap-rap-rap.

A harsh flashlight beam cut through the fogged windows, cutting through the moment of intimacy like a blade.

"Park Ranger," a gruff voice called through the darkness. "You can't park here."

Nia's wide eyes darted to Lochlan's as her lips curved into a mischievous smile. A laugh bubbled from her as she turned to the fogged glass, drawing a quick rune with her fingertip. She whispered softly, her voice lilting with magic:

"Away you go, nothing to see,

Turn your back and let us be."

The rune glowed faintly, its light casting soft shadows across the truck's interior. Outside, the ranger's silhouette hesitated, his flashlight beam hovering uncertainly. Then he turned, his steps slow but steady as he wandered off into the shadows, the flashlight bobbing until it disappeared completely.

A glint of triumph in her eyes, Nia turned back to Lochlan and kissed him lightly, her lips lingering just long enough to tease. "We should go. Someone else might find us."

"I need to get you home," Lochlan said, his voice gentler now. "You haven't eaten, and you used a lot of magic tonight."

Her smirk softened, but something flickered across her face—brief but unmistakable. She looked down at her lap, her fingers toying with the hem of her skirt.

"Someone could have been hurt," she said quietly. "*You* could have been hurt."

The contrast between her words and the moment they'd just shared struck Lochlan like a fist to his chest. Her pain was palpable, and he couldn't let it sit there.

Lochlan reached out, brushing her hair gently away from her face. "It was an accident," he said softly. "And supernaturals heal fast."

Her head shot up, eyes wide with worry, a deep crease etched between her brows.

"At least you made the night exciting. They probably would've preferred a flower attack over our original plan."

Nia's lips twitched, then she rolled her eyes, her worry seeming to ease slightly. "Seeing you naked would have been far better," she muttered.

"There's always next time," he said lightly. "Come on. Let's get you home."

Something in her expression softened, the tension in her shoulders ebbing. "Yes, *love*," she teased, warmth threading through her voice as she tossed his own endearment back at him. The word settled over him like a spell, quiet and powerful.

Love.

He held on to that possibility all the way home. As he made her chicken Alfredo with pasta and warm bread and tucked her into bed, the memory of her voice wrapped around him like magic, a wicked hope whispering of forever.

25

Lochlan

"All Future Moon Celebrations Canceled Until Further Notice." –THE VIDET

Lochlan had been unusually productive that morning. He'd finished restoring another diary, wrapped up a project for New Chapter, and had nearly forgotten to stop for lunch. He credited Nia for that. After her sweet kiss before she left, everything just seemed... easier. The air felt lighter, the world brighter, and the tedious work of mending old bindings oddly satisfying.

Even the diaries and their daunting weight didn't seem so heavy today. Not while her kiss still lingered on his lips.

The only thing throwing him off was the color green—not ideal, considering his house was practically a forest. She'd been wearing a pale green wrap dress when she'd kissed him, and now he couldn't stop thinking about how the fabric had brushed against him, light and teasing. Now, without work to keep his mind occupied, his thoughts looped back to her.

He stood at the counter, cookies baking in the oven behind him, as he stared blankly at the lettuce meant for his sandwich. He had no idea how long he'd been standing there, motionless, holding the leafy green in one hand.

"What the fuck, man," a gravelly voice came from behind him. "Are you going to make the damned sandwich or what?"

Lochlan turned, blinking as if he'd been yanked out of a dream. He hadn't heard that voice in eight years.

"Don't leave, I'm sorry. We can make it work. It will be better."

His brother, Thane, stepped out from the shadows of the hall. Broad and built like a fortress, with neatly cut dark hair and amber eyes that usually scanned a room as if assessing it for threats. Now, though, his gaze was guarded—and fixed on Lochlan.

Lochlan stepped forward. Both men opened their arms, and he caught the flicker of warmth in Thane's expression, the softening around his eyes as they crinkled at the edges. The embrace was all back slaps and awkward angles, but Lochlan still lingered, wondering how Thane had appeared.

"How did you—?"

"The greenhouse." Thane stepped back, brushing a bit of lint from his coat like he hadn't just broken in.

"The greenhouse?" Lochlan repeated, frowning. "There's no way you got past Jade—and the ducks."

Thane's lips twitched. "Don't worry. She's enjoying an expensive slab of steak, and your ducks are eating the finest strawberries I could find. Echo is with them."

Lochlan blinked. "You still have him?"

Echo had been just a pup when Lochlan left. Thane always worked with dogs, treated them like extensions of himself: trusted, disciplined, efficient. Just like the tech he designed and built.

As for what those missions were, and why or how Thane deployed both his dogs and his tech? Lochlan had never gotten the full picture. He'd worked up the courage to ask, once, when he was younger. At the time, he'd thought his brother might be off thwarting terrorist plots, quelling rebellions, even dramatically rescuing a damsel or two. But Thane had never shared details.

He nodded now. "Echo's getting old, but he's still sharp. I didn't see a reason to send him away."

Lochlan raised an eyebrow. "From high-security missions for the crown to distracting dogs and ducks. Are you finally slowing down, Thane?"

A flicker of amusement crossed Thane's features. "Since when are you so feisty?"

"Since you broke into my house," Lochlan shot back, crossing his arms. "Why are you here?"

Thane tilted his head, studying Lochlan like he was trying to place a puzzle piece that didn't quite fit. "I've been busy."

"Right. Preparing to take the throne, cleaning up our family's messes, fighting off the crown's enemies—or whatever it is you do—must be exhausting." Lochlan leaned against the counter. "Did you pencil me in between a coup and a crisis? Or am I the crisis?"

Thane gave the barest shrug. "The timing worked."

"And this is the first time in eight years 'the timing worked?'"

Eight years since he had left everything behind, since the fire that consumed his father's legacy—and his own. Generations of carefully cultivated plants, the collection within the greenhouse as old as the castle itself, all gone in an instant when his sister, Drusilla, had burned it in a fit of rage.

The scars along his calves pulsed with phantom pain at the memory. The skin had long since healed, but the ache beneath it lingered—flaring up when the weather turned cold, when he pushed himself too hard, or when the past refused to stay buried. They were a permanent reminder of everything he'd lost.

"It's time to come home," Thane said quietly.

A humorless laugh escaped Lochlan. "Home?"

Thane's expression didn't change. "You're third in line, Lochlan. We need to show... a strong family bond."

"That will be a little hard when there is no family bond," Lochlan said flatly. "Why now?"

Thane's jaw tightened, his gaze shifting away for the briefest second. Lochlan didn't know what specific problem or threat had brought Thane, but he knew enough to guess. There was always someone trying to dismantle the last vestiges of power the monarchy still clung to—oversight of international military operations, approval for government spending, and so on—the people ever-more hungry for democracy and eager to take power.

Good. Let them. As far as Lochlan could see, the royal family was no more fit to wield that power than anyone else. Possibly less.

His existence had been a gift to the Dover Coalition—in an era rife with dissatisfaction about the way the country was being ruled, he was living proof that the queen herself wasn't perfect, that her judgement could be compromised. Rumors of corruption and greed came on the heels of those related to her infidelity; perhaps she was no more faithful to her vow to protect her country than the one she took to her husband the king. The moment the world learned about Lochlan, cracks in public opinion had started to form—and as people dug deeper and learned more, they seemed less convinced the queen was a fit ruler, or that a royal family should be ruling at all.

But there was nothing Lochlan could do about that now, even if he'd wanted to.

"You and Drusilla will do just fine without me."

Thane's expression didn't waver, his stoic mask firmly in place. But there—a brief hesitation, a fracture in his composure just wide enough to reveal the faintest hint of vulnerability.

"We need you."

The words hit Lochlan harder than he wanted to admit. *We need you.* It was all he'd ever wanted from his family, wasn't it? To feel needed, wanted, to be seen as more than an outlier, more than the spare heir they had no use for. He'd spent years convincing himself he didn't care and that their approval meant nothing to him.

But it did.

No matter how cold his mother's gaze was, or how cruel Drusilla had been, some foolish part of Lochlan had always wanted to belong and be accepted—even loved—by the people who should have been his family, whose love he should never have had to hope for or earn. And now, after years of silence, Thane had come.

And Lochlan knew his brother meant it: he really believed they needed Lochlan.

That was the worst part. This wasn't a formality or a rehearsed diplomatic plea. Thane had chosen to come here, to say it himself, to ask for Lochlan's help.

"No." His tone was flat, final. "I owe you nothing."

Thane didn't argue. Instead, he reached into his bag and pulled out a bundle of brown cloth. He unfolded it carefully to reveal a small pot.

Lochlan's breath caught. Sage-green leaves, speckled with tiny stars, peeked out from the soil. The plant looked fragile, impossibly delicate, but the magic radiating from it was unmistakable. Lochlan couldn't look away.

Thane glanced at him. "Do you recognize it?"

Of course he did.

It was from the greenhouse. The one built around an ancient sequoia tree, its magic older than the royal family or even the kingdom itself. A vanilla orchid had once thrived there, its purple petals and star-speckled leaves born of a wayward spell, producing vanilla with a rare chocolate undertone.

Drusilla had started with the orchids, ripping them from the tree before setting the greenhouse itself ablaze. Lochlan had tried to save what he could, but the fire consumed everything. He'd nearly burned with it—and would have, if Thane hadn't pulled him out.

"No," Lochlan said, his voice disbelieving. "It burned. All of it did."

"The tree survived," Thane said evenly. "And this isn't the only plant that made it."

"More things for our sister to burn," Lochlan said, bitterness in every word.

"I've kept them hidden from her," Thane replied, "and constructed a secret entry for the herbalists. We walled off the original entrance."

Memories of his father flickered through Lochlan's mind—himself as a boy, chasing after a man whose broad hands worked with steady grace. His father had been soft-spoken, with a quiet brilliance that drew people in without ever demanding their attention. When he wasn't overseeing the castle's herbalists, he'd take Lochlan everywhere. To the countryside, where wild herbs tangled at their feet. Across distant towns to study flora in temple gardens and roadside ditches alike. They'd wandered through museums, old estates, forgotten groves. Always learning.

Always together.

After his father's early death, the other herbalists had tried to fill the void, but it had never been the same.

"Things will be different now," Thane said.

Lochlan let out a humorless laugh. "You may be a brilliant spy and our esteemed soon-to-be king, but you can't see what's right in front of you. Is our mother still cold and cruel? Is Drusilla still psychotic and spoiled?"

"Our mother has asked about you," Thane said, softer. "She's worried. About this… marriage. It isn't right. You should be with us. Not with that witch."

"I'm a witch!" Lochlan's voice thundered as his fist slammed against the counter.

He pushed away the small, unwelcome desire to believe his mother's concern was real. It wasn't care—not for him, anyway—and it certainly wasn't love that had her asking questions. Lochlan knew better. He wasn't the same young man who'd once desperately wanted to belong to the family he'd only ever watched from a distance.

He knew now how much of that life was only artifice: fake, constructed, and hollow.

Thane studied him for a long moment, as though trying to reconcile the brother he remembered with the man standing before him. Finally, he nodded once and placed a black card on the counter. "I'll be in the area for a bit longer. If you need me, or…"

He trailed off, but Lochlan could still hear the words: *If you change your mind.*

Thane turned and headed for the back door to the greenhouse.

Lochlan followed, finding Jade playing with Echo, a black shepherd. She was trying to tug a rope toy from his jaws. The larger dog held firm, his graying muzzle set in quiet determination, though his wagging tail betrayed his enjoyment.

Jade gave a playful growl, yanking the rope hard enough to make Echo stumble slightly. Echo retaliated with a deliberate tug, pulling Jade a few steps closer before suddenly letting go. Jade tumbled backward in surprise, landing in a pile of leaves. Echo let out a huff that might have been the canine equivalent of a chuckle.

"Echo." The dog immediately snapped to attention at Thane's call, bounding to his side. Thane paused at the greenhouse door, his hand resting on the frame. "Take care, Lochlan," he said finally, almost hesitant.

Lochlan opened his mouth to say something, but the words wouldn't come. He wasn't angry with his brother—not really. He just wished things could be different.

In the end, he managed a small nod.

Thane didn't press. He let the moment hang, the silence between them filled with everything they had and hadn't said, before he turned and disappeared through the back door.

The hunger Lochlan had felt earlier was gone. He grabbed the book he'd finished repairing, bagged up the fresh cookies he'd baked, and left to find the one thing he knew could make him feel better.

26

Nia

*"They don't work! Did you see how
she couldn't even do a simple spell?"*
—WOLVENLOVER1111

Nia sat at her desk, a smile tugging at her lips—that had been happening a lot today. As she jotted down notes, Ivy's voice crackled over the phone. She'd started the day hiking to connect with nature, and somehow pivoted to planning the biggest charity gala for the end of the year mid-hike.

"You want to do a silent auction?" Nia repeated, straining to hear over the wind on Ivy's end.

"I'm sure I can get Becket to volunteer," Ivy said, undeterred. "Would you give up Lochlan for a night?"

Nia froze mid-sentence, her pen hovering above the page. "Wait. You're not actually planning to auction people, are you?"

"For dates," Ivy said breezily. "We'll get influential people to volunteer!"

Nia scoffed. "Becket and Lochlan are not influential."

"Lochlan is a prince. Becket is pretty. And a lawyer."

"I mean, sure. Becket makes sense, he's single and all," Nia muttered. "But Lochlan is…"

Her voice faltered. She didn't need to finish. Nia could practically hear Ivy's grin on the other end.

"He's what, Nia? Say it."

Nia clenched her pen, staring down at her notes as though they could shield her from the truth. *Lochlan is taken.* That was true, privately. But publicly? To her father and everyone else? She was supposed to be finding ways to convince everyone she wanted to get rid of him.

A gentle knock broke through her spiraling thoughts. Nia spun in her chair, her gaze snapping toward the door of her office. Almost as if their conversation had invoked him—

"Lochlan is here," she said softly, more to herself than Ivy.

"Does he look hot?" Ivy's teasing voice came through the phone. "You sound like he's standing there all tall and handsome and sweet."

Nia's cheeks warmed as she continued to stare at him. *Yes,* she thought, because of course he looked hot. She still hadn't quite recovered from the memory of the night before. But something about him now was… different. Restless?

"I'm hanging up now," Nia said firmly, cutting off Ivy's teasing before it could escalate.

"Ask him if he'd be willing to be auctioned off at—"

Nia ended the call.

Lochlan's mouth curved into that devastating half-smile, and for a moment, Nia forgot how to breathe. *How was he even free to be shoved into this arranged marriage by her father? How had no one scooped him up yet?*

If he ever ended up on an auction block, people would lose their damn minds.

"Auctioned off?" One dark eyebrow rose and his lips twitched.

"We can talk about it later," she said, standing and smoothing down her dress. His eyes tracked the movement of her hands, slow and deliberate, before flicking back to her face. Her heart kicked up a notch—or ten.

Lochlan's gaze shifted, landing on one of the pots clustered at one corner of her desk. With restless energy, he reached out, brushing his fingers over a rough-edged leaf. Nia leaned forward as red flowers bloomed under his touch, the vibrant color spreading like fire.

"Whoa," she said, her voice soft with wonder. "I didn't know it had flowers."

"Episcia," he said, lifting the plant with careful hands. "They bloom if they get enough sunlight."

He walked it over to the table by the window, setting it down where the light streamed through. He lingered, his fingers brushing absently over the pot as though he was settling himself. His posture was relaxed, but Nia could still feel the tension rolling off him.

"I got it because the leaves reminded me of dragon skin," she admitted.

Lochlan glanced back at her, his expression shifting, surprise softening the harsh angles of his features. "Most people only like pretty, easy things." He stepped toward her slowly. "You're pretty. But you're not easy."

Her grip tightened on the edge of the desk as she looked up at him, their shoes nearly touching. "You think I'm pretty?"

"You walk into a room and I forget everything else exists." He toyed with a strand of her hair before adding, "I've never seen anyone carry their fire like you do. I misspoke, pretty doesn't cover it."

Her breath caught. "What brings you to this side of Stella Rune?"

"I had a book to drop off a few doors down," he said casually, though the tension in his shoulders betrayed him. "I thought I'd stop by. I... needed a distraction."

A distraction?

Before she could unpack the weight of his words, he stepped closer.

"I needed you," he said, his honesty cutting through what little remained of her defenses.

The world tilted as his hand brushed her cheek and his lips met hers. There was no hesitation, no pause to question. He kissed her like it was instinct, like they'd done it a thousand times before.

Her hands slid to his chest, her fingers curling into the fabric of his shirt as she leaned into him. The kiss was sure and familiar, but still sent a jolt through her, as if she hadn't already memorized the way he tasted.

He broke away just enough to rest his forehead against hers, their breaths mingling in the intimate space between them. "You make it hard to think," he murmured, his voice unsteady.

Her laugh was soft, shaky. "Then don't think. Let me be a distraction."

His eyes closed briefly, his expression torn between restraint and surrender, and then he kissed her again—deeper this time. His hands slid down to the back of her dress, fingers gathering the soft fabric.

"This damned dress," he muttered against her lips, frustration laced with desire. There was a mixture of reverence and urgency in the way he tugged at it, like the dress had been taunting him all day.

She felt everything—too much and just enough. Confidence surged through her veins, different from the usual self-assurance she carried. With him like this, needy and open, she felt untouchable. Like a siren pulling him under, leaving him powerless to resist.

"The dress, it's magic," she whispered when they finally broke for air, her voice low and teasing.

Behind Lochlan, shadows uncurled, fast and fluid, racing across the window and snapping the curtains shut. Stella Rune vanished in an instant, swallowed by darkness and silence. The only light came from the scattered lanterns and candles she'd placed around the office. Their flickering warmth painted the room in gold.

"Mmm." He leaned in to claim her mouth again, but she tilted her head back, just out of reach. His brow furrowed, his gaze locking on hers, making her pulse trip.

Satisfied with his attention, she slowly grasped the ties at her waist that kept the dress wrapped around her. With a quick tug, the fabric gave way, falling open like a spell undone.

"Damn." The word came out rough as his eyes swept over her. Her bra, a light silk that shimmered in the low light, paired perfectly with matching underwear that left little to the imagination. Semi-sheer tights clung to her thighs and waist.

His hands slid slowly up the length of her legs, palms gliding over the soft mesh—practical, she'd told herself this morning. Nothing about it felt practical now. All she could focus on was the way his fingers lingered, his grip firm enough to make her breath hitch.

"Do you have another pair of these?" he asked, his tone almost too casual, but the intensity in his gaze gave him away.

"Yes?" she managed to whisper.

The seams tore before she fully registered his movement, the sound sharp in the quiet room. Her gasp turned into a soft cry as he swept her onto her back atop the desk, his hands firm yet careful.

He froze.

"I didn't mean—" His eyes widened slightly, as if startled by his own boldness. "I just... acted. I'm sorry, I shouldn't have—"

She lifted her head, breathless, and curled her fingers around his forearm. "You should," she murmured. "That was hot. Don't stop unless I ask you to."

His gaze locked onto hers, dark and blown wide with want. He stared down at her, breath shallow, lips parted, every inch of him taut with restraint and need.

"What do you want to do next?" she asked, her voice low, coaxing.

It sent a thrill through her, the way he studied her like he was learning a new kind of magic—careful, focused, awestruck.

Her breath hitched as his thumb traced the silk covering her nipple, teasing her through the delicate fabric. She arched toward his touch, her pulse thrumming with a rhythm only he could conjure. He played her body like a spellcaster weaving quiet, potent magic. His hand tightened at her waist, anchoring her as his attention dipped lower, the air shimmering between them, charged with unspoken power.

She pushed herself up on her elbows, her breaths uneven as she watched him descend, the contrast between his calm precision and the raw desire in his eyes leaving her dizzy.

When his lips pressed against her through the thin silk of her underwear, it wasn't tentative. It was deliberate. Maddeningly restrained. Her body ached again, every nerve lighting up as he kissed her there, his breath hot against her.

"Is this alright?" he asked, his voice rough, hungry.

Her heart skipped, words catching in her throat as she nodded quickly, unable to do anything else.

But he wanted words, she remembered that as he punished her with a nip to the sensitive skin of her inner thigh, making her cry out.

"Yes," she gasped, her head falling back, her fingers gripping the edge of the desk. "Goddess, yes."

One sharp twist, and her underwear tore free in his hands, the ripping fabric a delicious sound that sent shivers down her spine.

"Loch!"

There was no time for protests—not that she had any—because his mouth was on her. His tongue pressed against her slick heat, and the first moan rumbled from his chest. The low, guttural sound reverberated through her, unraveling her inch by inch. Her knees shot up reflexively, her body yielding to the tidal wave of pleasure surging through her.

He paused, just slightly, lifting his head enough to ask, "Am I doing this right?"

"Yes," she breathed, hips moving toward him. "Don't stop."

That was all he needed.

She hadn't realized how desperately neglected she was until now. The warm drag of his tongue circled her clit before he sucked gently, so careful she almost laughed. *Am I doing this right?* If he only knew. What he was doing was maddening. His fingers spread her open, the pads of them massaging with a rhythm that sent sparks racing across her skin. She was warm, wet, and completely at his mercy.

The room was steeped in him—his magical, intoxicating scent, like stepping into a sunlit greenhouse, layered with something richer, warmer, like buttery caramel. It was driving her mad, mixing with the slick sounds of his focus and her breathless cries.

When he pushed a finger inside her—then a second—her mind shattered. Coherent thought slipped away entirely, replaced by raw, aching need.

Had it been minutes? Seconds? It didn't matter. Her hips moved of their own accord, grinding against him as she chased release with reckless abandon. Her body was completely lost to him.

"Loch," she whimpered, her voice catching as her head fell back. Her chest heaved as she gathered herself, her words tumbling out in a breathless rush. "You're so good at this. So fucking good."

Her hand slid to his hair, fingers tangling in it as she gasped again. "You're perfect, Loch. Every part of you. Your mouth—oh, goddess— your mouth is everything."

He moaned in response. Her gaze flicked downward, catching the subtle motion of his right shoulder pumping back and forth. Realization hit her like a lightning strike, blooming hot across her cheeks. He was stroking himself, his control slipping as he devoured her with the same intensity she craved.

"Loch," she said again, her tone low and urgent.

Her hand twitched toward him instinctively, but he stopped her with a smoldering look, his eyes dark and possessive, making her melt.

"Don't."

His voice left her trembling, her heart racing. He shifted slightly, and her gaze caught it—her torn underwear still clutched in his fist, stretched tight over his cock.

"You like this, want this?" he murmured, before dragging his tongue up her slick heat. "Watching me fall apart for you?"

"Yes," she gasped, her hips bucking into his mouth as her orgasm hovered just out of reach. "Don't stop. Please don't stop."

His lips grazed her clit as his fingers curled inside her, finding the perfect spot. "I couldn't if I wanted to," he murmured, his voice dripping with hunger. "Not when you're like this, wanting and waiting for me."

Her head fell back, stars bursting behind her eyelids, but her gaze kept returning to him. The sight of his cock sliding against the silken fabric of her underwear, his hand flexing with every stroke, was burned into her memory—a permanent entry in her spank bank, ready for frequent revisits.

"You're perfect," he groaned, his words punctuated by a harsh suck that made her cry out. "So fucking perfect. I feel you, Nia. Will you come for me?"

"Yes!" Her voice broke, raw and unrestrained.

"Then give it to me, love," he demanded, his tone firm yet coaxing, his fingers driving into her harder, his tongue unrelenting. "Let me feel you."

The combination of his words and his touch shattered her. Her release surged through her like a tidal wave, pleasure so intense her whole body trembled against him. Her cry filled the room, unbridled and wild, as every nerve in her exploded.

The deep, guttural moan he let out tore through her as his release followed hers, a perfect, messy symphony.

When the haze began to clear, her gaze dropped to him. He was still nestled between her thighs, his lips glistening with the evidence of her undoing. His chest heaved, his dark eyes heavy-lidded but blazing as they met hers. He looked utterly wrecked, and the sight made her heart race all over again.

Her gaze darted to his hand, the slick fabric stretched taut. The ruined silk between them wasn't just a casualty—it was a trophy, undeniable proof of just how far gone he was for her. She'd never look at fine fabric the same way again. Heat flared in her cheeks. "I didn't realize I was into that," she admitted, the words tumbling out before her mind could catch up with her mouth.

His brows lifted slightly, amusement and heat mingling in his expression. "Good to know," he murmured, his voice like a caress. He dipped his head back down, pressing a lingering kiss to her sensitive center.

"I didn't know what I was doing," he admitted softly. "I just knew I wanted to taste you."

She blinked. That was him not knowing what he was doing? Her body was still trembling from it. If that was inexperience, she was in serious trouble.

"I couldn't tell. We were quick," she said after a beat, her tone light but her heart racing.

His expression shifted, his eyes narrowing just enough to make her stomach flip. It wasn't annoyance—more like a silent, smoldering challenge.

"It means," she added quickly, a grin tugging at her lips, "we can go again, right?"

The tension in his shoulders loosened as he leaned in, his mouth brushing against her knee, then her thigh. "I don't think I'll ever get enough of you."

27

Nia

"A duchess and a prince sitting under a tree..."
—MESSY_IVY

The canal was calm at this hour, the water reflecting the low-hanging sun in ripples of gold and amber. The air carried the faint scent of blooming jasmine, mixing with the warm tang of Nia's steak and cheese sub, which was perched on her lap.

She sat in her fresh clothes on a thick blanket Lochlan had grabbed, now spread under an ancient oak tree. A short way behind her, half-hidden by wild ivy and stone, lay one of the town's many secret tunnel entrances, the same one they had emerged from not long ago.

It was a strange thing to reconcile—how assertive and provocative Lochlan had been in her office, yet how reserved and sweet he was now. She glanced his way as he stood near the water's edge, tossing small, red bits to the ducks bobbing nearby.

When he wandered back, the lazy smile on his face was enough to make her pulse stutter. She nodded toward the bag in his hand, curious. "What were those?"

"Freeze-dried strawberries."

She frowned. "Ducks like strawberries?"

"They like pretty much anything."

"Huh," she said, taking a bite of her sub. "I didn't know that. And you just... carry dried strawberries in your bag for the local ducks?"

"Ah, no." He rubbed the back of his neck, a blush creeping up his cheeks. "Those are my ducks."

"You have ducks?" She blinked. "Why didn't you tell me?"

He shrugged. "We haven't exactly told each other much, Nia."

That stung. She realized it was true, and hated how selfish she felt for never asking more about his life. "Well," she said, trying to make up for it, "tell me about the ducks."

He nodded toward the canal where the three of them floated. "Taco's the black one. He was my first. I found him near one of the beaches with a broken wing right before winter hit. Celia's the orange one, and Cynthia's the brown. Taco and I raised them from eggs."

"Eggs?" she asked.

"Yeah." He leaned back against the tree, gazing at the water. "A few years ago, I was consulting on a dig site for the town. They'd unearthed some tombs and the area was a mess. Trees ripped apart, nests destroyed. I found a clutch of eggs in the remains of a nest—three of them had broken, but two were still whole. I waited for the mother to come back, but she never did. So I brought them home."

"And Taco helped raise them?"

"Yeah. I guess he figured since I took care of him, he'd pass on the favor."

"But he's a boy," Nia said, frowning.

"Meaning he can't be motherly?" Lochlan gave her a pointed look.

Her lips pressed together. "I didn't mean it like that."

He smirked but didn't push further. "They live in the greenhouse," he said. "They eat bugs in the mornings, and when they want, they use a magical doggy door to swim in the canal. Jade likes hanging out with them."

Nia felt a fresh pang of guilt. She hadn't even asked to see the greenhouse. It felt like a piece of him she'd ignored. Now that her new magic had grown, she could almost sense it—the life and warmth of it calling to her. "Can I see it?" she asked.

He looked at her, surprised. Then he smiled. "Of course."

They walked along the canal. The ducks followed in the water, quacking softly, their tails wagging. The setting sun bathed the path in gold, and Nia's heart felt lighter as they crossed a small bridge. Lochlan slowed, his expression tight, as though he wanted to say something but couldn't.

"What?" she asked, a flicker of worry tightening her chest. "Is it whatever happened before... what made you want a distraction?"

He hesitated, then gave her a faint smile. "You mean what happened before I ruined your very pretty clothes?"

She grinned, trying to ease his nerves. "It was a good kind of ruin," she said, nudging his arm. "But yeah, it was unexpected."

Lochlan exhaled sharply, his shoulders sinking. "Maybe I shouldn't have—"

She cut him off with a wave of her hand. "I liked it. A lot, actually." Her cheeks warmed as she said it, but she pressed on. "But I am curious about why you seemed... different."

"It wasn't fair to you," he said, his voice low. "I was wound up, upset, tense. I took that tension out on you. Not in a bad way, but..." His jaw tightened, and he looked away. "You deserved better."

She touched his arm, her fingers light. "Better than that?"

He gave her a hesitant smile.

"Lochlan, I'm here, okay? Just maybe let me in on what's going on next time."

"I'll try."

"Good," she said. "So, are you going to tell me what happened?"

He hesitated, his fingers curling slightly around hers. "My brother stopped by."

"Your brother?" she asked, startled. "The crown prince?"

"Yeah," he said, dragging a hand through his hair. "It's been eight years."

"That's... a long time." She studied his face, looking for clues to his mood. "How did it go?"

Lochlan shrugged in a way that seemed more habit than actual indifference. "It wasn't the worst visit, but it wasn't the best either."

Her brow furrowed. "What does that mean? Lochlan, come on, he's your brother."

"Half-brother," Lochlan said. "We share a mother."

She hesitated. "I didn't think princes just stop by for visits like that. I mean... you're a prince too, but... goddess. I'm rambling. Wait—was he mean to you?"

Her body went rigid, her mind racing. If his brother had hurt him, she'd—

"You make everything better," Lochlan interrupted, his voice soft. A small smile graced his lips before it faded. His gaze shifted past her, and she turned to follow it. Far off, a cluster of men stood near the edge of a property across the water, their figures indistinct in the fading light. They weren't talking. Just standing there.

A chill crept up her spine.

"Let's go inside," she said, voice steady. "Show me the greenhouse."

He led her to the back and opened a vintage glass door, its surface fogged. Warm, humid air enveloped them, carrying the scent of damp earth and thriving plants. The ducks waddled past them, their little feet slapping against the floor as they greeted Jade with cheerful quacks, nibbles, and tail wags.

Nia's eyes darted around the space, taking in the haven Lochlan had built. Fairy lights crisscrossed the ceiling, casting a soft glow over the lush greenery. Plants were everywhere—vines draped from shelves, flowers bloomed in hanging baskets, and rare herbs thrived in carefully arranged pots.

Against one wall sat a wooden duck cottage, complete with a ramp leading to the raised floor. Nearby, a couple of wicker dog beds were scattered, each piled high with plush bedding.

"It's beautiful," she said, her voice almost a whisper. She reached out to touch the delicate leaves of a nearby plant, feeling the life humming through it. Her connection to Lochlan's magic let her sense the care and energy he'd poured into this place.

"The ducks like it," he said with a small smile. "And so does Jade." His dog was now curled up on one of the beds, eyeing Taco and Celia lazily as they waddled around.

"You created a haven," she said, turning to him.

He shrugged, glancing around. "I needed somewhere to put all of this," he said, gesturing vaguely at the plants. "It just… came together."

She tilted her head, studying him. "Would you ever want to create something bigger?"

Lochlan's gaze flicked to hers, and for a moment, a shadow crossed his face. "I don't know," he said after a pause.

She wanted to press, but something in his expression stopped her. "Sorry," she said instead. "I don't want to push. I just—after that harvest, I wished we'd had your help sooner."

"No, it's okay," he said taking a deep breath. "My brother stopping by has me revisiting a lot of old wounds."

Lochlan led her to a small outdoor kitchen area, where they sat down.

Nia was quiet, sensing he needed space to share at his own pace. Jade left her duck-watching perch and jumped onto the chair beside him, resting her head in his lap. Lochlan rubbed her ears absentmindedly.

"My father passed away thirteen years ago," he said quietly. "Five years after that, I left Dover."

"I'm so sorry," Nia said.

"Thank you. It was hard without him. I tried to adjust, but..." He paused, his hand stilling on Jade's fur. "That was when it came out I was the result of a royal affair. Suddenly, I wasn't just Lochlan—I was a prince, thrown into this life of titles and duties I never wanted."

She reached for his hand, and he gave her a small, grateful squeeze before continuing.

"There was one place I could escape to—an atrium greenhouse my ancestors built, the same one my father worked in. It was filled with life. Plants everywhere, like this, only on a much grander scale. I could hide there, get away from the cruelty of my sister, the distant coldness of my mother."

His fingers tensed slightly against Jade's fur. "Thane—my brother—was never unfair to me. He just... wasn't there. He had his own responsibilities, especially after his own father passed. Maybe we could have been closer, if I hadn't been hidden away for so long before being thrown into their lives."

He paused again, taking a deep breath. "Eight years ago, my sister, Drusilla, snapped. She burned the greenhouse to the ground."

Nia's heart ached for him. She could tell there was more, but didn't push.

Lochlan's gaze drifted toward the flickering lanterns along the garden path. "She found me that night. Cornered me, like she always did, throwing words like knives, cutting deep because she could. I ran to the greenhouse, where I always went when I needed a refuge. But this time she followed." His jaw clenched. "She didn't just want to hurt me. She wanted to destroy something I loved."

Nia stayed silent, her stomach twisting.

"She ripped the orchids from the trees. Pulled vines down like they were weeds. Then she set it all on fire." His voice was flat, but something in it sent a chill down Nia's spine. "Thane tried to stop her, but it was too late. The fire spread too fast. It climbed the walls, scorched through everything, filling the air with smoke so thick I could barely breathe." His fingers curled into his lap. "I tried to save what I could. I wasn't thinking. I just—I had to save something. The orchids, my father's book of pressed herbs, anything."

Lochlan closed his eyes.

"The fire didn't care. It crawled up my legs, burned through my clothes, my skin—"

He stopped. But Nia didn't need him to finish; she'd seen his scars.

"Thane pulled me out." The words were quiet. "I don't even remember him grabbing me. One second, I was running through fire. The next, I was outside on my back, choking on smoke, my legs burning, the greenhouse collapsing in front of me."

His grip on Jade's fur loosened and he exhaled slowly.

"I fought him." He let out a bitter laugh. "I tried to get back in. He held me down, told me to stop." Lochlan looked at her then, his golden-brown eyes darker in the dim light. "I left a few days later and never looked back."

A lump formed in Nia's throat. She didn't know what to say. What could she say?

"And your brother just stopped by to say hi?" Her tone was dry, laced with disbelief.

"No." Lochlan sighed. "He asked me to come back to Dover."

"Why?"

"It doesn't matter."

Anger surged through Nia, but she kept it in check. How dare his brother ask him to go back to a place that had caused him so much pain?

And worse—what if he did go?

The thought left her unsettled in ways she didn't want to name.

Jade suddenly jumped off the chair, chasing after the ducks as they waddled toward their little cottage. Nia stood and moved to Lochlan, straddling his lap before he could say a word. She brushed his hair back, her fingers soft and gentle.

His eyes darkened, his breath hitching. "Nia…"

She kissed him once, then pressed her lips to his cheek, his neck. The scent of him—mixed with her own—was intoxicating. Beneath it was that underlying sweetness, it made her want to taste him.

"Do you need a distraction?" she whispered.

His hands gripped her thighs, pulling her closer. "I need you."

28

Nia

"Their signs don't match - and it will end in horror."
—THE GREENWITCH 1969

I need you.

The words echoed in her mind as Lochlan carried her up the stairs. She kissed him the whole way—slowly, purposefully, nothing like the desperate, frenzied encounters they'd shared before. This was uncharted territory.

When he placed her on the bed, still nestled between her legs, his movements were unhurried. He brushed her hair away from her face, his fingers lingering as they slid to her cheek, then down her neck. He paused at her pulse point, his thumb pressing lightly.

"Do you feel that?" Nia asked, her voice low, rough. "How wild my heart beats for you?"

He answered with a kiss—soft and searching.

"This is so new," Nia whispered, her breath mingling with his. "So different from anything I've ever known. It scares me."

Their lips met again, the air between them thickening.

"I'm frightened too," Lochlan admitted, his forehead resting against hers. "That you'll open your eyes and realize I'm not meant for you, or your world, or..."

"I would never. I just..." Nia shook her head, her voice steady despite the maelstrom inside her. "I don't know how to leave space for someone else. But I want you to take up that space. I need you. And I need you to be patient. I need..." Her voice broke, and she kissed him roughly. "So much."

The thought scared her. She'd spent so long shying away from forever. And yet, as he looked at her now, she couldn't help but think that maybe... he was forever.

Before her thoughts could spiral further, she moaned low in her throat, chasing him—chasing distraction. At that moment, she didn't want to think. She just wanted him.

Lochlan's hands tightened around her hips, his control fraying at the edges. "Keep needing me like that, and I'll become desperate."

"Don't hold back," she murmured, her eyes locking with his. "I want to see every part of you—the messy, beautiful, desperate parts, too."

A groan rumbled from deep in his chest, and he kissed her again, this time with none of the restraint he'd shown earlier. His honey-colored eyes met hers, holding them with a reverence that left her breathless.

"Tell me if you want me to stop," he said, his voice quiet but firm.

"Don't stop," she said, the certainty in her voice surprising even herself. "Please."

Lochlan stood, his frame towering in the dim, golden light of the bedroom. Shadows danced along his body, emphasizing the quiet power he carried in his broad shoulders and the heavy lines of his chest, rough and real.

He pulled his shirt over his head, the fabric sliding free to reveal the expanse of his torso. She mirrored him, peeling off her own shirt, her gaze fixed on him, hunger rising with each inch of revealed skin.

He unfastened his pants, pushing them down slowly. The anticipation made her pulse quicken. As they pooled at his ankles, he stood before her in just his boxers, the tension of his arousal straining against the fabric.

She sat up on the bed, her eyes drinking in the breadth of his body, but as her gaze drifted lower, the breath caught in her throat. Faint silver scars peppered his thighs, becoming denser as they reached his calves, until they stopped abruptly near his ankles.

A pang of sorrow and understanding struck her—these were the remnants from the fire that had threatened to destroy the greenhouse he loved.

She leaned forward, pressing her lips to his stomach, then trailing kisses down to his thigh, her mouth lingering over one of the silvery marks above his knee. The touch drew a low, guttural groan from him, and when she glanced up, his eyes blazed with something raw and unguarded.

"Don't look at me like that," he said, his voice rough, almost desperate.

"Like what?"

"Like nothing else matters."

Her lips curled into a mischievous smirk as she stood, catching his mouth with hers in a heated kiss. Then she pressed her hands to his chest, guiding him back until he hit the bed.

"Nothing else matters," she murmured, her voice rich with promise.

His breath hitched as her shadows slid across his stomach, gripping the waistband of his boxers and tearing them apart with an audible rip.

"Repayment from earlier," she teased with a sly grin.

He chuckled, the sound low and dark, but stopped as she took off the rest of her clothes, her movements unhurried. She crawled up his body, her lips marking a path over his skin, every kiss a declaration.

When she straddled his lap, her hands explored his chest, her nails grazing along the firmness of his stomach. She let a single finger trace his length, her touch featherlight but enough to make him twitch and groan beneath her.

This was dangerous—the way his reactions made her feel. He had said he needed a distraction earlier, and now she understood completely. Nothing else existed outside of this, outside of them.

A flicker of nerves crept in, but she pushed through it. "I went to the healer for contraceptive magic last month. And I've been checked for illnesses—I'm clean."

"I was tested in college," he said, his voice low and husky. "And I haven't been with anyone since."

She shouldn't like that as much as she did, but it sent a thrill racing through her.

Leaning down, her lips brushed the edge of his ear as she whispered, "Good."

She felt slick and slippery as she ground against his hardness, her body aching for more.

"So, there's nothing stopping this from happening," she murmured, her voice teasing as she moved again, rolling her hips against him.

His hands gripped her waist in response, fingers squeezing and massaging as if steadying himself. A groan escaped her lips, and his grip tightened. "I guess not," he said, his voice strained.

She captured his lips as he slid against her entrance, the tease driving them both wild. He cursed softly against her mouth as she worked him in, every movement agonizingly hot and unbearably slow.

The room seemed to shrink around them, the air thick and electric, crackling with every measured thrust. His ragged breaths fanned against her neck, each one a reminder of just how much she unraveled him.

Her thighs began to tingle, the telltale pressure building low and insistent. She sat up abruptly, her nails dragging lightly along his chest as she fought to regain control, desperate to delay the orgasm that teased her from a distance.

"Too soon," she murmured, her voice trembling with both pleasure and frustration. She shifted slightly, adjusting the angle, her body humming with anticipation as she chased that perfect, dizzying edge without giving in just yet.

He sat up too, arms tightening around her waist like he couldn't stand the space between them. She didn't stop moving—pressing down hard before rising and falling in a rhythm that stole the breath from her lungs.

"You beautiful witch," he whispered against her lips, the words coming out like a reverent curse.

His hands roamed her body, firm and searching, gripping her ass, holding her as though he was terrified she might disappear. His mouth found her neck, his teeth nipping lightly before his tongue traced along her skin. When he captured her nipple in his mouth, she gasped, the sensation sending bolts of electricity through her.

It was too much—and yet she wanted more.

She felt like a wave ready to crash, wild and unyielding, against the jagged rocks that were Lochlan. His grip tightened, one hand on her ass as the other held her steady. His mouth stayed hot against her breast, and with a low, guttural growl, he thrust deeper into her, the angle making her cry out.

The pleasure was everywhere—on her skin, deep in her soul, a storm she couldn't control.

She tried to hold back, to make the moment last, but she was powerless against the pressure building inside her. Lochlan wasn't going to let her hold back, either.

"Let me have it, love." His breath was warm as his voice vibrated through her body. "Fall apart for me. Let me feel every piece of you."

His words undid her completely. She couldn't stop it—the orgasm tore through her like lightning, the intensity leaving her breathless and weightless. Lochlan caught her scream with his mouth, kissing her deeply as her body convulsed with pleasure, the connection between them heightening everything.

She floated somewhere beyond reality, lost in a magical space where nothing else existed but this moment, this man, and the fire burning between them.

Lochlan flipped her, his strength controlled as he pressed her firmly into the mattress. His fingers found her slippery heat, teasing and stroking and unrelenting, as if he held the power to command the rhythm of her pleasure. Each touch sent a jolt through her, reigniting and prolonging the blinding intensity of her climax.

She trembled beneath him, her body taut, caught in that unbearable edge between ecstasy and overstimulation. He groaned deeply as his own release overtook him, his body stiffening against hers, spilling into her with raw, unrestrained need.

A low, obscene curse escaped his lips, and she laughed—soft and breathless. Her body felt like it no longer belonged to her, and it was both thrilling and terrifying.

As the haze of their release ebbed, he leaned close, pressing soft, lingering kisses to her flushed skin. Between them, he murmured words—low, fervent, and unintelligible. She didn't need to understand them to feel their weight.

They were a mess—slick and tangled, her thighs damp with the evidence of their pleasure. It only made her want more, a temptation that left her aching to feel him again, though her eyes were heavy. Her breaths slowed, her body reluctantly sinking into the blissful exhaustion creeping over her.

A small, satisfied smile played across her lips as he kissed her face, her shoulders, her collarbone.

For now, nothing else mattered. Wrapped in Lochlan's arms, her skin still tingling and her body still humming, she let her eyes drift closed.

DIARY ENTRY
MY TWENTY-THIRD WINTER

I think we both knew the world was already shifting beneath our feet.

The question was whether we were brave enough to shift with it.

It began with whispered conversations at night, dreams and fears tangled with exhausted breaths and half-finished thoughts. I don't know when it changed from fleeting ideas to something real, but one day, I looked at him and realized he had already been building it—long before I ever spoke the words aloud.

A world where not only supernaturals would work together in harmony, but also one in which humans and supernaturals could exist together.

Not as conquerors and subjects. Not as hunters and prey. But as equals.

I have spent years running from the dark corners of my past, from the scars left by what the Videt once was. But today, I walked through the halls of what it is becoming. There were humans and witches working side by side, scholars and descendants of warriors shaping something new. And there he was, standing at the center of it all, watching his vision take root.

I stopped in the doorway, watching him as he spoke with a group of advisors. His expression was intense—so deeply focused that he didn't see me at first. But when he did, his face softened, just for a moment.

It struck me then, all at once.

I had been raised to believe that power meant control, that strength was measured in obedience and the ability to command it. But this? This was what true power looked like: not domination, but the ability to bring about change, coexistence, peace.

When I finally stepped forward, he met me halfway. He didn't ask if I was ready. He didn't need to. He already knew my answer. I had spent so long in the shadows. No one knew my name, my story—except him. He let me feel safe. Let me heal. Let me learn what life could be.

Now, I'll stand beside him and let them see me. Let them know that from darkness, light can rise. I'll do whatever it takes to make this dream real. Speak to those who are afraid. Listen to those who don't yet understand.

And whatever my wolf needs, I will give.

29

Lochlan

*"I accidentally married a wood devil—and now
I'm cursed. What do I do?"* —MESSY_IVY

Lochlan stepped into Becket's office just as a flurry of tarot cards flew past his head, smacking into the wall beside the door.

"Foul cards!" Becket cursed, throwing his hands up dramatically.

"You know, Beck," Lochlan said dryly, using Nia's shadow magic to gather the scattered deck. "The cards are just a conduit. It's not actually their fault."

Becket shot him a glare. "Don't start with me, you… you…" He trailed off, scanning Lochlan as if searching for the perfect insult, then pointed an accusatory finger. "You're getting some, you smug bastard!"

Lochlan froze. Heat crept up his neck as his memories betrayed him— Nia's breath against his skin, the way she'd looked at him, let him in. His stomach tightened, not just with want, but with something he wasn't ready to name. Something that felt too close. Too risky. Too easy to lose.

Becket's grin widened. "Oh, you are."

Lochlan rubbed a hand over his face, trying to will away the flush creeping across his skin. "Beck."

"No, no—don't Beck me." Becket leaned forward, all keen eyes and mischief. "You're blushing. I don't think I've ever seen you blush over a girl. This is fantastic."

Lochlan shook his head. "You need better hobbies."

"I disagree. This is exactly how I want to spend my afternoon."

Lochlan rolled his eyes, but the warmth lingered. It was too soon to examine or untangle everything that last night had shifted inside him— too soon to admit how deeply it was sinking in.

Which meant he needed to stop thinking about it. Now.

"Have you warded since the attack?" Lochlan asked, tapping his temple to indicate what he meant: The Sword invading Becket's mind. He wasn't ready for his father-in-law to hear about where he might be going.

Becket muttered something under his breath as he stood and headed for a shelf crowded with herbs and crystals. He grabbed what he needed and returned to his desk, creating a quick circle around it with deft, practiced movements. His words were low and steady as he threaded the spell together with ease.

Lochlan watched, a faint but familiar discontent settling over him. This kind of spell magic—fast and intuitive—was second nature to people like Becket and Nia. They'd grown up with it, woven it into the fabric of their lives without hesitation.

He hadn't.

His magic had always been slow, methodical: a tool for coaxing plants to thrive, for breathing life into paper worn thin with age. Even his work for the Videt relied on that care and patience—restoration spells, delicate repairs, unweaving damage without unraveling the past. But Nia's shadows came to him as naturally as breathing. It was as though something deep inside him had been waiting for the chance to bloom, and now emerged with startling speed.

Still, it wasn't like Becket or Nia, who seemed to wield their magic with intuition and ease—whether shadows, or seeing, or spell work. Lochlan didn't feel it in his bones. At least, not usually. Only when it mattered, he realized. Like that night in the Videt ballroom, surrounded by chaos: he'd acted quickly, intuitively and confidently—to help Nia.

His thoughts turned to his mother and sister. They had never made him feel that way, never needed his help, or helped him when he was in need. They'd cast him aside and made his life hell.

He thought of the day he was crowned prince. *His acknowledgment*— that was the phrase they had used, as if he hadn't existed before they'd chosen to take notice. The ceremony had been held in a grand hall before diplomats and carefully selected members of the public on his fourteenth birthday. His mother had placed the crown on his head, her hands stiff, her expression formal and unreadable.

Not once had she wished him a happy birthday.

Thane had been there, at least. His older brother had returned from a mission just for him, guiding him through what to expect, telling him he'd be there the whole time. And he was—until he wasn't. The moment the formalities had ended, he'd slipped away for another mission before the night was over.

That had left Lochlan alone in the ballroom, seated at the far end of the main table where, ironically, no one acknowledged him. No congratulations, no conversation, just the clatter of silverware and the low hum of voices speaking over or around him. His sister, Drusilla, had barely spared him a glance—until she got up to dance. As she passed, she'd bumped his chair hard enough to send his cup tipping forward, spilling juice down the stiff, uncomfortable suit he'd been forced into.

Minutes later, a palace worker had leaned down to whisper in his ear. "The queen has dismissed you. I will escort you back to your room."

Dismissed.

The rest of Lochlan's time in the castle had been just the same. His mother never spoke to him. Thane was never there. Drusilla was always cruel.

Yet here he was, considering going back.

Becket dropped into his chair, spinning it slightly before settling in. "Spill."

Lochlan leaned against the edge of the desk, arms crossed. "I don't know where to start."

Becket arched an eyebrow. "Oh, I don't know. Maybe start with how I had to hear about the catastrophe at the full moon celebration from the Stella Rune Gazette? The Gazette, Lochlan! They say you and Nia don't seem to work—terrible match, doomed for disaster. How your bad influence is why she couldn't do the spell." He smirked. "Yet, here you are, strolling into my office like you just bedded a goddess."

Lochlan *had* basically bedded a goddess.

The media's take didn't faze him—he was used to being picked apart, to them getting things wrong. Still, the idea that he'd been the reason Nia struggled with the spell sent a flicker of irritation through him.

"Nia and I have an… agreement." He cleared his throat. "But that's not why I'm here."

Becket leaned forward, eyes narrowing. "The plot thickens. And I'm guessing that's not the only thing that's been thickening."

Lochlan let out a reluctant chuckle, shaking his head. He exhaled, his humor fading as he met Becket's gaze. "Thane came to visit."

The smirk vanished from Becket's face. He cursed softly, leaning dangerously far back in his chair, the legs creaking under his weight.

"He asked me to come home," Lochlan said, his voice carefully even, masking the conflict swirling inside him.

Becket's jaw tightened, his usual teasing tone taking on a harsh edge. "That place is no home."

Becket had always been protective when it came to this topic. He'd been there during those early years of freedom, the drunken nights when Lochlan had finally let pieces of the truth slip out, the details of why he'd left, why he'd never looked back.

"Maybe things have changed," he said quietly, though the words felt hollow. "It's been eight years."

Becket didn't say anything. Lochlan could feel the weight of his gaze, but looked away. His own thoughts were enough to handle without trying to guess what Becket was thinking. The truth was, this wasn't the first time he'd let the idea of returning to Dover creep in. Watching Becket's family—loud, chaotic, full of love—had planted a seed. Lochlan's own father had been incredible but it had always been just the two of them. After he died, that sense of belonging had disappeared.

He hadn't realized just how deeply and fiercely he'd longed for family, community, people who were his, until he spent those school breaks surrounded by everything he'd never had. And now, the possibility dangled in front of him. If he didn't go back, he'd never know. If he did...

"Have you talked to Nia about this?" Becket asked, leaning forward in his chair.

"I told her some of the history," Lochlan replied. "And my brother's request."

"And the possibility of leaving?"

Lochlan looked away. He hadn't. He couldn't. The thought of telling her made his chest tighten.

Unless she'd go with him.

Becket sighed and pinched the bridge of his nose as if he'd heard Lochlan's thought. "Magic has to be hidden there," he said, his tone wary.

"Magic is hidden here," Lochlan shot back.

"Not like that." Becket's gaze hardened. "It's shunned there, Lochlan. Forbidden. It's thought of as dangerous and wrong. Here, we can use it. We've got places where we can actually be free. And you—" He hesitated. "You're finally using it. I've seen it."

Lochlan's gaze dropped to his lap. His fingers brushed against the ring Nia had given him, the token that was meant to ground and protect him, protect his life with her. Here.

"I don't want you to go," Becket said, quietly. "But maybe it's a good idea to get closure."

"Maybe," Lochlan murmured, though his voice lacked conviction and unease coiled in his stomach.

What would Nia say?

Wulfric's elderly assistant offered Lochlan a drink as he stepped into The Sword's office. He declined with a polite shake of his head.

Wulfric peered at him over his glasses, seated behind the imposing desk that dominated the room. A single sheet of paper was in his hand, its crisp edges catching the light as he glanced between it and Lochlan. His expression was unreadable. Silence stretched between them, tense and uncomfortable.

It was the opposite of how Lochlan had felt when they'd first met.

One of the older herbalists at the castle had told Lochlan about Stella Rune: a town where magic was everywhere but glamoured from humans.

His father had spoken of it once, wistfully, as a place he'd always wanted to see.

When Lochlan finally left Dover, desperate and alone, he'd followed that faint thread of hope. He applied for a groundskeeper job at the Videt, anything to stay afloat. Instead of handing him a rake, Wulfric handed him a lifeline: a scholarship to Videt Hall, the hidden school for the magical elite. Housing, food, tuition—all covered. It had reshaped his future and, at the time, felt like a miracle.

Now, Lochlan wasn't so sure.

Wulfric had once been his mentor, a guide for a lost witch trying to navigate a new world. But that same presence now felt more like a looming shadow.

Lochlan took a breath. "I stopped by the ballroom and offered my assistance with the cleanup."

Wulfric's lips twitched, though his gaze remained steady on the paper. "I appreciate that." Then, with a slight tilt of his head: "And where is the cause of the chaos?"

It wasn't spoken with anger or condemnation. In fact, there was something smug—maybe even proud—in his tone.

"She's at the Charis Foundation," Lochlan said evenly.

Wulfric nodded, his expression unreadable. "And why have you asked to speak with me?"

"I need to leave for Dover."

At that, Wulfric set the paper down and his face hardened. "For what purpose?"

Lochlan hesitated but pushed forward. "I have family business to attend to."

Wulfric's eyes narrowed. "Is my daughter going with you to that witch-hating cesspit?"

"I don't know." The words tasted bitter. "I haven't asked her yet."

Wulfric exhaled sharply, shaking his head. "I don't like how this distance bodes for my bargain." He folded his hands on the desk. "But, if it were up to me, I wouldn't let her go."

Lochlan nodded, careful to keep his expression unreadable. They had just one family dinner, one witch event, and a public appearance left. Three opportunities to convince Wulfric this marriage didn't work. Three chances to secure the annulment Nia wanted.

But did she really want it?

Lochlan exhaled slowly. That was the deal—prove this marriage was a mistake, and they'd be free. Wulfric had stacked the odds against them, forcing them into shared moments, into each other's space, hoping they'd fail at failing.

And Lochlan? He was failing spectacularly.

The autumn festival, the stolen moments, the way she had laughed, warm cider in hand, her fingers wrapped around his like she belonged there. Then the desk—her gasping beneath him, the sharp rip of fabric, and later, the sex. Fuck, the sex. He shouldn't be thinking about this. Not here. Not now. Not with Wulfric staring at him like he could see every filthy thought running through his head.

But Nia was consuming.

And did any of it mean she wanted to stay married to him? That she wanted him—more than she wanted to prove her father wrong?

He didn't know.

Lochlan had spent years believing Wulfric had taken an interest in him simply because he saw potential, because he'd cared. But the doubt that had been gnawing at Lochlan, the feeling something wasn't quite right, suddenly felt undeniable.

"I've studied the history of this town, of the Videt, and it states that there was an accident within the Cabot family, leaving you the new Sword."

Wulfric nodded. "A very bloody accident."

Lochlan had read the real accounts, the truth buried in that first diary he had repaired. The history books said there'd been a poisoning at a wedding, blamed on a grieving grandmother who couldn't bear what her family had become, and had died of natural causes a few days later. Wulfric hadn't drunk the wine, which left him the sole survivor—and the new Sword, with a new life and wife.

But that wasn't what had happened. Wulfric had killed them. All of them. To save Luna. And as far as he knew, they had never married.

"Nia doesn't know this."

It wasn't a question.

"No."

Frustration burned in Lochlan's gut. This man had saved Nia's mother from something horrific, had torn down a corrupt and coercive lineage and built something better in its place. But the official records barely scratched the surface. The truth—the messy, complicated truth—was locked in the pages Lochlan had pieced back together.

"You let her think the worst of you," Lochlan said, his voice tight.

"I did," Wulfric admitted. "If she left my protection, she needed to do so entirely on her own, as she has done. Any affiliation with me is a liability for her." He leaned back slightly, as if considering something. "I believed she needed to be entirely under my protection and supervision, or entirely outside and apart from it, if she was to be safe. But now I see how strong she is. How capable she has become. And I see a different path ahead."

One that required Lochlan and Nia to be married. Someone beloved by regulars and witches, someone with ties to human royalty.

Lochlan swallowed hard. "Was this your plan from the start?" His voice was calm, but a dangerous edge sharpened each word. "When you gave me that scholarship, were you grooming me for Nia?"

Wulfric studied him for a moment. "I offered you a chance to build something for yourself. You chose to take it."

Lochlan's hands curled into fists at his sides. "That's not an answer."

"Tell me, Lochlan—if you'd known where this road would lead, would you have chosen a different path?"

Of course he wouldn't have.

If Lochlan had never come to Stella Rune, never taken the Videt's offer, he wouldn't have met Becket. He wouldn't have found a passion for restoration. He wouldn't have met Nia.

Wulfric's lips curved into a small smile. "That's what I thought." After a beat, he said, almost idly, "You haven't told her yet, have you? About the diaries."

Lochlan's jaw clenched. "You told me not to." His voice was rough with something close to exhaustion. "Because you want to tell her the truth?"

"When the time is right."

Lochlan exhaled sharply. "Goddess help me, you're frustrating."

Wulfric chuckled. "Now, about Dover. How long will you be gone?"

"A week, I think."

"Three days."

Lochlan blinked. "I didn't realize this was up for discussion."

"If it wasn't up for discussion, you shouldn't have come here."

Lochlan exhaled slowly, steadying himself. "It's almost a full day there by train. How about I check in with you after day three?"

"Fine, fine," Wulfric said, waving him off.

Lochlan turned to leave, eager to put distance between himself and this conversation, but before he reached the door, Wulfric's voice caught him again.

"You don't need that place, Lochlan," he said, pointedly. "You don't need them. Blood doesn't make a family."

Lochlan swallowed hard. The words twisted something inside him. He'd spent years repeating this same thing to himself like a mantra. But now, with everything laid bare—Nia, the bargain, the doubts clawing at his ribs—he wasn't sure if Wulfric was offering him comfort, or tightening the chains he'd unwittingly walked into.

30

ℒochlan

"Long Train Ride? What to Bring."
—THE STELLA RUNE GAZETTE

The train station in Stella Rune exuded an otherworldly charm, with its wooden beams arcing gently over the platform and the glowing lanterns casting it all in warm light. Lochlan couldn't help drawing comparisons to the station he'd left behind all those years ago in Dover—cold, concrete, and unremarkable. This place, with its faint hum of glamoured magic, felt alive.

Soon he'd be leaving it to return to the world he'd once thought of as home.

Standing inside a phone booth tucked within the station, he traced his fingers over an old privacy rune carved into the wood. Its faint glow was barely noticeable, but its presence was a small reminder of the magic he now carried more easily, though still struggled to fully claim.

Movement caught his eye: deep red hair that glowed even under the station's dim lighting. Nia. She stood in the entrance, her gaze sweeping the room like a predator surveying its territory. She hadn't noticed him yet, and for a moment, he watched her.

Damn, she was beautiful.

He'd texted her to meet him here, and though she hadn't seen him, she moved with the confidence and purpose of someone who knew where she was going. As Nia passed the booth, he reached out on instinct, his fingers brushing hers in a fleeting touch that startled her to a stop.

Her laugh was soft, almost amused as he clasped her hand firmly, guiding her into the cramped space. She stepped closer, her green eyes sparkling with curiosity. "What is this?" she teased, her voice low and warm. "Hiding from someone?"

He shook his head, a faint smile tugging at the corner of his lips. Being in her presence made everything easier.

Her gaze dropped, catching on the duffle bag at his feet. The humor in her expression faded. "Oh," she murmured, the weight of realization thick in her voice. "I ask you to take up space, and this is what you do? Leave?"

Lochlan shifted uncomfortably, searching for the right words. "I need to go to Dover," he said quietly. "To figure some things out."

The silence that followed felt thick with things neither of them seemed ready to say. Nia pressed her lips into a thin line. Then, with a small nod, she lifted her chin in that practiced way that made her look untouchable.

"Okay," she said, her voice suddenly crisp, distant. "You go. I'll take care of Jade. And the ducks."

Lochlan blinked at her, caught off guard. "Really?"

"Of course." She stepped closer, running her hands up his chest before resting them at the back of his neck. Her fingers found his hair, twirling the strands in a slow, deliberate way that sent goosebumps racing down his spine.

"I, uh… I left some food in the fridge. For the next few days," he said, stumbling over the words.

"For the ducks?" she asked, one brow arching in challenge.

"For you."

Her answering smile was wicked. Dangerous.

"You know," she said, tugging his hair hard enough to make his breath hitch, "I managed to take care of myself just fine before you came along."

"And I bet the delivery drivers miss you." His grin widened as she rolled her eyes, the urge to kiss her nearly overwhelming. "And I'll be back as soon as I can."

"What about my father?" she asked suddenly, the question sharp enough to catch him off guard.

Lochlan hesitated. "I sent word to his office," he said carefully, avoiding her gaze.

Her eyes narrowed skeptically. "You sent word?"

"He seemed fine with it," Lochlan added, guilt twisting like a knife.

Before she could press further, a whistle cut through the moment, the announcement of the train's imminent departure echoing over the station intercom.

"Nia—"

Her kiss silenced him, soft and lingering and bittersweet. When she pulled back, her voice was steady, but her eyes betrayed a flicker of uncertainty.

"Hurry back, Loch. I'll be waiting."

Lochlan nodded, throat tight as he grabbed his bag. Turning toward the platform, he forced himself to move forward. He didn't dare look back—not yet. If he did, he wasn't sure he'd have the strength to keep going.

At last, he reached the train and climbed aboard, his legs stiff with hesitation. The doors slid shut behind him and he turned. Through the window, his gaze swept the platform and—

Nia burst out of the station lobby, her steps quick, her face unreadable.

She stopped at the platform's edge, her eyes darting across the windows as, just for a moment, her mask slipped. Raw, unguarded sadness flickered over her face, a stark contrast to her usual confidence as her gaze searched the train until—

Their eyes met.

In an instant, Nia pulled herself back together with practiced ease. She straightened, flicking her hair over her shoulder as her smirk returned, and with it a playful wink that sent a sharp ache through Lochlan's chest.

Why hadn't she offered to come with him? No, that wasn't fair. He hadn't given her the chance.

The real question was: why hadn't he asked her?

Lochlan's stomach tightened. The answer was tangled up with his doubts and unspoken fears. Maybe he hadn't wanted to burden her with the weight of his journey—or worse, maybe he wasn't ready to face what her presence might mean.

The train began to move, pulling him slowly away from her. Lochlan stood frozen, his hand braced against the train door, watching until she was a shadow in the distance. Only then did he turn and head toward his cabin.

Sliding the door open, he stopped short.

Echo—massive, his fur the color of coal—was sprawled across one seat, lifting its head to chuff at him with mild interest. Before Lochlan could process the sight, the tiny bathroom door creaked open and Thane stepped out, his expression smug and satisfied.

"Well, this is going to be a long ride," Lochlan muttered, tossing his duffle onto the luggage rack. His attention shifted to the dog. "Hey, old boy. You're looking good for your age." A small smile tugged at his lips. "Is Thane being mean? I bet he is."

The dog chuffed again, his tail giving a lazy thump against the seat.

Lochlan crouched to scratch behind Echo's ears. "Jade says hello."

He glanced toward his brother and caught Thane's smile.

Lochlan no longer felt the fury Thane had stoked by sneaking into his home and asking him to come back. The past day had dulled it, but amplified the gnawing questions of what he might miss or never have the chance to know if he didn't return. So, here he was, leaving behind a woman he wanted more than anything to see a family who'd never wanted him.

Goddess, it sounded stupid when he thought about it like that.

Maybe this whole trip was a mistake.

"It'll be great," Thane said, breaking the silence.

"Mind reading?" Lochlan lifted an eyebrow, straightening. "I didn't realize you were a witch, too."

Thane gave him a wink. "I don't need to be a witch to know you're already second-guessing. Or catastrophizing. But it really will be fine, little brother."

Lochlan dropped into his seat. "We'll see how right you are soon."

Thane didn't reply, his grin yielding to his usual stoicism as he leaned back in his seat.

Lochlan turned his gaze to the window. The countryside stretched out before him like a dream: rolling hills speckled with wildflowers shimmered in the evening light, and cliffs tumbled into sparkling blue waters. Magic clung to the landscape like a secret, subtle but undeniable.

The train plunged into a tunnel and the world outside disappeared, replaced by the low, steady pulse of motion that filled the cabin. Lochlan shifted in his seat, his thoughts wandering to Nia—the way her kiss had lingered, full of promise. Echo snuffed softly in his sleep, his tail twitching once before settling again. Thane sat with his arms crossed, his gaze distant.

Lochlan leaned back against the seat and closed his eyes. The rhythmic hum of the train filled his ears, a steady reminder of the journey ahead, and the growing distance between him and the world he'd left behind.

31

Lochlan

"A Prince for the Masses—Here Is What We Know."
—A PAGANS BLOG

A knock jolted Lochlan awake. Groggy, he blinked as Thane moved to the cabin door, sliding it open just enough to let the person on the other side speak.

"Fifteen minutes, Your Highness," a crisp voice announced.

Lochlan sat up, rolling the stiffness from his neck as his gaze drifted to the small window. The lush, magical scenery of Stella Rune was gone, replaced by gray lines of stone and steel. The city outside rose like a fortress, cold and imposing, its silhouette broken only by the gleam of a distant palace. Even the forest beyond the city seemed hostile, its trees clustered darkly, barring entry.

He turned his attention to his brother, who had shut the door with a quiet click and was now adjusting the stiff collar of a meticulously pressed uniform. It was a jarring contrast to the sweater and jeans Thane had worn earlier, his casual clothing replaced by polished boots and regalia that radiated authority.

"Who was at the door?" Lochlan asked, stifling a yawn.

"Royal guard," Thane replied, checking the watch on his wrist. "We've got fourteen minutes before they escort us to the palace."

Lochlan nodded absently, pushing himself up and stepping into the cramped bathroom. The dim light reflected a worn and wary version of himself. He splashed cold water on his face, hoping to wash away some of the fatigue and anxiety that clung to him.

As he wiped his face dry, his phone buzzed in his pocket. A news notification flashed across the screen. Lochlan swiped it away before he could process the words. The recent headlines were irritating, and he wasn't ready to face whatever was being said.

His chest tightened when he noticed two missed texts from Nia in the hours since he'd left. The first was a photo of Jade sprawled across his pillow, one paw flung dramatically over her face, the second a single sentence:

Nia

I think she misses you.

Lochlan stared at the screen longer than he meant to, his throat constricting. Did Nia miss him too? He smiled faintly, his thumb brushing over the screen as he typed.

Me

Good morning, love. Almost there.
I'll text you when I'm settled.

A second knock at the door forced him to pocket the phone. He steeled himself, bracing for the next chapter of this journey. As the train came to a halt, Lochlan moved to leave, but Thane stopped him with a hand on his arm.

"We have to wait for the guards."

A moment later, the door slid open, and a pair of royal guards stepped inside. Their polished uniforms and rigid movements made the cramped cabin feel even smaller. Lochlan followed Thane as they were escorted out in a formal procession.

A cold wind greeted them on the platform, a startling contrast to the warmth of the train. Beyond the train, a crowd of people were held back by barriers, their voices rising in a chaotic mix of cheers and shouts. Lochlan caught a glimpse of signs waving in the air, some too blurry to read, others loud and clear:

Marry me, Prince Thane!

Put a baby in me Prince Daddy!

Lochlan shook his head, suppressing a startled laugh as his brother smiled wide and waved to the crowd, his composure unshaken as the screams grew louder. The guards ushered them quickly into a waiting SUV. Lochlan settled into the seat, grateful the blacked-out windows muffled the chaos outside as the door shut behind him. Thane pulled out a sleek black tablet and began reading.

The drive to the palace was brief and uneventful, the SUV closely following the speeding escort cars. The scenery outside blurred past as they approached the imposing gates, where another crowd had gathered, their cheers barely audible from inside the vehicle. Instead of entering through the main gates, they were directed to a side entrance, shielded from prying eyes. The SUV rolled to a stop in front of a red-carpeted entryway.

As Lochlan stepped out, a man in a sleek suit—a palace attendant— approached briskly, clearly intent on taking charge. Before he could say a word, Thane stepped forward, his tone clipped and firm. "I'll handle it. Bring the bags to his room."

The attendant hesitated, flustered, but quickly obeyed, bowing slightly before signaling to other staff.

Lochlan adjusted his coat, his gaze drifting to the palace staff around them. Their stares were impossible to ignore, each one assessing, bowing slightly as he passed. It made his skin crawl. He couldn't help but wonder how Nia would react to all this pomp and formality. She'd probably roll her eyes and mutter a biting observation about ridiculous traditions. The thought brought on a small smile.

He missed her already.

Instead of leading him inside, Thane veered away from the castle entrance and staff and toward the palace wall, gesturing for Lochlan to follow as Echo trailed close behind. The hidden path at the back of the sprawling estate was unfamiliar, its narrow trail opening into a secluded garden Lochlan didn't recognize. Beyond it rose the massive greenhouse.

Flashes of memory surged, unbidden and raw: glass cracking in the sudden heat; the all-consuming desperation to save whatever he could; the blinding pain of burns and loss as Thane dragged him out.

Thane narrated details of the restoration process, gesturing to this part or that, but the words barely registered for Lochlan. He stepped through the doors, his gaze drawn to the large sequoia tree anchoring the space. At its base, faint vines of orchids clung stubbornly, their blooms vibrant against the rough bark.

Thane had told him the truth—it had grown back.

Herbalists wove among the plants, their movements purposeful and graceful, each step like part of a sacred dance. Their hands glowed faintly with magic, trailing soft golden light as they tended to leaves and stems with reverent care. The air was thick with the scent of earth and life— rich, loamy soil mingling with the crisp tang of herbs and the sweetness of blooming flowers. Around them, the greenery pulsed faintly, the plants responding to the touch of their caretakers.

Colors bloomed in vivid, almost dreamlike intensity: emerald leaves glittered with morning dew, and blossoms in shades of sapphire, ruby, and amber seemed to hum with their own quiet energy. It was a world alive and vibrant—a striking contrast to the cold stone of Dover.

Thane's voice cut through the haze. "Your father's work and greenhouse were too important to abandon. They just needed... protecting."

Lochlan moved deeper into the space, taking it all in. He should have felt something—pride, perhaps, or connection—but all he felt was an unexpected emptiness. The greenhouse was enchanting, but it felt foreign, now. Whatever spirit his father had imbued into this place, it was gone, and however lovely and magical a place it was, it felt like someone else's project now.

Thane, who had been subtly watching him, leaned in. "It's yours, if you want it."

The words should have stirred something in Lochlan, but he felt no desire, no draw to the place he'd once treasured above all others—instead he felt hollowed. His father's garden was gone. Though Thane had done the right thing in restoring the plants other witches would help thrive, none of it replaced or made right what Lochlan himself had lost.

Without a word, he turned and strode back the way they'd come, his pace brisk as he cut through the meticulously kept royal gardens. The pristine hedges and vibrant flower beds were beautiful, but they felt lifeless, devoid of the warmth he craved.

"Lochlan?" Thane rushed after him, his steps quick, his concern palpable. "What is it?"

He shook his head. Grief moved through him like a wave, harsh and flattening. He hadn't expected this. He hadn't expected to feel empty.

Then he saw her.

He hadn't anticipated running into Drusilla so soon after arriving. She stood to one side of the path, eyes glued to her phone, oblivious. He could slip away before she noticed. But courage—or maybe just stupidity—stirred inside him. He had come back for a reason, and he would see it through.

"Drusilla."

Her head snapped up, her gaze locking onto him like she was seeing a ghost.

Lochlan's magic stirred—not the herbalist magic that sought life, growth, and care, but the shadows. They crawled toward her, clawed at her. Not physically, not in a way anyone could see, but he felt the shadows coiling inside him, reaching and searching for something within his sister.

He shut them off, jolted by the power.

It wasn't just reflexive—it was aware. He hadn't fully understood the depth of what he shared with Nia until now. The shadows weren't just a tool to wield; they felt. They sought out pain, fed off it, connected him to it. And if he pushed harder, if he let himself sink into it, he suspected he could feel anyone's darkness.

Drusilla approached slowly, her lips curling into a predatory smirk.

That look—it was nothing like their mother's cold indifference. If he really considered her, she looked much more like her father. Lochlan and Thane could have passed for full brothers—they had their mother's deep skin tone, hair, and eyes, while Drusilla favored the late king with his fair skin and dark hair.

Drusilla reached Lochlan just as Thane caught up, breathless.

"Well, look who found the balls to show his face," she said, sharp as a blade. "The bastard whose very existence is causing the monarchy to crumble."

Thane scowled. "Drusilla, don't be so crass."

"No," Lochlan said evenly. "She isn't wrong. But she missed the part where it's our mother's fault. I'm just the evidence of her failures."

Drusilla's eyes darkened. "How dare you talk about the queen like that."

"She's never shown me an ounce of care or respect. Why do I owe the same to her?"

Drusilla stormed closer, ready for a fight, but Lochlan didn't flinch. He only tilted his head, measured, controlled. "Careful, Drusilla. We aren't children anymore. You wouldn't want your fans knowing how much of a bitch you actually are."

Her nostrils flared. "No one would believe a bastard."

Thane groaned, rubbing a hand over his face. His gaze flicked around the garden, as if wary of attracting curious eyes and ears. "For fuck's sake, stop it."

Lochlan barely heard him.

He had kept up with Drusilla over the years—not out of nostalgia, but morbid curiosity. The girl who had tormented him had grown into a woman the public adored. She played the role well, standing at the queen's side, exuding grace and charm: a picture-perfect princess, beloved by the people.

But Lochlan suspected there was more beneath the polished surface, cracks she fought to keep hidden. And now, as she stood before him, shaking with anger, her mask slipping, he felt it. The shadows thickened at the edges of his vision, responding to something deeper than thought. And this time, he didn't recoil. He let them reach for her.

The bright, manicured gardens seemed to grow darker, dimmer.

Then it hit him.

The sting of her loss: a sharp, aching grief that hollowed her chest. The anger curling inside her, desperate for an outlet. The betrayal, the way their mother's lies had unraveled, exposing secrets she'd never wanted to know.

It crashed into him like a wave—her pain bleeding into him and summoning his own.

He had buried his agony. Drusilla? She'd turned it into a weapon.

That wasn't an excuse.

She gasped, stumbling back. "What are you trying to do to me, you evil witch?"

"Evil?" Lochlan let out a cold laugh. "Drusilla, you set fire to an entire building. You bullied and tormented me for years. Why? Why did you hate me so much?"

"Because you're here!" she snapped. Her voice wavered though her rage did not. "Because the moment people found out about you, it ruined everything." Her hands curled into fists at her sides, trembling. "You're the reason we're about to lose everything, that the kingdom is on the brink of collapse. You're the reason my father is dead!"

Lochlan's breath caught.

"Oh, Drusilla," Thane murmured, his voice softer now, almost pitying. "Dad died because he was sick. You know his heart was weak. He'd had problems since he was a child."

"No, no," she whispered. "No! It was because of him!" Her wild gaze snapped back to Lochlan. "And when he died, I wanted you to lose something you loved as much as I loved him." Her breath shuddered. "Your precious greenhouse, full of witches."

Lochlan couldn't speak. He understood now. Drusilla was lost in her anger, trapped in it, controlled by it.

There would never be reconciliation with her.

"You could have killed someone," Thane said, his tone no longer soft. "You could have set the whole palace on fire."

Drusilla turned on him, her expression twisting. "Oh, now you care?"

she snapped. "You always take his side! But you couldn't, not if you'd cared about Dad the way I did."

Thane's jaw tightened. "You think I didn't care?" His voice was ice. "I'm the one trying to hold this kingdom together. I'm the one making sure it doesn't collapse under the weight of our family's mistakes." His gaze flicked between them, heavy with meaning. "And we need Lochlan—all of us—to show what a true family looks like."

Drusilla let out a bitter laugh. "We were never a family."

She turned and stalked off, the click of her heels echoing as she fled down the stone path.

Lochlan exhaled, tension coiled in his shoulders as he watched her disappear into the palace.

For a moment, Thane said nothing, his gaze distant.

"You asked me to come, told me things would be different," Lochlan pushed, his voice rising. "But clearly they aren't."

"They can be. Will be. I just…" Thane rubbed the back of his neck, his composure slipping. "I need time."

"Time for what?" Lochlan asked, crossing his arms.

Thane sighed and glanced at him, his voice steady but low. "The Ceremonial Commission of the Silver Guard is in two days."

"Goddess, that's a mouthful," Lochlan muttered dryly.

Thane gave him a pointed look but didn't take the bait. "It's a big deal. I need you there, by my side. The Silver Guard is the kingdom's elite battalion, sworn to protect its most sacred sites and the royal family. Every five years, we commission a new group of soldiers in a public ceremony. It's tradition—an important tradition. This year, we need to show the family is strong. United. Like we want the kingdom to be in their support of us."

Lochlan's eyes widened in disbelief. "And you want me to do what, exactly?"

"Just be there," Thane said, his tone pleading. "Stand with me. Smile. Wave. It'll be fine."

Lochlan shook his head, his laughter bitter. "You're asking me to pretend the last eight years didn't happen? That I wasn't driven away in the first place?"

Thane stepped closer and put a hand on his shoulder. Lochlan met his earnest gaze, seeing something there he hadn't expected—Thane didn't beg. But this was as close as Lochlan had seen him come.

"Please," Thane said quietly. "Don't do it for them. I need you there... for me. Because I'm trying to hold this together, and I'm running out of people I can trust. Out of moves. If you're not by my side, The Dover Coalition—and the public—will take it as another sign of our weakness. They'll move fast, using any perceived crack in our leadership, our unity, our family, as an excuse to remove any power we have."

The words hit Lochlan like a punch to the gut. A breath whooshed out of him as his mind churned. "I'll think about it," he muttered, his voice rough.

"Don't think too hard." Thane gave him a crooked smile before gesturing for Lochlan to follow. They walked in silence through the palace corridors, Thane was quiet, which was good, as Lochlan's thoughts swirled in a tangled mess.

Drusilla's fury still rang in his ears. He had expected her resentment, but not the depth of the emotions behind it, the way her grief bled into rage, rage to hate, how she'd blamed him for everything. And then there was Thane—standing between them, trying to bring together what had already and irreparably fallen apart.

When they reached the grand suite, Thane pushed open the doors, gesturing for him to step inside. "Try to get some rest," he said, gently.

Lochlan didn't answer. He stepped forward and heard the door click shut behind him. The suite was a masterpiece of opulence: polished wood, shimmering fabrics, and gold accents gleamed in the soft candlelight. But it felt stifling, a gilded cage rather than a retreat.

His gaze landed on the bed.

A sleek cat was curled up in the center of the plush covers, its fur a glossy obsidian. At the sound of his steps, the creature stretched languidly, its collar glinting with a small scroll. It wasn't like the other delivery cats from Stella Rune—this one was friendlier, purring loudly as it rubbed its head against his hand.

"Are you a better class of delivery beast?" he asked, his tone wry.

The cat chirped in agreement, its tail curling in satisfaction.

"Well, aren't you full of yourself," he murmured, gently untying the scroll from its collar.

The note was from Nia. Lochlan sat on the edge of the bed, letting her words sink in.

I know we can text, but I thought you might need a little magic from home. —N

Lochlan's chest tightened as he read it again and again.

Warmth spread through him, cutting through the cold detachment of the palace. The cat curled against his side, its presence a small, comforting piece of Stella Rune—of home—in a place that felt as far from that as possible.

32

Nia

*"I'm worried—there was a delivery brawl in
the town center. How will I get my food?"*
—MAGICALPOSTMATE45

Nia sat behind her desk at Charis. Afternoon sun streamed through the windows, catching on a dust mote parade, while Jade snored from an old armchair Nia had dragged into the light so the dog could sunbathe.

Her phone buzzed beneath a stack of donation receipts.

Mira

5 minutes out.

Me

I hope you have coffee.

Mira

Mira was an ex-mark turned friend. Years ago, Nia had tried to extort the witch, convinced she was running underground fights and selling black market potions tied to a string of deaths. But Mira hadn't been the culprit, just a daughter cleaning up her family's mess. As the new head of her community, Mira had begun quietly dismantling the criminal empire her mother left behind.

Now she was a donor. And, occasionally, a source of news and names. When Mira caught wind of terrible things planned or done, she passed along the intel and the identities of those responsible—marks for Nia to bother.

Normally, Nia made the ride out to Darkwood where Mira lived. She rarely came to Stella Rune unless she was checking on Salt, a club she owned in town. But the trip was three hours each way by motorcycle, and Nia hadn't felt great about leaving Jade alone for so long.

That morning, she'd texted Lochlan:

Me

Can Jade come to work
with me today?

Lochlan

Yes, you can take Jade. What did
you eat this morning?

Me

Coffee.

Lochlan

...and?

Me

Coffee.

Lochlan

I'm going to start hiding snacks in your purse.

Me

You're ridiculous.

Lochlan

Maybe. But I'm also serious. Let me take care of you.

She'd blushed the whole way to work. Even Jade chasing floating fairies through the morning light couldn't distract her.

Not because Lochlan had said anything explicit. But that quiet insistence, the certainty... it felt like he'd spoken the words into her skin.

Let me take care of you.

And he did. After they'd had sex for the first time, she'd drifted off. He must have gone downstairs, because when her bladder woke her, he was gone. When she came out of the bathroom, he was back—with food. A perfect, thoughtful plate: strawberries, cheese, crackers, chocolate. No questions. No big declarations. Just his warm, steady care.

And then he'd left for Dover.

Logically, Nia knew he had every right, and she trusted there was a good reason. But goddess, she hated it.

Her phone had buzzed again, just before she'd reached Charis.

Lochlan

Food will be waiting for you at work.

She'd shaken her head and muttered, "Utterly ridiculous." But her heart had still raced. And she'd found Joel waiting by the Charis door, holding a paper bag in one hand and a steaming coffee in the other.

Now, sipping from that same cup, Nia pulled a black notebook from her drawer. She flipped through the pages and scanned the latest names. Anything to distract from the fact that a text and a breakfast bag had her swooning like a teenager. Pathetic.

Hayden Sutherland - $100k Dover Community Foundation (for Housing) (Received)

Blake Rumi - $25k Charis (Received)

Jackson Runner - $85k Feeding Children, SR Pantry, SR Animal Shelter (Received)

Gregor Mcgruff - $45k Dover Repro-Health

Every recent mark was confirmed and received. Except Gregor. His payment had been due over a week ago.

She added a follow-up to her calendar for tomorrow. If he didn't respond, she'd leak the photos: proof of him setting fires, using his magic to commit arson for insurance payouts. It wouldn't just smear his name. It would drag down his husband, too, along with the tidy little empire they'd built in Fern. All those cozy, family-run establishments with their curated shopfronts whose business relied on wholesome reviews and glowing press.

Before she could finish writing "leak photos," Jade chuffed.

Nia looked up to see Mira standing in the doorway, two coffees in hand.

Nia grinned. "You're my favorite person."

"You say that to anyone with caffeine."

Nia stood, kissed her cheek, and took the coffee. "Still true. Who drove you?"

Mira tipped her chin toward the window, where Wren, her bodyguard, stood with his arms crossed and expression unreadable. Beside him was Glenda, a seventy-year-old wolven with no sense of personal space, openly admiring his biceps and tracing the tattoos curling down his forearm.

Nia laughed and dropped back into her chair as Mira took the one across from her.

"Thanks for meeting me here. I've been a bit busy..." Nia trailed off, fidgeting with the ring on her finger.

Mira's hazel eyes shifted to Jade, stretched out like royalty on her chair by the window. "And you have a new child."

"She's not mine," Nia said quickly. "She's—"

"Your husband's."

Nia flushed. Mira blinked slowly, then smirked.

"You didn't come to hear about that," Nia said, clearing her throat and straightening a stack of papers.

"No," Mira said. "But I'd like to."

Nia pretended not to hear. "You said you had someone for me?"

"Mr. Bell hasn't been very kind. To his wife, or the environment." Mira handed her an envelope.

Nia opened it. Inside were club photos, a hotel receipt, and a zoning notice clipped from a Dunlowe paper.

"He was at Ember last week," Mira said. "Got drunk, got handsy, and got loud. I caught enough to piece together his little project—an industrial build north of here. If it goes through, runoff cuts straight through unprotected forest and hits the ocean."

Nia flipped to the next photo: Bell with someone who was very much not his wife.

"He's been to Salt a few times, too," Mira added. "Word is he'll be back there tomorrow night."

"Reg or sup?"

"Reg."

Nia nodded. Regulars had a way of being drawn to magic, always chasing the feeling that anything was possible, without knowing what it really was.

"You did all the work for me," she said, closing the envelope and adding Raymond Bell to her black notebook before snapping it shut. "This'll be boring."

"It was easy." Mira shrugged. "But you get to pick the amount. Where he donates. And you get to see the look on his face."

Her smile sharpened. "Speaking of donations, I've come into some… funds."

Mira took a sip of her coffee. Nia didn't ask. When Mira had extra cash, it usually meant someone worse didn't.

"I need a place to unload it," Mira went on casually.

Nia drummed her fingers along the edge of the desk, her gaze drifting to the page she'd been doodling on earlier.

Manor of Magic

House of Comfort

House for Witches

Place for Wayward Souls

"How fast do you need to unload it?" Nia asked.

"I have time. Why?"

"Ivy and I are working on something… big," Nia said. "And we could use the support."

"Legal or illegal?"

Nia tilted her head. "Legal. And it'll help young supernaturals."

Mira's eyes widened, her face brightening. "I'll support whatever you and that chaos witch are up to."

The front door slammed open.

"Is Mira here!?"

Ivy barreled in, all blonde hair, bright colors, and no brakes. Mira stood, arms already open.

"I haven't seen you in forever," Ivy said, voice muffled against the witch's shoulder.

"You were at my club a month ago," Mira said. "Got on stage with that vibrating broomstick and corset? Half the room forgot how to breathe. You got a standing ovation, at least from those who weren't too horny to join in."

Ivy giggled, blushing hard. But then her eyes landed on the sun-soaked armchair and its occupant.

"Oh my goodness, is this Jade?" she squealed, moving cautiously closer, like she was approaching a unicorn grazing in the wild.

The dog perked up, tail thumping wildly before she launched herself at Ivy.

They both went down in a tangle of limbs and laughter.

Nia shook her head, smiling.

Mira chuckled and glanced out the window. Her bodyguard, Wren, was now surrounded by four elderly women, one of whom was trying to feed him spice cake.

"I should go," Mira said. "I'm checking in on Salt, then heading back to Darkwood. Text me when you have more details about your project?"

"Will do."

They saluted each other, half-serious.

Mira turned toward the door, then paused. "You have a delivery."

Nia blinked. "What?"

She followed Mira into the front room and found Becket standing there with two large boxes in his arms and sweat dotting his brow.

"Becket? Put those down."

Mira slipped past him and out the front door, presumably to rescue Wren from his admirers.

Nia looked Becket up and down. "What are you doing?"

"Hello to you too," he said, smiling faintly. "These are the leftover jars, volunteer vests, and a bunch of other things from the harvest."

"Oh." Nia eyed the boxes. "I thought Ivy was handling that. With Todd from the food pantry?"

Becket just smiled.

Nia narrowed her eyes.

Ivy appeared a second later, hands flying. "Oh, sorry, Beck! Those go in the back."

Becket followed her down the hall without hesitation.

Nia watched them go, her brow relaxing. She knew they'd hung out a few times since the autumn festival. But what did that mean? Ivy was supposed to be taking a break from dating, and Becket didn't exactly seem like the dating type.

Maybe they were just friends. Maybe.

She was still suspicious.

"We're grabbing a late lunch," Ivy said. "Want to come?"

"I have Jade," Nia replied.

"We're going to Drift," Becket added. "They're dog-friendly. She's been there before."

At the sound of her name, Jade came bounding out from the back, tail wagging as she nudged up against Becket like he was her long-lost best friend.

Nia laughed at the dog. "I guess that's decided. But let me check in with your daddy."

Ivy grinned. "Oh, do you call Lochlan that?"

"If she did," Becket said, deadpan, "the poor man would combust."

Nia waved them off as she ducked into her office and grabbed her phone.

Me

Thinking of chaperoning
Ivy and Becket at Drift.
Can Jade and I join?

She glanced at her desk with a nagging sense that she was forgetting something. Before she could place it, her phone buzzed.

Lochlan

I don't think chaperoning would've worked for us.

She rolled her eyes, already smiling when the next message came in.

Lochlan

Yes. But don't let Jade eat too many hush puppies. I miss you, love.

Her face warmed.

Whatever she'd been about to do was lost to the flush of pleasure and comfort that washed over her with Lochlan's *love*.

Drift was the kind of quiet that carried charm. Heating spells kept the ocean wind at bay, and the place smelled like salt and coastal comfort food.

Nia hadn't been here often. Its proximity to the Videt made it inconvenient—too easy to run into Wulfric.

As if thinking his name had summoned the darkness, her father rounded the corner, flanked by two guards and a fae man she didn't recognize.

"Pyronia," he said, sounding almost pleased.

"Well," Nia muttered, "there goes my appetite."

Wulfric smiled and glanced over her companions. "Hello. I've never met your friends before."

"Probably," Nia said, "because I wasn't allowed to have any."

Her father ignored this, of course, and extended a hand to Becket, who took it without hesitation.

"It's an honor, sir. I'm Becket—but you already knew that."

"My apologies for the intrusion," Wulfric said. "I needed to ensure my daughter remained married."

"Of course," Becket replied. Then the witch actually bowed.

Nia rolled her eyes.

Wulfric turned to Ivy, who was openly glaring at the most powerful supernatural alive.

"You must be Ivy," he said, smiling. "The other half of Charis and a brilliant witch."

Ivy crossed her arms. Jade growled low from under the table.

Wulfric withdrew his hand, unfazed. "I shall leave you to enjoy your afternoon."

Nia stared after her father, the weight of his presence lingering long after he'd gone.

Once, she'd loved him fiercely. She used to race into his study, shadow magic curling around her fingertips, eager to show off the newest trick she'd mastered. He would lift her into a spin and tell her she was perfect, how he loved to see her mother's legacy live and burn through her.

He had hired the best tutors. Bought every charm and ward the experts recommended. She was the perfect witch to wield such a gift, and he'd made sure she knew it. Magic didn't always pass from parent to child: it could come from any ancestor. But her mother's power had chosen her.

"You know," Ivy said, "your dad's kind of hot."

Nia groaned. "Ivvyyy."

"What?" Ivy grinned. "I can dislike the man and still think he's nice to look at."

"Why do you dislike him?" Becket asked.

Ivy lifted her piña colada and took a sip. "One, because he was a horrible dad."

Nia sighed.

"And two," Ivy continued, "he denied my application to Videt Hall."

Becket blinked. "What? Why?"

"Probably because I was a gutter rat—"

"Ivy!"

"What?" Ivy shrugged. "It's true. I didn't have the best grades, and I came from the system. But my test scores were great. Still wasn't enough."

"You are definitely enough," Becket said quietly.

Ivy grinned and punched him in the shoulder. "You're such a good friend."

Nia smiled. Good. Just friends. It was nice to see Ivy keeping that promise to focus on herself for once.

"If you'd gotten into Videt Hall," Nia said, "we'd never have met."

"True," Ivy said.

A server dropped off bread for the table and a small plate of hush puppies for Jade.

Nia snapped a photo and sent it to Lochlan.

Last night, she had rummaged through his clothes and found one of his old college shirts. It was recently worn, soft and threadbare. The shirt was almost comically large on her, but it smelled like him: pine and soap and something warm she couldn't name. She'd worn it to bed like some kind of sad wife whose husband had been gone for years at sea, not for a couple of nights in a cushy castle.

She'd almost taken a picture of herself in the shirt. But they had only slept together once, and it didn't feel like they'd reached sexy photo-sending territory yet.

Still. She'd wanted to.

Nia wondered what he was doing in Dover.

"So, you two met in college?" Becket asked.

"Yep!" Ivy said brightly. "What about you and Lochlan?"

Becket hesitated, his shoulders tightening slightly. "The same. We met at Videt Hall."

Ivy leaned in. "It's okay. You guys deserved it. And look at you now."

Nia barely heard them. She was watching her phone. Waiting. Lochlan didn't text back.

Maybe he was busy. Caught up in whatever power games his brother needed him for. Maybe there were deals to make, alliances to manage, the kind of work he couldn't tell her about. Or maybe his horrible sister had—

"How's our witch?" Becket asked pointedly.

"What?" Nia blinked. "Lochlan?"

Becket raised an eyebrow.

She coughed and grabbed her margarita. "I'm not sure. He usually just asks about Jade."

"Right…" Ivy dragged the word out with a smirk.

"You're among friends," Becket said. "Spill. Are you sad? Do you miss him?"

"It's been two nights."

"But who's counting?" Ivy grinned. "Why'd he go back again?"

"His dumb big brother talked him into it," Becket said.

"Ooh. Family drama?"

"So much family drama." He sounded genuinely aggrieved.

Nia looked back at her phone one more time. She hoped Lochlan was okay. And if he wasn't—well, she might just head to Dover and kick someone's ass.

33

Lochlan

"Prince Lochlan Returns Home—But Where Is His Wife?"—THE DOVER CENTENNIAL

The corridor was as still as a crypt. Even Lochlan's own footsteps felt intrusive, their echoes ricocheting down the yawning halls lit by high, arched windows. His shadow stretched long and distorted across the stone floors, as if reaching futilely for something it could never quite grasp.

This wing of the palace had once felt alive—a hive of constant movement and peaceful purpose. He could almost hear the distant chatter of staff, the soft swish of skirts, the hurried click of heels, and the subtle hum of hidden magic woven through the mundane tasks of running a royal household.

Now, it was all silence and shadows.

Only certain staff had the privilege of wielding magic openly—those like his father, whose gifts healed or created things too beautiful to be denied. Others worked in silence, their talents whispered about but never acknowledged. In the kingdom's earlier years, magic had been celebrated and, later, weaponized as witches forged tools of war and walked beside kings.

But with the rise of technology, magic had been set aside. Not banned, but quietly pushed out. The royal bloodline held no magic, and what they couldn't control, they feared. Across the kingdom, supernaturals had been taught to suppress or hide their gifts, and to pass as regulars.

Stella Rune was a rare sanctuary, where the Videt protected what others had chosen to forget. Magic was freedom—wild, boundless, infinite. Lochlan had learned that in Stella Rune, and Nia reminded him of it every day.

He didn't know what he was searching for in the abandoned wing, only that he'd followed the pull of old memories and found desolation instead of consolation. This place had once been his sanctuary, the home he'd shared with his father and others like them.

Now, it felt empty.

Just like the greenhouse.

But it wasn't just here, Lochlan realized, that hardly anyone roamed the halls—it was the entire palace. He'd noticed but hadn't thought about it earlier: fewer staff, fewer guards. Evidence of the slow erosion of funds, presence and function, as though slow rot spread throughout the palace itself.

Lochlan's stomach twisted. This place hadn't evolved; it had been left behind. And he wasn't sure what he hoped to find—or what Thane hoped bringing him back would change. He began to think there was nothing left for him to discover, or revive, nothing to rebuild. Like a tree rotted from the inside out, the palace wasn't just lifeless; it was hollow.

But for Thane, he would stay, at least for a little while. He'd seen the crack in his brother's resolve, that fleeting moment of vulnerability, and it lingered in his mind.

On his way back to his room, Lochlan caught the faint murmur of voices carrying down the corridor. Light spilled from the narrow crack of a door left ajar, flickering across the otherwise dim hall. Against his better judgment, he stepped closer, keeping to the shadows.

"Now that Prince Lochlan is home, we should arrange a public outing," a clipped, officious voice said. Lochlan recognized it immediately even after all this time—the palace advisor, Malrik. "Something philanthropic to get him out in the open. The people will eat it up."

"I have asked him to attend the Silver Guard Ceremony," Thane said.

A derisive scoff followed. Lochlan tensed. It had been years since he'd heard her voice, but even by this small sound he recognized his mother.

"I don't see how he could change anything," Queen Lavinia said, her voice cool and cutting.

Malrik went on, undeterred. "Things are different now. The public loves a prince. And I think they will love him."

"Why should they? And why should we want him here?" Lavinia snapped. "He left us. I don't see what good it would do to parade him around. It solves none of your problems."

Thane didn't raise his voice, but still commanded the room. "The Dover Coalition needs to see we're a strong family. Lochlan being here shows them they're wrong about us. The people—" He paused, just for a moment. "—I know how much they love a prince. Two will only help. And the fact that he's a witch? That certainly won't hurt."

"We can't say that publicly," Lavinia hissed. "You know that."

"No," Thane agreed. "But his community already knows. They're watching, and some may even come out in support. The supernaturals still wield power and influence, in more ways than even we are aware. That influence and support could help us."

Drusilla's voice sharpened. "I won't stand and smile next to that vile piece of—"

Lochlan had heard enough.

His pulse hammered in his ears as he threw the door open and stepped into the chamber.

The room was bathed in golden candlelight, soft and flickering against the high stone walls. A fire burned low in the hearth, filling the space with a quiet warmth at odds with the tenor of the conversation. Malrik—a thin, sharp-looking man—stiffened at the intrusion. Thane, standing near the queen's chair, looked wary.

But it was his mother who caught Lochlan's attention.

Queen Lavinia sat poised, dressed in rich midnight silks, her crown resting lightly against her dark hair. She looked at him with cool, assessing eyes, as if truly seeing him for the first time.

Lochlan met her gaze. "I'm not here to solve your problems."

"Lochlan—" Thane began.

But Lochlan cut him off. "If my presence helps, fine. But that's not why I came."

Lavinia stared at him, her expression unreadable, though her posture shifted almost imperceptibly. She waved a hand. "Leave us."

Drusilla left quickly, glaring at Lochlan as she did. The advisor hesitated, but at a pointed look from the queen, he bowed and slipped out. Thane followed, but not before squeezing Lochlan's shoulder in silent reassurance.

Then it was just the two of them.

For a long moment, neither spoke.

Finally, Lavinia sighed, the sound thoughtful. "You remind me of Galan."

The words hit him harder than he expected. Galan—his father. A name he hadn't heard spoken in years.

"But I look like you," Lochlan said cautiously.

"Yes." A pause. "But you are like your father. Kind. Calm."

An incredulous laugh escaped him before he could stop it. "What the fuck is this?" His voice was harsh and edged with disbelief. "You've never said anything like this before."

Lavinia's lips thinned. She tilted her head slightly. "You came here for closure."

Lochlan hesitated. "I came to see if there was anything here for me."

"There isn't," she said simply. "Not within these walls, at least."

He clenched his jaw.

Her gaze didn't waver. "Tell me what you want, Lochlan."

He studied her, searching for—he didn't know what. Maybe he never had. But he did want to know—

"Did you ever care about my father?" He hesitated. "About me?"

Something flickered in her eyes, but it was gone before he could name it. When she spoke, her voice was measured, quiet.

"I have always been bound by duty," she said. "It was in my blood. In everything around me. But I rebelled in the only ways I knew how. I sought distraction—wherever I could find it. In the city, hidden behind a disguise. In the unseen corners of this castle. With Galan."

Lochlan swallowed, his throat tight. "And me?"

She let out a slow breath. "You were proof I couldn't run free."

His stomach twisted, but he said nothing.

"I could be queen and still have my freedom—until you became real. Until you were undeniably your father's son. And so I hid you." Her tone was even, but there was something beneath it, raw and worn thin with time. "I tried. I tried to act as if it never happened, tried to be a good queen, a good wife, a good mother to the children my husband gave me."

Silence stretched between them, thick with unspoken things.

Then, finally: "I grieved when your father died. And you... were a reminder of what I had lost. Of what I couldn't have." She lifted her chin slightly, her voice unwavering. "I cannot change how I feel or undo what

I've done. But you can learn from my mistakes. Live the life you want, Lochlan. Not the one others have told you to live."

Lochlan exhaled slowly, tension leaving his shoulders in a rush.

This was the most she had ever said to him, the most honesty she had ever given. And while it wasn't enough—it would never be enough—at least it was real.

"I don't care for you as I should," she finally admitted. "That is a reflection of my choices and the way I have chosen to fulfill my duty, but it is not a reflection on you."

Lochlan didn't reply right away. He should be furious. But, once again, all he felt was empty. Maybe that was his answer: there really was nothing left for him here.

But Thane had seemed so desperate, so sure Lochlan could help.

"And what about Thane?" He ran a hand through his hair. "What about the kingdom?"

His mother studied him for a long moment before answering. "Thane is bound by duty and always has been. He will never stop trying to do what he believes is right." A faint pause. "And he is right that the people will love you. But I do not believe anything you or he does now will be enough to turn the tide. Too many mistakes were made over the centuries. The monarchy neglected our outer provinces. Ignored calls for reform. Hoarded resources while others went without. We ruled as if loyalty was owed, not earned. The doubt and distrust my infidelity brought forth? That was merely the nail in the coffin."

Lochlan frowned. "And if the kingdom falls?"

"It won't fall—not truly," she said, her voice quiet but firm. "We may lose much of our remaining power, but we will still be royalty by blood."

He narrowed his eyes. "Then why not step down graciously, on your own terms?"

Her lips curved into something that wasn't quite a smile. "Speak with your brother about that."

Lavinia rose, the candlelight casting long shadows over her sharp features. Lochlan wasn't sure what he saw in her expression—regret, finality, or something else entirely.

"You've changed since you left here. You're stronger, now. I was concerned about your hasty marriage, but…"

"Because I married a witch?"

She shook her head.

"I don't believe I have anything to worry about. Good luck with the ceremony tomorrow," she said, smoothing the folds of her gown. "And good luck with your life, Lochlan."

She hesitated, just for a breath. Then, softer, almost too quiet to catch— "Your father would be proud."

Lochlan didn't know what to say to that.

So he said nothing at all.

And as she walked away, he realized this was all the closure he would get. Not the kind that made amends or paved the way to the relationships and love he'd hoped for and craved.

But the kind that would finally allow him to leave Dover behind for good.

34

Lochlan

"A Long-Awaited Heir - Welcome Home Prince Lochlan!" –THE DOVER CENTENNIAL

Lochlan woke to a soft purr. His gaze fell to the sleek black cat curled against his side, its small frame rising and falling in steady rhythm, warm against the cool morning air. He exhaled slowly, letting the animal's peaceful slumber soothe him.

He had slept restlessly.

His mother's words still lingered in his mind. *Live the life you want, Lochlan.*

What did he want? He had an answer now, but this didn't make saying it any easier.

A faint glint of light caught his eye: a scroll tucked neatly into the cat's collar. With tired fingers, Lochlan untied the parchment. His chest tightened as he scanned the familiar, bold handwriting:

Loch,

If I didn't miss you so much, I'd tell you
to take your time, just to prove I could be less
dependent on you. But alas, I have a confession.
I tried to heat up the food you left. And I
ruined it. Completely. Utterly. The disaster was
so bad I had to throw the pan away.

That's why I had coffee for breakfast. So thank
you for sending food to the office. I've only had
takeout since. The delivery people no longer need
to worry about going out of business.

I sound ridiculous, don't I? But I'm blaming you.

Come home soon. —N

P.S. I read to the ducks and gave them snacks.
They like me better than you now.

Lochlan read it twice. Then again. Nia's humor made him smile, but it was the vulnerability—the quiet confession beneath the teasing—that was a balm to the raw and ragged edges of his emotions. He reached out and ran a hand over the cat's soft fur. The creature leaned into his touch with a low, contented purr, and he allowed the small, grounding moment to steady him.

A knock broke the peaceful moment. A palace attendant opened the door and entered a moment later, carrying a perfectly pressed suit.

"It's time to prepare for the ceremony, Your Highness."

Lochlan swallowed hard. He had never been comfortable with titles. *Prince* had always felt borrowed, like it belonged to someone else and might be taken back at any moment. But today he would try and own it. He would stand beside Thane, who'd never asked him for anything before, and do what he could to support him. Not because he expected it would make any difference to the kingdom, but because—prince or not—he was Lochlan's brother.

"I'll be ready."

The forecourt of the palace brimmed with tradition: rows of soldiers in formal dress, green and gold banners overhead, and the steady beat of a slow march echoing across the court. Lochlan stood beside Thane, the morning sun casting long shadows across the freshly polished stone. On Thane's other side, Echo sat tall and alert, the massive dog as much a sentinel as any of the soldiers before them.

A new regiment stood in crisp formation, freshly sworn into service. On the grand balcony overlooking the proceedings from above, Queen Lavinia and Drusilla watched impassively.

Thane stepped forward, his uniform pristine and presence commanding. Lochlan had always admired that about his brother—his ability to slip so easily into the role of the prince, the warrior, the future king.

A hush settled over the gathered crowd as Thane began to speak.

"Our kingdom is built on the foundation of those who came before us," he began, his voice carrying through the courtyard. "For centuries, my family has ruled, not only by blood, but by duty."

A well-placed pause. Lochlan saw it coming before it happened—the moment Thane made the speech personal.

"My father served in these very ranks. So did I." His gaze swept over the soldiers before him. "I stood where you stand now. I trained beside those who have carried the weight of this kingdom's safety on their shoulders. And in doing so, I learned that strength is more than battle, that leadership is more than issuing commands."

He let the words settle, then added, "The true test of a soldier is not in how they fight—but in how they protect."

A murmur of agreement rippled through the audience. Thane was good at this, the delicate dance of appealing to tradition while asserting his own principles. He continued, touching on the changes in warfare, on how this new generation of soldiers might not see battle in the same way their predecessors had, but their role was no less vital.

"Weapons evolve. Strategies change. But courage, duty, and heart still define us."

Lochlan found himself proud. For all the distance and resentment, and despite their bitter history, the monarchy and the kingdom they ruled still mattered to Lochlan. Their role, this place, was tied to history, to a legacy that was greater than any one person, and would endure in one way or another, whatever changes were on the horizon.

But this wasn't Lochlan's place or role. His duty lay in Stella Rune, with the Videt, with the archives, with Wulfric.

With Nia.

He just had to find a way to tell Thane.

Lochlan knew Wulfric would want him to maintain his ties here, to keep one foot in this world even as he built his life in another. And he would, in his own way, but from a distance.

Thane finished his speech to resounding applause, the soldiers standing at attention, the gathered nobility murmuring their approval. Lochlan let his gaze drift over the crowd, half-expecting to see nothing but a blur of faces and stiff courtiers.

Instead, he saw signs held high. Some bore Thane's name. Others his own.

Lochlan blinked.

Lochlan for King (of My Bed)

Lochlan & Thane, marry me and my sister!

Oh, for fuck's sake.

He wished Nia were here to see the sheer absurdity of it. As Thane shook hands and posed for photos, Lochlan pulled out his phone and snapped a quick picture of the crowd. The moment he did, people erupted into cheers.

Thane caught sight of it, let out a laugh, and promptly swiped Lochlan's phone. Before Lochlan could protest, his brother slung an arm around his shoulders, grinning wide as he angled the camera for a selfie. The crowd behind them went wild, their cheers doubling as Thane snapped a few shots.

With a final wave to the enthusiastic spectators, Thane passed the phone back, clapping Lochlan on the back before they were both swiftly ushered away by Malrik through the palace doors and into a private parlor. Echo padded in behind them, his nails clicking softly against the marble floor as he took his place at Thane's side.

Thane poured them each a glass of water and handed one to Lochlan. "Did you see that crowd? It's the biggest we've seen in years."

"What did you do to make them come?" Lochlan asked, raising a brow at the palace advisor.

"Me?" Malrik sipped his water, looking almost amused. "That was all you."

"Not a chance," Lochlan chuckled, shaking his head.

Thane only smiled. Malrik flipped open his tablet, tapped a few times, then turned the bright screen toward Lochlan.

"Prince Lochlan Returns Home, but Where Is His Wife?"

"Prince Lochlan Seen Volunteering for Those Less Fortunate." The accompanying photos showed him at the Stella Rune harvest.

"Prince Lochlan's Wife—What We Know."

His name filled the headlines, an endless scroll of speculation and gossip, despite the fact that he had only been here for three days.

"People know I'm married," Lochlan huffed. "What's with the signs?"

"It's not about facts; it's about fantasy." Malrik shrugged. "They know you're married, but they don't care. Thane isn't in a relationship, but the moment he so much as looks at someone, the papers are ready to print wedding announcements."

Lochlan frowned. "I didn't realize... they really care about what we're doing?"

Thane and Malrik exchanged a look.

"Yes," Malrik said plainly.

Had Wulfric known this would happen? Had he foreseen that Lochlan, of all people, would have some sort of pull? Wulfric's plans had always been far grander than the marriage he had forced upon Lochlan and Nia. That much had been clear from the start. But the true scope of those plans was only now beginning to reveal itself through the diaries Lochlan had painstakingly restored.

How Wulfric had reshaped their world. How he had rejected the notion that magic should rule. How he had built a system to protect humans—one that, in time, sought coexistence, not dominance. And now, somehow, Lochlan was entwined in that vision. Did Wulfric hope he would be the bridge between the magical world and the human one?

Could he be?

Lochlan suddenly felt an urgent, pressing need to get home—to keep building his relationship with Nia. To fix the remaining diaries. To find the rest of the pieces that would let him see the whole puzzle and how he and Nia fit into it.

"I have to go."

He pushed past them without another word, his mind set. Thane caught up only when they reached Lochlan's room. The black messenger cat stretched lazily on the bed, yawning a greeting.

"You're leaving?" Thane asked as he stepped inside. His brows pulled together. "And—how did a cat get in here?"

Lochlan barely glanced up as he scribbled a note, tied it to the cat's collar, and scratched behind its ears. "Take this to Nia."

The cat chirped and vanished into the shadows. Echo lunged after it, but a loud thump followed, and the dog spun in circles, searching for a feline that was already long gone.

"I have to get home," Lochlan muttered, shoving clothes into his bag.

Thane shook his head, no longer watching his dog. "*This* is your home."

"No. Stella Rune is my home. Nia is my home. And I need to get back to them."

"Look, I'm sorry about our mother," Thane's expression tightened, his stance bracing for a fight. "And I can never make right what Drusilla did—"

"Thane, stop." Lochlan turned to face him. "You never have to account for or make up for what either of them did. You saved my life—goddess, take more credit for the things you do." He took a steadying breath. "But this isn't about them. It's about me, and Nia, and the world we live in, and… so much more. I will be what I can for you. And for the kingdom, if it comes to it. But Nia, the people like us in Stella Rune, in the home I've found and built, they have to come first for me."

Thane searched Lochlan's face, his jaw tight. Then he sighed and rubbed the back of his neck. "I don't get it. But I get it." A pause. "There's a convening in a little over a week with leaders of the government and representatives of the opposition. If we work together, I think we can turn the tide—come to a compromise that still preserves the legacy our forebearers built, and push back against those trying to end our rule."

Lochlan hesitated. "I'll see what I can do."

"Lochlan?" Thane's voice was soft. "I don't want you to leave. I… I feel alone in this fight."

Lochlan pulled his brother into a hug, tight and too short, before stepping back. "I will always be your brother. But this isn't where I belong, Thane. And I think we both know it."

Without waiting for a reply, he turned and strode out, his steps steady as he descended the staircase. This—returning to Nia, to Stella Rune, to the diaries that might help guide his path—was the only thing that felt right.

The only pain he felt was for Thane.

35

Nia

"The Unwanted Heir spotted fleeing the castle. What does it mean?" –THE DOVER CENTENNIAL

N ia had been pacing for ten minutes, Lochlan's note crumpled from how tightly she'd gripped it. Her bare feet made soft sounds against the hardwood floor as she moved in relentless circles. Jade's bright eyes followed her from the couch, the dog's head tilted in quiet curiosity.

Three days. That's how long it had been since he'd left, and she had hated every second of it—more than she'd thought possible.

And now this: a note, cryptic and devoid of the details she craved.

I'm coming back.

"I don't even know if this is good or bad!" Nia muttered, her frustration bubbling to the surface. She waved the note at Jade as if the dog might provide answers. Jade's ears perked, but she remained lounged on the couch.

Nia sighed and raked a hand through her hair, then grabbed her phone to check the train station schedule again. She'd already memorized it, but still, she scanned the screen. He was either arriving soon or at midnight. There was no way to know for sure.

Lochlan hadn't texted her back and she hated that, too—the way her chest tightened every time she glanced at her phone, the way her thumb hovered over the screen, waiting for a response that didn't come.

It wasn't like her to be like this, tethered to someone else's timeline or absence. She was strong. Independent. She'd spent years building herself into the kind of woman who didn't need anyone. Sure, maybe she had a dependency on food delivery services. And, yes, she'd grown to like having Lochlan around, with his quietly steady presence that made the house feel full, that made her old life feel lonely.

But she wasn't going to just sit here waiting and worrying.

Jade let out a low whine, as if sensing her spiraling thoughts. "I know, I know," Nia murmured, stopping long enough to scratch the dog behind her ears. "But I can't mope here like some kind of lovesick fool hovering over my phone."

Even as the words left her mouth, she wasn't sure she believed them. She *did* want to be there when he got home. She wanted to see him walk through the door. She wanted to know if he was okay after whatever he'd faced in Dover.

She wanted to know if they—if she and Lochlan—were okay.

Her chest tightened again. If she stayed, she'd drive herself mad overthinking, rehearsing conversations that might never happen. She needed a distraction.

She shot off a quick text:

Me

Heading out for a bit. If you're home
before I'm back, find me at Salt.

Then, just in case, she grabbed a scrap of paper and wrote a short note and the address, leaving it on the counter where he'd be sure to see it. Satisfied—or pretending to be—Nia snatched her leather jacket from the hook near the door and pulled on her boots. She turned to Jade, who was watching her with big, soulful eyes.

"You've been fed, the TV is on, you'll be fine, right?" Nia asked, though she already knew the answer. She patted the dog's head anyway, the motion soothing. "Watch the house while I'm gone, okay? Bite your dad when he gets home for making me worry."

Jade gave a little huff, her tail thumping a few times against the couch cushion.

With a deep breath, Nia stepped out into the cool evening air. Her boots struck a steady rhythm against the pavement, her steps quick and purposeful. She left the polished charm of the historic district behind, turning into a quiet lane lined with shuttered businesses and back entrances. She liked this part of Stella Rune—the edges where people came to lose themselves for a while, to slip away from the polite smiles and carefully trimmed hedges of the town center. Here, it was wild but comfortable, and nothing needed to be hidden.

Halfway to the club, a strange sensation washed over her.

It started as a whisper of unease, a flicker at the fringe of her awareness as she reached the edge of downtown. She slowed, her eyes sweeping the street. The glow of the neon signs reflected off the damp pavement, but their colors felt muted, the shadows around them deeper. She glanced at a nearby alley. The darkness filling it seeming to breathe, to shift in a way that made her skin prickle.

Her hand brushed against the inside pocket of her leather jacket, feeling the edges of the envelope tucked safely inside. She had done this before—countless times. She knew the power of leverage, how to wield it for good even when it meant walking dangerous lines.

Still, her fingers tightened around the envelope.

The sound of footsteps echoed faintly behind her, matching her own in a way that felt too precise, less like an echo, and more like she was being followed. Nia stopped, her breath catching in her throat as she turned to scan the street behind her.

Nothing.

The sidewalks were empty and the faint hum of traffic in the distance was the only sound. She searched the shadows, her heart pounding faster, her grip on the envelope tightening as she turned back toward the club.

"Get it together," she muttered under her breath, forcing herself to keep walking.

The club's sign came into view, its garish neon spilling onto the street in a cascade of electric pink and green. The sight loosened the knot of fear in her chest, the familiar buzz of the place pulling her forward. She focused on the steady rhythm of her boots, the warm chaos of the club ahead offering an escape from the gnawing unease still clinging to her.

As she reached the door, a flicker of movement caught her eye.

She glanced back over her shoulder. In the distance, a figure jogged toward her. For a moment, her pulse quickened as a prickle of fear crawled up her spine. Then the man stepped under a streetlamp, his features illuminated by the warm, steady light. Dark hair, broad shoulders, the easy, loping stride. A man she would now recognize anywhere.

Relief flooded her, stealing her breath.

Lochlan.

Nia didn't think. She moved. Her boots barely made a sound as she crossed the pavement, closing the space between them. When she reached him, she didn't hesitate, wrapping her arms tightly around Lochlan's middle and pulling him close.

The scent of him hit her first—fresh, clean, unmistakably him—as she buried her face against his chest, letting herself breathe him in. Her hands gripped the worn fabric of his jacket, anchoring herself to him.

Lochlan's arms came around her, his hands spreading across her back in a way that felt both protective and desperate. He leaned back just enough to catch her gaze, his honey-colored eyes scanning her face as though searching for reassurance.

Then he cupped her cheek, his fingers warm against her skin, and kissed her swiftly.

He tasted of toothpaste and exhaustion, the kind of weary relief that made her chest ache. His breath caught as he sighed against her lips, and she smiled.

"You're here."

"I'm here," Lochlan replied, his voice low and rough.

Her smile widened against his lips, and she kissed him again, lingering this time, as if trying to convey all the things she couldn't bring herself to say.

"I would have waited," she said breathlessly, her words muffled against his chest. "But I didn't know when—"

Lochlan let out a soft chuckle, the sound warm despite the weariness clinging to him. "My exit was a little dramatic," he admitted. "I forgot my charger and couldn't get one on the train."

She leaned back, one brow arching. "And?"

He paused. "And I found nothing I went looking for," he said softly. "But discovered everything I needed to."

She searched his face for answers.

"Later." He shook his head, a small, rueful smile tugging at the corner of his mouth. "Now, why did you want me to meet you at Salt?"

"Work," Nia replied, her grin wide and unapologetic.

She turned on her heel and led him toward the club door without waiting for his reaction. Lochlan followed, his steps quickening to match hers. The stairs down were narrow and dimly lit, the soft glow of multicolored lights and the faint thrum of bass vibrating up from below.

Inside the club, the air was balmy and alive with the rhythm of slow, sensual music. Couples moved together on the dance floor, their bodies swaying as if drawn by invisible strings. Pressed up and along the walls, pairs kissed and whispered in low voices, their laughter mingling with the pulsing beat. On stages at either end of the room, dancers moved with hypnotic ease, their silhouettes fluid in the low light.

Nia let her eyes flicker to Lochlan, watching his reaction. His gaze swept over the room, taking it all in—the dimly lit bar, the haze of smoke curling in the air, the charged hum of desire. It wasn't always this spicy. Some nights, it was just a dive bar. Others, an open mic night. But tonight, there was something in the air that made people open to anything. Maybe a love witch had wandered in. Or a nymph, letting their magic curl through the room.

"Never been here before?" she asked, her tone teasing, though she couldn't quite mask her curiosity.

He shook his head, his expression unreadable.

A twinge of guilt struck her, sharp and unexpected. She stepped closer, touching his arm lightly. "Hey, I'm sorry," she said, her voice softening. "I should've asked… or explained. We can leave if you want."

Lochlan turned to her, his gaze steady, and the faintest smile curved his lips. "No," he said, his voice firm. "You asked me to come for a reason. Let me get my bearings."

Nia studied him for a moment, searching for any hint of unease, but she saw only calm determination.

"Alright." She nodded toward a table, her grin returning. "Let's sit and get a drink."

Lochlan followed her as they wove together through the crowd. Nia noticed the way people turned to watch them, their gazes lingering on

Lochlan and the way he carried himself—confident but unassuming, like he belonged anywhere, even if he didn't realize it yet.

After slipping into a secluded corner booth, Nia caught the bartender's eye with a subtle nod. Mairead, a fox-eyed fae who always seemed to know what you wanted before you said it, offered a wink in return and disappeared.

Lochlan rested his hand on the table, his fingers drifting across the worn wood until they paused on a faintly etched rune. His brows lifted. "So, who's your next victim?"

"Victim?" Nia scoffed. "You make it sound so sinister."

The bartender approached, setting their drinks on the table. Nia gave the woman a quick smile and a quiet thank you, her fingers brushing the cocktail napkin as she slid her drink closer. Her gaze caught on the black scrawl on the napkin's edge:

He has company.

She let her gaze follow the bartender's retreat, her eyes moving steadily across the bar until they landed on her mark. He sat near the end of the counter, his obnoxious tie practically glowing under the dim lights.

Nia leaned in toward Lochlan, resting her hand on his thigh as if they were just another cozy couple in the crowd. Her lips brushed his ear as she whispered, "See the man at the end of the bar? Terrible tie?"

Lochlan's body tensed slightly under her hand before he turned his head just enough to catch sight of the man in question. He nodded once, his expression neutral.

"That's Raymond Bell," Nia said, keeping her voice low. "He's a reg from a couple towns over—Dunlowe. He's helping fund a development that would tear down a stretch of unprotected forest just north of town. If it goes through, the runoff hits the ocean inside a week."

Lochlan's brow furrowed, his gaze flicking back to her. "And?"

"And," Nia said, her lips curving into a wicked smile, "I have proof he's been cheating on his lovely wife. If I give her the evidence, their prenup is void. He loses half of everything."

"Why not just give her the evidence?" Lochlan asked, his voice tinged with curiosity.

"Oh, I will," Nia replied. "But I need to stop this transaction first."

For a moment, Lochlan said nothing, his gaze lingering on her. Then, without warning, he leaned in and kissed her.

The contact was swift and unexpected, but it ignited something hot and electric between them. Nia's pulse spiked as his hand slid up to cradle her jaw, his lips firm and warm against hers. All thoughts of her work and marks dissipated, replaced by a heady rush that left her momentarily breathless. When they pulled apart, Nia's heart was still racing, her lips tingling.

Lochlan's eyes were dark and focused, his smile slow. "I missed you so much."

"It was just a few days."

Don't ever leave like that again, was what she wanted to say.

They watched as Nia's mark slid into an empty booth. He leaned back like he owned the place, but the effect was ruined by the way his eyes darted across the room, barely masking his nerves. His fingers drummed an uneven rhythm against the table's edge, impatient—like a kid waiting his turn for a game he hadn't been invited to play.

Nia pulled the envelope from her jacket and whispered a quiet spell. The magic worked instantly. Across the room, the man shifted, startled, his frown deepening as his fingers curled around the envelope that had appeared in them.

Nia and Lochlan watched from their dim corner as the man opened it with trembling hands. At first, his expression was unreadable. But as he flipped through the contents, his face grew pale. Each new photo made his jaw clench tighter, his hands gripping the edges like they might slip away. His gaze darted around the room, his bravado crumbling under the weight of his own secrets.

Without a word, he stood and rushed out of the club, his steps quick and uneven.

Nia leaned back, exhaling slowly. "I knew this would be boring," she said, her gaze following the man until he was out of sight.

"What was in the envelope?" Lochlan asked.

She leaned in closer. "Oh, just a collection of photos. And a note explaining that if the same amount he was about to funnel into his little land grab doesn't show up as three separate donations by tomorrow night, those photos will end up in his wife's inbox. And her lawyer's."

She ticked the causes off on her fingers. "Fifteen to the Children's Foundation, twenty to the Housing Trust, and fifteen to the Coastal Conservation Fund. All local. All in need. And not a cent left for bulldozers."

Lochlan raised a brow, clearly impressed. Then, with a suddenness that made her breath catch, he reached out and grabbed her hand, pulling her closer, the kiss that followed stealing the air from her lungs.

When he pulled back, his gaze burned into hers. "You're bold and beautiful and a little bit wicked," he said, his voice admiring.

Heat rose to her cheeks. "I've been told."

Lochlan looked thoughtful. "How do you know he'll donate?"

"I've been doing this a long time. That was the face of a man who'll pace around, freak out… but in the end, he'll do the right thing. They always do, when the stakes are high enough."

"How many millions have you raised this way?" He shook his head, bemused. "They should build a statue in your honor."

The blush deepened. "Keep talking like that," she murmured, leaning closer, "and I might just have to have my way with you."

Lochlan glanced around the club, then back at her, his smile slight and gaze heated. "Seems like the right venue for that."

Her lips parted in surprise and the laugh that bubbled out was low and throaty. "Careful," she said, her hand slipping to rest on his thigh again. "I might take you seriously."

Lochlan's smile shifted into something more dangerous.

"I am serious."

36

Lochlan

"Thank Goodness HE'S BACK!"
—PRINCES&PIES444

She was his home.

The thought hit Lochlan like a sucker punch, knocking the breath from his lungs. He hadn't planned for this—the warmth that settled low in his chest every time she looked at him, the ache that refused to be ignored. He'd learned so much in Dover: the truth of his sister's misplaced cruelty, pieces of his mother's past, the realization that his relationship with Thane was only just beginning. He had finally let go of the pain he'd carried for so long, it had become a part of him.

But none of this compared to the quiet certainty of being with Nia.

Her laughter still hummed in the air, low and throaty, and the sound curled inside him, leaving him feeling warm and restless in their dimly lit booth. She was still flushed from their kiss, and her fingers pressed a little higher up his leg, staking her claim.

Goddess help him.

Even as he basked in her closeness, guilt flickered through Lochlan as he thought about Wulfric's plans, Luna's diaries, and the threat to his job and livelihood if he didn't keep these secret. A seed of deceit had sprouted and grown between him and Nia. But he pushed these thoughts away, telling himself that if he could just finish the diaries—and give Nia that piece of her mother's life—maybe it wouldn't matter he'd kept it from her.

Maybe.

Nia was in her element here, the faint pulse of the club lights casting her in a glow, her lips quirking in a mischievous way that made Lochlan's thoughts scatter. And those eyes—gods, those eyes. Green and teasing, they locked on him with a focus that made the air between them feel heavy and charged as her body leaned ever so slightly closer.

What was he supposed to do? Be thoughtful? Assertive?

As if reading his mind, Nia leaned in, her lips heated, possessive, her tongue finding his with an urgency that left him dizzy. Lochlan groaned, his hand sliding up her side to tangle in her hair as her nails scraped lightly against his leg, a silent taunt that had him cursing softly against her mouth.

The tight space, the press of bodies in the club beyond, the low thrum of music vibrating in his chest—it all faded until there was only her. Her taste reminded him of fairy wine, dark and heady, her kisses leaving him drunk and aching. His body responded before he could stop it, his cock straining against his jeans as her hand shifted dangerously close.

She must have felt it, because her grin against his lips was pure mischief. Her teeth grazed his bottom lip before she shifted her attention to his neck, her lips and tongue finding the sensitive skin just below his ear. Lochlan's hand tightened in her hair as she kissed her way down, her teeth nipping lightly at his pulse.

"I'm going to lose my mind," he muttered, half to himself, half to her.

Nia laughed softly, pleased.

His eyes darted to the shadowed corners of the club, searching for something—anything—that could give them some semblance of privacy. But there wasn't much in a place like this, and Nia was in pants: tight, unforgiving pants that made it impossible to do what he wanted to do.

"What's wrong, Loch?" she murmured, her breath warm against his skin.

Her lips found the hollow of his throat, her tongue teasing against his skin as she pulled back just enough to meet his eyes. "What are you looking for?" she asked, her voice low and playful.

"A place where I can peel those pants down and taste that pretty little—"

Nia didn't let him finish. She silenced him with a kiss, her lips slanting over his with a fervor that made him groan. Her hips shifted slightly, and the faint sound she made—a soft, breathy moan against his mouth—nearly drove him over the edge.

Grabbing Lochlan's hand, Nia pulled him out of the booth. The noise and lights of the club blurred around them as she led him toward a door tucked discreetly near the back. His heart hammered, his body buzzing from her touch, her kiss, the promise in her eyes.

She pushed the door open and stepped inside, tugging him after her. It was a small office, cluttered but private, the faint scent of old paper and spilled alcohol lingering in the air.

Lochlan glanced around, his brow furrowing as Nia flipped the lock. "Are we allowed in here?"

She turned to him, her lips curving into a smirk that sent a shiver down his spine. "The owner owes me a few favors. Looks like it's time to collect one."

Before he could respond, she was on him, her hands gripping the front of his shirt as his back hit the door with a soft thud, the sound swallowed by the sensation of her lips moving against his. His hands moved to her waist, as he turned her, guiding her back against him in one smooth motion. The soft gasp she gave sent a jolt of satisfaction through him, and he tightened his grip, fingers pressing into her hips as if daring her to pull away.

She glanced over her shoulder, her eyes dark with heat, the corner of her mouth curving into a knowing smirk that made his breath hitch.

"Don't keep me waiting," she murmured.

He didn't need to be told twice.

Lochlan's hands moved to the waistband of her pants, his fingers finding the button and peeling them down with care. The sight of her bare skin beneath sent a rush of heat through him, and he swallowed hard as she bent slightly, bracing herself against the edge of the desk.

He dropped to his knees behind her, his hands steadying her hips as he leaned in, his breath grazing her skin. Lochlan didn't hesitate, his tongue flicking out to taste her, and the sound she made—a sharp gasp followed by his name—nearly unraveled him.

"Nia," he murmured against her, his voice reverent, thick with need. He buried himself there, his tongue moving in slow, deliberate strokes, savoring her taste. She was intoxicating, every sigh and moan she gave spurring him on.

Lochlan's hands slid up her thighs, his grip firm, keeping her steady as he continued, his own moans muffled against her skin.

"Loch," she gasped, her voice strained, her hips moving involuntarily against him.

He groaned into her, the sound sending a shudder up her spine he could feel as his hands gripped her hips, holding her steady, keeping her exactly where he wanted her. He could stay here forever—drowning in her, unraveling her inch by inch—but her legs were shaking, her body strung tight, every muscle locked as she fought to stay upright.

Her breath hitched, her moans edged with desperation. He felt it—knew it—the tension coiling low in her belly, winding tighter with every lick of his tongue, every maddeningly slow stroke.

And then he eased off.

A teasing drag. A lingering kiss to her backside. A deliberate pause that sent her keening against the desk, her fingers gripping the edge so tightly her knuckles had gone white.

"Loch," she gasped, her voice raw with frustration.

He savored the way her body trembled, the way she pushed back as if she could chase his mouth, as if she could force him to give her what she needed. Not yet. His hands traced slow, soothing patterns along her thighs, a contrast to the vivid heat pulsing between them. Another teasing stroke of his tongue. Another retreat.

She let out a desperate, broken sound and pressed her forehead to the desk, her back arching, hips shifting—begging without words.

"Please," she whispered, wrecked, her thighs quivering beneath his palms.

Goddess, he could feel her heartbeat against his tongue. He could push her over the edge in an instant.

But not yet.

Instead, he pressed one last, lingering kiss to her skin and rose, his hands gliding up the curve of her spine as he straightened. His lips followed, ghosting over her shoulder, a fleeting touch meant to soothe and promise all at once.

He reached for his waistband, unzipping his pants, too close to the edge himself to bother getting them off completely.

"Can I?" he asked, his voice low and tight with restraint.

Nia glanced over her shoulder, her hair falling messily around her face, her eyes dark and hooded with want. She smiled. "I might die if you don't," she murmured, her voice shaky but teasing.

That was all he needed. Lochlan's eyes dropped, taking her in under the low, golden light of the office. The way her hips swayed, seeking him out, made his breath catch. His gaze lingered, drinking in how wet she was, glistening and ready for him, and a low growl rumbled in his chest.

He gripped himself, guiding himself to her entrance, savoring the unbearable heat as he slowly pushed forward. The moment he sank into her, she gasped, her fingers curling against the desk's surface, and he couldn't hold back his own groan. The tight, slick heat of her surrounded him, and it was almost too much.

"Fuck," Lochlan rasped, his forehead dropping to her shoulder for a moment as his hands dug into her hips. He pumped into her with slow, measured thrusts, his control hanging by a thread. "I'm going to go quick," he admitted, his voice rough and raw.

Her hips rolled against him, a desperate rhythm that nearly undid him. "Don't," she said, her voice catching on a moan. "Let me come now. Then you can come in my mouth."

His movements stilled, his breath catching in his throat. Just the image her promise conjured nearly pushed him to the brink. He could see it so clearly—Nia on her knees, looking up at him with those stunning, wicked eyes, her lips parted and eager.

Lochlan's hands tightened on her hips, his chest heaving as he struggled to hold himself back.

"Loch?" Nia's voice was breathless, laced with need and impatience.

He could barely process her words, his mind clouded with the overwhelming sensation of her warmth gripping him. "Just... need..." he groaned, his voice cracking as he thrust into her slowly, every movement stealing more of his control. "Fuck," he bit out, his head falling forward. Words failed him.

Somehow, he managed to reach around her, his fingers finding her clit. He circled it, the slow, teasing motion making her gasp and jolt beneath him. Each stroke of his fingers was timed with the languid roll of his hips, and her body responded immediately, matching his rhythm.

She panted, her hips meeting each of his thrusts.

"You…" Lochlan rasped, punctuating the word with a thrust. "Better… come." His voice was low and guttural, every word drenched in the strain of holding himself back.

And then she did.

Nia cried out, her body seizing around him, her walls clenching and pulsing in a way that made him curse sharply. He had to think about anything else—about plants, ancient books, goddess-damned mushrooms—but nothing could compete with the sensation of her falling apart around him.

She cursed loudly, her fingers clutching at the desk's edge like it was the only thing keeping her grounded. Her head dropped, her body shuddering as she rode out the wave of her orgasm, her thighs trembling with each aftershock.

"Loch," she gasped.

"I can't," he groaned, his voice desperate, raw. He was right there, teetering on the edge, and it would only take one more thrust—

"You better," she said, her tone teasing despite the breathlessness in her voice.

Lochlan pulled out, and before he could fully process what was happening, she was on her knees before him.

Nia looked up, her face flushed, her breath still ragged as she reached for him. Her fingers wrapped around his cock, slick and hard, and he jerked violently in her grasp.

Her pants were still bunched around her ankles, her shirt disheveled and giving him a tantalizing glimpse of her breasts, her nipples hard beneath the fabric. She was a vision—messy, radiant, and perfect.

"Fuck," Lochlan muttered, his voice breaking. "Fuck, fuck." His head tipped back, his hands braced against the desk for support as his body tightened in anticipation.

He didn't deserve this—her, like this, looking at him with those sinful eyes, her lips curved in a wicked smile. He was going to die, right here, and there wouldn't be a better way to go.

She was gentle at first, her tongue tracing him with slow strokes that left him trembling. Testing. Teasing. Lochlan groaned, every muscle in his body taut with the effort to stay upright.

When she took him deeper, her lips gliding down his length, his vision flashed white-hot, and his head tipped back in a silent gasp. Then she moaned—soft, indulgent, like she liked the way he tasted on her tongue—and the sound vibrated through him, sending a pulse of pleasure that struck deep, leaving him trembling.

His balls drew up tight, his thighs tingling as if the ground beneath him had disappeared. He hunched over instinctively, one hand bracing on the desk behind her, the other tangling in her hair. She followed him, her hands gripping his ass as she pulled him deeper into her mouth, taking him as far as she could manage.

He would have pulled back—should have pulled back—but she moaned again, the sound rippling through him like fire. His control shattered, and he couldn't stop the desperate grind of his hips as the tension inside him coiled too tight, too fast.

"Nia," he choked, his voice wrecked, barely recognizable. "Fuck— don't stop. I can't—I'm going to—"

Her nails dug into his ass, and that was it. He shattered, his release hitting him like a lightning strike. A hoarse, guttural cry tore from his throat as his body jerked, every nerve alight.

Her lips stayed locked around him, her eyes rolling closed as she moaned softly, the sound sending little sparks across his skin, his chest heaving, his knees shaking as the last of his strength left him.

When she finally pulled back, it was slow, her lips releasing him with a soft pop. When she looked up at him—flushed and proud and radiant—he felt like he could float away to the stars.

Lochlan's breath came in uneven gasps, his head spinning as he stared down at her. He felt everything all at once: guilt and joy, exhilaration and awe, power and vulnerability. She made him feel like a god, and yet like he was utterly at her mercy.

He reached for her, his thumb brushing over the corner of her mouth as if he could somehow anchor himself to her. To hold on to this. To the impossible way she made him feel.

To her.

Lochlan hoped that maybe—just maybe—he could.

37

Nia

"Motorcycles on the Rise—Stella Rune Desperate to Stop the Noise." –*THE STELLA RUNE GAZETTE*

It was Monday afternoon, and the tunnels were mercifully quiet. The distant drip of water echoed through the stone corridors, blending with the low hum of glowing runes etched into the walls, their faint golden light flickering. Nia took a deep, slow breath and let the peaceful stillness settle over her.

After the heat of the other night, and the night after that, and *this morning*, she wasn't exactly complaining. She needed a moment to breathe, to collect herself, to pretend Lochlan wasn't slowly, relentlessly reshaping the world as she knew it.

Nia swore she could still feel his touch—those hungry, purposeful hands, his low, growling voice that made her breath hitch—and just the memory had her fighting to keep her expression neutral. The cool autumn air didn't stand a chance against the warmth that spread through her, making her grateful for the quiet solitude of the tunnels.

Of course, it didn't help that Lochlan was right there beside her.

His dark hair fell into soft, messy waves, brushing against the collar of his burgundy coat. The scruff along his jaw—thicker now, giving him an even more rugged edge—added to the unfair appeal. Nia's gaze drifted to his hands, the way they casually cradled his coffee cup, his fingers long and strong.

Focus, Nia.

Not that anyone in the tunnels would notice or care. The unspoken rule of these underground paths was simple: what happened in the tunnels stayed in the tunnels. No one gossiped, no one tattled. Even Tashy, who'd handed over their coffees with her usual wink, wouldn't breathe a word.

Her green skin had darkened with a blush when Lochlan flashed one of *those* smiles at her. "Thank you, madame," he'd said, his voice as smooth and rich as the coffee he'd ordered.

Nia had to bite back a grin as Tashy all but melted into the counter. She couldn't blame her.

"So," Nia said as they turned down the next passage, her own coffee warm in her hand. "Where to first?"

Lochlan glanced down the dimly lit corridor. "I don't know," he said, his brow furrowing slightly. "Is there any real map of the tunnels? Something comprehensive?"

Nia laughed softly, shaking her head. "No maps. But name something, and I'm sure we can find it."

He hesitated, his expression thoughtful but a little sheepish. "I'm not even sure what to ask for," he said finally, a self-deprecating smile tugging at his lips.

Before he could retreat further into his own thoughts, Nia reached for his hand, her fingers sliding easily into his. "Okay," she said, tugging him gently down the next passage. "How about this? I've noticed you don't carry any quick spells."

Lochlan blinked, his steps faltering slightly as they passed a row of small, glowing shops carved into the stone walls. Their entrances were arched and shimmered with spells; faint, colorful light spilled out onto the tunnel floor. One shop was cluttered with shelves of tiny glass bottles filled with swirling liquids while another showcased enchanted trinkets that sparkled with magic. The warm hum of quiet conversation buzzed in the air, blending with the subdued crackle of spell work being tested behind the counters.

"You've gone through my things?" he asked, arching a brow at her, his tone hovering between teasing and genuinely curious.

"You know I have," Nia said quickly.

He'd found his shirt under her pillow. He hadn't said anything, just dragged her under him and kissed her so slowly, from her lips to her breasts, her stomach, and then when he'd nestled between her legs, he practically feasted for a ha—

She blinked, refocusing. "I just... your pockets are always empty. And I've never seen you pull anything out when we might have used a quick spell."

"Right," Lochlan murmured, contemplative.

She glanced at him, suddenly uncertain. "Not that there's anything wrong with that," she added, her voice faltering. "I mean, you're obviously more than capable. It's just, you never know when a quick spell might come in handy and I figured—"

"Nia," Lochlan interrupted gently, pulling her from her spiraling thoughts. "It's fine. I don't mind." He squeezed her hand and kissed her knuckles.

The tension in her chest eased, and she offered a small smile before leading him down the tunnel. The faint scent of dried herbs drifted toward them as they turned a corner, and the golden glow of a familiar shop spilled into the passage.

The air was heavy with magic, and Nia felt it brush against her skin as they stepped inside. Shelves lined the walls, crowded with jars, vials, and tins. Bundles of herbs hung from the ceiling, their scent blending with the bite of salts and potions. Baskets of spell components were scattered on the floor, and the counter held an orderly display of bottles and scrolls.

Nia stepped up to it, pulling a few small tins from her coat pocket, then a couple more from her purse, and finally one last one from a hidden pocket in her skirt. She placed the containers on the counter in a tidy row, her movements precise and practiced.

"I need a stock-up," she told the shopkeeper, a wiry woman with sharp eyes and streaks of silver in her hair. Then, gesturing toward Lochlan, she added, "And he needs his first traveling spell kit."

The shopkeeper's eyes shifted to Lochlan, narrowing slightly as they swept over him. Nia frowned, her gaze darting between the two.

"Hey," she said, her tone light but with an edge, "keep those eyes to yourself."

The shopkeeper scoffed, crossing her arms. "I wasn't looking like *that*. I'm assessing his needs."

Nia's suspicion lingered, but before she could press further, Lochlan stepped forward as his attention was caught by something on the shelf.

"This is an amazing selection," he said, sounding both impressed and curious. He pointed to a bottle near the top, its pale green label faded but legible. "How do you procure *moonlace root*? I've heard it's tricky to grow."

The shopkeeper's demeanor shifted, her expression softening. "Good eye. My uncle grows them up the coast in his greenhouse. He's been working with moonlace for decades."

At the mention of the greenhouse, a shadow of unease crossed Lochlan's face. Nia caught the way his fingers tensed against the counter, his posture stiffening. Though his expression smoothed a moment later, she had no doubt his thoughts had gone to Dover.

He'd told her about it the night he came home—sleepy and blissed from another round in bed, his guard lowered just enough to let the words slip free. About his sister and her misplaced hatred, about the greenhouse that once meant something and now meant nothing at all. About his mother. There was no grief, only the quiet understanding that what he'd been chasing all those years—the sense of belonging, a place and purpose to be a part of—had never been in Dover.

He told her how he had stood beside Thane, how he was proud of his brother. He'd even showed her the absurdity of the crowd that had gathered for them, the signs waving in the air. Lochlan thought it was ridiculous. But Nia agreed with Thane. She was unsurprised the people of the kingdom would appreciate and admire him, if he let them.

And if she ever saw Dru-bitch-face in person, she'd have a few things to say herself.

When they left the shop, Nia's pockets were heavier and her purse was weighed down with tins and herbs. Lochlan carried a small, neatly packed tin, turning it over as they walked. He carefully inspected the labeled compartments, his expression unreadable.

"So," he said finally, glancing at her. "I just... carry this with me?"

Nia hesitated, feeling a bit sheepish. "You don't have to," she said, brushing a strand of hair behind her ear. "I just thought—"

"No, no," Lochlan interrupted, his tone soft as he leaned in and pressed a kiss to her cheek. "This is great. Really." He paused, his thumb brushing over the edge of the tin. "I've seen people with these kinds of kits before, but..." He trailed off, uncertain. "I didn't start doing magic outside of herbalism for a very long time. Not until I met Becket. Even then, I was worried I'd mess something up or..." He sighed. "Look foolish."

Nia's heart ached at this. She squeezed his hand, trying to think of the right thing to say. But before she could, a bright, cheerful voice echoed through the tunnel.

"Lochlan!"

They both turned. An older woman strode toward them with the kind of bubbly energy that seemed determined to fill any space.

"Oh no," Lochlan muttered under his breath, his voice tight with dismay. "Naked Nancy."

Nia choked on a laugh, nearly spilling her coffee. "What?"

Before he could respond, the woman in question came shuffling toward them, her heeled boots clicking unevenly against the stone floor as her hands flapped wildly, like she was trying to corral their attention.

But she certainly wasn't naked.

"My goodness," Nancy exclaimed, her voice breathless and chipper. "I can't believe I'm running into you again, Lochlan! We hardly see you at—"

"Yes," Lochlan cut in sharply, his tone overly bright. "Yes. Hello, Nancy." He gave her a tight smile, looking distinctly uncomfortable. "Well, we're on our way somewhere. Was there, uh, something you needed?"

"Oh gosh, no," Nancy said, waving him off as if the question were absurd. "But when I see Lochlan about, I *have* to make sure I say hello. It's such a rare sight!"

Nia blinked, her head swiveling between them. Nancy's cheerfulness was practically buzzing off her, but Lochlan looked like he wanted the ground to swallow him whole. He shifted awkwardly, looking more than anything like a cornered animal as Nancy continued to beam at him.

Then, as if she'd only just noticed Nia, Nancy's wide eyes flicked to her, and she seemed genuinely shocked. "Oh, my word," she said, straightening abruptly. "Hello, hello! Excuse me for being so rude." She extended a hand toward Nia, her small fingers wiggling expectantly. "I'm Nancy."

Nia, a little bemused, shook her hand. "Hello, I'm Nia."

Nancy's face lit up as if someone had just handed her a free kitten. "Of course you are," she said, nodding knowingly. "Well—"

"Wonderful seeing you, Nancy," Lochlan cut in, his hand already tugging gently at Nia's arm. "Truly. But we've got to get going."

Nancy didn't seem the least bit deterred. "Oh, yes, of course! But make sure you stop by next time you're at the arch—"

"Will do!" Lochlan called back, already steering Nia deeper into the tunnels.

The laughter she'd been holding back bubbled out as Lochlan glanced back over his shoulder, as if checking for signs of pursuit.

"Loch," she said between giggles. "Wait. What was that?"

Lochlan didn't answer immediately. Only when they turned another corner, and the air grew cooler and the tunnel dimmer, did he finally seem to relax.

Nia nudged his arm. "Seriously. What was that about?"

"What?" Lochlan asked, feigning innocence. He rubbed the back of his neck, his expression sheepish. "Oh. I just didn't want to get caught up with her."

"Naked Nancy?" Nia prompted, her grin widening.

Lochlan's groan echoed through the narrow space. "Yeah," he muttered, his hand falling back to his side. "There was an incident at Mabon, and…"

He trailed off, but the words hung there.

Nia froze. Mabon. The equinox celebration, the night that had upended their lives and forced them both into a marriage neither wanted. The comfortable, weightless bubble they'd been living in suddenly felt fragile, on the brink of popping.

She hadn't thought about the bargain—hadn't thought about proving her father wrong, about earning the annulment she'd once craved, in days.

Did she still crave it?

And why was Lochlan acting so strange about Nancy?

Nia's gaze flicked to him, watching the way his shoulders remained tense, his easy charm from moments ago gone. Nancy had clearly rattled him, and not in the way an overenthusiastic acquaintance normally would. Something about it didn't sit right.

Nia pushed the feeling aside and blamed it on the lingering bitterness her father evoked. But her unease remained, lurking at the edges of her mind like a shadow she couldn't quite shake.

The tunnels wound endlessly behind them, their footsteps echoing in a soft rhythm against the stone walls as they neared an exit. Nia barely had time to register the gentle tug on her hand before Lochlan pulled her into an unlit alcove.

"What are you—"

His hands framed her face, thumbs brushing her cheeks as the kiss pulled her under, deep and dizzying, until everything else—the encounter, the bargain, the weight on her shoulders—slipped away.

For a moment, there was only him.

When they broke apart, her head tipped forward, her forehead coming to rest against his chest as she caught her breath. His satisfied chuckle vibrated against her ear, making her smile.

"I didn't know I needed that…" she murmured. "But I did."

His lips brushed her temple before easing away. "Don't stop needing me."

They stepped into the crisp autumn air, the warmth of their kiss lingering between them. For a fleeting moment, Nia considered saying something—a joke, or maybe a tease—but Lochlan froze beside her, his body rigid. The shift yanked her from the softness of the moment, her smile faltering as she followed Lochlan's gaze across the street.

A man stood there—tall and broad-shouldered, his posture confident, at ease.

Recognition hit her like a slap, cold and jarring. Gregor—the man from her office weeks ago, the one who'd screamed in her face until her shadows restrained him. The memory came rushing back: the fury in his voice as he spat curses at her, the way his face had purpled with rage when she had calmly walked him out. She'd forgotten about him, forgotten to follow up.

Nia's gaze flicked to Lochlan. He had stepped in front of her, his stance protective and shoulders squared. His hand hovered near her arm, like he was ready to pull her away.

The man's eyes moved to Lochlan first, narrowing slightly as if sizing him up. His gaze shifted to Nia. His expression changed: not overtly hostile, but calculating in a way that made her spine stiffen. A flicker of unease bloomed in her chest, along with the sense that she was forgetting something. But the thought slipped just out of reach.

A bus rumbled down the street, briefly blocking her view. When it passed, the man was gone.

"Well," Nia said, exhaling sharply. "That was creepy."

Lochlan didn't respond immediately. His jaw was tight as he scanned the street, his eyes lingering on the spot where the man had stood.

"You've run into past marks before?" he asked finally, his voice even but tense.

"Sometimes," Nia said, keeping her tone light. "Stella Rune's the kind of town people like to visit."

"And nothing happens?" He turned to her, the lines of his face sharper than usual.

"Nope." She smiled, keeping her tone breezy. "It's either awkward small talk or they pretend not to see me."

Lochlan didn't look convinced. His gold eyes locked on hers with an intensity that made her pause. For a moment, the only sound was the faint hum of the town around them.

"Would you tell me if something wasn't right?" he asked.

Her smile was small as she reached for his hand, squeezing it gently. "Of course."

But as they walked on, her thoughts lingered—not just on the man's expression, but on Lochlan's reaction. The way he had stepped in front of her, shielding her without a second thought. It was instinctive, protective. And yet, doubt gnawed at her. Did he think she wouldn't confide in him?

Would he confide in her?

DIARY ENTRY
MY TWENTY-FOURTH SPRING

I remember the morning he named our baby. The air was cool, the sun casting its first rays over the meadow, gilding the world in soft gold. We moved in silence, my hand in his, the quiet broken only by the rhythmic rustle of grass beneath our feet.

The beast rarely speaks on these walks—he is always a grump so early in the day. I love the mornings and have come to cherish our strolls: their peace, his presence, the way these things make the world feel lighter, brighter.

He stopped suddenly, his gaze catching on something flitting through the dawn light. A butterfly, its wings glowing like embers, delicate and bold, landed on a wildflower. He murmured, as though the word had always been meant for her:

"Pyronia."

I followed his gaze, curious. He knelt, his fingers brushing the petals near where the butterfly rested, his movements careful, reverent. "Born of fire," he said softly, "and yet it lives in beauty. Resilient. Undiminished."

As he spoke, I felt the faintest movement beneath my hand resting on my belly. A flutter, as if she, too, recognized the name meant for her. He stood, his green eyes finding mine, raw and unguarded in a way that still surprises me. "That's who she will be," he said, his voice quieter. "Our little flame. A spark the darkness can't extinguish."

My beast had named her. And in that moment, I loved him more—for seeing her the way I did, as something bright and beautiful in a world that had tried so hard to destroy us.

Pyronia.

Even now, I can't think of the name without feeling the sun on my face, without remembering that gentle stirring inside me. She will carry it with pride, I know. Our flame. Our promise.

38

Lochlan

"I keep pulling the fertility card, WHAT DOES IT MEAN?" –THE GREEN WITCH 1969

Becket was leaning against the windowsill in Lochlan's office, one hand dramatically pressed to his chest like he'd been sitting there, neglected, for hours instead of thirty minutes. "Are you even listening to me?"

"Of course."

"What did I say?"

"No idea."

"Dude."

"Don't be so dramatic," Lochlan muttered, eyes still on the diary spread across his desk. Becket had been here for a while, but Lochlan had only half-registered the conversation. His focus had been wrapped up in restoring the final pages.

"I see your wife more than you."

Lochlan glanced over, one brow raised. "Nia mentioned something about you and Ivy?"

Becket sighed and reached for the carved paperweight on the windowsill, turning it slowly in his hands. His thumb traced the edges with too much focus, like he was stalling. "Just friends."

"That's all you want, isn't it? *Just friends* and a roll in the sheets. You've never wanted more before."

"And you never thought you'd end up married. Never thought you'd confront your mother or sister."

Lochlan's expression sobered. He had told Becket everything about Dover. "Things change."

The look Becket gave him in return could only be described as: no shit, asshole.

Lochlan leaned back. "You know, a few weeks ago, I was desperately trying to figure out how to keep Nia. Are you saying…"

"I'm not saying anything." Becket nudged at the corner of the rug with his shoe. "My sister gave Ivy a reading. Told her to stop chasing relationships when she hasn't learned to love herself."

"Zora's a powerful seer. She's probably right."

Becket threw his hands in the air. "Why did I even come here?"

"Beck," Lochlan said gently, "I think you might also be looking for the wrong kind of love."

Becket squinted at him. "I don't feel comfortable taking advice from a man who's keeping a massive secret from the wife who may or may not still want to annul their marriage."

Lochlan didn't argue. He turned back to the diary on his worktable and slid the final page into place. Magic stirred through the paper like breath—soot and water damage faded beneath his fingers. The fibers healed. The words became clear. They now showed a near-perfect account of a life a daughter and man still mourned. Once the next volume was delivered and repaired, the record Nia's mother had made of her life would be complete. Then, Lochlan would share these with Nia and tell her the truth—about the diaries, about her father, about everything.

"I know," he said quietly. The threads of deceit he'd spun felt too tangled up with everything else he had with Nia. If he unwound them now, he was afraid everything else would unravel, too.

Becket stepped closer and gave his shoulder a quick squeeze, just as his phone buzzed. "Hey, Pixie, one sec."

Lochlan arched a brow. Pixie was Becket's nickname for Ivy, and he said it with a wide grin. The pout from moments ago vanished like it had never existed.

His poor friend. Lochlan knew the feeling too well.

And Becket wasn't wrong. Lochlan had no room to judge, not with what he was still hiding.

He followed Becket out, locking the office behind him. By the time they reached the front door, a Videt courier was already climbing the steps.

Becket waved, phone still pressed to his ear as he rounded the corner, heading toward a tunnel entrance.

"Perfect timing," Lochlan said, working to project a calm he did not feel as he signed the delivery slip. The worker handed over the package with a polite nod before retreating down the steps.

Resting on top of the package was a note, written in Wulfric's precise hand.

You and Nia will join me for dinner tonight.

Lochlan turned to go back inside and close the door, but froze mid-motion. Nia pulled into the spot behind his truck, her sharp green eyes locking onto the delivery worker as she cut the engine. His pulse kicked up. Thankfully, they were already halfway down the block.

Nia swung off the bike in one fluid movement, pulling off her helmet as she walked toward him. Her vibrant hair spilled free, catching the light.

"Hey," she said, her gaze flicking to the package in his hands.

Before he could respond, she leaned in, brushing her lips against his in a kiss that was far too brief for his liking. When she pulled back, her attention lingered on the package, a hint of curiosity creeping into her expression.

"What's that?"

Lochlan forced a smile, gripping the package a little tighter. "Oh, just a book," he said, keeping his tone casual. "A new volume for me to repair."

Nia raised an eyebrow, skepticism flashing in her eyes, but she recovered quickly. "Okay."

Lochlan shifted his weight, clearing his throat. "What are you doing home so early?"

Her lips quirked into a smirk, but there was something guarded in her expression. "Last-minute meeting came up," she said, waving a hand vaguely toward the house. "I wanted to change before heading out again."

"Oh," he said. "Your father's summoned us for dinner tonight."

The words hung awkwardly between them. She studied him for a long moment, unreadable, before giving a small nod and stepping past him toward the front door. Lochlan followed her, his grip on the package firm as they walked upstairs together. He could feel her watching him out of the corner of her eye, her curiosity palpable and unnerving.

When they reached the top of the stairs, he hesitated for just a moment before unlocking the office door.

"I'll just drop this off," he said, his voice too quick, too forced. Lochlan didn't need to look back to feel the weight of her gaze as the door clicked shut behind him, blocking her out.

Inside, he leaned against the door for a moment, exhaling a long breath. His shadows stirred restlessly at the edges of his vision, a mirror of the unease coiling in his chest.

He left the package unopened on his desk: the final piece.

When he walked into the bedroom, he stopped short. Nia stood by the closet, changing into something more businesslike. Her back was to him, her movements efficient as she pulled a blouse from a hanger. She was in just her bra and slacks, the curves of her body catching the soft afternoon light streaming through the window.

Lochlan couldn't help himself. He crossed the room, his hands finding her waist as he pressed a kiss to her shoulder.

Nia laughed, swatting at him playfully. "I have a meeting."

"Who's the victim?" he teased.

She rolled her eyes, turning back toward the closet. "I'm meeting with the owner of the manor we went to for Becket's event," she said, slipping the silky shirt over her arms. "I want to turn it into a place for young supernaturals."

Lochlan raised an eyebrow, intrigued.

Nia continued as she buttoned her blouse. "We have spaces like this for humans—places for kids and families. But those with children whose magic is still a little wild can't use them. It's too risky. They might be seen and get in trouble."

Lochlan frowned, confused. "I thought the Videt had this kind of place?"

She turned and gave him a pointed look. "That one is reserved for the families of people who work there. Those with money and means."

Lochlan felt like a fool. He hadn't known—hadn't paid attention. The unease he'd felt earlier settled back over him. "You're right," he said after a moment. "That's an amazing idea."

Her expression softened. A small, pleased smile lifted her lips. "Yeah?"

"Yeah."

Nia slipped on her heels, then hesitated. "Would you want to go with me?"

Lochlan opened his mouth to respond, but his thoughts immediately went to the diary waiting in his office. The final piece. He was so close to finishing, to coming clean, to finally giving Nia everything.

Her face fell, just a fraction, but enough to make his chest tighten.

"I have that new project that got dropped off," he said quickly, forcing the words out. "And I need to get started. It's… important."

Nia blinked, nodding too fast. "Oh, okay."

She turned back to the mirror, her movements hurried as she straightened her blouse and grabbed her bag. The smile she gave him as she leaned in for a quick kiss didn't quite reach her eyes.

Before he could think of anything else to say, anything that might make it better, she was gone.

As the sound of the door closing behind her echoed through the house, regret twisted in Lochlan's chest. He hadn't just been avoiding telling Nia the truth. He'd lied to her, hurt her, hidden what was her right to know.

He told himself he would make it right.

Just as soon as the last diary was done.

39

Nia

"The Sword—Leader, Protector, Zaddy."
—A PAGANS BLOG

The old manor stood at the edge of Stella Rune, nestled on twenty acres of rolling land. Thick woods framed the property, giving it an air of seclusion. For a building so old, it was in remarkable condition: the stone walls stood tall and sturdy, their surface dappled with ivy that climbed toward the roof like an offering to the sky.

Nia ran her hand along the banister of the grand staircase, its wood polished and warm beneath her touch. Sunlight filtered through the tall windows, casting golden patterns across the floor. Everything about the manor felt like it was waiting—for life, for purpose.

"This place is gorgeous," Ivy said, stepping out of a side room with a wide grin. "It's perfect."

Nia's throat tightened as she looked around, her vision blurring slightly. She felt a wave of emotion rise, unbidden but welcome. "Yeah," she said, her voice catching. "It is."

It would be nothing like the house she grew up in. That hollow, empty manor with too much space and not enough warmth. This place—their place—would be filled with laughter, with people, with life.

Near the doorway, Rue watched with quiet amusement, her keen eyes flicking between them. The woman was short and curvy; she looked like a ridiculously sexy nymph with mocha-colored hair. But she wasn't a woodland creature that lured lovers. She came from a long lineage of fae, a bloodline as old as Stella Rune itself. Most people wouldn't see her pointed ears or the wild eyes that, in the afternoon light, appeared more purple than blue. They'd see whatever glamour Rue chose to wear, the illusion of smooth, human features. But Nia was a witch. Fae magic couldn't fool her so easily.

"What will you do with it?" Rue asked, curious.

Ivy's grin widened. "Everything."

Rue laughed, the sound rich and full.

Nia knew the manor was a piece of Rue's past she was sloughing off, something left to her that she'd never asked for. Nia could relate. Inherited titles, roles, expectations—they had a way of weighing you down until you had to decide: live for them, or live for yourself.

Rue had made her choice.

What would Nia choose?

Everything had been good—great, even—until now. Something with Lochlan had begun to feel... off. He'd been cagey, and that wasn't like him. When he'd locked himself in that office—an office she was now kicking herself for never searching or questioning—her stomach had twisted. Now she wondered: why was it always locked? What was he doing in there?

The thought nagged at her.

"What will we do?" Nia said, turning back to Rue, shoving her worries aside. "For starters, we'll host an after-school program for young supernaturals—not just for those from Stella Rune, but the surrounding areas. It's in the perfect location."

Ivy's expression softened. "Maybe even turn some of the rooms upstairs into safe spaces?"

The idea hung in the air, heavy but hopeful. Nia reached out to grab Ivy's hand and give it a firm squeeze. "An orphanage of sorts?"

"I'm not sure yet," Ivy said, her gaze sweeping the room again. "But something."

Rue clasped her hands in front of her, her gaze sweeping the grand hall before settling back on Nia and Ivy. "There are two other houses on the property," she said, her tone practical. "They used to be staff quarters. You could turn them into housing, or something else. There's also an empty greenhouse—it's massive. And a barn that can hold five horses or other livestock."

"Goats?" Ivy asked, her eyes lighting up with interest.

Rue's eyes flickered violet as she smiled. "Anything you want."

Nia, still taking in the sheer scale of the place, frowned slightly. "How much does it cost to run a property like this?"

Rue flinched. "Around four hundred thousand a year," she admitted, her voice quieter.

Ivy winced. "Ouch."

Rue offered a tight smile. "I'm willing to donate for the first year," she said. "And I can help fill it with whatever furniture you need. I've been left with a lot of pieces." Hesitation crept into her tone. "But, you know…"

Ivy tilted her head, her brows drawing together. "What?"

Rue's thoughtful gaze shifted between Nia and Ivy. "You could get funding through the Videt," she suggested, her voice cautious. "They have grants and other resources—"

"No," Nia said flatly, the word leaving her mouth before Rue had even finished.

Beside her, Ivy turned, her brow furrowed. "But Nia, you do have an in—"

"I said no," Nia interrupted. Her chest tightened as she looked at Ivy, then back to Rue. "I want this to be separate from him. This is our biggest venture, and I want it to be on our own. We'll figure it out."

Ivy didn't look convinced. "Nia," she said, her arms crossing, her tone teetering between persuasion and frustration. "Think about it."

The silence stretched uncomfortably.

"I'll give you two some privacy," Rue said gently, breaking the tension. She offered a small, understanding smile before slipping out of the room, humming a lilting tune that faded as she walked away.

Ivy turned and gave Nia a pointed look.

"No, Ivy," she said. "I won't say it again."

Ivy held her gaze, her expression shifting from mild annoyance to quiet curiosity. She tilted her head slightly. "What's wrong?"

"Nothing," Nia scoffed, waving a hand dismissively.

But the word fell flat as she said it. Her thoughts drifted to Lochlan. He should be here. She'd asked him, wanted him close before signing off on something this big. But...

She rubbed her temple, sighing. Was he acting weird? Why couldn't she just ask him?

"Something's off with Lochlan," she admitted, hoping saying it out loud would help. It didn't.

Ivy frowned. "That man is head over heels for you."

Nia gave her a skeptical look, her chest tightening. "I really thought things were good," she said softly. "He went to Dover, he got his closure, but I still feel like... he's holding something back."

Ivy tilted her head, her curiosity clear. "Like what?"

"I'm not sure," Nia admitted.

Ivy studied her for a moment before raising an eyebrow. "Have you used your powers on him?"

Nia's eyes widened. "Of course not. That wouldn't be fair."

Ivy smirked. "So, you've never used them on me?"

Nia burst out laughing, the tension easing just slightly. "I don't need my powers to know what lurks in your darkness." She gave Ivy a playful wink.

Ivy shook her head. "If Lochlan is holding back—" She wrapped an arm around Nia's shoulder and gave her a squeeze. "—I think he'll let go of it eventually."

Together they took in the room one more time. Nia could see it so clearly—young supernaturals running through the halls, their laughter echoing through the grand space. Tutors trained in every manner of magic guiding them, helping them flourish. The libraries they could build, the resources they could provide—it was all right here, waiting to happen.

"I don't want you to force anyone to donate to this place," Ivy said, her voice hesitant. "I want it to be a hundred percent free of anything... bad."

Nia turned toward her, and for a moment, the weight of Ivy's past seemed etched into her features, every struggle and hard-fought victory written on her face.

She remembered a night their first year at Stella College, when Ivy had finally told her the truth. Sitting on the floor, knees pulled to her chest, she'd said, *"They didn't know I was a witch. Just that I was wrong somehow."* She'd bounced through group homes, always too much, too strange, until she learned to suppress the chaos. It wasn't until she was a teen that she even heard whispers of Stella Rune: a place where witches could be safe. Where she could be herself.

Nia reached for her hand. "We'll make it work," she said, "and we'll do it on our own."

But as the words left her lips, doubt crept in.

The idea of going it alone, in general, didn't feel as certain as it once had. She wanted more than just independence. She wanted to be part of a team. And she and Ivy were—and had been—a fantastic team. But Nia realized she wanted that in other areas of her life, too. She wanted more. Someone more. No, not just someone.

She wanted Lochlan.

This thought tangled with the reality ahead of her: the final family dinner tonight. Another performance to prove Lochlan shouldn't—couldn't—be that person.

But could he?

She wasn't sure of anything anymore.

40

Nia

"Fae Politics - And Why We Are Worried."
—THE WEEKLY HEX

Nia's motorcycle rumbled up the long and winding drive, the sound a steady, grounding hum beneath her. Wulfric's manor loomed ahead, its tall windows catching the last light of the day. She hated the way it stood there: an imposing figure against the horizon, a shadow she could never quite outrun.

This was the last family dinner she and Lochlan were required to attend. After this, there would be one last public event and then Samhain—a supernatural gathering where Wulfric would decide whether to grant their annulment.

She had told herself she wanted that. Hadn't she?

For so long, she'd clung to the idea of freedom. She had vowed never to be controlled again, never to let anyone else dictate her life: not her father, not a husband or wife, not anyone.

And yet…

Her fingers tightened around the handlebars. She wanted to know what she and Lochlan could be, freed from her father's manipulations. If they chose each other, what would that look like? Could she let herself choose him?

The thought sent a warm, hopeful flush through her. But doubt immediately followed, swift and chill. Lochlan had been acting secretive. Hadn't he? Or was she looking for problems because she wasn't ready to admit how much she wanted this?

As Nia approached the house, she pulled her bike behind Lochlan's green truck. The air was cool and carried the faint scent of pine and smoke—maybe they were barbecuing again. Probably, knowing her father.

Nia headed for the grand entrance, ignoring the sense of dread that crept over her as she pushed the heavy doors open without waiting for the butler. As she stepped into the foyer, voices drifted toward her from the sitting room, low and tense. She paused, her hand brushing the edge of the door frame.

"I should be the one," Lochlan said.

"No, son. This is my plan, it has to be—" Wulfric stopped abruptly before turning smoothly toward the doorway where she stood. "Pyronia. You're here."

She hesitated, scanning their faces. Wulfric's expression was unreadable, his mask perfectly intact. Lochlan looked tense, shoulders rigid and jaw tight, but her breath caught with a flicker of relief just at seeing him.

"Did I interrupt something?" Her voice was steady despite the way she could feel the rough energy in the room prickling over her skin.

"No," Lochlan said quickly.

"No," Wulfric echoed, his tone a touch too polished, too rehearsed.

Nia's gaze moved between them. Lochlan had been off today, but standing here with her father, she didn't blame him. Wulfric made everyone uneasy. The sound of approaching footsteps made her jump slightly as the butler appeared, his expression as calm and collected as ever.

"Miss Pyronia," he said with a polite nod before glancing toward Lochlan and Wulfric. "Dinner is ready."

He turned and led them through the house. Nia followed reluctantly, trying to keep her thoughts from knotting up with every step.

"How was the meeting?" Lochlan whispered.

"Fine."

Lochlan hesitated. "Was it really, or—"

"You'd know if you'd gone."

Regret tugged at her, quiet and immediate, as soon as the words left her. But she didn't take them back. It felt good to be near him again, but that didn't change how frustrated she felt.

They stepped outside and it was just as she remembered: heating spells kept the crisp evening air at bay, while the soft glow of enchanted lanterns cast a warm, golden light over the table. Despite the cozy setting, unease gnawed at her.

Lochlan had already taken a seat. The intensity in his eyes made her pause. There was something raw there—longing, or pain, maybe—but she brushed it aside, choosing a seat across from him. As she settled into her chair, the restless feeling in her chest grew, leaving her feeling oddly out of place.

Wulfric lingered near the grill, murmuring something to the chef before taking his seat at the head of the table. His gaze swept across the scene, pausing briefly on the space between her and Lochlan.

"You came separately," he said, his tone casual but curious. "Why?"

"I had a meeting on the other side of Stella Rune," Nia replied.

Wulfric's gaze shifted to Lochlan, his expression unreadable. "And you're upset Lochlan didn't attend with you?"

Nia exhaled but didn't answer. It hurt more than she felt was reasonable or wanted to admit.

Wulfric's gaze moved from Lochlan to Nia, pinning her in place. "And what was this meeting for?"

"None of your business," Nia snapped.

Wulfric's jaw tightened, but he let it go, leaning back in his chair. "This is our last family dinner," he said, his voice carefully measured. "Which public event will you be attending as a happy couple? Hopefully, it will have fewer… vines than the last."

Of course, he had to bring up the chaos of the full moon celebration.

Lochlan shifted, clearly uncomfortable. "We haven't decided," he said carefully.

"Floating lights ceremony," Nia said at the same time.

The moment the words left her mouth, she flinched. She'd planned to bring up the idea today, somewhere between her meeting and this dinner, but hadn't had the chance. The new moon of October was always special in Stella Rune. When the sky was at its darkest, the townspeople celebrated by releasing lanterns along the canal and out into the ocean, their soft glow carried by the tides.

Two years ago, Ivy had spearheaded a campaign to switch to an eco-friendlier alternative, replacing the traditional lanterns with ones made from seaweed paper and candles crafted from beeswax. It had been the only time Nia had seen Ivy genuinely furious, her usual affability turned to righteous rage as she'd fought the town council to make the change. Now, the ceremony held even more meaning.

Nia had wanted to share that with Lochlan. She just hadn't planned to float the idea under her father's calculating gaze.

Dinner was quiet and awkward, every attempt at small talk withering before it could take root.

Nia thought about how little time they had left to prove themselves to her father. How this dinner, with its silence and tension, was the perfect way to reinforce the idea that she and Lochlan didn't work. But she hated it. Hated how much the uneasy tension between them bothered her, how much it hurt to see the look on Lochlan's face when she'd brushed him off.

When Wulfric finally dismissed them, his frustration with the lack of conversation apparent, Nia didn't hesitate. She threw herself onto her motorcycle and tore down the dark roads, thoughts and doubts chasing her all the way home. She beat Lochlan back and slipped inside the house, quickly greeting Jade before bolting upstairs.

Passing the locked door of his office sent a fresh wave of irritation through her, but she ignored it and headed straight for the bathroom. She turned the water as hot as it would go and stepped under the spray, hoping it might scorch away the tension of the evening.

But all she could think about was Lochlan and the quiet tension at dinner, the way he'd closed himself off. She didn't know what he was working on, or why he'd been so cagey about that package. Maybe it was nothing. Or maybe it was something. She couldn't tell, and the not-knowing ate at her. Still, she didn't think pressing him tonight would help either of them.

Lochlan was cautious, thoughtful. He always took his time. And if she pushed too hard now, she might only make him retreat further. But this was about more than that. The real question Nia needed to answer was this—

Did she trust Lochlan?

The scalding water cascaded over her, painful and clarifying. She wanted to trust him. And he'd earned that, hadn't he? Not just her affection or desire, but her trust. He'd stood by her, taken care of her, been devoted to her, despite her father's manipulations and her own doubts.

However tense or uncertain she might feel, as far as she knew, Lochlan hadn't done anything to break that trust.

So, she'd wait.

For now.

41

Lochlan

"Marriage Mishaps on the Rise—Will the Videt Step In?" –A LEGAL THREAD

Lochlan sat on the edge of the bed, his elbows resting on his knees and hands clasped tightly as he stared at the floor. The faint sound of water running in the bathroom filled the otherwise quiet house.

Dinner had been torture, and he knew why. Nia was too smart not to notice something was off. He hated keeping things from her, hated the way her guarded looks cut through him.

He just needed time.

Before coming upstairs, he'd quickly fed Jade, who had stared at him with those big, judgmental eyes. It felt like everyone—even the dog—knew he was hiding something.

Now, he was here, waiting.

The water shut off and a few moments later the bathroom door opened. Nia stepped out, wrapped in a towel, her damp hair clinging to her shoulders. She stopped when she saw him, her brow furrowing slightly as their eyes met.

Lochlan swallowed hard, the words coming before he could stop them. "I'm sorry."

"For what?" Nia tilted her head slightly.

Lochlan looked up at her, his throat tightening. "For not coming today."

And for so much more.

"I have a feeling it was important," he added.

Her expression softened as she stepped closer. He stayed seated on the edge of the bed, his hands still clasped in front of him, as she reached out and ran her fingers gently over his face.

"I didn't tell you how important it was," she said quietly. "I could have told you. But I didn't."

She was feeling bad? Guilt twisted in his chest like a knife. No, this couldn't be right. He was the one who should grovel. He was the one keeping secrets, who needed to confess.

But then she leaned down, kissed him, and all his thoughts dissolved.

She was so warm, her skin still damp from the shower, her hair leaving droplets on his cheeks as her lips moved against his.

Lochlan kissed her back, letting her warmth and the soft press of her lips distract from the tension still lingering in his chest. But when she reached for the hem of his shirt, pulling it up and over his head, his heart kicked into overdrive.

The towel dropped to the floor, and for a moment, all he could do was stare. Nia didn't give him the chance to overthink. She pushed him back onto the bed, her hands quick to undo his pants and slide them down his legs.

He thought about slowing her down, his hands instinctively brushing her hips. But her grip was firm, insistent, as she guided him to her entrance, her body pressing flush against his.

"Nia—"

"Loch." she murmured, cutting him off as she sank onto him.

This—sex with her—was as easy as breathing. They moved together effortlessly, like they were made for it, no thoughts, no worries. Except—

A voice in the back of his head: a quiet alarm bell, ringing faintly under the heat of their bodies. He shoved it down, tried to ignore it, to ignore everything else as she took him deeper, her hands braced on his chest.

Nia rode him like she couldn't get enough, her head tilting back as she cried out, her release shattering through her. The sight of her undid him and a heartbeat later he followed, his hands gripping her thighs as he came hard.

For a moment, there was nothing but the sound of their heavy breathing, the warmth of her body still pressed against his.

Lochlan reached for the towel she'd discarded, cleaning her up with gentle care before slipping off the bed and heading to the bathroom. When he returned, she was already drifting off, eyes heavy. She dragged herself from where she'd been curled in the blankets, and padded to the bathroom half asleep. When she came back and crawled onto the wrong side of the bed, Lochlan slid in beside her. He carefully gathered her into his arms, shifting until she fit snugly against his chest.

He pressed a kiss to the top of her head.

Within seconds, her breathing fell into a soft, steady rhythm.

Lochlan didn't sleep.

His mind refused to quiet, every secret he'd kept from her swirling in his head like a storm he couldn't outrun.

L.L. CAMPBELL

Lochlan sat at his desk, holding a piece of paper that had slipped from the last diary. The restoration of the volume itself was nearly complete—pages soothed of their burns, ink coaxed back from the brink of oblivion. But the letter he held had been hidden deep within its spine, fragile and forgotten.

He had just finished repairing it.

The ink had darkened as his magic settled over it, the words growing crisp and whole once more. He hadn't meant to read them. But the moment they surfaced, he hadn't been able to stop himself. The letter was addressed to Nia.

From her mother.

Lochlan's chest tightened, the weight of his discovery crushing. He'd known the diaries contained pieces of Nia's past—known they might hurt her as much as they helped her—but this was different. This wasn't history he was restoring. It was *her* history he was holding.

And he'd kept it from her.

The quiet of the house felt suddenly suffocating. Nia had been off lately, her energy guarded, her distance unspoken but unmistakable. She could feel his secrecy, even if she didn't know its object or shape.

Whatever Wulfric had promised or threatened or wanted, he couldn't do this anymore.

Lochlan scrubbed a hand over his face. The diary sat open before him, the letter resting atop its pages like a confession. Nia didn't deserve this.

He was going to fix it.

Before he could second-guess himself, Lochlan was out of the office and then the house, his feet automatically steering him through the tunnels to the Videt, his resolve solidifying with each step. He stormed past Francine without a word, ignoring her startled greeting. His focus was singular, his frustration fueling every step as he pushed open the heavy doors to Wulfric's office.

A blustering elder stood in the middle of Wulfric's office, his face red with indignation and his hands gesturing wildly as if he and The Sword were mid-argument. The sudden intrusion left him flustered, his eyes narrowing at Lochlan, who'd entered without so much as a knock.

"I need to speak with you."

Lochlan fixed his gaze on Wulfric, ignoring the elder, who straightened, puffing up with self-importance.

"Have some decency," he barked, his tone dripping with disdain.

Lochlan didn't flinch, and instead of retreating stepped deeper into the room.

"Leave us," Wulfric said, low but commanding.

The elder's smugness lingered for a heartbeat too long before he realized The Sword wasn't speaking to Lochlan—he was glaring at the elder. The older witch's self-satisfaction evaporated as he stammered, bowing before hastily exiting the room.

The doors slammed shut behind him, leaving Lochlan and Wulfric alone in the charged silence that followed. Wulfric leaned back in his chair, his expression unreadable as he regarded Lochlan with a quiet, expectant air.

"I'm done," Lochlan said, his voice steady despite the weight of the moment.

Wulfric arched a brow. "With what, exactly?"

"The lies," Lochlan replied.

Wulfric's lips twitched, something that wasn't quite a smile ghosting at the edges of his mouth. "Which ones?"

"All of them."

For a long moment, Wulfric studied him, his gaze sharp and searching. His expression shifted from carefully projected indifference to understanding, then something closer to pride.

"I heard what you said yesterday," Lochlan went on. "I disagree. I need to be the one to tell her, and it needs to be now. It can't wait until Samhain."

His chest ached at the memory of Nia walking in on them at the manor, suspicion flickering behind her eyes. The distance between them had widened every second he'd held on to Wulfric's secret.

No more.

Lochlan pulled out his phone and messaged Nia before he could talk himself out of it.

Me

Can I meet you at your office? Please. I need to talk.

He would bring her home and show her everything. He only hoped he wasn't too late.

42

Nia

"Not All Is What It Seems in Stella Rune?"
—THE STELLA RUNE GAZETTE

Nia walked briskly through the streets of Stella Rune, the cool morning air brushing her cheeks as the town slowly came to life. Early commuters filled the roads, their footsteps steady and purposeful, echoing her own.

She told herself she felt better after last night. Not because everything was fixed, but because for a moment they had simply been themselves. Awkward. Sweet. Honest. And it had felt perfect.

Lochlan wasn't hiding anything. Maybe she was just looking for reasons to doubt the match her father had forced on them both.

Lost in thought, she didn't notice the figure in front of her until it was too late—they collided, the impact jolting her out of her reverie.

"Oh!" Nia stumbled, steadying herself as she looked down. Recognition flickered almost instantly. "Naked Nancy?"

The woman blinked, startled, then let out a light laugh. "Oh, my apologies, dearest…" Her voice trailed off and her brow furrowed as she hesitated. "What did you just call me?"

Nia shook her head. "Nothing. You're Nancy, right? I met you the other day."

Nancy's face lit up as she clasped her hands together. "Yes! Wow, yes." She paused, her eyes softening with fondness. "I'm sorry if I interrupted your afternoon with Lochlan. My, I just love that boy."

Nia forced a polite smile. "How do you know him?"

Nancy tilted her head, looking momentarily baffled. "We've been working at the Videt together for years. He's so quiet and reserved, but always patient and kind. Just a lovely young man."

Nia's ears began ringing. The bustling noise of the street faded into the background as her thoughts, questions, and doubts all coalesced around a single possibility.

"Wait. At the Videt… in what department?" she managed to ask, suspicion building.

"In the archives. Oh, everyone else was so surprised when you two ended up together, but I wasn't." Nancy smiled and patted Nia on the arm. "I mean, I know how close he is to your father. I just think it was serendipitous."

"Close to…" Nia's stomach dropped, her throat tightening further. "My father?"

"Of course!" Nancy said, as if this were common knowledge. "It's only natural, after your father got him that scholarship. Then an internship. Goodness, but you should know all this already!"

Nia forced out a stiff nod, her lips pressing into a thin line. "I should," she said quickly, the words clipped. "I do." Clearing her throat, she straightened. "Will you excuse me?"

Nancy's smile faltered, but she nodded, stepping aside to let Nia pass. Nia turned on her heel, heading back the way she'd come as her thoughts spiraled. Wulfric had orchestrated this marriage—had manipulated events, pulled strings, forced them both into the marriage they never agreed to.

Or at least, a marriage *she* had never agreed to.

Lochlan had said he hadn't wanted this. He'd acted like he was just as much a pawn as she was. But what if that wasn't true? What if he'd known all along? What if, from the very beginning, he had been working toward this—toward *her*?

She thought about dinner the night before, the tension in Lochlan's voice, the way her father had glanced at him. She thought about the argument she'd overheard, the cryptic remarks.

And, then, she thought about everything she'd chosen not to see, not to look for.

When she reached the house, the sight of Lochlan's green truck parked outside sent a fresh wave of unease through her. Inside, she called his name.

No answer.

Her pulse pounded as she strode straight for the locked office door. Her hand hovered over the doorknob for a moment, her pulse quickening. What was she expecting? Proof that she wasn't crazy? Reassurance that it was all nothing, that she was overthinking?

She turned the knob.

It was unlocked. For a fleeting second, she wondered if maybe she was wrong. Maybe it really was nothing.

Then she pushed the door open and stepped inside.

The familiar smell of damp soil and greenery hit her first, the space filled with Lochlan's plants and tools. Her gaze swept over the room, lingering on the small, personal touches that reminded her of him.

And then she saw them.

Journals.

They were laid out in a careful row across his desk, pristine and arranged with precision. Her breath caught in her throat as she stepped closer. She recognized the leather bindings, the delicate engravings. They looked identical to the one she carried with her, the one she had protected for years.

Her mother's journal.

Nia's breath grew shallow, her chest tight as she reached for the first one. Her hands trembled, her fingertips reverently grazing the leather cover before she finally flipped it open.

She expected to find earlier passages that built on the pieces of a story she already knew. Instead, her mother's familiar handwriting greeted her, its curves and flourishes unmistakable, but the time marking at the top of the page was later than the entries in the journal she carried with her.

Her eyes skimmed the opening lines, her pulse pounding in her ears.

I don't know where this path will lead us, but for the first time in forever, I feel a spark of hope. The beast has set me free, and though the future is uncertain, I am not alone. I can even feel him now, watching over me. He will keep me safe. It's a promise I cling to, a beacon in the dark.

Nia's fingers tightened on the page.

The words didn't make sense. This entry picked up just after where her diary had left off, yet it told a story she hadn't imagined.

Nia turned the pages, devouring the words, unable to stop. Passage after passage unraveled everything she thought she knew. Her father, Wulfric, hadn't been the villain she'd believed him to be. He'd dismantled the dark legacy of his family brick by brick, building something extraordinary in its place. Her mother's words were no longer filled with anguish and dread, but love and hope as she recounted how Wulfric had saved her, how she'd fallen for him, how they had conceived Nia.

Her mother wasn't scared, she'd written. Not with Wulfric by her side. The story of Nia's name was there, too, written in her mother's delicate script. Every word painted a picture of a life filled with love and purpose. Nia's vision blurred as she read, tears slipping down her cheeks. Everything she'd believed—about her father, her family, her mother's life—it was all wrong. Her father had told her only part of what happened when she was younger. He'd blamed himself, told her how it was his fault, that he hadn't been able to protect her mother. That it was why Nia had been kept hidden.

She hadn't understood then why he blamed himself so deeply for her mother's death. His words had seemed hollow, tainted by grief she couldn't begin to comprehend. But when she had found that first diary at seventeen—when she'd read those passages painting a picture of a monster coming for her mother—it had all made sense.

The journal in which her mother had spoken of her fear, of the horrible man she was fated to and would be forced to marry, had been Nia's answer, her vindication for turning her back on the lonely isolation of her father's stifling protection. It was what had empowered her to run, why she chose to forge a path on her own; she couldn't bear to stay, not with what she'd believed she knew about him, what she believed he had done to her mother.

But now, surrounded by the journals, these undeniable pieces of Luna's life, Nia realized just how wrong she had been. The truth radiated from each carefully written line, shattering the image Nia had clung to for so long.

Wulfric hadn't just loved her mother. He had been her partner in something bigger. Luna had believed in a future where humans and supernaturals didn't just exist side by side—but lived together, thrived together. And her father had believed in it, too, fought for it, standing at her mother's side, working toward a world where their daughter could grow up without fear, where she and all witches like her would be free from the need to hide who and what they were.

And Wulfric had adored Nia, too. Loved her enough to shield her from truths he thought too heavy for a child to bear. To protect her from the threats that had already stolen her mother from them both. Luna had known the dangers of the Anti-Glamour Coalition and embraced a new path that defied them anyway; she'd understood the risks, but believed change was worth it.

Nia's fingers trembled as she reached for the last diary and found a folded letter tucked between its pages. Her name was written across the front in looping script.

Nia unfolded it, her hands shaking.

My dearest daughter,

I hope you aren't reading this. If you are, then I have passed, and that thought alone makes my heart ache. It feels strange to write this, when I have spent so long feeling safe—when I have spent so long believing I would see you grow, hold you, tell you all of this myself.

But the tides have turned again.

There are some who do not wish to see our vision come to light. They fight against it, clawing to keep the world as it is, separate and broken. But your father and I believe in something better. We dream of a future where humans and supernaturals are not at odds but woven together, building a stronger world than either could alone. A place where the next generation—your generation—can thrive in harmony, not fear.

And so we fight on.

I do not know what the world looks like as you read this. I do not know what your father has told you, or if he's alive. I hope he is. I hope we will both survive this. I don't know what you have been made to believe. But please, my love, trust in this—I love you. He loves you. You have been cherished since the moment we knew you existed.

I wish I could tell you how much of me already belongs to you. How I wonder what your laugh sounds like, if you have my nose, if your magic will bloom bright and wild, like fire in the dark.

Don't fear it, my love.

If you ever find yourself lost, if you ever stand in the shadows and wonder if you are meant to be there—know this: your magic is not cruel. It is beautiful. It is endless. It is yours to shape.

And so are you.

With all my love, Mom

Tears splashed onto the page, smudging the ink. Nia blinked rapidly, pulling her sleeve down to blot them away before they could do more damage. Her chest burned with frustration, a storm of emotions swirling inside her.

She was angry—so angry—with herself, with her father, with Lochlan.

Why hadn't they told her? Why had they just let her continue on, clinging to half-truths and assumptions? They hadn't fought her. They hadn't pushed her. They had just… let her.

"Nia?"

She whipped her head around so fast, pain twinged down her neck.

Lochlan stood in the doorway, his expression caught somewhere between guilt and dread, like a man walking into his own execution.

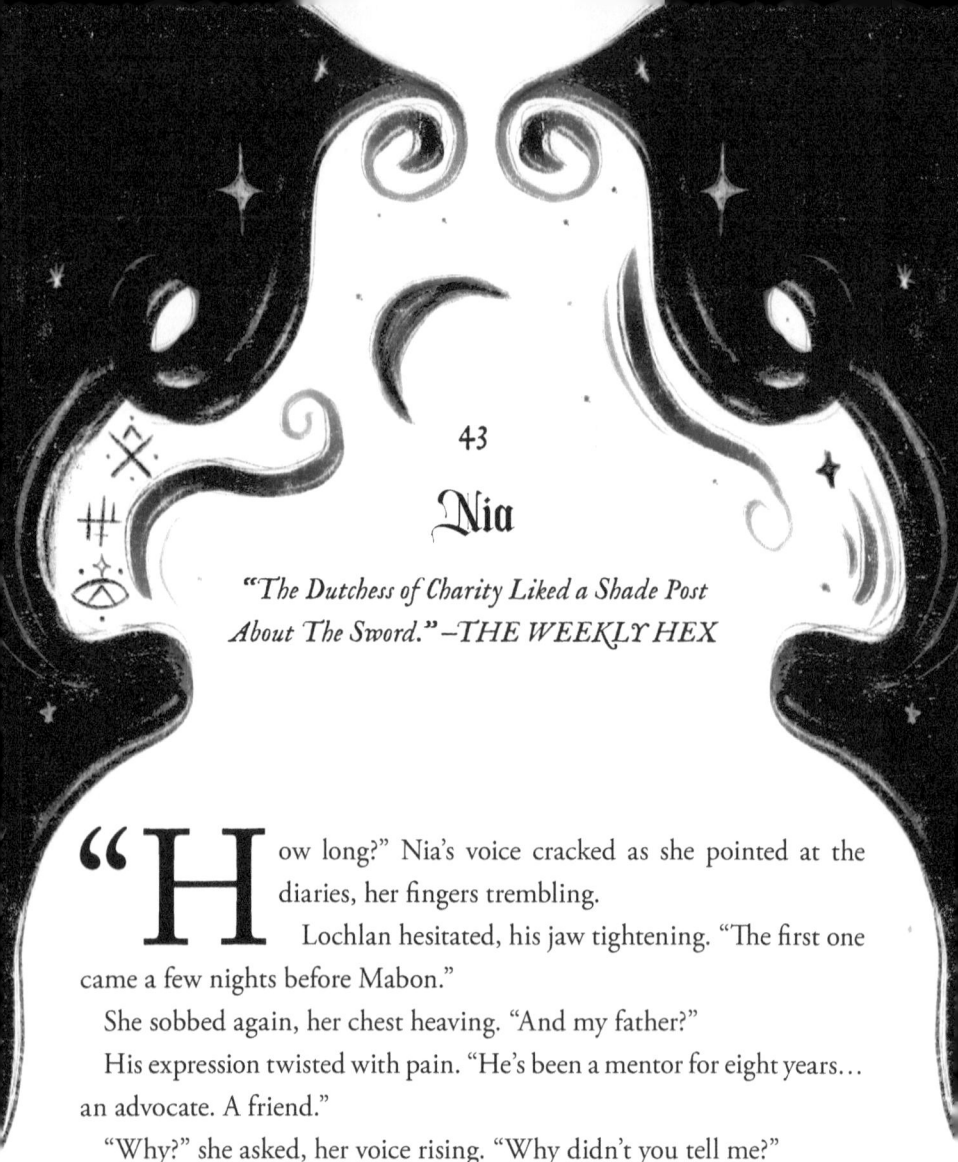

43

Nia

"The Dutchess of Charity Liked a Shade Post About The Sword." –*THE WEEKLY HEX*

"How long?" Nia's voice cracked as she pointed at the diaries, her fingers trembling.

Lochlan hesitated, his jaw tightening. "The first one came a few nights before Mabon."

She sobbed again, her chest heaving. "And my father?"

His expression twisted with pain. "He's been a mentor for eight years… an advocate. A friend."

"Why?" she asked, her voice rising. "Why didn't you tell me?"

"He told me not to," Lochlan admitted, his voice low. "And threatened me when I told him I wanted to come clean. I didn't know what to do."

Nia stared at him, the tears blurring her vision. "You asked me not to lie. To be honest with you. But this whole time, you were both lying to me. And he's been lying to me for so much longer."

She stood abruptly, the chair scraping against the floor as she stormed past him, her steps quick and unsteady as she descended the stairs.

"Nia, wait!" Lochlan called after her, desperate.

She spun on him, her fury like a tidal wave. "No! You don't get to tell me what to do." Her voice broke as the tears spilled faster. "You lied to me, and it hurts. I don't know what to do, where to go. It just hurts so much."

Lochlan reached out, his hand moving toward her like he could somehow fix everything with a touch.

Nia recoiled, her whole body jerking back as though he'd struck her. "How could you?" Her voice shook, betrayal twisting in her chest.

Lochlan froze. For a moment, he looked lost, his mouth opening and closing before he finally spoke as his hand dropped to his side. "I... needed time," he said, his words halting and unsure. "I wanted to give you all her diaries once they were repaired. So you could have a piece of her, have the whole story."

Nia's stomach churned as she watched him, his shoulders sagging as he laughed bitterly.

"It sounds so stupid now." He ran a hand through his hair, his voice breaking as he continued. "I didn't want to hurt you. I just... I love you so much it scared me. The idea of losing you scared me. The idea of Wulfric taking away everything else I've known and worked for if I told you..." He shook his head. "I didn't know what to do."

The words hit her like a physical blow. She stood there, staring at him, unable to move or speak.

Lochlan's gaze dropped to the floor, his voice quieter now. "But I went to your father this morning," he said. "I told him I'm done lying to you."

Nia let out a short, bitter laugh, the sound harsh even to her own ears. "You went to him?" she said, her voice breaking. "Again, you went to him, instead of coming to me? I feel like... I'm going to explode."

Lochlan took a step closer, his expression desperate. "What do you need?"

"I don't know," she admitted, her hands shaking as she wiped at her face. "I hate this. You lied to me. And you were working with him?"

Lochlan flinched. "Not like that. Not with the marriage." His voice was raw, pleading. "I swear to you, Nia—I didn't know. I had nothing to do with it." His throat bobbed as he swallowed hard. "When Wulfric told us what he'd done, I was as blindsided as you were. I had no idea he was your father, no idea what he was planning—I didn't know he had a daughter at all."

She shook her head. "More lies."

"No." He took another step forward, his hands curling into fists at his sides. "I won't lie to you. Not now. Not ever again." His exhale was slow, unsteady. "I knew he had plans, that this marriage wasn't just about you. Or me." His jaw clenched. "But I didn't understand, couldn't guess what they were. Not until Dover."

Her breath caught, fury slicing through her like a blade. "Dover," she repeated, voice low, shaking. "So you knew then. And you still kept it from me?"

Lochlan didn't answer.

Nia's vision blurred again, but she refused to blink. "How could you look at me every day, knowing what you knew, and say nothing?"

"I wanted to tell you." He looked brittle, breakable, like something within him had collapsed. "I should have told you."

"Damn right you should have."

Lochlan took a ragged breath. "Please," he said, his voice breaking. "Don't give up on this. On us."

She didn't trust herself to answer.

"I'll leave," he said quietly. "I'll give you time. Just… stay here. Please."

He backed away, his steps slow and measured, as though worried the wrong move might shatter her.

"I'm sorry," Lochlan whispered, more to himself than to her. "I wanted this so much… and I was afraid of losing it all."

Nia stayed rooted in place, watching as he opened the front door and slipped out, the soft click of the latch echoing in the silence. The moment he was gone, her knees buckled. She crumbled to the floor as sobs wracked her body, loud and messy. Jade padded over, her wet nose nudging Nia's arm gently as the dog curled against her, offering quiet comfort as Nia clung to her warmth.

The back door burst open with a deafening bang.

Nia's head shot up, her heart caught in a battle between fury and hope.

But it wasn't Lochlan.

44

Nia

"Goblins are asking after the duchess! Did something happen?" –*WOLVENLOVER*₁₁₁

Nia barely had time to register what was happening before a canister clattered to the floor, rolling to a stop just feet away from her. Smoke billowed out in thick waves, curling around her ankles and filling the room with a damp, earthy scent.

It smelled almost like a field in the early morning—rich and strangely familiar.

Her chest tightened, her body reacting before her mind could catch up. She staggered back, coughing as her lungs filled with cloying smoke. Her vision blurred, the edges of the room warping as her legs weakened beneath her. Her eyes felt unbearably heavy, and she blinked rapidly, trying to fight the weight dragging her down.

Moon moss.

The thought flitted through her hazy mind as the smoke coiled around her, the scent conjuring a memory: Lochlan had made this same thing and used it on the Lunaflor.

Lochlan.

Her chest ached at the thought of him, but the sound of a deep, guttural snarl snapped her focus back to the kitchen. Jade. She stood protectively between Nia and the door.

The dog lunged, tearing at a shadowed figure.

A man screamed in pain, raw and visceral.

"Don't hurt my dog!" Nia rasped, coughing and inhaling more smoke. *My dog.*

The words rang clearly in her head even through the fog. Jade *was* hers—her protector, her companion—and she loved her fiercely. She didn't know who was there, or what they wanted, but she knew one thing for certain: she would not let them harm Jade.

Nia reached for her magic, her fingers curling as shadows and vines tumbled forth with sluggish, desperate movements. She could feel her power responding, but it was slow and uncertain, and wielding it felt like wading through water.

The haze in her mind made everything harder—her focus was fractured, her control slipping. Vines lashed out, cracking chairs and sending splinters flying. Through the chaos, Jade scurried back and pressed herself against Nia's side. The dog's low growls rumbled against her as Jade crouched, ready to spring again.

Nia's breath caught as she saw them—three sets of feet stepping into view through the smoke, just inches from where she lay on the floor.

Her throat burned, her voice barely a croak as she forced the words out. "Get out of my home!"

My home.

The thought was clear and tangible, even as her body felt less and less so. This was her home. No matter how she'd gotten here, or what had happened between her and Lochlan, this place was hers. This house was home.

He was home.

And she wanted to keep both so badly it hurt.

A voice broke through the haze, wavering with nerves. "Is this… magic?"

"It wasn't supposed to go down like this," said another, higher but still masculine.

Jade's growls deepened, vibrating against Nia's side as she curled closer.

This was the last thing Nia felt before the world tilted, the hazy light narrowing to a pinprick just before everything went black.

45

Lochlan

"Have You Seen Lochlan's Big Brother? How Do We Summon Him?" –MESSY_IVY

He had made Nia cry.

The thought was enough to make him consider walking off the cliffs of Stella Rune and letting the ocean swallow him. Instead, he'd ended up here, wandering aimlessly through the tunnels, his shoes scuffing against the uneven stone floor. The air was cold and damp, the walls too close, pressing in like a punishment he couldn't escape. It was fitting. He deserved this.

He'd made a mistake.

No—he was the mistake.

His mother's voice rang in his head: *"A mistake from the beginning."*

Lochlan dragged a hand through his hair, gripping the strands at the back of his neck. If he had just come clean from the start, this wouldn't have happened. Maybe Nia would have hated him in those early days— hated him for being connected to her father. But wouldn't that have been better? At least then they could have had a chance to work through it. His chest tightened as the question hung in his mind, heavy and unanswerable.

Would they work through this?

Her tear-streaked face flashed before his eyes. The memory hit him like a punch to the gut and he fought the urge to crumble right there in the cold, damp tunnel.

What could he do to fix this?

Nothing, at least not here in the tunnels, he realized. Every step away from home felt more wrong than the last. He should have stayed. He should have gone to her, told her what he'd feared and wanted, how much he cared for her, until there was nothing left to hide.

Goddess help him, he was an idiot.

Lochlan stopped, dragging in a shaky breath as he glanced over his shoulder. The pull to go home was so strong, he imagined he could hear his ducks quacking in the distance. Long, rapidly waddling shadows stretched up the tunnel walls, distorted in the dim light.

"Taco?"

It wasn't his imagination: a small, black figure emerged from the gloom, its neck stretched out and wings flapping furiously as it barreled toward him.

Lochlan had seen a lot of ridiculous things in his life, but nothing quite matched the absurdity of a duck running. Taco's legs churned, his head bobbing in time, and his wings flailing in a way that didn't seem remotely aerodynamic. Celia and Cynthia emerged from the shadows, circling him in an erratic flurry of feathers and quacks.

"What's this?" Lochlan muttered, his heart pounding as the ducks nipped at his ankles, herding him back the way he had come.

He stumbled, nearly tripping over Taco as he let out a massive, exasperated quack.

"I need to go home?" Lochlan asked, feeling a mix of incredulity and rising panic.

Taco's commanding quack reverberated through the tunnel.

Lochlan's stomach twisted with fear.

Nia.

He turned and ran, the sound of his boots pounding against the tunnel floor mingling with the frantic chorus of quacks behind him. As Lochlan rounded a corner, a group of witches gasped, their conversation cutting off as they watched him sprint past.

"What the—?" one of them began, dissolving into laughter as Taco and the other ducks waddled after him, their wings flapping wildly.

"Are those *ducks*?" another asked.

Lochlan ignored them, yanking his phone from his pocket as he ran. His thumb hovered over Nia's contact for a split second before he pressed call.

It rang.

And rang.

"Come on, Nia," he muttered, his heart hammering harder with every unanswered tone.

The call clicked to voicemail.

"Nia, it's me." His voice trembled. "I—something's wrong. Please call me back."

He shoved the phone back into his pocket just as the tunnel's end came into view, the late-morning light spilling into the opening as he burst through, chest tight as he sprinted toward home.

Lochlan reached the front door and threw it open, slamming it against the wall as he stumbled inside. A strange smell lingered in the air, faint but unmistakable—damp and earthy, with an edge that made his stomach twist. He tried calling Nia again, the phone pressed so tightly to his ear it hurt.

Nothing.

"Nia!" His voice cracked as he stormed through the house, shouting. "Jade?"

The quacks of his ducks echoed behind him as they waddled in his wake, hopping awkwardly over the overturned furniture and tangled vines. The ducks clustered near the remains of a canister on the floor, pecking curiously at the metallic shell.

Horror froze Lochlan, like ice in his veins

"No," he whispered, his heart racing as he turned and bolted for the stairs.

He took them two at a time as he called her phone again. The ringing barely registered before he heard it—but the sound wasn't coming from the line.

It was coming from inside the house.

The sound grew louder as he neared the office. He pushed the door open, the sight inside hitting him like a punch: her phone sat on his desk, next to her mother's diaries.

He sank to the floor, knees hitting the wood hard.

"Where is my dog," he whispered. "Where is my wife."

They weren't here. Lochlan's hand trembled as he pulled his phone away from his ear. His thumb hovered over Becket's name for a split second before he stopped.

He called his brother instead.

46

Lochlan

"A Concerning Uptick in Duck Activity—Should We Be Worried?" –THE STELLA RUNE GAZETTE

Eight hours.

Eight agonizing hours, and still no sign of Nia or Jade.

Lochlan paced the length of the living room with his phone clutched in one hand. His brother was on the way, but the train would take hours—hours Lochlan didn't know if they had.

Thane had answered on the first ring, his voice bright with excitement. "Hey little brother! Are you coming to—"

"Thane." Lochlan had barely managed to choke out his brother's name.

Thane's tone had shifted instantly, somber and intense. "What happened?"

"Nia and Jade are gone." Lochlan had gripped the phone tighter, voice raw. "I think they were taken."

Silence. A heartbeat. Then—

"I'm on my way."

And the line had gone dead.

Lochlan glanced over his shoulder at Ivy and Becket, both seated at the dining table with their laptops open. Their screens cast pale lights over their faces, each focused, though Lochlan had no idea what they were working on. Searching, tracking, hacking—whatever it was, it wasn't happening fast enough.

The tension in the room was suffocating.

Helen and Jimmy from the bookstore were out canvassing streets and alleyways, asking anyone and everyone in town if they'd seen Nia and Jade. Natasha and the other goblins were searching the tunnels and canal, hoping to find any clues as to where they'd gone.

But Lochlan knew they wouldn't find Nia. Not like that.

He didn't know who had her, or why, but his gut told him the truth he didn't want to face. Nia had been taken, and Jade had either been kidnapped with her, or managed to escape during the fight. The thought of Jade running scared through the streets—or worse, lying hurt somewhere—made his chest tighten painfully. And Nia…

He couldn't finish that thought.

Wulfric and the Videt were doing their part, working with magic Lochlan didn't pretend to understand. Wulfric's frustration was razor-sharp, his scowl deepening with every passing minute. "It's useless," he growled, making Ivy glance up. "The block is still there. I can't see her thoughts at all."

They were trying everything—spells, tools, methods Lochlan didn't have words for. But none of it was working. Every failed attempt felt like another weight pressing down on him.

The front door burst open. Lochlan turned, his heart leaping at the thought of Nia walking through that door. But it wasn't her.

It was Thane.

Dressed in all black, he strode inside with a large bag slung over one shoulder. Echo padded in beside him, his sleek black shepherd's head low as he sniffed the floor.

Without a word, Thane dropped his bag on the counter and pulled Lochlan into an embrace. Lochlan closed his eyes for a moment, letting his brother's steadiness anchor him.

Thane pulled back, one hand firm on his shoulder as he met Lochlan's gaze.

"Tell me everything."

Lochlan hesitated, his shoulders slumping slightly. "I was a fool," he admitted, running a hand through his hair. "I left her when she was upset. After what I'd done—"

"Logistics, Lochlan," Thane interrupted, his tone cutting off the spiral of guilt.

Lochlan exhaled, dragging his focus back to the facts. "I left here around nine this morning," he began. "About twenty minutes later, the ducks found me and brought me back home."

Thane gave him a look, one brow lifting.

Lochlan sighed. "Logistics."

Thane nodded, motioning for him to continue.

"When I got back, there was a smell in the air," Lochlan said, his voice tightening. "And an empty canister of what we think was a sleep-inducing substance. The house was a mess, and Nia and Jade were gone."

Becket looked up from his laptop, his expression grim. "We asked the neighbors if they'd seen anything, but no one has come forward."

Across the room, Ivy began to pace, her hands twisting nervously. "What if it was someone she… you know." Her voice trailed off, leaving the rest unspoken.

Lochlan dragged a hand down his face but nodded. "It could be."

Thane glanced at him sharply. "What?"

"There was a man," he said, his voice tight with anger and regret. "I've seen him once before, but the other afternoon, he was watching us. Nia said it was nothing. But he'd threatened her before, yelled at her, in her office."

"So it was something," Thane said. "Who is he?"

"I'm not sure," Lochlan admitted, raking a hand through his hair. "But I think she coerced him into giving money to some charity."

He'd tried to remember, but if Nia had mentioned the name of the organization the purple-faced man was supposed to donate to when they'd argued in her office, he couldn't remember it through the haze of stress and panic.

"I wonder..." Ivy's fingers flew over her keyboard as she searched. Her movements were frantic, her breath coming faster. "Nia put a note in here, but we don't have any record of receiving the funds and—" She froze, her eyes widening as she looked up. "Wait. The man who threatened Nia. Was he a big guy?"

Lochlan nodded, his brow furrowed. "Yes?"

Becket leaned back in his chair, his expression thoughtful. "You think it's the same man who came up to you at the autumn festival?"

Ivy snapped her fingers. "Yeah, I bet that's him! He said he wouldn't be donating, which I didn't really think was strange. People back out all the time. But he looked really unhappy—maybe even angry—about it."

The room fell into a tense silence as the pieces slowly came together.

"But who is he?" Lochlan demanded.

Ivy shrugged helplessly, her eyes darting back to her laptop.

Before Lochlan could press further, Wulfric's growl of frustration cut through the room like a thunderclap. They all turned to see him gripping the elder—the same one Lochlan had interrupted earlier that day—shaking him with barely restrained fury as the man attempted to scry for Nia.

"I'm trying!" the elder yelped.

"Try harder!" Wulfric roared. The lights flickered violently, casting long, sharp shadows as his anger radiated through the room. "You fucking bird brain!"

"Yes, birds!" The elder flinched, his eyes wide with panic. "All I see is chickens, thousands of them!"

Ivy gasped, rushing forward to stand between the elder and Wulfric, who was towering over the older man in a state of rage. "Chickens?" She grabbed the elder's hand. "Do you see a farm?"

The elder hesitated, glancing nervously at Wulfric, who stood seething behind her. Finally, he nodded.

Ivy turned to Lochlan and Thane. "Jackson Runner. He's the CEO of a poultry distribution company. Nia was talking to him the night of Mabon. He didn't look very happy, either."

Thane was already at his laptop, his brows knit in concentration. "Runner Enterprises has a facility that houses chickens in the farmland just outside Stella Rune," he said. He pulled out his phone, pressed a button, and began speaking. "Alpha team, rally at thirteen Perseverance Lane."

A voice on the other end of the line responded, though Lochlan couldn't make out the words.

Thane checked his watch, his tone hardening. "Make it ten minutes. I'll be there in twelve, I expect the team ready for extraction upon my arrival. I'll send instructions en route."

He put down the phone and turned back to his laptop. Across the room, Wulfric's guards were also on their phones, their low voices an undercurrent in the tense atmosphere.

One of them ended his call and looked up, his expression firm. "We will handle this."

Thane didn't even look up from his screen. "Are you trained in kidnapping extractions?"

The guard hesitated. "Er…"

Wulfric cursed under his breath.

Another guard stepped forward. "We're trained to protect against magical attacks."

"Great," Thane said dryly, flipping the screen of his laptop. With a swift motion, it transformed into an improbably sleek, streamlined tablet. He tapped at it quickly before snapping the protective case into place. "You can be my anti-magic insurance. Stay behind me and out of my way."

Ivy blinked at the device, her mouth falling open slightly. "Witchcraft?"

Thane gave her a quick wink as his fingers flew over its surface. "No, miss. Just good old technology."

Becket raised an eyebrow. "Right. We all agree Thane's hot and mysterious. Can we stay focused for five seconds?"

Ivy stuck her tongue out at him.

Before either of them could respond, Lochlan spoke. "I'm going with you."

"No," Thane replied flatly, not even looking up.

"You think I'm just going to sit here?" Lochlan snapped, stepping closer, his frustration boiling over.

"You aren't trained." Thane said, his attention fixed on a detailed map. His fingers moved rapidly across the surface, zooming in on the warehouse and the surrounding terrain. "This place is out in the sticks," he said, his voice clipped. "Only one way in by road, and if they're smart, they've got eyes on it. We'll go through the back farm on foot." His gaze flicked to the guards, his tone dry. "Hope you don't mind some cow patties"

Lochlan stepped closer, his jaw tight. "I'm going."

Thane glanced at him sidelong, his expression unreadable. After a beat, he sighed. "Fine. But stay close to me or Echo, and follow my lead. No heroics." He turned back to his tablet, his voice lowering. "I've done this before. You haven't. If you come, I need to know you'll follow orders."

Lochlan bristled at Thane's words but held his tongue.

Thane's attention was back on the tablet. "We've got nine minutes before my people are in place. The guards can handle any magical interference, and Echo's trained to sniff out anyone or anything hiding along the approach path."

At the sound of his name, the sleek black shepherd let out a low bark, his ears perking up as his tail wagged in a subtle but eager display of readiness.

Lochlan hoped Echo could help them track down Jade, too.

Thane shut the tablet with a decisive click and grabbed his gear, slinging the pack over his shoulder. Confidence Lochlan found himself envying in that moment radiated off his brother like heat.

"Move out," he commanded, heading for the door. "We're not leaving her in there a second longer than we have to."

47

Nia

"The Best (and Worst) Ways to Get Out of a Magical Contract." –A LEGAL THREAD

Nia woke to a pounding headache and muffled sounds, as though the world had wrapped itself in cotton. The first thing she registered was clucking—dull and incessant. The next thing was the smell.

Wherever she was, it stank.

Her eyes fluttered open, vision swimming before gradually clearing. Darkness pressed against the outside windows; it had been hours since she'd collapsed on the floor. She shifted on the ground, the coarse texture of sawdust scraping against her skin.

Then she saw Jade.

Her dog was crammed into a cage far too small for her, growling low and steady. Nia's chest tightened as anger burned away the mental haze.

Chickens. Dozens of them surrounded her, feathers shifting and restless, but they stayed clear of Jade and her cage.

Nia tried to move, but her arms were bound tightly behind her, secured to a pole. She tugged at the ropes, frustration building as her gaze darted around the space.

She recognized it.

The foul smell of badly cared for chickens and the faint creak of metal beams—she'd been here. Months ago, she'd snuck into this very warehouse to take incriminating photos and videos. This was Jackson's operation.

Her eyes narrowed at the distant second-floor office overlooking the pens, where three figures moved behind opaque glass.

"Fucking Jackson," she muttered, venom infusing every syllable.

She pulled harder at the ropes, but it was useless. Her head throbbed and her body felt weak. Across the room, Jade let out a low growl, her cramped body shaking with tension. Nia clenched her jaw, forcing down the panic rising in her chest. She had to focus. She had to get Jade out. And herself, too.

Taking a deep breath, she ignored the painful throb in her skull. The moon moss they'd drugged her with left her abilities dull and sluggish. Focusing on the floor, Nia coaxed a thin stream of shadow to creep forward, gliding across the sawdust like an inky thread. It took far more effort than it should have. The thread of shadow thinned, flickered, her breath catching as it reached the cage and—

The latch clicked open.

Nia sagged back against the pole as Jade burst free, her body surging forward as chickens scattered, their wings flapping frantically. Feathers flew through the air as they scrambled away.

"Good girl," Nia whispered hoarsely.

Relief flooded through her as Jade bounded forward. The dog wasted no time, her teeth going straight to the ropes that bound Nia's hands. She tugged and gnawed, her strong jaws working quickly.

The three figures behind the glass had stopped moving.

"Shit," Nia hissed under her breath. She turned to Jade, who was still frantically chewing at the ropes around her hands.

"Jade, leave me," she whispered urgently, her voice trembling. "Go for help."

The dog's jaws worked faster, growling as if she could sense Nia's panic.

"Jade, no," Nia said again, her voice softer but desperate. "Go for help. Please."

Jade whined, pausing just long enough to nuzzle her face against Nia's cheek in a quick, reassuring lick. The dog turned and bolted into the shadows, her pale body disappearing into the maze of sawdust and feathers.

The door to the office opened with a labored creak.

The three men descended the stairs, their eyes fixed on her. Nia's anger flared. At the front was Jackson Runner, the CEO of this hellhole. He looked every bit the part—well-groomed and dressed in crisp, clean clothes that screamed professionalism despite the filth of the setting. Behind him loomed Gregor, the big, imposing man she'd fought before. He might have been terrifying to most, but Nia knew better. She'd kicked his ass once, and she could do it again. And then there was Raymond Bell, the man from the bar. He lagged behind the others, his face pale, his eyes darting around nervously. Of the three, he was the only one who looked scared shitless—probably because he was a regular.

Whatever he'd seen when they took her from her home had clearly left its mark.

Gregor was the first to speak. "You didn't lock the cage?" He rounded on Raymond, glaring.

Raymond flinched, his hands shaking as he stammered, "I-I did!"

"Clearly not!" Gregor snapped, his massive form radiating frustration. Nia smirked, tilting her head as if she found the whole situation amusing. "Well, well, well. Three grown men against little old me. What's the matter? Afraid?"

Jackson's eyes narrowed, but before he or the others could reply, she lunged forward. The ropes dug into her skin, pulling taut, but the sudden movement was enough to make all three men flinch. Their uncoordinated reactions were pitiful, and a bark of laughter burst from her lips.

"Pathetic," she shook her head, smiling wryly.

Jackson's face twisted in anger. "We're done with your games, Nia. You think you can threaten us like this, do business like this, and there are no consequences?"

"Boo freaking hoo." Nia shook her head. "You've all got more money than you know what to do with and you've lied, cheated, and stolen to get it. I'm just trying to level the scales."

"The scales aren't yours to balance!" Gregor snapped, his deep voice echoing through the cavernous room, startling a few chickens.

The air thickened with heat as flames erupted in his fists.

Nia eyed the fire with icy defiance. "You think you'll get out of paying for what you've done by threatening me? Please."

Let them try.

Jackson's mouth curled into something smug. "You think this is about money?" He let out a short, humorless laugh. "You're still playing small, Nia." He leaned in, voice dropping. "We're going to expose how Charis really operates."

He tossed a black notebook at her feet, its pages full of names and amounts they donated.

Nia's breath caught.

Her notebook.

Shit.

Jackson must have seen the flicker of hesitation in her eyes. He grinned. "You think people won't care that their beloved foundation was funded by people like us?" He gestured toward Gregor and Raymond. "You think the public won't be interested in how you convinced us to donate, how charitable the Duchess of Charity really is? The blackmail, the extortion, the threats?" His voice dripped with mock admiration. "You're not a saint, sweetheart. You're just better at hiding your dirt."

Nia forced herself to keep her expression neutral, even as a nauseating panic clawed up her throat. Charis wasn't a cleanly run business, not in the traditional sense. But it worked. She'd made it work. What did it matter if she coerced corrupt businessmen, threatened to expose politicians, twisted the arms of criminals, and occasionally partnered with them, if in the end it funneled money where it was actually needed?

But now...

For the first time, she saw it differently.

She'd always been willing to take risks—and pay any consequences incurred. But this wasn't just about her. If word about their funding got out, it wouldn't just ruin Charis—it would destroy Ivy's reputation. It would cast a shadow over every person the foundation had ever helped, turning their success stories into scandals. It would ruin future projects, the space she and Ivy had envisioned for young supernaturals.

It would hurt Lochlan.

And Wulfric.

The way she'd generated funding for Charis would be seen as confirmation their family had manipulated the system—and misused their magic—to claim and maintain power. Everything her father and mother had worked to build, the path to coexistence they'd fought for, would be threatened.

For the first time since she woke up, true fear curled in Nia's chest.

But she couldn't let them see it.

She lifted her chin. "Oh, it is my place to balance the scales." A slow smile spread across her lips. "And you're in deeper than you can imagine. Kidnapping the daughter of The Sword?"

She felt a surge of pride as the words left her mouth. It was the first time she'd said that title without bitterness or resentment. After seeing her father through her mother's eyes, she was finally beginning to understand the man he truly was. She just hoped she'd get out of here and have the chance to tell him that.

Not to thank him—oh no.

To yell at him for letting her go through life thinking he was a monster. And Lochlan.

She hated that she'd spent their last moments pushing him away, convincing herself she couldn't trust him. But was that really what had kept her from choosing him? Or was it because trusting him—really, truly trusting him—meant giving up something she had never been willing to before now?

Control.

Her entire adult life, she had relied on herself. No one else. Not even Ivy. Because no one else had ever been safe enough to rely on. But Lochlan...

Lochlan was different.

He had lied, yes. But not to manipulate her. Not to control her. Not even to keep the truth from her. He'd lied because he hadn't known how to tell her the truth in a way she could hear and accept without blaming him.

He'd lied because he didn't want to lose her.

And she knew—she *knew*—no matter what happened with these ass hats, no matter what they leaked, he was coming for her. And whatever happened next? They would be okay.

She loved him.

For the first time, she let herself believe love didn't have to mean losing herself. And if she got out of this, she wasn't going to waste another second pretending otherwise.

Raymond's brow furrowed "How can she be the daughter of a sword?"

Jackson rounded on Gregor. "The Sword?" he hissed, panicked.

"You didn't know?" Gregor's massive shoulders shrugged. "I don't live here, so it's not like I could keep eyes on her all the time while you were gone," he muttered. "But I never saw them together, and people say they haven't talked in years. I heard their relationship is rocky."

Nia let out a dry chuckle. "You heard wrong."

Jackson's head whipped back toward her, his face paling. "They can't trace her here, right?"

48

Lochlan

"Prince Thane Absent from Pinnacle Meeting—What's the Real Story?"—THE DOVER CENTENNIAL

A single light glowed in the warehouse looming ahead, the building's edges barely visible in the darkness. Inside, Lochlan knew there were thousands of chickens—and somewhere among them, Nia.

His chest tightened, the urge to charge in almost unbearable.

In the cow farm behind him, Wulfric, Ivy, and Becket were under close watch by Videt guards and two of Thane's trusted men. Wulfric had fought to join the mission; in the end, Lochlan and Thane had won that argument.

Now, Lochlan was crouched behind a wire fence, hidden among the tall grass, waiting. For what? He didn't know. Every second felt like a year. He just wanted to see Nia, to know for certain she was still there, whether she was hurt, if—

"There's movement." Thane's voice crackled through the earpiece Lochlan wore, his whisper deafening in the stillness.

Lochlan's gaze darted to Thane, who was focused on his tablet. The infrared scan glowed faintly, showing a small blob weaving through the field toward them. The clicks of weapons being armed echoed through the night. Lochlan's pulse quickened, his hand instinctively tightening on the hilt of the knife Thane had given him.

The Videt guards around him murmured quietly, their voices tense. "Could be a spell," one of them whispered.

"Wait!" Lochlan whispered, his eyes locked on the screen. He watched the blob carefully, his heart racing. "Jade?"

The heat signature on the tablet moved with more urgency. Lochlan's breath caught as a white shape burst through the tall grass ahead. Jade cleared the fence in a single bound, landing in Lochlan's arms.

"Jade!" The dog whined and licked his face, her whole body vibrating with anxiety. His hands moved quickly across her fur, feeling for anything out of place, afraid of what he might find. But there was nothing. No injuries, no blood—she was unharmed and whole.

Relief washed over him.

"Jade has been found," Thane whispered through the comms, his voice steady and clear. "Prepare for extraction."

Two of Thane's men moved forward with swift, practiced motions. They cut through the wire fence, the faint metallic snip barely audible over the pounding of Lochlan's heart. The group slipped through two by two, crouching low to keep their movements concealed.

On the far side, Echo and Jade took the lead, their noses working furiously as they sniffed at the air and ground. The two dogs seemed to communicate with each other in some unspoken way, pausing in unison as their bodies dropped low, their focus fixed on a large door ahead.

Thane gave a hand signal. The team fell into position, two men on each side of the door. In precise coordination, they wrenched it open with a piercing, metallic groan.

Chaos erupted.

A flood of chickens burst through the opening, wings flapping wildly as they scattered in every direction, their startled squawks mingling with those of the Videt guards.

One stumbled back, yelping like a child as a particularly angry hen flew at his face. "Get it off!" he shouted, swatting helplessly. The others recovered quickly, forming magical shields to deflect the onslaught of birds. But the dogs had already darted through the rush of feathers, slipping into the warehouse.

"Go!" Thane barked, cutting through the noise.

The team surged forward, Lochlan right behind them. Inside the warehouse was a chaotic swirl of motion and sound, shadows flickering against the walls as the team burst through the door. At first it was impossible to make out anything. Lochlan's eyes scanned the space, his heart lurching as he searched for the glow of red hair and—

Nia.

She was tied to a pole in the center of the space, her hands bound behind her back.

Relief slammed into Lochlan so hard it nearly knocked the breath from his chest. She was alive. But rage at the fact she was tied up, that she had been captured and might be hurt, followed close behind that relief. His whole body tensed, the magic within him rising, begging for release.

A man Lochlan recognized from the bonfire—Jackson—stood off to one side with Raymond, their expressions twisted with fear and uncertainty. A third man, the one who'd threatened Nia in her office and whom they'd seen on the street, raised his arms.

A stream of fiery magic hurtled toward Nia and the shadows she was clearly trying to conjure. But something was wrong. Instead of the bold, beautiful magic Lochlan had come to know and admire, Nia's shadows looked faint and frail, nothing like the ones she'd used to easily fend off and restrain this man before. They wouldn't be enough to stop him or his flames this time.

Lochlan didn't think—he moved.

His hand shot to his spell kit, fingers closing around a small opal vial. The mixture inside—moonlace root, distilled and potent—gleamed like frozen starlight.

He smashed the vial in his palm.

The crushed glass bit into his skin, mixing the powerful extract with his blood. Cold bloomed instantly along his fingers, an eerie chill shooting through his veins. His bloodied fingertips carved a rune in the air, like writing in untouched snow, and the moment the final stroke connected, the air crackled with energy.

Frost raced outward as the glowing rune solidified into jagged ice.

A wall of shimmering, blue-white ice erupted between Nia and the fire, the flames crashing into it with a violent hiss. Steam billowed. The icy barrier groaned but held, its surface spiderwebbing with frost, reinforcing itself against the heat.

The enormous man snarled in fury and frustration.

"Cover me!" Thane's voice roared through the cavernous space as he charged the man head-on. There was no hesitation, no finesse, just brute strength and sheer determination as Thane collided with him, slamming his shoulder into the other man's chest. They fought, fast and brutal—no weapons, no magic, just fists and feet. Gregor's sheer size gave him an advantage, but Thane's speed and ferocity more than made up for it. In a matter of seconds, he had the bastard hog-tied.

Echo and Jade circled Jackson and Raymond like wolves closing in on prey, their teeth bared. Jackson had gone pale, while Raymond looked seconds away from bolting.

Lochlan barely noticed, his focus solely on Nia.

He dropped to his knees beside her, his knife cutting through the ropes binding her, careful and swift. The moment she was free, Nia collapsed into him, her arms wrapping tight around his neck as she buried her face in his shoulder. They sank to the ground together, Lochlan holding her so tightly it almost hurt. His grip was desperate, terrified—he was afraid if he let go, she might vanish.

His hands moved over her on instinct, brushing her hair back, checking her neck, his thumbs grazing the raw red marks on her wrists where the ropes had been.

"Are you hurt?" His voice was rough, breathless. "Nia, talk to me. Are you hurt?"

She cupped his face, her fingers cold but steady against his skin. "Loch," she whispered.

He scanned her face for any sign of pain. "Tell me what to do," he said, his tone low and dangerous. "And I'll make it right. Just tell me what you need."

Nia answered by kissing him, quick and firm, soothing the storm that raged in his chest.

"I need you," she whispered against his lips. Her arms slid around his neck, pulling him into a fierce embrace. "At first, I was terrified. Then I woke up and…" She let out a short, incredulous breath, almost a laugh. "And I saw who it was, and I just—"

Her words broke off as she shook her head, a wry smile tugging at her lips.

Lochlan blinked down at her, the tension in his shoulders easing slightly. "You what?"

"Laughed," she admitted, her smile widening. "It's ridiculous. Chickens everywhere. Jackson, Gregor, and that little coward Raymond from the bar? Really? I mean, who gets kidnapped by a poultry CEO and his minions?"

"You, apparently." A reluctant chuckle escaped Lochlan as his forehead touched hers.

Nia's eyes met his. "The whole time, I kept thinking about us. About how we left things." Her expression faltered, a flicker of regret passing over her features. "I hate how we left things."

Lochlan's breath caught, and he opened his mouth to respond, but just then a fresh wave of chickens burst through the space, squawking and flapping as they scattered in every direction as someone shouted from the door.

Lochlan stood, leaving Nia on the ground putting his body between her and the door.

Wulfric stormed in, his gaze sweeping over the scene: the bound men, the feathery chaos, Lochlan, and finally, on the floor behind him—

"Nia." Wulfric's tone was cold and cutting as he stepped over a squawking hen. "This marriage is over. I will grant your annulment."

49

Nia

"Urgent Recall: Chicken Breasts Pulled From Shelves Due to 'Unspecified Contamination.'"
—*THE STELLA RUNE GAZETTE*

Among all the clucking and drifting feathers, her father's words took several moments to sink in.

This marriage is over.

Nia's brows knit together as she looked between her fuming father and Lochlan, his expression a mix of confusion and regret and—sadness.

She shuffled to her feet too quickly. The world tilted, her balance faltering. Lochlan reached out instinctively, his hand ready to catch her, but she grabbed the pole she'd been bound to and steadied herself. Straightening, she turned to her father.

His expression was no longer furious, but pale and worried in a way that twisted her heart.

For a moment, Nia almost laughed at the absurdity of it: Wulfric, the great and terrible Sword of the Goddess, frightened. The sight was so at odds with his fearsome reputation, she might've laughed, if she hadn't been so angry.

"How dare you!" she snapped.

Wulfric blinked, taken aback. "Pyronia—"

"No," she cut him off, her voice rising with every word. "You don't get to do this. After everything—after the lies, after manipulating me, after forcing me into this marriage in the first place—you don't get to decide when, or if, I will or won't stay married. How dare you!"

Wulfric blinked, confused. "How dare *he*!" He pointed at Lochlan. "He failed to protect you. He doesn't deserve you!"

Nia's hands clenched into fists. "Deserve? How dare you talk about what I deserve." Her voice rose with frustration, the words spilling out like the dam holding them back had finally broken. "I deserve the truth! And you kept it from me. You told Lochlan to keep it from me. You let me believe you were a monster—believe you were the reason my mother died!"

"It was safer." Wulfric said, stiffly. "A way for you to have the freedom you craved, without incurring the risk that being my daughter carried. The belief I was monstrous let you leave the identity that placed you in danger behind, allowed you to leave it with me."

"But you let me hate you!" she continued, her voice breaking. "You could have told me the truth, instead you let me believe the worst."

Wulfric ran a hand over his face.

"Losing your mother is a pain I carry every day," he admitted, his voice rough. "Losing you would end me." His next words were slower, more careful. "After she was taken from us—and you, still in her belly, were almost taken too—I realized the cost of the dream we'd built together. And it was too much." Wulfric shook his head, jaw tight. "The world we wanted, a world where regulars and supernaturals could truly coexist? People weren't ready. They wouldn't accept it. They would fight it. And I couldn't risk losing you to that fight, too. So I let it go. And then, so that you could have the freedom you craved, I let you go."

He studied her face, his own composure cracking.

"But I watched you grow from afar. I saw the ways you shaped the world on your own, how you fought for those who had no voice." He paused. "And I wondered—could you be the spark to finally ignite this change?"

The words caught Nia off guard. She swallowed hard, feeling them settle.

Perhaps she *could* be that spark.

She had built something—kindled in others the desire for the sorts of change she could see in Stella Rune and beyond. And though she might have to do things differently, she wouldn't let that spark flicker out.

Perhaps she could build it, spread it, share it.

"I arranged your marriage thinking a prince of this kingdom—one who bridged that world and ours—would be the perfect partner to help you spread that spark." Wulfric's jaw tensed and his voice hardened. "And it may even be true. But you cannot remain married to Lochlan."

Nia blinked, thrown by the sudden shift. "What?"

"He's already failed to protect you once," Wulfric said, his expression cold. "I will not hand my daughter over to someone who has proven he lacks the ability to protect her against the kind of attacks your future may hold."

Nia's stomach twisted with disbelief. "You think Lochlan is the problem? You think he's the reason I was taken?"

"He should have been with you, should have prevented it from happening at all," Wulfric snapped. His words were bitter as he added, softly: "A husband should protect his wife."

Nia let out a sharp breath, anger flashing hot. "You think you made a mistake forcing me to marry the wrong person, so now you get to decide what happens to that marriage now? Again?"

Wulfric's silence was answer enough.

Her hands curled into fists, shaking with frustration. "My future—*our* future—isn't yours to control."

She turned her back on Wulfric and stepped toward Lochlan, trembling as she reached for his hand, lacing her fingers through his. Lochlan didn't move. His expression was unreadable as she searched his face.

"I choose you," she said, simply.

Lochlan's lips parted slightly, his eyes wide as they searched hers—like he didn't quite trust what he was hearing. So she made it as clear as she could.

"I want to be married to you." She squeezed his hand. "Not because I have to, not because of some arrangement. Because I *want* to. Because..."

She swallowed, her heart pounding so hard she felt sure he could hear it.

"I love you."

Lochlan's breath hitched. His fingers twitched in hers, like he was afraid to hold on too tight, afraid she might take it back.

"I love the way you fight for me, even when I'm too stubborn to let you," she continued. "I love the way you make me feel safe and seen." Her voice faltered, and she took a shaky breath. "I don't want to lose you. Ever."

Lochlan's eyes met hers as he cupped her face gently, his fingers trembling against her skin.

"Nia, I—"

"I know," she said, cutting him off with a small, tearful laugh, her hand covering his where it rested on her cheek.

"You've had me from the beginning." Lochlan rested his forehead against hers. "You'll have me always."

The air between them felt charged as he pulled her to him.

"Ahem." Wulfric cleared his throat, breaking the moment. Nia and Lochlan turned to find him standing stiffly, arms crossed tightly over his chest. His stern expression faltered slightly as his gaze flicked between them. He sighed. "Well…"

But before he could say more, a frazzled-looking witch stormed into the coop, a smattering of chickens flapping wildly as they fled from her path. Leather pouches hung from her utility belt, vials and crystals jingling with every step. Her hands settled on her hips as she eyed the room with suspicion, her dark gaze landing on each of them in turn.

Aurelia Shade.

The Eraser Witch of Stella Rune.

Wulfric stiffened, his expression wary. "Aurelia." He tilted his head in acknowledgment.

"Wulfric," she grumbled. "Do I have you to blame for yet another infringement?"

Wulfric's jaw tightened, but his tone was respectful. "No… ma'am," he said to the witch who was half his age, clearing his throat awkwardly. Nia wasn't sure she'd ever seen her father look deferential before.

She bit back a laugh and turned to Lochlan, taking his hand and tugging him toward the exit, leaving Wulfric and his team to deal with Aurelia.

The air outside was cool and crisp, the country sky glittering with stars that seemed impossibly close. The chaos of the coop faded behind them, replaced by the soft murmur of witches and soldiers dressed in dark tactical gear milling about. Nia inhaled deeply, the fresh air filling her lungs as she tilted her face up to the sky and leaned against Lochlan's chest.

"Take me home, husband," she murmured, soft and sure.

Lochlan smiled down at her, his hand cupping the back of her head as he bent to kiss her, his words a quiet promise: "Yes, wife."

EPILOGUE
♥ *TWO WEEKS LATER*

This man. ♥ i love him so much.

Lochlan ♥

"Two heroic princes—how will we recover?"
—*PRINCES&PIES₄₄₄*

Supernatural reference ☺

Lochlan set the baking dish on the counter, the rich scent of melted cheese and herbs filling the kitchen. He wiped his hands on a towel and reached for two wine glasses just as Malrik's voice rang out through his phone, propped against a bowl full of Halloween candy. *get a guy who can cook. trust me.*

"So then I said, 'That's not a regulation formation, it's a—'"

"Malrik," Thane groaned from the other side of the screen, pinching the bridge of his nose. *Poor Thane ☺*

Lochlan smirked, half-listening as he poured the wine, the familiar cadence of Thane and Malrik's banter washing over him. Before he could sit, Jade's ears perked up. A second later, she leapt off the couch, nails clacking against the hardwood as she bolted toward the front door. ♥ Nia. ♥

Lochlan grabbed the glasses, turning just in time to see her sweep in, cheeks flushed from the cold, energy radiating off her in waves. She leaned into him, her lips pressing a quick, warm kiss to his before she plucked the glass from his hand and turned to the phone. "Hey, Thaney."

Thane groaned again, and Lochlan stifled a laugh as his brother dragged a hand over his face. "Not you, too." *I have a feeling they will be besties*

Malrik, for once, had fallen silent, which told Lochlan just how tense the situation in the palace had become. Thane had been pivotal in saving Nia, but he'd missed a major meeting with Dover's leadership to do so. He'd spent the last two weeks trying to make up for it, with Lochlan even putting in an appearance at the palace himself—this time with Nia at his side.

The brunch had been tense, a polite battleground where Thane debated members of the opposition while other leaders floated their own ideas, careful not to commit too fully to either side. Later, Lochlan and Nia had toured Dover's autumn festival with Thane, shaking hands and fielding cautious questions. Quietly, Nia had also reached out to Dover's hidden supernatural networks, trying to get a clearer picture of what they were up against. Magic lived deep in the shadows there, and they'd hoped to discover who was hiding and what could be done.

It hadn't mattered.

The Dover Coalition, who'd already controlled much of the government's power, had seized the opportunity to claim the rest, and had finally succeeded in passing resolutions that stripped the monarchy of its remaining power over the military, and both foreign and domestic affairs.

Lochlan exhaled, leaning against the counter. "What's the latest offer from the leadership of the esteemed DC?"

Thane snorted, grabbing a glass of amber liquid. "Oh, you'll love this. The monarchy is symbolically dissolved, but we still get to keep our titles—for tradition's sake." His voice dripped with sarcasm. "We're still princes, just without the pesky ruling part. Instead, we're expected to smile, wave, and be paraded around like show ponies at important events."

Lochlan's grip on his glass tightened. What did this mean for Wulfric and his plans? He'd bring him up to speed tonight.

"And Lavinia?" Lochlan asked. *notes her*

Thane took a slow sip. "Mom and Drusilla have taken leave—which is a delicate way of saying they packed their things and fled to one of the country estates before anyone could ask them to do any actual work to manage the transition of power." *There is so much to Thane, Its like he needs a book DO*

"And you?"

Thane exhaled, rubbing the back of his neck. "I still need to negotiate my position in the military. There's talk of making me a general in some kind of consulting role, which is just a fancy way of saying, 'We don't trust you to command armed soldiers, but we'd like to keep you around to look cooperative, and in case we can use your expertise.'"

Nia leaned into Lochlan, swirling her wine. "Come to Stella Rune. I'm sure Lochlan can find you something worthwhile in the Videt. And we all know my father loves a prince." *DO H* ☺

Thane groaned.

Lochlan smiled wryly, lifting his glass. "So, in summary: we're still important, theoretically, but no one actually wants us to do anything?"

"Pretty much." Thane raised his own glass. "To being very expensive decorations."

Nia grinned, clinking hers against Lochlan's. "Two very pretty decorations."

Lochlan grimaced, but they all drank.

"I'll send you the details on the latest transition offer," Thane said, setting his glass down. "We have a week to decide whether to accept or try to negotiate further."

Lochlan hated how defeated his brother looked. But a part of him thought maybe this was exactly what needed to happen.

They said their goodbyes, and Lochlan turned to Nia.

He leaned down and pressed a lingering kiss to her lips. "Hi," he murmured. "How was your day?"

"Amazing." Her smile was tired but genuine. "Long. And…" A hint of mischief lit her eyes. "I have a surprise."

Lochlan's brows lifted. "What kind of surprise?"

Instead of answering, she knelt to greet Jade, wrapping her arms around the dog and pressing a kiss to the top of her head. Jade wagged her tail, nudging Nia's chin with her nose before trotting toward the back door and slipping outside.

Lochlan crossed his arms, watching Nia with growing curiosity. "You're not going to make me guess, are you?"

She just smiled and pulled one of her mother's diaries from her bag. Moving to the bookshelf, she carefully placed it alongside the others, then selected a new one. He'd seen her do this often over the past two weeks, each time with the same quiet reverence. She carried the diary with her for days, reading it over and over again, and then, when she was ready, she would replace it with another. Both the routine and the deepening connection to her mother seemed to bring Nia peace.

But this time, after tucking the new diary into her purse, she reached into her bag again and pulled out two small vials of glowing orange liquid.

"What are those?" Lochlan asked.

Nia held up the vials, the luminescent liquid shimmering faintly.

"I had my final interview with Aurelia today," she said. "She's finished her investigation. All the regulars have had their minds wiped, and we are officially done."

Lochlan leaned against the doorframe. "And what about the charming trio?"

She smirked. "Gregor will do time for kidnapping. Jackson has a hefty fine to pay and has stepped down as CEO. And Raymond..." Nia shook her head. "His mind has been blissfully wiped, and he's in the early stages of being sued and divorced by his wife." *good good* .

The relief Lochlan felt was impossible to put into words.

"And these?" He nodded toward the vials, his brow arching.

Nia's smile widened as she twirled one between her fingers. "These are a gift from Aurelia." Her tone was light, but Lochlan could sense a hint of gravity. "Usually, she erases memories. But she can also give them back. I told her about our situation with the fairy wine and my father. How that night is a fragmented, horny haunting, and how I wished I could remember our hand-fasting ceremony." *I love this phrase*

Lochlan groaned softly, tipping his head back for a moment. "Of course you do."

"Don't roll your eyes at me," Nia teased, her smile playful but her gaze serious. "She says if we take these little guys, we'll remember everything that happened that night."

Lochlan's gaze flicked to the violently colored vials in her hand, unease *her so dramatic* curling in his chest. He'd never heard of such a memory recovery spell, let alone one that could reverse the effects of fairy wine. His mind churned with questions. How did it work? What would it feel like? And, most pressing of all—did he want to know?

The night of Mabon was a mystery he had grown to accept. And yet, the idea of uncovering the truth, of knowing what had happened, both tempted and unsettled him. *would you want to know? idk?*

Nia closed the distance between them, her touch warm and grounding as her hands ran down his chest. "We don't have to do this." Her gaze softened, her voice gentle. "I just thought... it was the last thing missing *She's a boobs & ass gal.*

I only added a dash because it fit better on the cover.

from our lives. I see glimpses every once in a while, but that's all they are: glimpses."

Lochlan's throat tightened as his doubts bubbled to the surface. "What if we remember and…"

"And?" *I really love how real he is. Like, he still has fears*

"And whatever you learn makes you change your mind," he said quietly.

It was Nia's turn to roll her eyes. Her lips quirked in a knowing smile as she let out an exasperated sigh. "Nothing," she said firmly, "can make me change my mind about you."

Lochlan hesitated, glancing at the vials before meeting her gaze. "But… who's going to hand out the candy tonight?"

Nia laughed, the sound easing some of the tension in his chest. "We're not taking them now." She shook her head. "Aurelia said to drink them before bed. When we go to sleep, we'll dream of our missing memories."

"All missing memories?" Lochlan asked, a thread of worry creeping into his voice. There were things he'd forgotten—memories he'd let go—that he didn't want to revisit.

"No," Nia said quickly, reassuring. "She did something with the fairy wine to narrow them down. Just that night."

Their eyes met, a quiet understanding passing between them.

"Do we have to do it tonight?" Lochlan asked.

Nia smiled, her expression gentle as she leaned in and kissed him. "We can do it whenever you want," she said softly. *These two.. I swear.*

Before Lochlan could respond, she turned and placed the vials carefully in the cabinet. The chime of the doorbell echoed through the house, and Nia darted toward the door, grabbing a headband with red horns glimmering with sequins and the candy bucket as she passed.

"Get Jade's costume on and grab the lawn chairs!" she called over her shoulder, her excitement infectious.

Lochlan grinned, shaking his head as he moved to find Jade.

Trick-or-treating lasted a little over an hour, the sounds of laughter and footsteps filling the crisp autumn evening. Lochlan sat in the lawn chair beside Nia, sipping his wine while they handed out candy. Jade, in her witch costume, had stolen the show. Kids squealed with delight, some even bringing fruit for the ducks, who waddled curiously near the edge of the yard. *I want ducks so bad* :—

Lochlan couldn't stop watching Nia—her laughter, her easy conversation with the neighbors, the way she leaned into him between groups of kids, her hand resting lightly on his leg.

It was incredible and even unreal, like he was dreaming, caught in some perfect illusion that might dissolve if he let himself believe in it too much.

But it wasn't a dream.

This was his life, the one he hadn't known he'd been missing. The one he never could have imagined for himself. A life built on love, on belonging—on her. *Sobs*

The stream of trick-or-treaters slowed, the earlier hum of excitement fading as porch lights glowed against the dark, their soft warmth casting long shadows on the cobblestone streets.

Then came the familiar sound of boots crunching on gravel.

Lochlan turned just as Becket strolled up, hands shoved into his jacket pockets, a crooked grin in place. "Well, if it isn't my favorite witches— the queen and king of hand-fasting and other hazards." He waggled his brows. "Ready to see what sort of chaos you can unleash at the Samhain celebration?" *I love that beck said the title*

Nia's smile turned wicked. "Always."

Lochlan glanced down both sides of the now-empty street. It felt... settled. A perfect kind of quiet. "Looks like our job here is done."

He turned to Nia, catching the shimmer of her dress as she moved.

The deep emerald fabric flowed around her like water, catching the soft glow of the porch lights.

She ran a hand down the fabric, her lips curving in a knowing smile. "I'll put Jade inside and grab a coat for the walk."

"Hopefully people will be naked by now," Becket quipped.

Lochlan groaned. The only person he wanted to see naked tonight was Nia. *poor loch will always be haunted by Nancy, lol*

As she disappeared inside, he let out a slow breath, looking once more at the quiet, waiting street. The night wasn't empty, far from it—it was full, of warmth, of possibility, of her.

And for the first time in his life, Lochlan felt like he was exactly who—and where—he was supposed to be.

EPILOGUE
Nia

"The History of Samhain—And Yes, They Were Naked Back Then." –THE WEEKLY HEX

T he witches are already naked," Nia said with a laugh, shaking her head as she scanned the celebration.

Lochlan looked at her with the same crooked smile that always made her knees weak. She leaned into him, soaking in his warmth.

Not all of the witches were naked—some still wore flowing clothing and others had clearly come straight from Halloween with the regs, their costumes a mixture of eerie and ridiculous. A vampire adjusted his plastic fangs. A woman in a cat costume had ditched her ears but kept the whiskers drawn on her cheeks.

Becket looked unimpressed. His gaze swept over the revelers, his lips a flat line. "I need a drink," he muttered, stalking toward the bar.

Nia watched him go, brows lifting. "What's with him?"

But before he could answer—

I hope you fell in love

♥ love a good mirror / call back

"Lochlan!" *oh No- na ha!*

Nia turned and felt her stomach drop. Naked Nancy hobbled toward them, arms flapping dramatically and other things jiggling. *lol*

Nia pressed her lips together to keep from laughing, but the corner of her mouth twitched treacherously. Lochlan, meanwhile, had gone rigid.

"I'll get drinks," he muttered, his gaze locked on the sky as he made a swift exit.

Nancy, undeterred, changed course and followed after him.

Nia couldn't hold back her laugh.

"Pyronia." Her father's voice came from behind her, gruff but warm.

She turned. This time, no tension curled in her chest, no resentment lingered between them. Instead, she smiled, bright and genuine, as she let him press a kiss to her cheek.

They'd both worked hard over the past two weeks to address the things that had kept them apart for years, and the air between them had cleared. Nia had made copies of her mother's diaries for him, though she didn't know if he would ever read them. They sat on a shelf in his new townhouse, the one he shared with his hauntingly creepy but loyal butler and his even more terrifyingly talented chef.

"I'm glad I caught you before the debauchery begins," Wulfric said, his lips twitching.

"Why?" Nia teased. "You're not about to marry me off to someone else, are you? Or thinking of getting hitched yourself?"

"Not tonight," he replied with a rare smile. *I don't think wolfie will ever find love again.*

Then he took a breath, as if bracing himself. "I know you didn't want me to interfere with your application, and I didn't. I swear. But I had to be the one to tell you." He paused dramatically. "The funding was approved."

Nia's heart skipped a beat.

"It's locked in for five years," Wulfric continued. "And after that, you're

I love this name ♥

eligible to have the House for Wayward Supernaturals permanently funded by the Videt." *I thought it would be wayward witches but that felt limiting.*

She barely processed his next words.

"I may even have offered the manor as a second location when I got the news."

For a moment, Nia could only stare at him. The words sank in slowly, their weight settling in her chest, filling her to the brim.

"Dad!" she squealed, launching herself at him.

He let out a startled laugh, catching her as she threw her arms around him. He held her tight. "I'm so proud of you," he said into her hair. "Your mother would be so proud."

Nia closed her eyes, emotion thick in her throat. "Thank you," she whispered. *✶ Sobs ✶*

"I never doubted you'd get it," Wulfric murmured. "Even after you insisted I stay out of it and demanded none of my council be on the approval committee."

She pulled back, shaking her head with a knowing smile. "Only because I know how persuasive you are."

She and Ivy had worked tirelessly on their proposal in the days since Nia's kidnapping. They had presented five- and ten-year plans to the Videt committee only the day before, outlining structure, programs, and long-term benefits for the supernatural community. It had been one of the most ambitious things they'd ever done—years of planning and dreaming transformed into a single comprehensive plan in a matter of days—but their vision of what the House for Wayward Supernaturals could be had kept both her and Ivy going.

And now? It would be real.

The thought of what this could mean, not just for Stella Rune, but for witches and supernaturals everywhere, sent another surge of pride and hope through her. There was still so much work to do. For their world.

For a future where supernaturals and regulars could finally coexist. And Nia had a feeling that this—the House, the work ahead—would be an essential part of it.

Lochlan arrived and handed her a drink.

"Fairy wine-free," he teased. "I spoke with Thane today," he said, turning to Wulfric. "He has news."

"Not now," Wulfric said, clearing his throat and wiping at his eyes. "We can talk tomorrow. Tonight I'll make my rounds and head out. Blessed Samhain." He smiled at them both before stepping away into the crowd.

Nia turned back to Lochlan, her heart still racing. "We got the funding."

"Of course you did," he said, warm and certain. He leaned down and pressed a kiss to her lips, the kind that said everything words couldn't.

She smiled against his mouth, her fingers curling in the fabric of his shirt. Lochlan had been there through every late night, every moment of doubt. His steady presence had been her anchor—and she couldn't imagine having done it without him.

A familiar voice broke through her thoughts.

"Nia!"

Ivy barreled toward them, her sheer dress catching the firelight in dazzling flashes. Nia set the drink aside and rushed to meet her friend halfway, grabbing Ivy's hands in excitement.

"We got the funding!"

"No." Ivy gasped, her face lighting up with pure joy. "You're kidding!"

"I'm not!"

They squealed in unison, laughing and jumping up and down like they were teenagers again. Ivy hugged Nia tightly, her voice muffled against her shoulder. "I knew we'd get it. Goddess, this is going to change everything." *I love Ivy so much and it's scary to think about writing her story.*

"I think it just might. And none of it would have happened without you."

"Don't you dare get sentimental now," Ivy teased, fanning her face dramatically. "I refuse to cry before the dancing starts."

"Good thing it's starting now," Nia said, grinning as she grabbed Ivy's hand and tugged her toward the fire.

The music swelled, a lively beat carried by drums and stringed instruments. Ivy let out a delighted laugh and spun in a circle, her dress catching the air like a shimmering cloud. Nia joined her, their laughter blending with the rhythm as they twirled and swayed.

From the edge of the firelight, Lochlan watched, an amused but hesitant smile on his face. He looked so out of place—tall and stiff among the fluid movements of the dancers. Nia broke away from Ivy and made her way to him. Grabbing his hand, she tugged him into the circle of dancers. *I am loch when it comes to dancing* ♡

"Nia," he began, reluctant.

"You'll be fine," she teased, her smile playful as she pressed a kiss to his cheek.

"The lack of fairy wine makes this hard," Lochlan muttered, his feet shuffling awkwardly as he tried to match the rhythm.

Nia stepped closer until her body was pressed against his. Her hands slid up to rest on his shoulders, guiding him gently. "You don't need to be drunk," she whispered, her voice low and seductive as her lips brushed his. "You just need me."

She swayed her hips in time with the tune, and Lochlan's body responded. His arms settled around her waist, pulling her closer as he followed her lead. *yeah he is!...*

"See?" she murmured against his ear. "You're perfect."

Lochlan's hesitant smile turned into something brighter, more confident, as the music carried them. In that moment, there was nothing else—just the two of them, moving as one in the glow of the firelight. Lochlan leaned in to kiss her, his lips brushing hers with a promise of something deeper. But Nia pulled back at the last second.

"Oh, no," she teased, dancing away and out of his grasp. "You're going to have to work for it."

The cool night air brushed over her skin as she shrugged off her jacket, letting it drop at her feet. A flicker of heat danced in her chest—her own daring thrill—as she reached for the hem of her dress. With a deliberate tug, she hiked it up just enough to free her legs, the soft fabric brushing against her thighs as she began to move.

She let the music take over, swaying her hips to the rhythm, her hands gliding along her body in a way that felt both freeing and provocative. A grin tugged at her lips as she twirled, the bare skin above her stockings warm in the firelight. Her gaze snapped back to Lochlan, daring him to follow her lead, to lose himself in the night, in this moment.

Lochlan let out a low chuckle, the sound sending a shiver down her spine. He pulled off his jacket slowly, tossing it aside. His fingers went to his cuffs next, rolling up his sleeves, revealing forearms corded with muscle. When he undid the top few buttons of his shirt, exposing the hollow of his throat and just a glimpse of his chest, her breath hitched.

His gaze was no longer hesitant. It was heated, ravenous. Same. ~~nia~~ *same*.

Nia felt her pulse quicken, heat pooling low in her belly. Goddess, that look... it was enough to make her slick, her thighs pressing together involuntarily. He took a step toward her, closing the distance, but she danced away, her laughter light and teasing as she beckoned him with a crook of her finger.

Lochlan chased after her, his steps growing bolder, more fluid with the music. She moved around him like a flame, her fingers brushing his arms, his shoulders, his chest. They danced through another song, and then another, their movements growing more tangled, more intimate. His hands found her waist, pulling her against him as her fingers threaded through his hair, mussing his waves until they were a glorious mess.

By the time the last song faded, Lochlan's shirt was gone, discarded somewhere in the shadows. His chest gleamed faintly in the firelight, his skin warm beneath her touch. Her own dress felt suffocating, the fabric clinging to her sweat-dampened skin.

She couldn't stand it any longer.

"Lochlan," she murmured, her voice low and breathless, "I need you."

She kissed him again, her lips lingering on his, teasing, before she broke away with a wicked grin. Then she ran, her laughter trailing behind her as she darted into the woods.

The cool night air kissed her skin as she let her dress straps slip from her shoulders, leaving it behind. Her underwear and stockings followed, piece by piece, falling into a trail of fabric between the trees. The moonlight guided her, filtering through the branches above as her bare feet carried her into a clearing.

She stopped in the center, the moon's silvery glow lighting up the open space. Her chest rose and fell as she caught her breath, her arms lifting to the sky. She spun slowly, the cool grass brushing against her feet, the night wrapping her in its quiet magic. *This is my favorite visual.*

When she turned, she saw Lochlan emerge from the shadows, his movements slow and his gaze locked onto hers. Her heart thundered in her chest as she watched him, his hands at his waist, undoing his belt, the soft sound of leather sliding free sending a thrill racing through her.

And then his pants fell, and she forgot how to breathe. *This too!*

She ran to him, her bare feet silent against the ground, and leaped into his arms. He caught her easily, his hands steady as they gripped her thighs, holding her against him. Her legs wrapped around his waist, and the heat of him pressed against her, sending a shiver through her entire body.

Lochlan's lips claimed hers again, his hand tangling in her hair with just the right amount of pressure, pulling her head back to deepen the kiss. A soft moan escaped her, her body melting against his, but then she felt the rough bark of a tree against her back as he pressed her to it.

His mouth left hers, trailing down her neck, his stubble grazed her sensitive skin and made her shiver. Each kiss was a mixture of teasing and reverence, and by the time his lips reached a peaked nipple, she was trembling.

"Lochlan," she breathed, both a plea and a command.

In answer, his hands slid down her sides, gripping her thighs firmly as he lowered himself. She gasped when he maneuvered her legs over his broad shoulders, the position leaving her entirely exposed to him, completely at his mercy.

He looked up at her, his gaze molten, a silent promise in his eyes before his mouth found her. *Cheese and rice sir . goddess !*

The first touch of his tongue sent her head back against the tree, a strangled moan spilling from her lips. He was thorough, savoring her like she was something decadent, something worth every second of worship.

Her hands flew to his hair, threading through the soft strands as her hips moved instinctively against him. Every flick, every stroke, drove her closer to the edge, but just when she thought she'd tumble over, he eased back, letting her teeter there, maddeningly close to release.

"Loch!" she scolded, half-laughing, half-growling as frustration built.

His voice rumbled through her, the vibration adding another layer of delicious torment. "Patience," he murmured, his voice rough against her skin. *he's so mean (smirks)*

"Patience?" she snapped, glaring down at him, her chest heaving. "I'm about to—"

But he silenced her with another long, deliberate stroke, sending her spiraling right to the brink again before pulling back.

"Loch!" she growled, tugging at his hair in protest. *fuck him*

When it happened again, she shoved him to the forest floor. *up*

"You're going to pay," Nia said, her voice low and dangerous. *Nia !*

Lochlan laughed, the sound husky and confident, the kind that could have distracted her—but she wouldn't let it.

"Make me pay love," he said, his tone a challenge. "We have forever."

So she did. *I tried every nickname*

Using the wetness pooling between her thighs, she slid against his hardness, deliberately not letting him inside her. His hands gripped her ass with bruising force, but he didn't push—he only groaned, the deep sound rumbling through his chest and driving her on.

She shifted her hips, teasing him with her slick heat, building herself higher as she rubbed against him. Her control was intoxicating, and the sight of him beneath her, his head thrown back, his lips parted in a desperate groan, made her thighs clench.

He was close. She could see it, feel the tension coiling through his body. *hehe not :*

"Nia," he ground out, her name a curse on his lips, his hands trembling as they tightened even more.

"No," she said, her voice breathless, grinding harder against him. "If you want inside, come now." Her eyes locked with his, daring him. She smiled wickedly. "And then maybe I'll let you go again."

He growled, deep and feral. Before she could react, his hand cracked against her ass in a sharp smack that sent a shiver up her spine. Then his hands were back on her, guiding her, sliding her up and down his length with effortless control.

"Goddess," she gasped, her head falling back as the sensations overwhelmed her. "Lochlan, fuck—"

The world went dark as she shattered, her climax ripping through her with a force that left her trembling. He followed her over the edge, his body arching beneath her.

When their breaths slowed and the world settled again, Lochlan pulled her against his side, tucking her close. His chest heaved as he let out a low, satisfied laugh, pressing a kiss to the top of her head.

"Smug witch," Nia teased as a satisfied smile spread across her face. She pressed her lips to his skin, trailing gentle kisses across his chest.

Lochlan groaned, the sound low and rough, vibrating against her mouth. "Your smug witch," he said, his hand brushing tenderly along her back.

She tilted her head up to meet his gaze, her smile widening. "My husband."

He shifted, turning them so that he hovered above her, his weight comforting and familiar. His eyes glinted with heat and mischief as he leaned down, capturing her mouth in a searing kiss.

"My wife," he whispered, his body already eager for hers again.

She laughed softly, her fingers framing his face as her heart swelled, warmth radiating through her. She'd never wanted this, or thought she needed it. Love was a living thing, both tender and unassailable. She would pour every part of herself into nourishing and nurturing it, and she knew Lochlan would, too.

Given time, their love would flourish and grow, strong and everlasting.

The End

I wish we got to see their wedding night. but I think this epilogue sums it up.

Authors Note

This book feels like an Enid to my Wednesday. It gave me my color back, the brightest, most beautiful colors, and it's so awesome to share it with such amazing readers.

Loch, Nia, and the rest of the Stella Rune cast brought me so much joy, and I believe it's the only book I could have put out after a graveyard full of abandoned projects.

Thank you for spending time in Stella Rune. For reading. For caring. It means more than I can say.

If you loved this book, consider leaving a review or telling a friend. It makes a huge difference for authors like me, especially in indie bookstores and cozy corners of the internet. And if you're just here for the magic and the kissing, that's more than enough.

Acknowledgments

I have a lot of people to thank for this book, but at the center are Chris, Scarlett, Alysha, Ash, Britt, and Laura. And those long flights and a delirious brain back in March 2024. That's where it all started: at the corner of writer's block and trying to nap through plane number five or seven. Two witches, waking up in a field, unnamed, freaked out, and naked.

Thank you to Scarlett, for always telling me to go write and for being there when I feel the most lost. To Alysha, for reading those early chapters and giving me a reason to keep going—and then sticking with me through all of it. To Ash and Britt, who are the biggest cheerleaders and best friends a witch could ask for. To Laura, my new editor, who came in at the perfect time. This book started as a jumbled stream of thoughts, and you helped me shape it into something I'm proud of. I feel less like an imposter because of all of you. To Chris, who makes every day brighter and worth living, and always has a hair tie in your pocket.

There are so many more people I want to thank. To Veronica, who doesn't love my books just because she's a best friend. My parents, for questioning my choices but supporting them anyway. Mackenzie and The Fix, where I put in the most work and found so much encouragement. To Frankie, for jumping in at the end and being such a great PA. Julia, who's always Team L, sells a fuck-ton of my books, and gave them the perfect indie bookstore home. Dani, the most brilliant smut dealer. Chloe, who keeps reminding me, "You need to love your own book." Mia, always encouraging and cheering me on. And Alix, for putting the finishing touches in.

To Charlotte and Bia, for bringing these characters to life. To the indie bookstores who joined me on this journey. To my street team, who always meets me with feral enthusiasm. The cover reveal team, the ARC readers, and every new reader—thank you. I couldn't be here without you.

L.L. Campbell grew up in the spooky corners of Massachusetts and now lives in Florida with her forever fiancé, Chris, their land hippo Sasha, and the ghosts of their favorite furkids. A witch with too many stories and not enough time, she's always daydreaming about new characters and the chaotic worlds they belong to. If she's not writing, she's probably reorganizing a playlist or pretending to be normal in public.

@authorllcampbell
www.llcampbell.com

www.ingramcontent.com/pod-product-compliance
Lightning Source LLC
Chambersburg PA
CBHW021843010726
47493CB00005B/1531